"WHAT THE HELL JUST HAPPENED?"

"She's something, ain't she? Looks like the lady got to your bail skip first."

"Who is she?"

"Name's Cassidy. She's a bounty hunter. Pretty amazing, huh?"

Luke was torn between annoyance and curiosity. "That's M. Cassidy?"

"Yeah, short for Emma. The guys call her Em."

Em Cassidy. He knew the name, thought it was a man. He watched the petite brunette—nine inches shorter than Digby's six-foot frame and no more than a hundred ten pounds—haul Skinner out the side door into the parking lot. Luke reached for his beer, took a last swallow, tossed a little extra cash on the bar, and followed the lady outside.

Also by Kat Martin

INTO THE FIRESTORM

KAT MARTIN

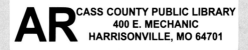

ZEBRA BOOKS
KENSINGTON PUBLISHING CORP.
http://www.kensingtonbooks.com

ZEBRA BOOKS are published by

Kensington Publishing Corp.
119 West 40th Street
New York, NY 10018

All Kensington titles, imprints, and distributed lines are available at special quantity discounts for bulk purchases for sales promotion, premiums, fund-raising, educational, or institutional use.

Special book excerpts or customized printings can also be created to fit specific needs. For details, write or phone the office of the Kensington Sales Manager: Attn.: Sales Department. Kensington Publishing Corp., 119 West 40th Street, New York, NY 10018. Phone: 1-800-221-2647.

Zebra and the Z logo Reg. U.S. Pat. & TM Off.

First Printing: February 2017
ISBN-13: 978-1-4201-3904-4
ISBN-10: 1-4201-3904-5

eISBN-13: 978-1-4201-3905-1
eISBN-10: 1-4201-3905-3

10 9 8 7 6 5 4 3 2 1

Printed in the United States of America

Chapter One

Seattle, Washington

The first thing she saw was the blood. Thickened into a syrupy dark red mass, it formed a scarlet river down the hallway into the entry of her sister April's home. Nausea hit her and her stomach rolled. The packages Emma was carrying, purchases she had made at the mall, fell from her nerveless fingers.

"Ginny! Ginny, where are you?" Emma Cassidy raced across the hardwood floor, a scream tearing loose as she spotted Eleanor Harris, the housekeeper, lying motionless in the hall, her head bent at an odd angle, her neck and chest soaked in blood.

Fear expanded inside her. "Ginny!" She ran past Eleanor, whose throat had been cut in a single long gash. The housekeeper's eyes were open, staring lifelessly up at the ceiling.

Emma started shaking. "Ginny!" Her voice cracked as she shouted her niece's name. Moving beyond the dead woman, she swallowed the tears and bile in her throat and continued down the hall. Her sister was at work. Emma raced toward her niece's bedroom, her lungs burning with the effort to breathe.

As she reached the open door, a sob escaped. Her pretty little fourteen-year-old niece sat curled up in bed, her back against the headboard, her jeans gone, her T-shirt in tatters, her arms crossed over her budding breasts. Ginny's fine brown hair hung in a tangled mess around her slender shoulders. A bruise darkened her cheek. Big brown eyes stared straight ahead as if she looked inward and saw nothing at all.

Emma's heart simply shattered. She dragged in a shuddering breath, her hands clenched into fists. She had to stay calm, had to be strong for Ginny.

"It's okay, sweetheart." Approaching slowly, afraid she would frighten Ginny even more, Emma crossed the floor to her bedside. "It's Aunt Em, Ginny. You're okay, sweetheart. You're safe."

But was she? What if the man who had done this was still in the house? What if he came back and murdered them the way he had poor Eleanor? Dear God, she needed to call the police but her cell phone was in her purse, lying among the packages scattered on the floor in the entry.

She wanted to reach out and pull Ginny into her arms, tell her everything would be okay, but she didn't dare. Not until the police were on the way. She pulled the sheet up over Ginny's half-naked body, leaned down, and kissed her forehead.

"I'll be right back, sweetheart. I'm not leaving you. I need to get my phone." Emma turned and ran toward the door.

The whisper of her niece's voice halted her before she reached the hall. "It was him . . ." she said. "It was . . . Rudy."

Emma couldn't move. Hearing his name spoken out loud made the horror somehow worse.

"He tore off my clothes," Ginny said in that eerie monotone that sounded nothing like her. "He tried to . . . tried to . . ."

"It's all right, honey." She swallowed. "Everything's going to be okay."

"Eleanor stopped him . . . but he . . . killed her."

"Oh, God."

A thick sob escaped Ginny's throat. "He says he's coming back for me."

Emma pressed her trembling lips together. "I've got to call the police, honey. I'll be right back." She had to get help but she could barely see through the thick glaze of her tears. She raced back down the hall, her sandals slipping in the housekeeper's blood, grabbed her purse off the floor in the entry, and dragged out her cell phone with a hand that could barely hold on to it.

It took three tries to punch in 9-1-1.

"This is police dispatch. What's your emergency?"

"There . . . there's been a murder. A woman named Eleanor Harris. And . . . and a young girl has been . . . has been attacked." Her voice broke. "Please . . . Ginny needs medical attention. She . . . she needs an ambulance." She swallowed past the heavy lump in her throat. "Rudy Vance . . . He's the one who did it. He might still be in the house. Please, you've got to help us."

"Ma'am, please stay calm and stay on the line." The dispatcher repeated April's address. "Is that correct?"

"Yes, that's right. It's my sister's house, but she's . . . she's at work." Fresh tears rolled down her cheeks. She kept the phone against her ear as she hurried back down the hall.

"The police are on the way," the operator said. "Ma'am, please stay on the line until they get there."

But Emma no longer heard her. She had to reach Ginny, had to keep her safe.

Two weeks ago, Rudy Vance, a man her sister had only just met, had broken into the house and raped her daughter. April had blamed herself, had barely been able to cope. Rudolph Vance had been arrested, but he had been released.

Emma bit back a sob. If only she'd been at the house with Ginny this afternoon instead of out shopping, maybe Eleanor wouldn't be dead. And Ginny. Dear God, what about Ginny?

As Emma rushed back down the hall, she thought of the man who had destroyed her family. The man who was still out there, free to do his evil again. The man the judge had released on bail when he should have stayed locked in prison.

She would find him, Emma vowed, a promise that burned through every cell in her body. She would personally make sure Rudolph Vance never hurt anyone again.

Chapter Two

Seattle, Washington
Ten Months Later

Sitting at the long, neon-lit bar in Rocker's Karaoke Lounge, Luke Brodie sipped a cold Corona and eyed his quarry. A bail skip named Skinner Digby leaned back in a chair at a round Formica-topped table a few feet away.

"You here for Skinner?" Eddie Mullens, the bartender, a string bean of a guy with gold wire-rimmed glasses, followed Luke's gaze to where Digby sat nursing a Jack and Coke. Eddie knew everything that went on in this part of Seattle. For a little cash once in a while, he kept Luke informed if anything interesting went down.

Luke took a sip of his beer. "Digby skipped on a DUI."

"Seems like small potatoes for you."

Luke was a bounty hunter. He went after FTAs, failures to appear, guys released on bail that didn't show up in court. He got twenty percent of whatever the bondsman had posted for their release and would have to forfeit if the fugitive wasn't rearrested. Luke specialized in the toughest and most profitable cases, bail skips whose bond sometimes ran into the millions.

"I need to ask Skinner some questions." That was the way it worked. You went after the small fish to get your hands on the big ones. "Figure I might as well make a few bucks while I'm at it."

Luke took a swallow of beer and returned his attention to his quarry. Digby had been flirting with a petite little brunette no more than five foot three in a tight black skirt and low-cut silver top who laughed at one of his dirty jokes.

Luke was getting irritated. Skinner, with his bulldog face and beer belly, was no ladies' man. Luke wished the woman would just take the free drink he offered and move on.

Instead, she sidled a little closer and leaned over to whisper in his ear, giving him a bird's-eye view down the front of her sparkly top at some very impressive cleavage. Skinner pulled out a chair, inviting her to join him.

Luke softly cursed. If the woman was going to hang around, he was going to have to make his move. He didn't like putting a woman in the middle of a situation that might go bad, but he needed to talk to Digby. The lady was giving him no choice.

He set the beer bottle down on the bar and came off the stool. Luke couldn't hear what the little brunette said, but Skinner snarled a curse and started up from his chair.

Luke couldn't believe his eyes when the lady grabbed Digby by the nape of the neck and shoved his head down, slamming him hard onto the top of the table.

Skinner groaned and his muscles went limp. The brunette twisted one of Skinner's arms up behind his back, pulled a pair of handcuffs from the handbag on her shoulder, and shackled his wrist, doing the same to the other one. Looking even more stunned than Luke, Digby swayed, his legs wobbly, as the brunette hauled him to his feet.

Sonofabitch. Luke turned to Eddie, who stood chuckling behind the bar. "What the hell just happened?"

"She's something, ain't she? Looks like the lady got to your bail skip first."

"Who is she?"

"Name's Cassidy. She's a bounty hunter. Pretty amazing, huh?"

Luke was torn between annoyance and curiosity. "That's M. Cassidy?"

"Yeah, short for Emma. The guys call her Em."

Em Cassidy. He knew the name, thought it was a man. He watched the petite brunette—nine inches shorter than Digby's six-foot frame and no more than a hundred ten pounds—haul Skinner out the side door into the parking lot. Luke reached for his beer, took a last swallow, tossed a little extra cash on the bar, and followed the lady outside.

It took him a minute to spot her beneath a lamppost at the edge of the parking lot. He sauntered into the shadow of a car in a nearby space, got a real good look at her this time.

Late twenties, petite, but curvy in all the right places, thick dark hair that hung in heavy curls around her shoulders.

A bounty hunter. That was a laugh.

The smile on his face slipped a little as he watched her handle Skinner. She had the guy sitting cross-legged on the grass, hands cuffed behind him. She was pressing him to answer her questions—exactly the same questions Luke wanted to ask.

"There's a guy you know," she said. "His name is Felix Riggs. He's your supplier. I want to know where to find him."

Felix Riggs. Same guy Luke was hunting.

Skinner just grunted. "Yeah, right. Like I'm gonna tell you anything. You damn near knocked me out, you bitch."

Emma lightly cuffed the back of Digby's head, and Luke bit back a grin.

"You skipped on a drunk driving charge," the lady said. "Third offense, Skinner. They're going to stick your butt in jail for at least a year. Tell me what I want to know and I'll let you go."

She'd let him go? Luke hadn't expected that. Now he was even more intrigued.

Digby sat quietly, considering his options. "Take off the cuffs, then I'll tell you what you want to know."

"Not a chance."

Digby shook his head. "If Riggs finds out I told you, he'll kill me. He don't like snitches."

Frustrated, Emma nibbled her bottom lip. It was plump and damp, and Luke felt a curl of heat he hadn't expected.

"You want to walk or go to jail?" she asked, pushing, but not quite hard enough, only willing to go so far.

Luke glanced around. If Digby didn't spill in the next few minutes, there was a chance the cops would arrive. Always somebody there to dial 9-1-1.

He stepped out of the shadows and Emma spun toward him, went into a wide-legged, self-defense stance. He pointed to the bail enforcement badge clipped to his belt and she relaxed.

"I didn't hear you walk up," she said.

Luke ignored her, zeroed in on Skinner Digby, crouched down in front of him. "The lady asked you nice and polite where to find Felix Riggs. You know who I am?"

Skinner grunted. "I know who you are. You're Brodie."

"That's right. I'm going to ask you the same question just one time. You don't answer, you won't have to worry about dealing with Riggs. You'll have to deal with me."

Skinner swallowed.

"Now . . . where is Felix Riggs?"

Skinner ran his tongue over his lips. There was a lump turning purple in the middle of his forehead. "Riggs is . . . he's out of town. Won't be back till Monday."

"Where can I find him?"

Skinner gave a sigh. "Hangs around the Polo Club. There's a bitch he's got the hots for."

"What's her name?"

"Lila Purdue . . . like the college, you know?"

"Yeah, I do." Luke rose to his feet, turned to the lady standing a few feet away. The moon was out. She was prettier than he had first thought, with big doe eyes, fine features, and a firm little chin. He was a boob man and from what he could tell, hers were prime grade A.

"Emma Cassidy," she said by way of introduction.

"Luke Brodie." He glanced down at Skinner, who was grumbling beneath his breath, then looked back at Emma. "Nice work," he said.

"Thank you."

Luke glanced across the parking lot. "Here comes Skinner's ride. I'll see you around." He started walking as a black and white patrol car rolled into the lot. *Interesting lady,* he thought, ambling over to his battered old Bronco. Pretty and feminine with a hot little body.

The very last person who should be running around trying to hunt down criminals.

Luke just shook his head.

He wondered why she was interested in Felix Riggs. Riggs wasn't wanted, though he should be since he was a low-life scum. Maybe he knew something about another bail skip she was hunting. Luke hoped like hell Emma Cassidy wasn't going to confront the guy. He didn't think she'd come out as unscathed as she had tonight.

None of your business, he told himself as he crossed the

lot, slid in behind the wheel of his beat-up old Ford, and fired up the powerful V-8 engine.

The Bronco, the perfect, nondescript surveillance vehicle, had been completely rebuilt. A powerful Ford Racing Aluminator XS 5.0 liter Coyote Engine—500 plus horses— idled like a predator under the hood. The Bronco had a Cobra jet intake manifold and fully CNC ported aluminum heads.

Welded restraints had been fitted into the back to hold any prisoners he had to transport to jail. Luke loved the Bronco. Like driving a rocket disguised as a paper airplane.

He checked the rearview mirror, saw little Emma Cassidy hauling butt-ugly Skinner Digby over to the patrol car. Why she would want to be a bounty hunter he couldn't begin to guess.

He'd never understood women.

Clearly that hadn't changed.

Emma watched Luke Brodie's rattletrap, black-and-tan Bronco pull out of the parking lot. The vehicle was old and beat to high heaven, but as she listened to the primal roar of the engine, it sounded more like a race car than an SUV headed for the junkyard.

She'd recognized Brodie the minute he'd stepped out of the shadows, though he'd moved into them as silently as a cat. Maybe it was the soft-soled, knee-high moccasins he was wearing. More likely, just the long-limbed, easy way he moved. She knew him from photos she had seen in a dozen different stories about him on the Internet, and from the research she had done.

Thirty-two years old, six-two, a hundred and ninety pounds, medium brown hair, and blue eyes. Tonight she had actually seen him in the flesh. Not just handsome, as he appeared in the photos, the man had a devil-angel face that would drive any red-blooded female crazy. His eyes weren't just blue, they were a fierce electric blue that had made her breath stall when they'd lasered in on her.

The snug, olive drab T-shirt and jeans he'd been wearing did nothing to hide the wide-shouldered, narrow-hipped, rock-hard body underneath.

She appreciated his help with Digby. She was still new at this, still learning the tricks. Interrogating a subject wasn't that easy.

Emma pulled her cell phone out of her purse and checked the time. It wasn't quite midnight. She was tired but high on her success. Digby's arrest had gone down just the way she'd planned.

Once she finished her paperwork, she was heading down to the Hide and Seek, a bar where some of the local bail enforcement agents hung out. Not Luke Brodie, who lived in Bellevue, on the other side of the lake.

It was almost one when she pushed through the door of what looked more like a biker bar than a local pub, with its worn board floors, long wooden bar, and rickety bar stools. Balls clattered against each other on pool tables in the rear.

Emma spotted Xavier Castillo, a bounty hunter friend, playing darts with another bail enforcement agent, Bobby Grogan, and Bobby's girlfriend, Melissa.

Xavier, the X-man, was as big as a house with skin the color of teak. He was part black, part Hispanic. He had no idea how to speak Spanish, didn't speak Ebonics, either.

Like Emma, he was still learning the trade, trying to break into the business. Emma wasn't certain the soft-spoken man had the right personality for the business, but she had only officially been at it six months herself.

Xavier waved, left the dart game, and walked over to join her at a scarred wooden table, flopped down in one

of the captain's chairs, making it creak with his colossal
weight.

Mattie Jackson, the owner, who also worked as a waitress, gave him the evil eye. "Easy, big boy, or you'll be
buying that chair." She was in her early forties, auburn-
haired and big-busted, popular with everyone who came
into the bar.

"Sorry," X said, color washing into his cheeks. For all
his size, Xavier was extremely shy, kind of a gentle giant.

Tray riding the palm of her hand, Mattie cocked her
head in Emma's direction. "You having your usual tonight?"

Emma smiled and raked back her long dark hair, tired,
but also stoked. "A cold Bud Light sounds great."

When Mattie turned to X, he held up his unfinished
beer. "I'm covered for now." He took a swig as Mattie
swivel-hipped back toward the bar. "So what's up?"

"I found Skinner Digby. He's cooling his heels at police
headquarters as we speak."

"Damn, that's good work. I would have gone with you,
you know."

"I know." They'd teamed up a few times. Emma doing
the locating, Xavier assisting with the capture. The problem was, X was kind of a Pillsbury Doughboy. Big but
harmless. It didn't take long for a truly hardened criminal
to figure that out.

Emma thought of Digby, his foul mouth and dirty jokes.
"From what I knew of Skinner, I didn't think he'd give me
much trouble."

Mattie walked up just then and set a cold bottle of Bud
on the table. "Word is you got your man tonight. Good
for you."

"Thanks. I got a little help from Luke Brodie."

Mattie's burnished eyebrows went up. "Watch yourself,
girl. That man is a real heartbreaker."

One look at him, and Emma had already figured that out. "I'm not interested in Brodie—at least not that way. And he isn't interested in me."

Mattie rolled her eyes. "From your lips to God's ears." The woman was always brutally honest. Still, Emma valued the budding friendship between them.

Mattie gave her a wave as she walked away. Emma appreciated Mattie's advice, but aside from professional curiosity, she wasn't interested in Luke Brodie or any other man. She didn't date. She didn't have time. She'd spent the last ten months training, completing the education requirements, and studying to pass the bail bond recovery agent exam.

Once she'd obtained the necessary licenses, she'd started learning the ins and outs, the skills and tricks of skip tracing and bounty hunting and generally getting ready for the mission she'd undertaken.

"You get that info you needed?" Xavier asked. He was one of the few people who knew her real quarry, the reason she had become a bounty hunter. Xavier and his sister, Benita, and Emma's close friend and roommate, Chelsea Davenport, a regional sales rep for a high-tech software firm.

Emma took a swallow of beer, felt the chill as it bubbled down her throat. "Skinner gave me a lead on Felix Riggs. I wasn't sure I was going to get him to talk. Then Luke Brodie showed up, and the guy started singing like a bird."

Xavier took a swig of his beer. "So you finally got to meet him."

Emma nodded. "Yes, and he was everything I imagined. He didn't even have to threaten Digby. He just sort of looked at him, told him to answer my questions or else. Digby couldn't talk fast enough."

Xavier chuckled. "Handsome S-O-B, ain't he?"

Emma glanced away. "I didn't really notice." That was a fat one. No way could a woman not notice a man who looked like Luke. "I recognized him from his pictures." That much was true.

Luke was one of the country's top bounty hunters and lived right there in Seattle so Emma had read every article she could find on him, even done a background check. Luke was ex-military, Army Special Forces, though there wasn't much about that in anything she'd read. When he wasn't hunting a skip worth enough for his efforts, Luke worked as a private investigator.

Brodie was famous—make that infamous—in the bail enforcement game.

"From what I hear, the guy's a regular man-whore," X said. "Got a different woman in his bed every night." He rubbed his chin. "Though I did hear, lately he's been a little off his game."

For whatever reason, she found herself defending him. "Luke's a busy man. Maybe his schedule's too full at the moment."

X chuckled. "A man's schedule's never too full for a good piece of—"

"Xavier."

"Sorry."

Aside from working as a private investigator, and recovering expensive stolen property like airplanes and jewelry, Luke had made a fortune bringing in some of the toughest, meanest, most elusive criminals in the country.

Emma reluctantly admitted she idolized Luke Brodie, and meeting him tonight, she hadn't been disappointed.

"So what's your next move?" Xavier asked, toying with his beer bottle, peeling off the label a tiny strip at a time.

"Digby gave me a location for Felix Riggs. He's out of town, but he'll be back on Monday. I want to talk to him."

She didn't give a rat's behind about the measly fee she was collecting for Skinner Digby. She had money enough to meet her monthly expenses: a small inheritance from her grandmother. But if Skinner's information panned out and she found Felix Riggs, she might have her first solid lead on Rudy Vance, the man she was really hunting, the man she had vowed to find, no matter how long it took.

"You gonna work out tomorrow morning?" Xavier asked.

"I usually take Sundays off. Tell Nita I'll be down at the gym at eight on Monday. I'm sure she'll be there. She never misses a class." Xavier's sister, Nita, was the exact opposite of her brother. She was in top physical condition, an expert in personal defense—the class where the two of them had met—and not afraid of anything or anyone.

"I'll tell her," X said.

Emma slid back her chair. "I'm heading home. Tomorrow I want to do some follow-up work on Riggs. I want to be ready when I talk to him." And on Sundays, as often as she could, she went to church. She was Irish Catholic. She'd have to tell the priest about Skinner Digby and the knot she'd put on his head, but since Skinner deserved it, the penance shouldn't be too much.

"Say hi to Nita for me," she said, "and enjoy the rest of your weekend."

Xavier waved as Emma headed out the door.

Chapter Three

Up early Monday morning, Emma pulled her long dark hair into a ponytail, dragged on tight black latex pants, strapped her full breasts into a snug-fitting sports bra, and headed for the gym on 42nd Avenue SW, not far from the West Seattle apartment she shared with her roommate, Chelsea Davenport.

Chelsea was a traveling sales rep, which made her the perfect person to live with because she was rarely home. The downside was Emma hadn't gotten to share her Skinner Digby-Luke Brodie story with her friend.

After church on Sunday, she'd enjoyed a relaxing afternoon. Then at eight A.M. on Monday, walked into Easy Fitness for her standing appointment with her trainer, Leonard Fox.

Mid-thirties, big, buff, and not bad looking, Len was a nice guy who did his job and kept his semiprivate lessons tough and professional. Len had a gorgeous girlfriend he was devoted to so Emma felt completely at ease during their hands-on training sessions.

As she walked onto the thick rubber mat in the workout room, she glanced around, saw Nita Castillo already there, running in place to warm up. Nita flashed a quick smile and returned her attention to Len.

"All right, ladies. How are we doing this morning?"

"Ready to kick some instructor ass," Nita said with a grin. She wasn't a lot better looking than her brother, but Nita had his same smooth, coffee bean complexion, which was a very nice feature, and at five-nine, with an amazing body, there was no doubt she was all woman.

"How about you, Em?" Len asked. "How you doin' today?"

"I'm doing great. I got to use the Face-pounder on a skip last Saturday night. First time. It worked perfectly."

Len flashed a grin. He was sandy-haired, a former Marine who had a way of teaching that made it seem more fun than work—most of the time. "Glad to hear it. I wouldn't want to think all the hours you've spent landing on your butt in here were wasted."

Thinking of the thousands of falls she had taken during her training sessions, Emma smiled.

Len clapped his hands, grabbing their attention. "All right, let's get moving. Both of you . . . give me fifty push-ups—now."

Emma inwardly groaned. She wasn't that good at push-ups. She could do a jillion sit-ups, which was why Len always called for the other.

She dropped down and got to work, got through the warm-up exercises; then they started on self-defense. Len moved her through the Grab, the Peel, the Hammer, did a few Inside Rolling Elbows, and finished with a Bear Hug. Nita made the moves look easy, which they weren't, then they role-played them together. When they were finished, Len put both women to work on the heavy bags.

The class finally ended. "I'll see you ladies on Wednesday," Len said.

"Let's hit the treadmill," said Nita as they walked into the main part of the gym.

"Sounds good." Over the past few months, the clank of weights and the sound of men grunting had actually become familiar.

"Xavier says you're going after Felix Riggs," Nita said as she climbed up on one of the machines. "You need to be in shape to take on that dude." Felix had a reputation. He was a drug dealer and an ex-con who had a way of staying off the grid. Now Emma knew where to find him.

"I *am* in shape," she said.

"Yeah, but still . . . I think you should take X with you."

That wasn't going to happen. This was her mission. It was dangerous and it was personal. Besides, she was only going to ask a few questions. "I'll think about it."

Emma spent an hour running next to Nita on the treadmill. When the hour was up, Nita kept running, but Emma had had enough. True, she needed to stay in shape. It was important to the job. But it wasn't a compulsion for her the way it was with her friend.

Emma was more fit than she had ever been in her life, and considering the amount of effort it had taken her to get there, she was proud of what she'd accomplished, an amazing change from her quiet life as a middle school teacher.

The bail enforcement job she'd undertaken was the biggest challenge she had ever faced. But the moment rapist Rudy Vance had been released on bail, gone back to her sister's home, murdered Eleanor Harris, and tried to rape little Ginny for the second time, Emma had had no choice.

Rudolph Vance was a sociopath, a killer who never figured on getting caught. A man with plenty of money, a fancy attorney, and no real evidence; three days after he'd been arrested for rape, he'd been released on bail.

The judge had made a terrible mistake. Even the three-million-dollar bond hadn't been enough to keep Vance from running. Rudy had disappeared, vanished into thin air, but he was out there somewhere. Out there and still a threat to her family.

For the past ten months, no sign of him had surfaced. But lately, word on the street was that Vance was back in Seattle.

Emma was determined to find him.

Luke parked the Bronco in the lot behind the two-story, freestanding brick building in Bellevue and walked into his office at Brodie Operations Security Services. BOSS, Inc., everyone called it. The office was done in chrome and black, with modern desks and a waiting area with deep black leather sofas and chairs. Photos of hot cars and speedboats hung on the walls.

Nice digs for a bunch of ex-cops and former military who now worked in the security business.

As he passed the conference room and the employee lounge and walked into the main part of the office, Luke spotted his older brother sitting at his desk with his cell phone pressed against his ear. Ethan was an inch taller than Luke, more muscular, same short hair, darker than Luke's, brown eyes instead of blue.

He was an ex-cop from Dallas, not far from where they'd been born. A few feet away, their cousin Nick, formerly a homicide detective in Alaska, now happily married and a dad, pounded away on his laptop keyboard. Luke's cousin Ian, another ex-cop, the owner of the company, worked upstairs.

Luke slid into the chair behind his desk and pressed the button on his laptop, powering it on. He looked up to see his brother walking toward him.

"You busy?" Ethan asked.

"I'm tracking a skip. You might remember him—Rudy Vance? Gangster, killer, child molester—none of which was ever proven."

"I remember."

"It's big money if I can find him. So far I haven't had much luck."

"You think he's back in town?"

"Rumor is he's back. Probably not for long. He must be working on something big to risk returning to Seattle."

"Or maybe he never left."

"Could be, I guess. But he'd have to have been in a very deep hole to stay out of sight for nearly a year." Luke leaned back in his chair. "You need me for something?"

"Val's putting together a little barbeque next Saturday. She was hoping you could make it. I've got Hannah this weekend. Dirk and Meg are coming, bringing little Charlie. Nick will be there with Samantha and the baby. And of course Ian, Meri, and Lily."

"Sounds like a real family reunion. I oughta fit right in."

Ethan didn't miss the sarcasm. "You won't be the only single guy there. Pete Hernandez is coming, Sandy Sandowski, guys I worked with on the fashion show tour. Some of Meg's girlfriends are coming too."

His head came up. "Lingerie models?" Meg was Dirk Reynolds's girl. Dirk was a PI who worked in the office, one of Luke's best friends. Lucky bastard was marrying a former La Belle supermodel.

Ethan smiled. "Carmen and Isabelle are planning to be there."

Luke had met the girls through Ethan when he was working as a bodyguard on the tour. Izzy and Carmen were two of the hottest females on the planet. But they weren't one-night stands. They were relationship kind of women, and that wasn't the kind for him.

Though lately, he had to admit, he wasn't interested in a string of one-nighters, either.

Luke inwardly sighed. He had no idea what was wrong with him. Probably just too much of a good thing. Maybe he ought to stop by the health store, pick up some vitamins or something.

"So, can you make it?" Ethan asked.

He always felt out of place with a bunch of guys and their families, though he did enjoy the kids.

Ethan's little Hannah and Ian's daughter, Lily, close to the same age, were cute as all hell, and Meg's little redheaded Charlie was a kick. Babies, not so much. Once Nick's kid got older, began to like baseball and football, he and Luke would get along just fine.

"What time's the shindig?" Luke asked.

"Starts at four o'clock. We'll have a couple of beers and barbeque some burgers, hot dogs for the kids. I'll tell Val you're coming."

Luke just nodded. He wasn't the kind of guy who would ever have a wife and kids. Too much water under the bridge. He didn't miss what he'd never have until he got around his friends and their families.

"You got any leads on Vance?" Ethan asked, pulling him away from the black mood he didn't want to slide into.

"I'm staking out a joint called the Polo Club tonight, looking for a second-tier supplier named Felix Riggs.

Word is, he was part of Vance's food chain. I got a hunch he still is."

Luke knew everything there was to know about Rudolph Vance. Part owner of International Cargo, the man had made a fortune in the import-export business, shipping and receiving goods from all over the world.

It hadn't come out until Vance was on the run that the feds had been trying to build a case against him. According to an agent friend of his, the feds believed Vance was into everything from drug smuggling to gunrunning. Problem was Vance was too smart for them. The authorities never got their hands on any proof.

It was his kink that had finally tripped him up, his perverted desire for underage girls. He liked them just as they were becoming sexually aware, their tiny breasts beginning to blossom, the girls more curious than wary.

The rape of a fourteen-year-old had gotten him arrested. Luke had been tracking him since the day he'd missed his court date, since before he'd gone back to the same house, killed the housekeeper, and tried to rape the girl again.

Vance was worth twenty percent of the three-million-dollar bail the bondsman had posted. Luke had followed every lead until it had gone as dead as the murder victim. But the guy had fallen completely off the grid.

Until now. If Vance was back in town, Luke was going to nail him. He hated a child molester worse than any human being on earth. Hell, he could always use a fat, six-hundred-thousand-dollar fee, but with scum like Rudy Vance, he might even haul the bastard in for free.

Chapter Four

Emma wasn't wearing her hooker-look tonight, the suck-in-the-horny male trick her mentor, Booth Childers, had taught her. Booth was an older guy, ex-military, mostly retired from the fugitive recovery business by the time she'd met him at the Hide and Seek.

Silver-haired, still a handsome man at sixty-five, Booth loved to sit at the bar and tell war stories about his days as one of the country's top bounty hunters. Emma loved listening to him. Booth said he liked her spirit, eventually took her on as a protégée and agreed to help her learn the trade.

He'd been a huge help until a month ago when he'd had a stroke. With no family in the area, Booth didn't have a lot of people to look out for him. Emma went by Oakmont, an assisted living facility where he was recovering, as often as she could, had gone over Sunday after church, and was glad to see how fast he was improving.

"I got a lead on Vance," she'd told him as the conversation progressed. They were sitting in overstuffed chairs in Booth's studio apartment looking out on the grassy, park-like setting beyond the window. "I found someone who might know where he is."

Booth Childers was another of the few people who knew she was hunting Rudy Vance.

"What's his name?" Booth asked, only half his mouth moving. One of his arms didn't work right and one of his legs, but he was going through therapy and doing better every day. Emma figured he'd be man-hunting again in no time, or at least telling more tales of his previous arrests.

"Felix Riggs," she said.

Booth made a kind of whistling sound through his teeth. "Bad hombre. Not the brightest bulb on the string, which is definitely a plus for you."

"I got the info from Skinner Digby." A smile of satisfaction spread over her lips. "Brought him in last Saturday night."

"Good work."

"Thanks." She didn't mention Luke Brodie. Booth knew him, surely knew his reputation with women. He would be full of advice she didn't want or need.

"When you going after Riggs?"

"Digby says he'll be at the Polo Club Monday night. Says he's chasing some woman who works there."

"You're just asking questions, right? He doesn't have a warrant?"

"No."

"How you planning to get him to talk?"

"I'm not sure yet. I'll have to play it by ear."

"You need to take some backup."

"I'm not going there to arrest him."

"Maybe not, but still—"

"I'll think about it." She should probably take the X-man, but he was almost more trouble than he was worth. Besides, she'd spent months training and been successful in bringing in a number of skips already. Emma had every confidence she could handle questioning Felix Riggs on her own.

"Any advice on how I should go in?" she asked.

"Yeah. I know the Polo Club. Bunch of druggies and lowlifes. Place like that, you need to keep a low profile. Don't draw unnecessary attention. They serve alcohol, so you can't go in there armed. Carry your Mace."

"All right. Anything else?"

"Be better if you could get to him outside. If you play it that way, don't hesitate to let Riggs know you're armed."

"Okay." She was licensed to carry concealed, and she knew the rules. She kept a little .380 semiauto in her purse, and she was a darned good shot. She planned to leave the gun in the car, along with her powerhouse Glock 19. She'd carry the Mace, just like Booth told her. The man was a pro. She'd do what he said.

They talked awhile longer, Booth making her promise to let him know how the op went down.

Op. She was getting used to all the military lingo the guys used. There were other women in the business, of course, but most of them specialized in tracking, not making the capture. Skip tracers made a living from debt collection, repossession, finding deadbeat parents, missing heirs, any search that paid a fee.

Except for a lady named Michelle Gomez. The four-foot-eleven-inch, hundred-pound lady from Lockhart, Texas, was a world-renowned bounty hunter. Stumbling on an article about her in *Wired* magazine a few weeks after Vance's attempt to rape Ginny a second time, Emma became convinced she could learn to be a bail enforcement agent like Michelle, that she could develop the necessary skills to find Rudy Vance.

She was trained and ready and now she had a lead. From the retirement home, Emma drove by the Polo Club, just to scope the place out, get a feel for what she'd be facing when she returned on Monday night. It was a rough joint in a rough part of town. She understood Booth's warning.

It was ten o'clock the next evening when she pulled her five-year-old, white, four-door Mazda hatchback into the parking lot and backed into a space so she wouldn't get trapped if she had to leave in a hurry.

Instead of her short skirt and low-cut top, she was wearing worn jeans, a navy blue T-shirt, and sneakers. She'd pulled her dark hair into a ponytail and stuffed it through the hole in the back of a blue Mariners baseball cap. As small as she was, she looked more like a teenage boy than a woman.

A can of Sabre Red, police-strength pepper gel spray in a flip-top can rode in a holster strapped to her belt next to her bail enforcement badge. The .380 was in her purse on the floor of the passenger seat. Her Glock 19 was stowed handily out of sight beneath the driver's seat.

Emma got out of the car, pulled a lightweight windbreaker on to cover the badge and Mace, clicked the locks on the doors, securing her weapons, and headed into the bar.

It was happening again—Luke couldn't fucking believe it. The kid he'd seen walking into the bar hadn't been an underage teen, as he had first thought. It was Emma Cassidy. Even the windbreaker she was wearing couldn't hide her first-class set of tits.

He could not f-ing believe it. Sitting at a table in the back of the room, irritated she was getting in the middle of his pursuit—again—to say nothing of a potentially dangerous situation, he leaned back in his chair and watched her.

She was looking for the woman, Lila Purdue, that Skinner Digby had mentioned. When a voluptuous blonde sashayed out of the back in a pair of jeans with rhinestones on the pockets so tight, you could count the dimples in her ass, Luke figured Emma had found her.

They talked for a while. The sound of raucous laughter and the clank of beer bottles kept their conversation mostly private. Some loudmouthed biker shuffled through the peanut shells on the floor, told everyone in the bar he had to take a piss, and headed for the men's room.

Luke shook his head. Not a place for little Emma Cassidy, no matter how tough she thought she was. She said something to the blonde, smiled, and discreetly opened her jacket, flashing her bounty hunter badge. Amazingly, the blonde boomed a laugh.

Since Emma hadn't yet been tossed out of the bar, and figuring he might actually learn something useful, Luke shoved up from his chair and quietly moved close enough to hear, careful to stay out of sight.

"I just need to speak to him," Emma said to Lila. "He's not wanted for anything. I just need Felix to answer a couple of questions. You think you could get him to talk to me?"

"You came here all by yourself to get Felix Riggs to rat on one of his friends? If I was wearing a hat, I'd take it off to you, Emma. You are truly something."

Luke rolled his eyes. She was something, all right. A major trouble magnet.

"So what do you think? Can you get him to see me? All I need is a couple of minutes."

Lila cocked a hand on her hip. "Felix has the hots for me. He'd do anything I ask for a piece of ass. Trouble is, I got no inclination to give it to him."

"I can see where that's a problem."

The blonde gave Emma the once-over. "You got a real nice little body yourself, honey. How bad do you want the information?"

For the first time, Emma looked uneasy. "I'm pretty picky about who I sleep with. How about money?" She pulled out a roll of cash. "I've got five hundred dollars. How much information will that buy?"

Luke inwardly groaned. Flashing money was a bad move in a place like this. Emma had just made her first big mistake. Except for the mistake of wading into this pigswill joint in the first place.

The blonde glanced nervously around, thinking the very same thing. A big lumberjack of a guy came up off his bar stool. The short, barrel-chested guy next to him did the same. A big black dude with a shaved head parted the curtains and walked out of the back room.

Emma's gaze went from the men back to the blonde. "So I guess we aren't going to make a deal."

"Oh, honey, I wish I could help you, I really do. My best advice is to give Ivan, there, that roll of bills and get your pretty little self out of here."

When Emma stuffed the roll of bills back into the pocket of her jeans, Luke softly cursed. The money wasn't worth what these guys were planning to do.

Emma just smiled. "No answers. No money. Tell Felix I'll see him another time."

Turning, she started for the door. When Ivan stepped in front of her, all six-foot-five inches of him blocking her way, Luke had to give her points for moxie.

"You'd be wise to let me pass," she warned, craning her neck to look up at him.

"Is that so?" said the muscled-up black guy from behind her. A foot wider than she was, he clamped his arms around her and flashed a leering grin at the other two over the top of her head. Emma stepped to the outside and backstopped his knee, knocking the guy off balance, then whirled and shoved him backward so hard, he crashed into a table, spun, and went sprawling across the floor.

Luke felt a jolt of heat that went straight to his groin. Why watching the pretty little lady take that big bastard down should turn him on he had no idea, but he couldn't look away.

Emma started again for the door but Ivan blocked her way. Her hand moved so fast, Luke almost missed it. Down to the snap on her Mace, can up, spray in bozo's face, and run like hell for the door.

Luke couldn't stop a grin as she raced outside and the door slammed behind her. Chaos ensued in the bar, giving him time to slip out the back and make his way around to the parking lot.

The bad news was, by the time he got there, three long-haired, bearded lowlifes in black leather jackets had Emma pinned against the side of her car. The lady had already taken down three grown men—true, they were drunk, and her small stature and level of skill had surprised them and given her an edge, but still . . .

Luke figured it was time to level the playing field.

Chapter Five

Emma was scared. It hadn't happened a lot during her brief career as a bail enforcement agent, but she was scared now. So far she'd been able to hold her own, but that was about to change.

She'd unlocked her car and almost made it to the Glock beneath her seat when the three stooges from hell grabbed her and pinned her against the car door. Her ball cap went flying. One of them dragged the scrunchy out of her hair, sending her dark curls flying around her face. Her heart was beating like crazy, her mouth dry as dirt.

She had to suck it up and she had to do it now.

"Let go of me," she said with cool authority, or at least hoped it sounded that way.

"You hear that, Badger?" stooge number two said. "She wants you to let her go." The men guffawed in unison.

Badger leaned over her, pinning her with his body, his breath hot and foul on her face. He was big and beefy, and the determined look in his eyes made her inwardly cringe.

"I thought you was a boy till I seen them pretty boobs. We gonna have us some fun tonight, lady."

Unfortunately for Badger, he turned to look at the others as he laughed. Emma twisted, jerked her knee up, and slammed it into his privates, just the way Len had taught her. Badger let out a yowl that could be heard for miles around and collapsed to his knees, grabbing his crotch and gasping for air.

Emma bolted, only to find herself trapped again by stooge number two. When he grabbed her shoulders to block her way, Emma did an Inside Rolling Elbow, bending her arms, jerking her right elbow up and slamming it into his face. There was an eerie crunch of bone, then blood sprayed all over the front of her windbreaker.

Nausea rolled through her. It was one thing to practice self-defense, another to actually see the results of what you'd done.

The instant of hesitation cost her. She hadn't realized the guys from the bar had poured out into the parking lot and formed a semicircle around her.

"You're gonna pay for that, lady," stooge number three said. Big and brawny, he had an ugly scar down the side of his face that made her stomach roll again. "Strip her out of those clothes," he said to the others. "Let's get this party started."

Emma made a sound in her throat as he grabbed hold of her windbreaker and jerked her forward.

"I wouldn't do that if I were you."

Her insides were shaking. Emma sliced a desperate glance toward the sound of the deep male voice. Luke Brodie stood behind the half circle of men, long legs splayed, face as hard as steel.

"The lady's with me. Let her go."

Once more standing, Badger shifted nervously, his face still waxy pale. "We didn't know she was yours, Luke."

They knew each other? Badger turned to stooge number three. "That's Brodie. Best do what he says."

Stooge number three carefully released his grip on the

front of her jacket, brushed off a piece of lint that didn't exist, and took a step backward.

"No harm done," Luke said with a hint of a Southern drawl that reminded her he was from Texas. "Emma can be a real handful. You can see what I have to put up with."

The men chuckled uneasily.

Luke jerked his head, silently commanding her to move toward him. Emma clamped down on the urge to run in the opposite direction and walked a step at a time over to where he stood behind the circle of men, who had turned and now faced in his direction.

"Get in the Bronco," he commanded. Though she would rather have driven her own car home, Emma didn't argue, just gave the lot a quick perusal, spotted his battered old Ford, and walked toward it.

By the time she had closed the door and settled herself inside, Luke was behind the wheel.

"Put on your seat belt," he growled, strapping his own on, which surprised her only a little. He probably knew driving without a belt took thirty years off a person's life. From what she knew of him, Luke Brodie wasn't stupid.

When the Bronco shot backward, spinning its wheels, she realized what a smart move the seat belt was. The car fired out of the lot and shot off down the street at supersonic speed.

"Luke, I really appreciate—"

"Don't talk. Don't say one single word."

"But—"

"Not a word, Emma." He swore foully, making Emma's face heat up. "I can't believe you went into a place like that by yourself."

"I needed to talk to—"

"Did you hear what I said? I'm hanging on by a thread, here, Emma."

Luke was really mad. She wondered if she should be frightened, though the image she had of him didn't include Luke as a woman-beater.

He turned the corner and the car slowed a little. She figured that was a good sign.

"What did you think was going to happen when you went in there tonight?" Luke asked. She had a hunch he didn't really expect an answer.

"Actually, I was doing pretty well until I pulled out the money. I didn't handle that right. I'm pretty new at this. I should have made the offer in private. I should have—"

"Stop right there." Luke pulled the Bronco over to the curb and shoved the SUV into Park. "There were a dozen things you should have done, Emma, starting with staying away from the Polo Club and forgetting about Felix Riggs."

"He was supposed to be there. You helped me get the name. What did you think I was going to do with it?"

"I was hoping you weren't crazy enough to go after him alone."

She frowned. "Wait a minute. What were you doing there?"

"Riggs has information I need."

Her eyebrows shot up. "I can't believe it! I thought you were helping me question Digby the other night, but you were getting information for yourself!"

"What, you thought I was just being Mr. Nice Guy? I've got a job to do. I do what it takes to get it done."

A hard lump settled in Emma's chest. She pretty much idolized Luke Brodie. She'd thought he was one of the good guys. How could she have been so wrong?

Then she thought of the way he'd looked standing in the parking lot, like an avenging angel swooping in to rescue her from half a dozen ruthless men. "You saved me tonight. You could have just gone your own way and left me there."

Those amazing blue eyes zeroed in on her face. "I might not be the man you thought I was, darlin', but I'd never leave a woman to deal with that kind of scum by herself."

She felt better. Just because Luke was looking for Riggs didn't mean she was wrong about him. He'd saved her butt tonight. She owed him and she wouldn't forget it.

She thought of Riggs and her lost opportunity and disappointment slid through her. "I didn't even get to talk to him."

Luke slammed a hand down on the steering wheel. "No, dammit, and you aren't going to. Whatever skip you're chasing isn't worth being raped or killed. You get me?"

Emma sighed. "I get you." But she still had to talk to Riggs. She and Lila had kind of hit it off. With the right persuasion, she had a feeling the woman might help her.

"My purse is in my car. I unlocked the door when I came out, but I wasn't fast enough to get inside."

Those blue eyes sliced toward her again.

"The thing is, my weapons are in there. You think those guys will steal them?"

"No. They think you're mine. They won't touch your stuff."

"Yours? As in your girlfriend?"

"I don't have girlfriends."

"What then? Your night's entertainment?"

He pulled the Bronco into the traffic. "I guess so."

Emma rolled her eyes and leaned back in the seat. They thought she was spending the night with Luke. Having hot sex with man-whore Luke Brodie. For all the money in Vegas, she wouldn't admit to the little zing that skipped the length of her body.

"Where are we going now?"

Luke slowed and pulled a U-turn, started back toward the bar.

Her eyes widened. "We're going back to the Polo Club? Seriously? You want to butt heads with those guys again?"

His mouth edged up. He had the sexiest mouth she'd ever seen. God, she wished she hadn't noticed.

"We're not going in. We're going to surveil the place, see if we can spot Riggs—something you should have done instead of going inside without backup."

"We? So you're going to help me again?"

"Hell, no. I just don't want to drive you home, then drive all the way back. You're here. You can just sit tight until I finish what I came here to do."

"Talk to Riggs."

"Not here. Not after your little episode in the bar. He wasn't inside when I got there. I'm going to wait, see if he shows up. If I spot him, I'll track him to wherever he's roosting at the moment."

"Good idea." Emma leaned back in the seat.

Luke pulled up at a stoplight and his attention swung back to her. "Let's get something straight. I did you a favor tonight. That's it. We're done. I'm tracking a skip and you aren't involved."

"Who is it? Who's the skip you're tracking?"

He hesitated. "I guess it doesn't matter. I've got the contract. I'm looking for Rudy Vance. He's a—"

"I know who he is," she said, unable to keep the edge out of her voice. If she closed her eyes, the awful, heart-wrenching memories would surface. She'd had nightmares for weeks, still had them on occasion. She'd finally learned to deal with what had happened and move forward. Which meant finding Rudy Vance. She couldn't afford to be distracted, couldn't lose her focus.

She hadn't known Luke was after Vance, too. She didn't tell him Booth had stuck out his neck for her, gone to S & B Bailbonds and talked Arty Bernstein, one of the owners, into signing a side deal giving Emma the paperwork she needed to keep her out of jail if she found Vance and arrested him. She'd known there was another bond agent involved. She should have figured it would be Brodie.

Even if she found Vance, her fee wouldn't be the twenty percent Luke would be getting, but Emma didn't care.

The light turned green. Luke started driving. He rounded the block two times, scoping it out before finding a place to park where he could watch the bar without being seen.

Turning off the engine, he reached behind his seat, pulled a pair of binoculars out of a canvas bag and looped the strap around his neck. A big mercury light behind the building made it bright enough for him to see.

He tossed her a radio. "You know how to use this?"

She nodded. "Booth showed me."

"Booth Childers?"

"Booth's been helping me. He's kind of my mentor. Or at least he was."

"Yeah, I heard. Too bad about that."

"He's doing better."

"Booth's a good guy. If you're serious about the business, you do what he tells you."

She just nodded.

He handed her a long-handled heavy black Maglite to use as a weapon. She had a flashlight just like it with a slightly shorter handle next to the driver's seat in her car.

"Watch the front door. I presume you know what Riggs looks like."

"I know."

"Fine, you see him, you give me a heads-up on the radio. Whatever you do, do not get out of the car."

He was gone before she could reply. Emma watched as he headed for the back of the building. He was wearing jeans tucked into the same knee-high moccasins he'd had on the first time she'd seen him, walking with the loose-limbed, easy gait she'd noticed before.

Wide shoulders filled out his dark green Henley. His long torso tapered down to a very nice behind. There was enough light to notice the sun streaks in his short brown hair just before he disappeared out of sight.

Emma turned her attention to the front door of the Polo Club. With any luck, Riggs would eventually show up. They would wait until he left, then follow him to wherever he lived, and Luke would make him answer their questions.

Emma almost smiled. Bounty hunting was a whole lot easier when you were working with Luke Brodie.

Chapter Six

Luke crouched down in the deep grass twenty yards from the back door of the Polo Club. Seattle summers were cool, the high today only seventy, dropping into the fifties at night. A half moon shone overhead as he stretched out on his stomach and propped himself on his elbows to watch the back door. The mercury light lit the back porch and a portion of the lot. Luke figured on staying until the place closed down before he gave up and went home.

Waiting was a big part of the job, and he was good at it. He'd been a special ops soldier. If the mission required it, sometimes you waited for hours without moving a muscle. Luke hoped Emma didn't fall asleep. He needed eyes on the front door as well as the back.

At the sound of an engine running, he turned to see a black Cadillac Escalade drive up to the back door. The vehicle parked in one of the employee spaces and two men got out.

Adjusting his binoculars, Luke peered through the lens to confirm one of them was Felix Riggs. It was well after midnight. He figured Riggs would drink for a while, maybe con the buxom blonde out of a piece of ass. Though he had his doubts about that.

Thinking of the blonde made him think of Emma and how close she had come to disaster. She was pretty, with her thick dark curls and big doe eyes. Lately, he hadn't had the slightest interest in the female sex, not until he'd watched petite Emma Cassidy take on that big behemoth, Ivan Dorell. He hadn't felt a shot of lust like that in weeks, hell, longer than that.

It took balls to go into a rough joint like the Polo Club, big brass ones to go toe-to-toe with Ivan and his thugs. She'd stood up to Badger and his biker buddies, too.

It was a crazy thing to do. She had to be forty degrees off center to do something that dangerous. Hopefully, she'd figure out that hunting riffraff like Digby and Riggs wasn't worth the piddling fee paid for the capture of most bail skips. And the work was hard to come by. It was the big fish that paid big money, guys like Rudy Vance.

Riggs could be the key to finding Vance. Luke fixed his binoculars on the back door of the Polo Club.

Emma's neck felt stiff and her eyes burned as she watched the entrance to the bar. If felt like hours since Luke had left. She hoped he hadn't gone inside without her.

She tried to stretch in the passenger seat. After brawling with half the lowlifes in Seattle, she figured by morning she'd have bruises all over her body.

She rubbed the back of her neck, rubbed her eyes, and sat up a little straighter in the seat. She didn't want to fall asleep; she had a job to do. She wanted to talk to Riggs even more than Luke did.

Emma jerked upright at the sound of the door swinging open. Luke slid in behind the wheel.

"Riggs and his buddy just pulled out," Luke said. The powerful engine fired up and he jammed the Bronco into gear. "I'm dropping you in the lot beside your car. Get in and lock the doors, then drive the hell home."

As the Bronco lurched toward the parking lot, Emma snapped her seat belt. "I'm not going home. I'm going with you."

"The hell you are."

"The hell I'm not."

His mouth curved an instant before his frown fell back into place. He pulled up in the front lot behind her car, reached across and unsnapped her belt, then shoved open the car door. Emma forced herself to ignore the tingle as his arm brushed her breast.

"Get out."

"He's in that big SUV, right?" Emma watched the red glow of taillights getting dimmer as the vehicle that had just pulled out of the lot drove off down the street. "If you don't hurry, you're going to lose him."

Luke's jaw clenched. "Goddammit!" He slammed her door, straightened behind the wheel, and jammed his foot down on the gas. The Bronco fishtailed and leaped forward. Thank God she'd snapped her belt back on or she would probably be halfway through the windshield.

"I swear, lady, you are a real pain in my ass."

"I just need to ask Riggs some questions. I won't get in your way."

Luke blew out a breath. "Who are you looking for? I'll see what I can find out."

She didn't want to tell him. He wasn't going to like the answer. "Rudolph Vance."

"You're looking for Vance? Bullshit. I've got the contract on Vance."

"Arty is letting me look for him, too. It's kind of a favor to Booth."

Instead of getting angry, Luke relaxed. "Vance has

been off the grid for the past ten months. The odds of you finding him are slim and none."

"I found Digby, didn't I? And Digby gave us Riggs."

A muscle jumped in Luke's cheek as he slowed the Bronco, staying three cars back from what she could now see was a black SUV. Typical gangster mobile. No originality. But she had known that from the profile of Riggs she had done.

He was a follower. He'd worshipped Rudy Vance, wanted to be part of his inner circle.

"How'd you connect Riggs to Vance?" Luke asked.

"He showed up in the profile I've been building. Riggs attended a couple of Vance's parties. He was in some photos I found. I ran down the names of the men acting as security that night. Riggs was one of them. It was before the murder, before the feds began to suspect Vance was doing a lot more than importing airplane parts and exporting lumber and frozen fish."

"Like smuggling drugs and running guns. You need to let this one go, Emma. You said yourself you're new at this. Vance is out of your league."

Emma leaned back in her seat, kept her eyes on the road. "The car's turning left up ahead."

Luke made the turn just as the light changed, kept his distance, drove on past when the SUV pulled into a parking garage beneath an apartment building.

He made a quick U-turn at the end of the block, drove back, and turned into the garage, slowing down long enough for the driver to pull into a space. As Riggs and his passenger got out, Luke drove the Bronco up behind the car, pinning the vehicle in place. He turned off the engine, reached beneath his seat, pulled out a big semiauto, and stepped out of the Bronco.

"Stay here." He was gone before she could speak.

Emma grabbed the Maglite he'd given her, cracked open her door, and quietly stepped out of the SUV. No overhead light went on. She'd noticed the missing bulb before. Damn, she wished she had her gun or at least her Mace. But Badger had grabbed the can when she'd tried to use it on him, and her guns were in the Mazda.

She moved quietly into position behind Luke. She hadn't made a sound and yet she had a feeling he knew she was there. She could see his pistol in the waistband of his jeans at the small of his back.

He said something to the men. The next thing she knew the man with Riggs was on the ground moaning. He didn't look seriously injured but he was definitely finished resisting. Luke did a quick weapons search, turned back to Riggs, grabbed the front of his shirt, and shoved him up against the wall.

He did another quick weapons search, then searched Riggs's pockets. Out came a clear plastic bag of what Emma figured was probably cocaine.

"Take a walk," Luke said to the other man, older and heavier, with a pencil-thin mustache. The man groaned as he rolled to his feet and plodded off toward the entrance of the garage.

Luke turned to Riggs. "I'm looking for Rudy Vance. Where is he?"

Riggs shook his head, breathing a little too fast. "I got no idea." Riggs was in his forties, black hair and dark eyes, a terrible dresser in too-tight black slacks he must have thought were the latest fashion.

Emma figured the salesman had sold him a size too small. He wore loafers without socks and a wrinkled beige linen sport coat. His bed head wasn't the least bit flattering.

Luke held up the plastic baggie. "You don't answer my

questions, Felix, I'm calling nine-one-one. Cops will arrest you for dealing. Since I happen to know you're on parole, you're going to have a serious problem."

"Screw you. What do you want?"

"I need to find Vance. Any little tidbit you can give me will do. If you don't know where he is, then tell me why he's back in Seattle. Maybe he's got a deal going down. Maybe he's visiting a lady. If you want to walk away, you're going to have to give me something."

"I'm not giving you shit."

Luke reached into the pocket of his jeans and pulled out a folding knife. Emma barely heard the click as a four-inch blade popped out.

"You better start talking or this conversation is going to get real serious real fast."

Glancing down at the spray of blood from stooge number two's broken nose, fighting a memory of Eleanor Harris lying dead and bloody in the hall, Emma stepped out of the shadows and moved past Luke toward Riggs.

"Fuck."

"You don't have to swear, Luke." She smiled at Riggs. "I'm Emma Cassidy. I'm a friend of Lila's."

Riggs swiveled his head in her direction. "Lila sent you here?"

"No, but we talked about you. She likes you. A lot."

"She does?"

"Yes, she does."

"She'd already gone home when I got to the club. I was hoping she'd still be there."

"Lila said she was sure you'd be willing to help us. We don't need much, just some idea where Rudy might be. Luke's helping me, but I'm the one who's looking for him. Rudy and I . . . we were . . . you know . . . involved until he had to leave town. That's how I know you. I was at that

party on Bainbridge Island. You remember the party, right?
I saw you there that night. I'd really like to see Rudy again.
And I know he'd like to see me."

She had a good figure. She moved a little, opening the
jacket so her badge didn't show but the curve of her bosom
did. When Riggs's gaze ran over her breasts, she saw Luke's
mouth tighten.

"Yeah, I think I remember you." Riggs frowned at Luke.
"So what are you? Some kind of private dick?"

"That's right," Emma answered before Luke could ruin
her play with some snarky remark, grateful that for once
there was someone Luke didn't know. "I hired him to
help me."

"Like I said, I got no idea where Rudy is. I don't know
if he's back in town or not." He looked over at Luke, who
was holding the knife with a sort of casual intimacy. "But
I might know something."

"All right, go on," Luke said.

"Rudy's got an aunt. Once in a while, he'd stop by and
see her. If you're looking to find him, you might try talking
to her."

"What's her name?" Luke asked.

"Bernice Mills. She had a place over in Wallingford. Be
best if you didn't mention I told you."

"No problem." Luke folded the knife and slid it back
into the pocket of his jeans.

"What about my stuff?" Riggs asked, eyeing the baggie.

Luke opened the plastic bag and dumped the white
powder onto the cement floor of the garage.

Riggs hissed as if he were in pain.

"You ought to be thanking me, Felix. That stuff will ruin
your health."

Riggs ground his jaw. He turned to Emma. "Next time

you see Lila, will you tell her I helped you out? Maybe put in a good word for me?"

"Sure, I can do that."

"You won't forget?"

"No, I promise I won't forget."

"Get in the truck," Luke said to her darkly.

Ignoring his foul mood, Emma walked back to the Bronco, climbed into the passenger seat, and slammed the car door.

Luke drove out of the parking garage and headed back to the Polo Club. It was half an hour after closing. He needed to drop Emma back at her car, then haul his tired ass home.

He glanced over to where she sat in the passenger seat. "You're a damned good liar, I'll give you that. Maybe you're more suited to the job than I thought."

"I wasn't lying. I was improvising. I learned it from Booth."

He felt the pull of a smile. "Got to say it worked pretty well. You got Riggs to give up a lead. I'd say we're even."

"Would you really have used the knife?"

He checked his rearview mirror, signaled, turned a corner. "Probably not."

Emma's eyebrows shot up. "Probably?"

Luke grinned. She was really cute, with her big brown eyes and plump pink lips. He liked those heavy dark curls. Liked the way they framed her pretty face.

"Just holding the blade up is usually enough of a threat," he said. "Most people don't like knives."

She made a sound in her throat. "But you do."

He shrugged. "If it becomes necessary, I know how to use one."

There was something in her face the instant before she turned away and gazed back out the window. He didn't know much about her, wondered what her story was. Thought it might be interesting to find out.

They didn't talk again till he pulled into the Polo Club parking lot and stopped behind her little white Mazda.

"Time to go home, Em Cassidy." Luke flashed her a heated glance. "Unless you want to actually do what Badger and his boys thought you were going to do—go back to my place and be my evening's entertainment."

Emma scoffed. "Fat chance. From what I've heard, you'd sleep with a snake if it would hold still long enough."

Luke laughed. "Now you've hurt my feelings."

Emma cracked open the door. "Don't be surprised to see me at Bernice Mills's house—unless I come up with a better lead in the meantime." She started to get down, but Luke caught her arm.

"Hold on a minute. Truth is, you did a pretty good job tonight. You made a couple of mistakes, but overall, you did okay. If you want to go with me to the aunt's house, I'll call you before I go." He was lying. *Improvising.* No way was he taking her anywhere.

He didn't want Emma getting even more involved in the pursuit of a guy as dangerous as Vance. Once Luke found him and hauled his ruthless, perverted ass in, Emma would move on to another case.

She flashed him a smile. "That'd be great, Luke. I'd love to go with you. I really appreciate it." She handed him a business card. Her name and cell were the only things printed on it. "Give me a call and I'll meet you there or we can ride over together."

He took one look at her too-sweet smile and knew he was being played. "Jesus Christ, you aren't going to wait, are you? You're going to talk to the woman come hell or high water."

"I was improvising—just like you. And clearly I need to improve my technique."

"Fuck."

"You don't need to swear. Good night, Luke."

"Wait a minute!"

But she was already out of the vehicle. Opening her car door, she slid in behind the wheel.

Luke cursed foully. It shouldn't matter what Emma Cassidy did. She was her own person. She could do whatever she wanted. If the lady got into trouble, it was a lesson she needed to learn.

He shouldn't give a damn.

Trouble was, he did.

Luke watched her drive out of the parking lot. He only followed her partway home. He figured if Badger and his cronies were lying in wait for her, they would be easy enough to spot. Finally satisfied she'd be okay, Luke turned the Bronco and headed for his apartment.

Chapter Seven

Emma tried to make a yoga class at least once a week. Not today. She hadn't gotten home last night till nearly four in the morning, then overslept and didn't wake up until noon.

She'd been right about the aches and pains. As she'd rolled out of bed, a groan bubbled up from her throat. Going head-to-head with Ivan-the-terrible and Badger-the-stooge had been a lot harder than the self-defense drills she did with Len and Nita.

Emma dragged herself down the hall to the kitchen. With Chelsea away, she made herself a pot of coffee, then ate some yogurt and fruit for breakfast. Her shared two-bedroom, one-bath apartment was neat and clean but spartan. Emma had more important matters to deal with than decorating, and Chelsea was gone more than she was home.

She finished the strawberry yogurt, refilled her coffee cup, and carried it into her bedroom, over to the desk where her laptop was set up.

Her primary objective was to track down Bernice Mills. Riggs had given her an area—Wallingford—but no address. She hoped it wouldn't take too long to find her.

Emma tried to imagine what Bernice would be like, a woman with a close relationship to rapist and murderer Rudolph Vance. But even monsters had family. Robert Yates, a serial killer who'd lived in Spokane, had had a wife and five kids.

Taking a sip of coffee, Emma went to work on her computer. It didn't take long to come up with an address in the Wallingford area and a phone number for Bernice Mills, but the phone had been disconnected. She checked the utilities, but they'd been changed out of her name six months ago.

No death certificate filed that Emma could find. But bail enforcement agents were, first and foremost, skip tracers. Locating people was their specialty. Sooner or later, she would find Bernice Mills. She just hoped Luke Brodie wouldn't find her first.

It was late afternoon when she finished her initial search without much luck. She had more work to do but she wanted to go over and see Booth, check on him, and fill him in on the lead she'd gotten from Felix Riggs. She wished she could manage to do it without mentioning Luke Brodie, but she wasn't going to *improvise,* not to Booth.

When she arrived at Oakmont, he was taking an afternoon stroll around the courtyard with Barbara Wilson, one of his nurses. Barb was in her late fifties, blond and attractive, and clearly falling for Booth's macho charisma.

As Emma walked toward them across the grass, Barb glanced over and smiled. "Hi, Emma, your timing's good. Booth's just finished his walk." The nurse settled him in the wheelchair he hated, rolled it over beneath a shade tree, and left them alone to talk.

"I like Barb," Emma said, sitting down on a cement bench beside him.

"So do I." Booth's gaze followed the buxom nurse till she disappeared inside the building.

"I think she likes you, too."

Booth flashed a roguish, lopsided grin. "What can I say? I'm not dead yet."

Emma laughed. "Not even close," she said. "I came by to bring you up to speed on Riggs, like I promised."

"So you found him." Booth started nodding. "That's good work. He didn't give you any trouble?"

Emma took a deep breath. "Actually, I did have a little trouble at the Polo Club. By the way, that's a really stupid name for a dump like that."

Booth chuckled. "No question about it. What happened?"

"I had a run-in with a big goon named Ivan, then Badger somebody and two of his stooges showed up in the parking lot. They . . . umm . . . wanted me to . . . umm . . . party with them. Luke Brodie arrived and told them I was with him and that was pretty much the end of it."

Booth cast her a speculative glance, as if he knew there was a lot more to the story. "Brodie was there?"

She nodded. "He's got the contract on Vance."

"I should have figured," Boothe said. His knowing gaze ran over her. "So Brodie showed up and saved your ass, and the two of you went after Riggs together?"

"I'll admit I was in a pretty tight spot when he got there. He told Badger and the others to leave me alone and we left the club together, then we came back and staked the place out. Riggs arrived. When he left, we followed him to his apartment, and he gave us a lead on Vance."

Booth started shaking his head. "Luke Brodie works solo. There's only one thing he wants from a woman and it isn't help bringing in a skip."

Emma's face went red. "He didn't want my help. I told him I was going with him—I didn't give him any choice."

Booth started chuckling. "I wish I'd been a fly on the wall when that went down." Booth's crooked smile slipped away. "Brodie's a notorious womanizer, Emma. You aren't in his league."

"I'm not getting involved with Brodie. He helped me out. I'm grateful, but not the kind of grateful you're thinking."

Booth seemed relieved. "All right, then. I want all the gory details, so I can live vicariously."

Emma relaxed. The topic of Luke Brodie was over, at least for the moment. For the next half hour, she replayed the events that had given her Bernice Mills, Rudolph Vance's aunt. She hadn't found the woman yet, but she was sure she would.

From Oakmont, she headed home and went back to work on the computer. Wednesday morning, she had target practice, then she planned to head over to the house on Bagley Avenue that was Bernice's former address. She wanted to talk to the neighbors, see if any of them knew where the woman had moved.

As she sat in front of her laptop, she felt a tug of loneliness. Chelsea was rarely there. She wished she could talk to her sister, visit April and Ginny. But they were no longer living in Seattle.

An FBI agent involved in the murder case had stepped in, pulled some strings, and gotten them into witness protection. With Ginny underage and the victim of a rape and a second attempt, with Rudy Vance still on the loose and a deadly threat, April had done as the agent told her, packed their things, severed all ties, and left for parts unknown until Rudolph Vance could be found and arrested.

Her sister and Ginny were the only family she had left. Their parents had died in a small plane crash five years ago. April had been raising a nine-year-old daughter by then, her no-account ex-husband already long gone—

good riddance, as far as Emma was concerned. In the years since the divorce, he hadn't even sent his daughter a birthday card.

April and Ginny meant everything to Emma. The sooner she found Rudolph Vance, the sooner she would have her family back.

Emma awoke early enough to attend her Wednesday self-defense class. After an hour of training with Len and Nita, she drove over to Wade's, an indoor target range, and parked in the lot behind the building.

Dressed in khaki cargo pants, a black T-shirt, her hair pulled into a ponytail stuck through the hole in a black baseball cap with a gold fugitive recovery emblem on the front, she grabbed her gear bag, hooked the strap of her purse over her arm, and got out of her Mazda.

Wade's shooting range was a big cement block building in Bellevue. At the counter in front, Emma signed in, then headed for the gallery in the rear, her steps accompanied by the roar of gunfire echoing inside the walls.

Finding her assigned cubicle along the row of shooters, she opened her gear bag and took out a pair of protective glasses. She shoved them on, then set her earmuffs over her ears.

The Glock came out next. She dropped the clip to check the load and found the magazine full, as she had expected. Taking a double-handed grip and a wide-legged stance, she took careful aim at the man-shaped target forty feet away.

The clip held fifteen rounds. Holding the pistol steady, she pulled off one shot after another until the clip was empty, then hooked the earmuffs around her neck and shoved the glasses up on her head. With the push of a button, the target rattled toward the cubicle.

Under the cacophony of gunfire, she hadn't heard anyone approach. "Two nice groupings," Luke Brodie said, his deep voice sending a little shiver across her skin. "Four head shots dead center. One a little to the right. Nine heart shots dead center, one a little right. Nice work, Calamity Jane."

She smiled at his praise. "Thanks, Cool Hand."

The corner of Luke's mouth edged up. "You twisted a little on both those missed shots. Reload and I'll show you."

"What are you doing here?" Keeping the barrel aimed down, she dropped the empty clip and shoved in a full one, trying to ignore how close he stood.

"I wanted to talk to you."

"How'd you know where to find me?"

"You're in Bellevue, Emma. This is my neck of the woods. Besides, I called Booth and asked him. He said you practiced here on Wednesdays. I called Wade and he told me what time you'd be in."

"My, aren't we efficient?"

"Finding people is what I do, sweet pea." He moved even closer, close enough she could feel his heat, and suddenly it was hard to breathe. "Now turn around and take your shooting stance."

She pulled her glasses down over her eyes, set her muffs over her ears, widened her stance, and brought her weapon into position. Luke stepped behind her, so close she could feel the roughness of his jeans, the hard muscles in his chest and shoulders against her back. Wrapping his arms around hers, he steadied the weapon in her hand.

Emma closed her eyes and breathed him in. She didn't give a damn about hitting the target.

"Emma, are you paying attention?"

"Yes . . . yes, of course." She reminded herself to focus, felt his hand on her hip, adjusting her position, holding her in place. Emma took a calming breath and pulled off a round. It hit dead center, a perfect heart shot.

"Feel the difference?"

God, yes, and it felt amazing. She just nodded.

"Do it again."

She concentrated on keeping her hip in the position he'd shown her and cracked off another perfect round.

"Nice," he said, but he didn't move. "Damn, you smell good." He buried his face in the hair beside her ear and inhaled her scent. "What's that perfume you're wearing?"

"Night . . . Night of Passion."

"I really like it." He took a step back. The heat was gone but she felt light-headed.

He pushed the button, moving the target out another ten feet. "Try it one more time."

She had to get this right. If she missed, he'd give her another lesson and she didn't think she could survive it.

She took the proper stance, remembered to keep her hip straight, held the weapon steady. She practiced at this distance a lot. She pulled the trigger, fired six more rounds before they brought the target in.

"Perfect." Luke studied the man-shaped image riddled with bullet holes. "You're a helluva shot, Emma."

She relaxed, smiled at the compliment. "Thanks."

Luke waited until she'd finished practicing with the little .380 she carried in her purse; then she was done.

She smiled up at him, pleased with herself for shooting so well with him there watching. "Your turn."

"All right." They changed the target. Luke pulled his pistol from the holster clipped to his belt.

"What are you shooting?" she asked.

"M-9 Beretta nine mil. Custom grip." Luke stepped into the cubicle and took a double-handed shooting stance. He fired fifteen perfectly centered rounds, seven in the head, eight in the chest.

"Impressive," she said.

Luke just shrugged. "I've had a lot of practice."

She didn't have to ask what he meant. She knew he'd been Army Special Forces. They packed up their gear and walked out of the building, into the shade of a big cedar tree that overlooked the parking lot. The June weather was crisp and cool, the day crystal clear. It was a nice change from a string of wet weather.

"So what did you want to talk to me about?" Emma asked.

"Did you find Bernice Mills?"

"Not yet, but I will. I don't think she's living in Wallingford anymore. I planned to go over to her last known address as soon as I was finished here."

"Great. Let's go."

"Wait a minute. Now you want to work together? Or maybe you didn't find her and you're tricking me into giving you information."

He flicked her a *get real* glance.

"Okay, so you know as much about her as I do. Maybe you're just trying to find another way to keep me out of your hair."

"Now there's an idea I hadn't considered," he said dryly.

Emma rolled her eyes.

"Truth is, I gave it a lot of thought before I came over here. We both want Vance. You can help me track him down. Once I have a location, I'll take it from there. I'll pay you a fee for your help."

It was common for bounty hunters to work together to bring in a skip and share the fee. Still, she wasn't quite sure she believed him. "So you're actually going to let me work with you. You aren't improvising again, are you?"

Luke shook his head. "Not this time, darlin'."

The endearment sent a curl of heat into her stomach. She knew he'd said it to a thousand women, but still . . .

"I need to be sure this isn't some kind of joke or just a way to get rid of me. I want your word. I presume that's something you stand by."

He sobered. "I never break my word. And you have it. We work together to locate Rudolph Vance, then I take it from there."

"We work together to locate Vance, then we'll see."

"Dammit, Emma."

"We need to get going, Luke. If we don't find Vance's aunt, we'll be right back where we started. We won't have anything to argue about because we won't have a lead on Vance."

Luke blew out a breath. Amazingly he nodded. "We can leave your car here and pick it up on the way back." They started walking across the lot toward the Bronco. When his hand settled at her waist to help her climb into the passenger seat, heat radiated from her stomach straight to her core.

Emma hissed in a breath. Maybe this wasn't such a good idea after all. Maybe she should have kept working the case on her own. She didn't want to join the ranks of Luke Brodie's nightly entertainments. Not for all the money in Vegas.

But she did want Rudolph Vance, and Luke was her best chance of finding him.

Emma sucked up her courage, leaned back in the seat, and clicked her belt into place for the ride to Wallingford.

Chapter Eight

Damn, he wanted to take her to bed. Watching Emma Cassidy squeeze the trigger, seeing the way the muscles clenched in her fine little ass, the way her full breasts quivered when she pulled off a shot, just flat turned him on.

Emma was one hot lady. Pure temptation in a dynamite package. But it was more than that. There was something about the concentration on her face, the determination to get the shot exactly right, her unbelievable focus. She'd worked damned hard to get as good as she was. She was tough, and yet he had a feeling she was marshmallow-soft on the inside. He'd never met a woman quite like her.

Emma was driven, no question about it, motivated by something he hadn't yet figured out. Eventually he would. Figuring people out was what he did, and he was good at it.

She wasn't his type. Emma Cassidy was no one-night stand. He was reminded of that every time she blushed when he spit out a dirty word. Emma was sweet and she was sexy. The smell of her soft perfume drove him crazy. She wasn't meant for a battle-hardened guy like him. He needed to leave her the hell alone.

He would, he promised himself. *Maybe*.

In the meantime, he was doing her a favor, helping her

find Vance, letting her get involved in a way that would keep her out of danger. Or at least that was the plan.

The Bronco rolled up to an address on Bagley Avenue, a single-story wood-frame older home heavily overgrown with shrubs.

As Luke turned off the engine and cracked open his door, Emma pulled off the baseball cap with the bail enforcement logo on the front. She was out of the car and headed for the front door before he'd rounded the hood.

He caught up with her in a few long strides and grabbed her arm, pulling her to a halt. Freed from the cap, her ponytail bobbed enticingly. He wanted to free those pretty curls and run his fingers through them, see if they felt as silky as they looked.

"Take it easy," he said. "You never know what you're going to find behind that closed door. Better to take your time, check things out a little."

He pointed to the window. "See that? Someone's watching from behind the curtains."

"I see him."

"Looks like a kid. We're probably good to go."

She smiled. "I guess sometimes I get a little overeager."

Amusement slid through him. "I hadn't noticed."

Emma laughed. He really liked the sound.

"Okay, I'll tone it down."

Now that he'd seen the kid, he let her go first. They climbed the steps to a tiny covered front porch. "Go ahead and take the lead."

Emma stepped forward. Clearly she liked taking control. His thoughts went sideways. He liked taking control, too, especially in the bedroom. He wondered how that would work out.

Emma knocked on the door. Luke relaxed his usually straight posture to look less intimidating and came up with a casual smile. The door opened and a teenage boy no more than fourteen stood in the entry. He had thick brown hair and frayed jeans with holes in the knees, a faded orange T-shirt with a dinosaur that said RAPTOR TRAINER underneath.

Emma smiled at the kid. "Hi, I'm Emma, and this is Luke. We hate to bother you, but we're friends of Mrs. Mills, the lady who used to live here. We know she moved, but somehow we lost touch. Do you know where she's living now?"

"I got no idea. Sorry." The boy was texting as he talked. Emma's mouth thinned. She looked like she wanted to smack him in the head like she'd done to Skinner Digby, tell him he was being rude.

"Well, thanks anyway," she said with a smile that looked more like a scowl.

Luke started to turn, to head back down the sidewalk.

"You could try the lady across the street," the kid said when he'd finished his text. "I heard my mom say her and Mrs. Mills were friends."

Luke was surprised Emma didn't correct the boy's grammar.

"Thank you." Her smile this time was real. When she turned, Luke could read the excitement in her face. She was definitely still new at this. He didn't get excited till he was hard on the scent and ready to go in for the capture. Then he went dead calm.

He followed her across the street, trying not to notice the sexy little wiggle going on inside her cargo pants, but hey, he was a guy, wasn't he? Add to that, he hadn't been with a woman in more than three weeks.

He continued his scan of the neighborhood but didn't see anything out of the ordinary. A dog ran out of the shrubbery as they moved along the sidewalk and headed straight for Emma. A gangly black lab puppy that nearly knocked her down.

She crouched and gave the damned mutt a quick hug.

"Aren't you a good boy? Yes, you are." She rose again and scrubbed his shiny black head.

She pointed back the way the animal had come. "Go home, boy. You don't want to get lost. Go on now. Go home." As if the dog understood, it turned and trotted back the way it had come.

Luke just shook his head.

"So you don't like dogs?" she asked.

"We're working, Emma. Getting sidetracked in this kind of job can get you dead."

She flushed. "I wasn't thinking. Sorry."

Luke almost smiled. "I like dogs. If I were more settled, I'd have one. As it is, it just wouldn't work."

She sighed. "That's the reason I don't have one, either. I figure once this is over—" She broke off as if she'd said something wrong.

"When what's over, Emma? You talking about catching Vance?"

Emma just shrugged. "I won't always be a bail enforcement agent. Eventually I want to open a school that teaches women's self-defense. I've gotten pretty good at it."

"Can't argue with that. You did a helluva job the other night. Just remember it doesn't make you bulletproof."

She glanced at him as if he'd imparted some universal wisdom, continued up the walk, and rang the bell. Several long seconds later, an elderly woman pulled open the door. Heavyset, with short white hair, she had so many wrinkles she looked like a dried-apple doll.

Emma made introductions, saying they were friends of Bernice Mills who'd lost touch with her over the years. The conversation went back and forth, casual, no pressure.

"I saw you on the sidewalk with Scooter," said the older woman, whose name, they'd discovered, was Helen. "He belongs to Freddie Henson, the boy across the street. Scooter's a real nice dog."

"Yes, he is," Emma sincerely agreed.

"Well, as far as I'm concerned, anyone who loves dogs can't be a bad person. I'll just go write down Bernice's address and phone number for you." As the woman turned away, Emma's excited gaze swung to Luke. "*We got it!*" she silently mouthed.

Luke found himself smiling.

The lady returned with a folded slip of paper, which she handed to Emma.

"Thank you, Helen," she said. "We really appreciate it."

"If you don't mind," Luke put in, "we'd really like to surprise her."

"Oh, that should be fun. I won't spoil it for you." She smiled. "I was just about to brew a pot of tea. You and your husband are more than welcome to join me."

"I wish we had time," Luke said, before Emma felt the need to politely accept. "Maybe next time we're in the neighborhood."

"Of course." Helen's wrinkled face reflected her disappointment.

"Thank you again," Emma called over her shoulder as Luke urged her off the porch, back down the walkway. By the time they reached the Bronco, she was practically jumping up and down. "We did it! I almost can't believe it!"

"Nice job," Luke said. "Assuming Bernice is actually there, all we have to do now is get her to open up and tell us where to find Rudy Vance."

Some of Emma's enthusiasm faded. Neither of them thought it was going to be that easy.

As the Bronco roared along the highway at breakneck speed, Emma used her smartphone to search county ownership records on the address they'd been given for Bernice Mills.

"The property's in the name of Lyle McCarthy." Pensive, she glanced up from the screen. "I know that name. He's a partner in International Cargo. It's an import-export company. McCarthy's linked to—"

"Rudy Vance," Luke said. "You've done your homework, Emma. McCarthy's probably a straw man for Vance, who actually owns the house."

"Rudy's got plenty of money. He and his aunt were close. It makes sense he'd want to take care of her. I bet she still lives there."

"Let's hope you're right." His gaze went down the road to a street sign up ahead. "There's the turn." Luke drove into a neighborhood of moderately priced houses. The Bronco continued past a redbrick home at the address Helen had given them, but didn't stop.

Pulling up beneath a sycamore tree in front of a house down the block, Luke cut the engine. Digging out his cell phone, he started dialing the number on the paper Helen had given them.

"You're going to call her?"

"I want to see if anyone's home." He kept the phone pressed to his ear. When the line picked up, he hit the end button, severing the connection. "Woman's voice. Now I need to see if she's alone."

He slid the phone back into his jeans. "You're armed. I need you to stay here while I take a look around." He'd insisted she bring her Glock. The .380 was in her purse. She was definitely carrying some firepower.

"I'm going with you," she said.

"You can go. Just give me a minute to surveil the place. If it's clear, I'll come back and get you."

"What if Vance is in there? You might need backup."

The corner of his mouth edged up. "If he's there, I'll handle it." He reached behind the seat and unzipped his canvas gear bag, took out the pair of radios they had used at the Polo Club, handed one to Emma.

"Keep an eye out. If he's in there and tries to run, he might come your way. Be careful. And give me a heads-up if you see anything."

She wanted to argue, which Luke must have known.

He reached over and gently caught her shoulder. Heat radiated clear to her toes. "I need to be sure he isn't there before we go in," Luke said. "If I go by myself, I won't be spotted."

He was right. Of course he was right. He was Luke Brodie. "Okay."

The next instant he was gone. She hadn't even noticed the alley that ran behind the house until he disappeared behind a heavy row of dark green shrubs. The Glock was under her seat. She pulled it out and set it within easy reach. Rudolph Vance was a murderer. He wouldn't hesitate to kill again.

Emma watched uneasily until Luke reappeared, his moccasins moving soundlessly toward her across the grass. She should be thinking about Vance, but she couldn't help noticing his long, confident strides, how wide his shoulders were in comparison to his narrow hips.

Dangerous thinking. And unusual for her. She hadn't felt the least attraction to a man since the day she'd come home and discovered Rudy Vance had murdered Eleanor Harris and attacked her sweet little niece.

Luke reached the Bronco and pulled open her door. "She's alone. Let's go."

Emma followed him up on the sidewalk and they reached the house together. Luke rang the bell beside the front door, then stepped back to let Emma take the lead. Apparently he was satisfied with the way she'd handled things so far.

A thin woman answered the door. "May I help you?" She was younger than Helen, late sixties, Emma would guess, tall, fine-boned, and frail, with mostly silver hair.

"Mrs. Mills? I'm Emma Brodie and this is my husband, Luke." She cast him a glance, warning him to go along with the story she had thought up on the way, thanks to Helen. Luke seemed amused. "My husband used to work for your nephew, Rudy Vance. Luke's out of work at the moment, and I just found out I'm pregnant."

Luke's amusement faded.

"We heard Rudy was back in town," she said. "He was always very good to us. We're hoping you might know where we can find him. We're really hoping he might have a job for Luke."

"You're friends of Rudolph's?"

"That's right," Luke said.

"My nephew's never had many friends. Why don't you come in?"

Emma clamped down on her excitement. Being invited into the house was further than she'd ever expected to get. "Thank you. That's very kind."

As they walked into the entry, the glance Luke cast her way held a trace of respect. Emma surveyed the comfortable living room: a burgundy overstuffed sofa and chairs, doilies on the armrests, family photos on the table beneath windows covered with white lace curtains.

"If you have the time," Bernice said, "I can bring us something to drink."

"That would be lovely," Emma said. "As long as there's nothing alcoholic in it." She bit back a smile, enjoying Luke's discomfort.

"Of course not, dear."

Luke surprised her with a grin.

Bernice returned a few minutes later carrying a tray that

held a pitcher of lemonade and three glasses. Setting the tray down on the coffee table, she poured each of them a glass.

Luke took a sip. "This is great, Mrs. Mills. Tastes like homemade."

The woman actually blushed. No big surprise. With his brilliant blue eyes and amazing dark-angel face, Luke Brodie was incredibly handsome. Clearly, even much older women weren't immune.

"I always make my lemonade from scratch," Bernice proudly explained. "I don't really care for the frozen kind."

Luke took another sip, then wandered over to the window to examine the photos on the table, a bounty hunter trick that often yielded valuable information.

"Nice-looking family," he said, taking another sip of his drink.

Bernice walked up beside him. "That's my sister's daughter, Annabelle. She's with Eric, her second husband. Rudy's the boy in front, next to Eric's daughter, Cissy. Rudy's thirteen. Cissy's just nine."

"So technically you're Rudy's great-aunt," Luke said, while Emma made the same mental calculation.

"Yes, that's right. You know he was adopted. I think that was the reason he always felt so much an outsider."

Rudy was adopted? Emma was surprised she had missed that when she'd created her profile. She should have dug even deeper, a lesson she wouldn't forget.

"He never talked about his parents," Luke said.

"The three of them never really got along. They were just too different. I felt sorry for him. I never condemned him when he acted out, the way Annabelle and Eric did. I suppose that's the reason he felt closer to me than he did to them, at least in his early years."

Standing next to Bernice, Emma's gaze traveled to

another photo on the table. A pretty young girl in a white lace dress with light brown hair, a heart-shaped face, and warm brown eyes. Her features were familiar. Beyond familiar. Her heart jerked. The girl looked enough like Ginny to be her twin.

Emma's whole body went numb. "Is that . . . is that Cissy?"

"Why, yes it is. It was taken a few years later, on her fourteenth birthday."

Emma couldn't breathe. The glass of lemonade began to slip through her nerveless fingers, and would have crashed to the floor if Luke hadn't plucked it out of her hand.

"You all right?" he asked.

Emma swallowed. "Yes . . . I'm . . . I'm fine."

"It's probably the pregnancy," he put in smoothly. His blue eyes went to Bernice. "Maybe she should sit down."

"Yes, of course." Bernice led her over to the sofa. "Come, dear, sit right here."

Luke set their lemonade glasses on the tray as Emma sat down on the sofa. Bernice sat next to her while Luke took a seat in an overstuffed chair.

"I'm fine, really," Emma said. "I just felt dizzy for a moment." Luke was eyeing her strangely. She wondered what story she could come up with when he asked what had happened, which she knew he would.

"I probably ought to get her home," Luke said. "If you could tell us where to find Rudy, that would be really great, Mrs. Mills."

Bernice seemed to consider her answer. "I presume you're aware of Rudy's troubles."

"We read about his arrest in the newspapers when it happened," Luke said. "He was a good boss. I didn't figure there was any truth to it. I know he's not in jail. I heard he was back in the area. He's got a business to run. I thought maybe he could use my help, someone he's worked with before."

Bernice shook her head. "I'm afraid I can't help. I haven't heard from Rudy since before he was arrested."

Luke raked a hand through his sun-streaked brown hair. "I was really hoping you'd know where to find him. With the baby coming, I really need a job."

Bernice glanced away. She reached for her lemonade with an unsteady hand, took a sip, then carefully set the glass back down on the tray.

When she looked back at Luke, resignation lined her face. "You're Rudy's friend so I'm not sure I should tell you this. But you seem like such a nice couple, I feel it's my Christian duty. The truth is, there's a very good chance at least some of what they said in the newspapers was true."

Luke sat forward in his chair. "You think Rudy killed that woman, the housekeeper?"

"I don't know about that. I can't imagine Rudolph killing anyone, but what happened to that little girl . . ." She pressed her lips together, then released a slow breath.

"When Rudy was a teen, he . . . well, he became enamored of his stepsister, the little girl in the photo. He began . . . having relations with Cissy when she was nine years old. It continued for several years before Cissy finally came forward and told her father. When Rudy's mother confronted him, he said he was in love with Cissy, that he hadn't meant to hurt her." Tears welled in Bernice's eyes. "She was just a little girl."

An image of Ginny appeared in Emma's mind and her throat closed up, trapping a sob inside. A tremor ran through her. She had to get out of there, had to leave before she burst into tears.

"What happened to him after that?" Luke asked.

"His family sent Rudy to live with me and moved back

East. Once Cissy grew into a young woman, Rudy's interest in her seemed to fade."

"We need to find him," Luke said to Bernice. "Can you help us?"

"I told you the truth. I haven't seen him since before he was arrested. I don't know where he is."

"Take a guess. Is there a place he might go? Someplace he'd feel safe?"

Her gaze sharpened on Luke's face. "You aren't his friends, are you? I suspected the moment you walked through the door. You want to arrest him."

Luke didn't hesitate. "Yes," he said, taking the same risk Emma would have taken. "He's already hurt another little girl. We don't want him to do it again."

Bernice made a sound in her throat. She straightened on the sofa, took a deep breath, and slowly released it. "There was a house on Whidbey Island. I don't know if he owns it or rents it or what. If he's somewhere near Seattle, he might be there. Almost no one knows about it. Rudy rarely mentioned it to anyone. It was his personal retreat."

Luke rose from his chair. "Thank you, Bernice."

Emma moved silently toward the door. As Luke walked past, he leaned over and kissed Bernice on the cheek. "You did the right thing."

Striding toward the door, he walked out of the house.

Chapter Nine

Luke found Emma in the shade of the sycamore tree down the block, next to where he'd parked the Bronco. She was sitting on the lawn, her knees drawn up beneath her chin.

Luke sat down cross-legged on the lawn beside her. Plucking a long stem of grass, he twirled it between his fingers, giving her a little reprieve. But he wasn't about to wait long.

"What's going on, Em? What happened in there?"

She pulled a stem just like his, toyed with it. "Nothing happened. I was role-playing, is all. I thought it would give you an opening and it did."

Luke shook his head. "You're improvising and it isn't going to work. If I'm going to partner with someone, I have to trust them. I have to trust you, Emma. Tell me the truth."

She looked up at him and tears leaked from the corners of her eyes. Luke felt it like a punch in the stomach.

"The girl in the photo . . . I recognized her. She looks exactly like my niece, Ginny Hodges. Exactly."

"Ginny Hodges," he repeated, recognizing the name. "The fourteen-year-old girl Vance raped was your niece?"

Emma wiped away a tear that escaped down her cheek. "Yes."

With that one word, the puzzle pieces all fell together. "That's the reason you're after Vance, the reason you became an agent. You want Ginny safe."

"That's right."

"Vance went after Ginny two different times. The second time he killed a woman. Now that you've seen the photo, you know why he was obsessed with her. You don't believe she'll ever be safe until Vance is locked behind bars."

Something unreadable moved across her features. She released a shaky breath. "He told Ginny he was coming back and I believe him. He won't give up and I won't stop until I find him."

"Where's Ginny now?"

"She's in witness protection. Even I don't know where she and my sister are hiding. I just know I won't have my family back until this is over. I'm going to do everything in my power to make sure Vance never hurts anyone again."

He'd known there was a reason she'd put herself through the study, training, and difficult physical conditioning it took to become a successful bail enforcement agent. Now he understood Emma's determination.

Luke pushed to his feet and reached a hand down to help her up. When Emma placed her smaller hand in his, something fiercely protective moved through him.

"Come on," he said a little gruffly, hauling her to her feet. "Let's go."

As they reached the SUV, she pulled free of his hold. "You aren't going to work with me anymore, are you?"

He shouldn't. This was personal for Emma. Her being so emotionally involved put both of them in danger. "Whatever I decide to do, you won't stop, will you?"

"No."

"Then I guess I'm stuck with you until we catch Vance."

Emma blinked as if she hadn't heard him correctly. "You mean it?"

"Stupid, but yeah—I mean it."

For the first time Emma smiled. It made his chest feel tight. "We need to find that house on Whidbey Island."

"We need to regroup, gather some intel, find the house, and surveil it. If Vance is there, we'll nail him."

It was late afternoon by the time they got back to Bellevue. Emma wanted to head straight for the island, to start asking questions, try to locate the house. But Luke was right. It would be easier if they had more information.

Driving the Bronco into the parking lot behind a two-story, freestanding brick building on Bellevue Way, Luke parked in one of the spaces and turned off the engine.

"Home sweet home," he said as he grabbed his laptop out of the backseat and closed the door.

"You don't actually live here, do you?" Emma said, slamming her door and joining him at the rear of the vehicle.

He chuckled. "Mostly I live in my ride—or at least it feels that way." They started walking. "But I've got an apartment in Bellevue and a cabin up near Gold Bar. That's my bug-out spot when I need to get away. What about you?"

"I share an apartment with a friend."

His gaze shot to hers, stopping her forward motion. "Male or female?"

"Female. Her name is Chelsea Davenport." Her roommate was definitely female. Emma hadn't even had a date since before the murder, but she wasn't about to tell Luke that.

His shoulders relaxed. "Let's go inside."

As they reached the office door, she noticed the black and silver sign that read BRODIE OPERATIONS SECURITY SERVICES, INC.

Luke's gaze followed hers. "BOSS, Inc., we call it." He held open the door so she could walk into the office, which was very masculine and modern, with lots of black and chrome.

They passed a conference room with a long mahogany table surrounded by black and chrome chairs. A big flat-screen monitor hung on a wall at the far end of the room.

The main part of the office was lined with rows of desks. Luke tipped his head toward a powerfully built, dark-haired man seated behind his laptop. A man with a lean, sinewy build sat in the chair next to the guy at the desk.

"See those two jokers over there? The big one's my brother. The guy with the 'stache is Dirk Reynolds. Come on, I'll introduce you."

The men stood up as Luke walked Emma over to the black, Formica-topped desk.

"Ethan and Dirk, this is Emma Cassidy. She's a bounty hunter."

Dirk's hazel gaze started at her ponytail, traveled over her black T-shirt to the bottom of her cargo pants. He looked like he was waiting for the punch line. Ethan was eyeing Luke as if he'd gone over the edge.

"Hey, it's not a joke," Luke said. "You should have seen her in action over at the Polo Club. Pepper-sprayed that big dumb-ass Ivan Dorell and left him crying like a baby. And poor ol' Badger Stovall will never walk the same again."

Ethan's dark eyebrows climbed up. He glanced from Luke to Emma. "Wish I'd been there."

Dirk's lips twitched in amusement, moving the short-cropped mustache that curved over his mouth and ran down to an iron-hard jaw. Both men oozed confidence.

"We're working together to bring in Rudy Vance," Luke said. "We got a lead, a house on Whidbey Island. We need to find the location."

"Sounds promising," Ethan said.

"If you need some backup," Dirk said, "just let me know."

"We've got to find the place first. Even if we do, he might not be there."

"Still," Dirk said, "you could pick up something useful."

Luke nodded. "Let's hope."

"You're still coming to the barbeque on Saturday, right?" Ethan asked. "Val's counting on you being there."

Emma noticed the subtle tension that tightened the muscles in Luke's wide shoulders.

"We're closing in on Vance," he said. "I might not be able to make it."

"You don't," Dirk warned, "you're the one explaining to Meg."

Luke looked uncomfortable. "I'll try. I have to see how things shake out."

Emma felt his hand clamp around her arm as he propelled her toward a desk on the other side of the room. "It's nice meeting you," she called over her shoulder to the men. She could feel their eyes on her all the way across the room.

Luke set his laptop on his desk, sat down in the chair, and opened it, while Emma sat down in the chair beside him. Google Maps popped up and he pulled up Whidbey Island.

"I've been there a couple of times," he said. "The ferry terminal's an hour drive north of Seattle."

"We need to search property ownership records," Emma said, "see if any of the names jump out at us. I wish I hadn't left my laptop in my car this morning."

"You can use mine." Luke got up from his chair. "You found out Lyle McCarthy owned the house Bernice Mills lives in. Go ahead and see what you can do."

Emma took his place and went to work. She paid for

access to a Web site called ProspectNow.com. She brought it up and keyed in her username and password. A cursory search gave her the name and address of every property owner on Whidbey Island—a daunting number of people and companies.

She ran through the pages, but the name Rudolph Vance wasn't on the list, which wasn't a surprise. The police would already have checked for any property he owned when he jumped bail and disappeared. Lyle McCarthy wasn't listed either.

"None of the names on the list ring any bells," she said. "You recognize anyone?"

Perched on a corner of his desk, Luke turned the laptop to face him and scanned the screen, running through page after page of names in a lot less time than Emma had taken to complete the task. "I don't see a damn thing."

"There's always a chance he's just a lessee or a tenant."

"I don't think so," Luke said. "Vance is a control freak. No way is he taking orders from a landlord."

"I don't think so either. It doesn't fit his profile."

"We need to look into the LLCs that own property on the island, dig into the names on the corporate ownership rolls."

"I can do that. This Web site has a ton of information. But it's going to take some time."

"We need to narrow things down. Let's bring the map back up. Wherever he's hiding, it has to be someplace private. Vance has plenty of money. Take a look at the larger parcels, bigger chunks of ground with very few neighbors."

Google Earth brought them up close and personal with the area. There were some great spots on the island, large parcels fairly secluded, overlooking the water. Unfortunately, there were far too many possibilities to guess which property might be occupied by Vance.

"We can dig around for the next few hours," Luke said. "Or—better idea—" He reached over and caught her hand, tugged her to her feet. "We can get some help." He hauled her across the room toward the stairs. "Sadie's my secret weapon. She's been helping me look for Vance all along."

At the top of the stairs, Luke led Emma down a hallway past an office on the right with a big black granite desk and a black leather sofa along one wall. A handsome blond man worked behind a computer screen.

"That's my cousin, Ian," Luke said as they walked past. "He owns the company."

They kept walking, turned into a room full of computer equipment. A woman in her fifties with shoulder-length curly platinum hair sat behind one of three big screens.

Her gaze shot to Luke as he walked in. "Hey, sunshine. What's up? Sadie, this is Emma Cassidy. She's bail enforcement. We picked up a lead on Rudy Vance. We're hoping you can help us find him."

Sadie eyed her from head to foot in much the same manner Dirk and Ethan had done. Emma forced herself not stare down at her feet like a schoolgirl in front of the principal.

"We?" Sadie asked, her slightly darker eyebrows creeping toward her hairline. "As in the two of you working together?"

Luke's features went from friendly to defensive. "Em's got a personal stake in finding Vance, so yeah. We're working the case together."

Sadie's assessing gaze returned to Emma. "Luke works alone. Says something, he's letting you in. You do what he tells you, you'll be okay."

Emma managed a nod.

Sadie turned back to Luke. "So what can I do for you this time?"

Luke relaxed. "Vance may be holed up in a house on Whidbey Island. We need to figure out which one."

"You're thinking he owns the place?"

"He'd want the control, so yeah. We've done a preliminary search, but so far we haven't found squat. We're hoping you can find a way to narrow the search and come up with a location."

"Property's not in Vance's name or any of his cronies'," Sadie said. "If it was, I'd have turned it up when you first went on the hunt."

"I know, but you've got a list of his business connections. We're thinking the ownership might be buried in a corporation, someone on the board or in some way connected, something we haven't figured out. House is probably on a large, secluded piece of property. FBI was looking into Vance for drug smuggling and gunrunning so he's got plenty of money stashed away."

Sadie started nodding. "Gimme a little time. I'll see what I can find out."

"Nice meeting you," Emma said as Luke led her away.

Sadie's gaze held a note of something Emma couldn't read. "You be careful out there."

Emma nodded. She couldn't tell if Sadie was warning her of the danger posed by Rudy Vance. Or if that danger came in the form of the hard male body and amazing face that belonged to Luke Brodie.

Chapter Ten

When Luke returned to the first floor, Ethan and Dirk were gone, but Nick sat working at his desk.

"That's another Brodie," Luke told Emma. "My cousin Nick. He's married. Got a great wife and a baby boy about six months old." Luke waved at Nick but didn't take Emma over to meet him.

He knew his cousin would be just as shocked as the rest of his family and friends to see him there with a woman. He didn't bring women into the office, and he never worked with a partner—or almost never did. The guys didn't understand he was just doing Emma a favor.

"See you at the party on Saturday," Nick called out to him.

Luke made no reply, which, from the look Emma cast his way, she hadn't missed.

"Sadie needs some time to work," she said, changing the subject, for which he was grateful. "And my car is still at Wade's. I need to pick it up."

"The gun range isn't far. We can grab a burger on the way. You can bring your car back here and leave it in the lot or I'll follow you home and you can park it there."

"So we're definitely going to Whidbey?"

"That's right. If Sadie doesn't come up with a property location, we'll do some old-fashioned legwork. We'll show Vance's photo around, see if anyone recognizes him."

"You don't think we'll . . . umm . . . be there overnight?"

His mind shot ahead to spending the night with Emma, and blood pumped straight to his groin. Dammit, nothing was going to happen—even if they had to stay overnight. This was business, nothing more.

He tried not to think how sexy Emma had looked at the shooting range, but his mind wouldn't cooperate, and he bit back a groan. Focusing on a mental image of perverted Rudy Vance cooled his ardor, considerably.

"The day's mostly gone," he said, "so yeah, we could be there overnight. If we have to knock on doors, it's going to take awhile. You probably ought to bring a change of clothes."

Emma glanced away. He wondered if her thoughts had strayed in the same direction his had, prayed, for both their sakes, they hadn't.

"It's not a problem," she said. "I keep an overnight bag in the trunk of my car in case I have to go out of town on short notice."

"Booth's idea?"

She nodded. "He made me a list of things I should carry. Tactical lightweight handcuffs, Maglite, pepper spray, stuff like that. A go-bag was on the list."

"Guy knows what he's doing." Luke went over to his desk to retrieve his laptop, returned, and urged Emma toward the door.

From the office, Luke drove the Bronco to the nearest Burger King drive-thru; then they headed for Wade's to pick up Emma's car. Sitting in the parking lot under a shade tree, they downed the cheeseburgers, fries, and Cokes they'd ordered.

Since Emma's West Seattle apartment was out of the way, they decided to drive her car back to the BOSS, Inc. parking lot and leave it there until they got back from the island. The neighborhood was good and there were guys in and out of the office at odd hours, night and day, so the vehicle would be safe enough.

Luke knew exactly what Dirk, his brother, and his cousins would think when they realized whose car it was, but there was nothing he could do about it.

At Wade's, Emma picked up her car, then followed Luke back to his office parking lot. Retrieving her overnight bag from the trunk, she clicked the door locks, and started walking toward the Bronco.

A memory arose of the first time he'd seen her at Rocker's Karaoke Lounge, low-cut sparkly top showing a delicious amount of cleavage, short tight skirt clinging to her fine little ass, long dark hair curling around her shoulders.

Desire rose thick and hot, and silently he cursed. He needed a woman and he needed one badly. Only problem was, the woman he wanted he couldn't have. Not when he knew what Emma would think of him when he drove her home the next morning and never came back again.

Still, as she climbed into the passenger seat and strapped her seat belt over those luscious breasts, he found himself wishing his buddies were guessing right and Emma would be spending the night in his bed.

But he was pretty damn sure they'd be wrong.

As the ferry skimmed over the white-capped waves, Emma stood at the rail, the breeze blowing flyaway strands of hair against her cheeks. She loved being out on the water, loved the screech of the gulls and the tangy smell of the sea.

Luke stood beside her, nearly a foot taller, a man who exuded confidence in every move he made. She was hyper-aware of him: the heat of his body, the shifting of the hard muscles beneath his long-sleeved T-shirt and jeans, the way his amazing blue eyes slid over her like a caress.

It wasn't fair for a man to have that much sex appeal. Especially when Luke barely seemed to notice her existence, at least not as a woman. She was a bail enforcement agent. He was doing her a favor, nothing more.

She should be grateful, she told herself. It made it easier to resist temptation. Not that she had any intention of joining Luke's nightly brigade of women, but still . . .

She sighed as the ferry skimmed over the sea on its brief, twenty-minute voyage to the Clinton terminal on Whidbey Island, where they would leave the ship. They still hadn't heard from Sadie, but legwork was a big part of a bounty hunter's job.

"So how do we approach this?" Emma asked, breaking the silence, though she had been surprisingly comfortable in the quiet that stretched between them. "Vance isn't the kind of man to hang around some local bar. The profile I did said he was extremely conscious of his image. Expensive clothes, gourmet restaurants, fine hotels. No way is he going into a pub and ordering himself a beer."

"No, but he has to eat. If he's alone, he'll have to go to the grocery store or have food delivered to the house. He has to buy gas for whatever car he's driving. The entire population of the island is less than sixty thousand. He needs his house cleaned and his lawn mowed. We look hard enough, we'll find someone who knows something."

Emma had worked on her MacBook Pro on the drive up

the 405 Freeway north to the ferry terminal in Mukilteo. She'd pulled up Wikipedia information on Whidbey Island, and anything else of interest she could find on the Internet, reading much of it to Luke along the way.

"The island's fifty miles long," she said, remembering some of what she had discovered. "But the population's very rural. Only eight or nine towns and they're all fairly small. I think the best place to start would be Freeland or Langley. They've got a number of large private estates, something that would give Vance the kind of privacy he'd be looking for."

"Sounds good. We'll start in Freeland and cross over to Langley. Maybe we'll get lucky."

"Or maybe Sadie will call."

Which would certainly be easier than knocking on doors all over Whidbey Island.

It was after five when Luke drove the Bronco off the ferry in Clinton. Both carrying a photo of Rudy Vance, they decided to hit every grocery store and gas station in the search area—three stations in Clinton in case Rudy filled up when he drove off or before he drove onto the ferry, and two in Freeland.

No luck at any of their first three stops.

They went into the Clinton Food Mart, got nothing, then headed for the two gas stations in Freeland. Again, nothing turned up. At the Payless grocery store, they talked to several different clerks, flashed Rudy's picture, but no one remembered seeing anyone who looked like him.

"Maybe he changed his appearance so he wouldn't be recognized," Emma said as they walked back to the SUV.

"It's possible. But I talked to several of the women he

dated. They all said Rudy was vain. He's a decent-looking guy and a stylish dresser. His hair is beginning to recede, which he hates, but apparently, he keeps himself in good physical condition. He might change his looks a little, but I don't see him putting on weight or dressing like a bum. He might bleach his hair, but he'll keep it well groomed. He won't do anything that's a detriment to his appearance. Or at least that's my take."

"I agree. So we just keep looking. We've barely gotten started and we never thought it would be easy."

"We keep looking, no question. But I've been thinking about it, and it's likely if Vance is on the island, he isn't alone. He's got people working for him, running errands, doing whatever needs to be done. Rudy likes being king, likes having a bunch of ass-kissers around."

Emma started nodding. "Guys like Felix Riggs. I should have thought of that."

"I don't think he'd risk having more than a few of his most trusted people, not when there's the possibility of going to jail. We'll hit a couple more stores. If nothing turns up, we'll regroup and take another tack."

They showed the photo to a clerk in a grocery store called The Goose and one called The Star. No one recognized Rudy's picture.

"What if someone tells Rudy we're digging around asking questions?" Emma asked as they climbed back into the Bronco. "You don't think he'll run?"

"I think he might. But if we want to find him, we have to take the chance. We don't have any choice."

It was getting late, the sun setting over the water to the west. Clouds were beginning to drift over the island. Whidbey spent half of each month in a rainy, cloud-covered mist, but as the Bronco rolled along, the sky was clear enough to see the pines along the road and the lush green rural landscape around them.

"We'll head over to Langley," Luke said. "It's more touristy. Got kind of a quaint New England charm that draws people. Got B&Bs, better restaurants, lots of guest cottages. Seems a less likely spot to find Vance, but we'll give it a try."

Just then Luke's cell started ringing. He pulled it out and checked the caller ID.

"It's Sadie," he said to Emma as he pulled off into a wide spot on the road and turned off the engine. "Cross your fingers." He hit the built-in hands-free. "Hey, sweet pea."

"Hey, sunshine. I got news."

"Yeah? I hope it's good."

"I think I found your man—or at least the property you're looking for. There's a house on ten acres. From the satellite photos, it's real private. Property records show it's owned by a guy named Sam Cogan. Cogan is secretary-treasurer of International Cargo. I cross-referenced the island property ownership list with some of the people linked to Vance and that's how I ran across it."

"International Cargo. Makes sense. Vance is part owner. What's the property address?"

"I'm sending you a map link. The house is off Highway 525 in the Freeland area."

Freeland. They'd been right. Luke flashed a grin at Emma, who grinned back.

"The map shows how to get to Wahl Road. The house is on a dirt lane off Volcano. There's a pin drop on the map."

"Thanks, Sadie, you're the best."

"You gonna need backup?"

He looked at Emma, read the determination in her face. "We need to find out if he's there. If he is, we'll take him down, then call the police."

"Dirk's here. He's itching to get up there."

Emma shook her head. There was something in her eyes. . . . She needed this, Luke realized. Whatever happened, she needed to be part of the process. And she wasn't going to let him down.

"We're okay for now. If things look dicey, I'll call Dirk, wait until he can get up here before we go in. Thanks again." Luke ended the call and turned to Emma. "You ready for this?"

In answer, she reached behind the seat and grabbed her gear bag, unzipped it, and brought out her holstered Glock. Pulling the pistol, she dropped the clip to check the load, then shoved it back in with a heavy metallic click.

Emma was ready.

So was he.

Luke started the engine and pulled back out on the road.

Chapter Eleven

It was dark by the time they reached the property. Moonlight shining down from between the clouds made it easier to stake out the house to see if Vance was inside.

Emma prayed he was. She wanted this over and done. She wanted April and Ginny safe. She wanted her family back home.

Luke hid the Bronco out of sight in a copse of trees half a mile down the road. Emma dug a pair of black jeans out of her go-bag, then stood behind the door of the Bronco to exchange them for the khaki pants she was wearing. Pulling a windbreaker over her black T-shirt against the chilly mist, she blended into the darkness.

Luke did the same, shucking his jeans and yellow T-shirt, pulling on a black Henley and black cargo pants. He wasn't modest as he stripped off his clothes, and why should he be?

Emma stared at more hard muscle than she had ever seen: an amazing set of pecs, a chest banded with sinew, a ladder of muscle across a flat stomach, and a pair of biceps that made her mouth water.

"Keep looking at me the way you are and we aren't going to make it to the house."

Emma flushed and turned away. Thank God it was dark. "Sorry, my mind was somewhere else." Someplace naughty but nice.

When she turned back, he'd streaked his face with greasepaint. Emma reached into her bag, pulled out a tube of paint, and did the same. He changed out of his moccasins into military combat boots while she slid into a pair of sturdy hiking boots.

She was sure he was going to tell her to stay with the vehicle, out of harm's way, but he didn't. When he turned toward her in the moonlight, his features had morphed into the same hard mask he had worn the night he'd confronted Badger and his biker gang. The same mask he'd worn when he'd taken on Felix Riggs.

"Here's the plan," Luke said, totally focused on what lay ahead. "First we circle the house, figure out the layout, and check for security guards. If it's clear, we move in. Maybe the house is empty, maybe not. We need to find out."

"Do we split up here or wait till we're closer to the house?"

"Tonight you're with me. You're still new at this and we've never done a takedown together."

Uneasiness filtered through her. She didn't want Luke involved when she confronted Rudy Vance.

But maybe it wouldn't matter. They weren't even sure he was there.

Luke pulled his Beretta and Emma pulled her Glock. Holding it in a two-handed grip, the barrel pointed down, she turned to Luke. He put a finger to his lips, then signaled for her to follow him, turned, and slipped into the deep woods behind the house, moving so silently among the thick foliage, she was afraid she'd lose him.

Just as the thought occurred, he slowed. He was holding back, letting her keep pace with him. She covered him as he moved forward, then caught up with him. Covered him again then moved forward. Each time she caught up with him, he stopped to listen, make sure they didn't come up on one of Vance's security guards.

Emma's heart raced as he paused again. Long, silent seconds passed. No movement, just the wind sighing through the branches of the trees. An owl hooted somewhere in the distance and a small animal scurried through the grass a few feet away.

The house was a long, low, ranch-style with big plate-glass windows that looked out over the sea. A huge deck wrapped around the living area and bedrooms. There was a white floating dock, but no boats bobbed in the water. Luke moved again, then dropped down into the cover of the foliage. Emma crept into position a few feet away.

They made a full circle, ending back at the three-car garage behind the house. From a distance, the place looked dark and empty, but without going inside there was no way to be sure.

Luke indicated they should ease back into the trees where they wouldn't be heard.

"I don't think there's anyone home," he said, disappointment clear in his voice. "But we need to be sure. If Rudy isn't there, we might find something that'll help us figure out where he is."

"Are you sure this is the right house?"

"It matches the image on the satellite picture Sadie sent. It's private and expensive. It looks like something Vance would own."

"Maybe he's there by himself and he's sleeping."

"It's possible. I need to find the alarm." He pulled his Maglite out of a loop on the gear belt around his waist. "I'll move in, you cover me. I'll signal when to follow."

Luke headed for a window in the garage, shined the light

inside. A spot of yellow circled around the interior. The light fixed on something, then Luke was moving silently toward a door that led inside.

He pulled something out of his pocket, fiddled with the lock, and in seconds the door swung open. Luke motioned for her to follow, then disappeared inside. Apparently he had located the alarm system in the garage. Emma counted the seconds, praying the alarm wouldn't go off before Luke could manage to disarm it.

Hurrying toward the garage, she slipped inside and spotted him next to a box flashing a series of colored lights. His gun was back in the holster on his belt, his cell phone in hand. Emma held her breath as he worked the phone. Any second the alarm would go off, loud enough to wake half the island.

An instant later, the flashing red lights on the panel went dark, and relief trickled through her.

Emma glanced around. There were no cars in the garage. Not a good sign. The cell phone returned to a pocket in Luke's black cargo pants and the small set of tools was back in his hands. Lock picks, and clearly he knew how to use them. He twisted one of the picks a couple of times, turned the doorknob, opened the door, and motioned for her to follow him inside.

"The alarm. How did you—"

He grinned. "Wireless. Piece of cake. Let's go." He went in high, gun two-handed. Emma went in low, right behind him. "Stay alert," he said as they stepped into the kitchen.

Finding nothing there, they made a sweep of the house, clearing one room at a time. By the time they reached the master bedroom, it was certain the house was empty.

Despair settled over her but Luke seemed unconcerned. For him it was just part of the hunt.

Emma holstered her weapon. "Maybe he just went to

town or maybe he had something to do in Seattle. Maybe he's coming back."

"Let's find out." Using the bottom of his T-shirt so he wouldn't leave prints, Luke flipped on the light beside the king-size bed.

"What if someone sees the light and knows we're in here?"

"This place is way off the beaten path. Unless somebody's in a boat out on the water, nobody's going to notice." He walked over to the closet, used the T-shirt to slide open the mirrored doors. Men's clothes hung from an upper and lower rack: dress and casual shirts. Slacks and pants, all neatly separated half an inch apart. But there was a section that had been neatly cleaned out.

Luke walked over and used his T-shirt to carefully pull open the top two dresser drawers. Socks and briefs in orderly rows, a lot of them missing.

"Looks to me like our bird has flown."

Emma nodded, fighting another rush of disappointment. Reaching into her back pocket, she pulled out a pair of thin latex gloves and snapped them on. At the same instant, Luke's gloves made the identical snapping sound.

He looked up, surprised to see her wearing them. "Booth?"

She nodded.

Luke seemed pleased. "Okay, I'll start in here; you start in the kitchen. There might be some kind of local night patrol in the area so we need to get this done and get out of here, but we don't want to miss anything."

Luke set to work. The house was a little too warm. Emma stripped off her windbreaker and tied it around her waist, then headed for the kitchen, which was clean, she discovered when she flipped on the overhead light.

With its granite countertops and stainless steel appliances, the kitchen was a chef's delight. Opening drawers and checking cupboards, she made her way around the room, looking for something, anything that might be useful.

A stack of utility bills and a grocery list sat on the counter. The gas and electric bills were in the name of Sam Cogan, mailed to this address. She wondered how Vance paid them. A credit card number would be useful but there was no number on the bills.

The grocery list was interesting, all the food organic, mostly vegetables, nuts, and fruits. MARMITE was printed in big bold letters. She had no idea what it was, but it was grouped in with the other health foods. She made a mental note to check it out and set the list back down with the stack of bills.

She searched the trash under the sink, but it had recently been emptied. There was a paper towel in the bottom, something used after the can had been cleaned out. She found a plastic bag in one of the drawers, folded the paper towel and slipped it into the bag, hoping to find some DNA.

There was a good chance Rudy had been in the house, but someone might have been there with him, someone they could track down. She was about to head for the dining room when she noticed a spatter of dark spots across the bottom of the refrigerator. More of the substance sprayed in small dark red dots across the floor.

Her heartbeat kicked up as she crouched down to examine them, touched one of the spots with a gloved index finger, found it still slightly tacky. *Blood.*

She followed the drops to a wide swath that had been almost completely cleaned up. The faint trace remaining pointed toward the door leading into the garage, a pale but unmistakable blood trail.

With a steadying breath, she followed the trail out the

door they had come in through, down the steps to the garage, and flipped on the light.

In the dark she hadn't noticed the chest-style freezer against the front wall. Her mouth went dry as she realized the faint, smeared trail of blood stopped right in front of the box.

Her stomach was churning. She thought about calling Luke, but he was busy, and it might be nothing, a package of steaks that had dripped a little on the way to the freezer, something as harmless as that.

She stood there for several long moments working up her courage. Luke appeared in the doorway just as she reached for the handle and lifted the lid.

"Oh, my God!" The room spun and she swayed on her feet. Luke was behind her in an instant, his arms locking around her, pulling her away from the grizzly contents inside the freezer chest. Emma sagged against him, unable to catch her breath.

She was back in her sister's hallway, staring down at Eleanor Harris's blood-soaked body. Ginny was in the bedroom, hurt and needing her help. She must have made some kind of sound because Luke swore softly and eased her down on the floor of the garage. He gently pressed her head down between her knees.

"You'll be okay. Just give yourself a minute. It's always hard the first time you see something like that."

Her eyes filled. She looked up at him through a glaze of tears. "This isn't the first time. I'm . . . I'm the one who found Eleanor Harris."

Luke's body went rock solid. "Jesus." He crouched down beside her. Reaching out, he gently touched her cheek. "Just take it easy, okay? Take a couple of deep breaths and try to think about something else."

She closed her eyes and breathed deeply, swallowed past

the bile in her throat. "I—I'm okay." She wasn't, of course. She wasn't okay at all. "It's Felix Riggs, isn't it?"

Luke's features hardened. "It's Riggs."

"Vance cut his throat, just like . . . just like Eleanor."

"Yeah. We need to get out of here. We'll call the cops when we get to the mainland, feed them the info without getting involved."

She nodded, let him help her to her feet.

She thought of the dead man, Felix Riggs. "What do you think happened?"

Luke glanced back at the freezer, reached over, and closed the lid. "I don't know." She could almost see his mind working.

"Maybe Riggs found out we were bail enforcement and called Vance," he said. "Or more likely, called someone connected to Vance. No car here, so they picked Riggs up and drove him out here. Vance must not have liked what Riggs had to say so he killed him."

"Riggs told us about Bernice. Maybe Vance knows she helped us. You don't think she could be in danger?"

Luke blew out a breath. "Can't say for sure, but it doesn't seem likely. She's family, all he really has. And there's no way for him to know she's told us about the island."

"I hope you're right."

"We'll call her, give her a heads-up just in case."

Emma nodded.

That's when she heard it—the engine noise of a vehicle rolling up the dirt lane toward the house.

Chapter Twelve

Luke hit the overhead light, pitching the garage into darkness. He'd already doused the lights in the kitchen. As he moved to the window in the garage, he prayed whoever was in the vehicle had been watching the road, not the house.

The headlights bumped slowly up the dirt lane. When he turned to look at Emma, she held her pistol in a solid, two-handed grip. As her eyes locked with his, her features looked calm. She was back in control, ready for whatever might come. Luke breathed a sigh of relief.

He strode back to her. "Go out through the slider in the dining room and get into the cover of the trees. I'll reset the alarm and follow you."

"What if it's Vance?"

It could be. He planned to wait and find out, but he wasn't telling Emma. She'd seen enough blood and death for one night. And if it was Vance, the guy wouldn't go down easy.

"More likely it's someone Vance sent to get rid of the body." That much was true. "As soon as it's safe, I'll follow you. Give me five minutes. If I don't show up, meet me at the Bronco. Now go."

She gave him a look. She was trying to decide if he was telling the truth. Since he wasn't completely lying, after a moment, she turned and hurried up the steps. He heard the slider in the dining room open and close and quickly reset the alarm. As long as he didn't try to leave the house, the alarm wouldn't go off.

He took a position behind an old wooden rowboat that leaned bow upward against one wall. The garage door groaned its way open, automatically triggering an overhead light, and a dark brown Chevy Malibu backed into the garage.

The trunk popped open. A door on each side of the car swung wide and two men got out, one late thirties and balding, the other younger, early twenties, a muscle jock with thick black hair who looked part Asian or Latino. The bald guy went for the security alarm and punched in the code, turning it off.

The jock strode over to the freezer and flipped open the lid. "Fuck, I hate a goddamn corpse."

"Just do your job, Rio. Go get the plastic bag."

The kid went over to the trunk of the car, grabbed a big black leaf bag from inside, and returned to the freezer. The men lifted Riggs's stiff, but not-completely frozen body out of the box and worked it into the big black plastic bag. The bald guy hefted one end, the black-haired kid, Rio, lifted the other.

Luke stepped out from behind the boat. "Stay right where you are." He aimed his Beretta at the younger guy, hoping the older guy had more sense. "Don't move and don't go for your weapons."

They were stuck holding on to the bag. "Who the fuck are you?" the kid demanded as Luke approached the bald-headed guy, who was closer, and lifted a Sig .45 from the holster at his waist.

"Unless you killed the guy in the bag, I'm nobody you need to worry about. I just want to know where I can find Rudy Vance." He tossed the gun away, heard it hit the floor and slide up against the wall.

"We didn't kill him," the bald guy said, both men still holding opposite ends of the bag. "We're just the cleanup crew."

"Where's Vance?"

"I got no idea. He pays us to do his dirty work. That's all I know."

The sound of the kitchen door opening should have alarmed him. Instead Luke silently cursed, not surprised to see Emma at the top of the steps, legs splayed, arms straight, pistol steady in both hands. Luke cursed again, even as he thought how sexy she looked.

Dammit, he should have known she wouldn't leave when there was a chance one of the men in the car was Vance.

"He won't shoot you for lying," Emma said. "But I will." She leveled her gun at Rio. She'd read the men right. Rio was the wild card. "Where's Vance? Tell me or I'm going to blow out your kneecap. You can choose which one. Right or left?"

Luke's eyebrows went up. If he didn't know her, he'd believe she meant every word.

"You better tell her," he drawled. "They don't call her Calamity Jane for nothing."

The kid smirked and Emma pulled the trigger, the bullet slamming into the concrete floor, missing his knee by inches.

"You fucking bitch!"

"Vance took the boat and headed north," the bald guy said calmly. "That's all I know."

"What kind of boat?"

"No idea. Never been here before."

"Who called?"

"Just a voice on the other end of the phone. That's how it works."

Rio cursed. Jerking up the body bag, knocking it out of the bald guy's hands and using it as a shield, he pulled his pistol and fired. Luke's shot slammed through Rigg's dead body, hitting the kid chest-high. Emma screamed; the bag slid out of Rio's hands and the kid went down hard.

Behind him, the Chevy engine roared to life. Tires screeched as the car shot out of the garage. The bald guy hit the gas and careened off down the dirt road. Luke let him go. He didn't know where Vance was or he would have said.

Jesus, seeing the look on Emma's face, the guy would have given up his own mother.

Luke turned to find her kneeling beside the kid, who was unconscious but still breathing. Luke dialed 9-1-1, got an ambulance on the way, along with the sheriff, then crouched down beside her to see what he could do to help.

Emma had stripped off her windbreaker, wadded it up and pressed it over the blood oozing through the hole in the right side of Rio's chest.

"You didn't kill him," she said. "I thought you would."

"I should have. I took a risk. But I saw you'd ducked out of the line of fire. I don't like making someone dead unless I have to." He looked down, saw the shot had entered where he'd intended, not a kill shot but close. "He still might not make it."

There could be complications. With a bullet, you never knew.

"You did your best. Now it's up to him."

Luke nodded, relieved she saw it that way. He ripped open the kid's shirt and saw the tats across his shoulder and a sleeve of them running down one arm. Dark blue, bright red, and green in sophisticated Asian patterns. He ripped the shirt open wider, pulled out his cell, and took a couple of pictures.

"I shouldn't have taken that shot," Emma said, pressing harder on the fabric stuffed into the wound in Rio's chest. "The bullet could have ricocheted off the cement and gone anywhere."

"Heat of the moment," Luke said. "Rookie mistake. Calculated risk, though, and it got the bald guy talking." He gave her a look. "Probably be better if you didn't do it again."

Emma's lips tipped up a little. Damn, she had the prettiest lips.

"So what do we tell the police?" she asked.

"We tell them the truth. Why we're here, what we found, what happened when those two jokers showed up. And what we know about Vance, which is next to nothing. Maybe they can figure out who Rio is and his connection to Rudy—if there is one. We don't mention our sources, but we keep the cops informed. I'm not willing to risk Vance killing someone else just to collect a fee, even if it's a fat one."

Emma glanced away. It wasn't about the money for her, he knew. It was about justice for her family. She released a shaky breath. "You're right. We'll tell them what we know."

"What we know is Vance took a boat and headed north. What they do with that is up to them."

"So what are *we* going to do about it?"

"Find out how Rio's connected to Vance and try to figure out where the bastard landed the damned boat."

The distant sound of sirens ended the conversation. Luke looked out through the open garage door and saw red lights flashing as a vehicle barreled up the dirt road toward the house. Using the bottom of his Henley, he wiped the greasepaint off his face and Emma followed his lead.

The ambulance rolled to a stop and a pair of EMTs jumped out. Shoving a stretcher ahead of them, they ran toward the victim lying on the concrete floor. A sheriff's car roared to a halt behind them.

The kid hadn't opened his eyes, but his pulse was steady, his breathing not too shallow, and they'd been able to keep the blood loss to a minimum.

As a pair of deputies approached, Luke flipped open his bail enforcement badge, then pointed to the pistol in the holster on his belt. Emma did the same. The bigger man, heavyset, with a thatch of silver hair, stalked toward them.

"Keep your hands where I can see them and step out of the garage."

"No problem, Officer," Luke said.

While Rio was being stabilized and hauled off in the ambulance, the deputy and his partner took their weapons, then made notes on the details of the shooting. The coroner arrived to take charge of the body and string yellow crime scene tape around the house.

A detective named Sizemore showed up, and for the next two hours, Luke and Emma went over the events: finding Felix Riggs in the freezer, the two men showing up to get rid of the body and the resultant shooting. A story that never changed, even when he and Emma were questioned separately.

It was always easier when you were telling the truth.

It was after midnight when Detective Sizemore, a narrow-faced officious cop with a ruddy complexion and worry lines across his forehead, finally satisfied, got into his unmarked car and left the crime scene.

The heavyset deputy, Stankowski was his name, walked

over to where Luke sat next to Emma on a wrought iron bench not far from the garage.

"I don't much like you people," the deputy said. "You bounty hunters think you're above the law. You get involved and shit happens, just like tonight."

Luke's jaw went tight. He pushed to his feet. "You've got a right to see this any way you want. The way I see it, we discovered a murder and gave you information that might help you solve it. The kid fired on us first or he wouldn't be lying in the back of that ambulance. We've told you everything we know. Now, unless you're going to arrest us, we're leaving."

Stankowski grunted. "You can go. Just don't leave the state. We might have more questions."

"You know where to find us."

Emma stood up and Luke tipped his chin toward the road, urging her back down to where the Bronco was parked. They'd missed the last ferry. They needed a room for the night.

Luke's gaze sliced to Emma. Even in her work clothes with her hair slicked into a ponytail, the urge to have her burned through his body. Inside his cargo pants, he was hard.

"Are we going back to Seattle?" she asked.

He shook his head. "Not tonight. We missed the boat." Luke inwardly groaned. Just like he was about to. They'd be spending the night together, after all, but the chances of Emma winding up in his bed were about as good as the Bronco crossing the ocean without the ferry.

They found a little motel along the highway. The Pine Tree Inn sat on the same side of the road and right next door to Mannie's Roadhouse. The motel looked clean and the cars in the roadhouse parking lot were newer models. No bikers; a Prius belonged to someone inside.

The area looked like a safe place to stay. Besides, she was with Luke. He pulled the Bronco up in front of the motel office.

"I'll get us settled." Turning off the engine, Luke headed for the office door. By the time Emma caught up with him, he was talking to a sleepy-eyed clerk behind the counter.

"We need a room," Luke said, flipping out his credit card.

"Two rooms," Emma said, walking up beside him, tossing out a card of her own.

Luke's mouth edged up. "Two rooms. Preferably connecting."

Emma opened her mouth to argue, but Luke just smiled. "Options," he said. "The more the better."

Since Booth had said something similar, she didn't argue. Luke slid back her card. "I'll deduct the cost from your fee."

"What if we don't collect?" Emma asked.

Luke's jaw tightened. "Oh, we're going to collect."

Emma grabbed her room key and walked outside while Luke finished the details. Grabbing her go-bag out of the Bronco, she headed for room 110. Luke parked the Bronco in a space in front of his room next door as Emma slipped quietly inside.

Exhaustion rolled through her. She just wanted to get some sleep. She looked down at her black clothes and thought of Felix Riggs, stuffed into the freezer with his throat cut. She thought of the blood trail she had followed to find him, and pulled the black T-shirt off over her head.

A shower might help, a chance to wash away the scent of death that clung to her like rotten meat. She went into the bathroom and stripped off the rest of her clothes, wrapped a towel around her hair, and turned on the water, cranking it up nice and hot. The shower felt great, warm and refreshing, but the images remained in her head.

They didn't leave as she dried herself off and shook out her hair, walked back out of the bathroom. A glance at the double bed warned her she'd never be able to sleep. Her gaze went to the window. In the distance, she could hear the thrum of the jukebox in Mannie's Roadhouse.

There was still time for a beer or two before closing. Maybe a drink would help her fall asleep.

She tried not to think of Luke but he was there in the back of her mind, his beautiful body and amazing face. Sheer male temptation. Luke could make her sleep, no doubt about it. On another night, she might have smiled.

Wiping the thought out of her head, she went back into the bathroom and put on a light touch of makeup, then went to her overnight bag and took out the little jean skirt she carried, along with a plain white tank top. Sliding her feet into a pair of heeled sandals, she ran the brush through her hair, slung the strap of her purse over her shoulder, and headed for the bar next door.

Showered and ready for bed, Luke heard the soft click of the door closing on the room next door.

What the hell?

Striding to the window, he saw Emma crossing the lot to the roadhouse. She had changed out of her work clothes, into a sexy little skirt and tank, and taken down her hair. A shot of pure male possessiveness rolled through him, a feeling he had rarely known.

His jaw hardened. If Emma was looking for male companionship, he'd be more than happy to oblige. Grabbing a clean pair of jeans, he slid them on, grabbed a navy blue Henley and dragged it over his head, pulled on his moccasins, and strode out the door.

By the time he got to the roadhouse, Emma was poking money into the jukebox in the corner. Willie Nelson sang "Mamas Don't Let Your Babies Grow Up To Be Cowboys." Good to know Emma liked Country music.

Luke stood in the shadows, watching as she crossed the room. Mannie's was a locals' joint with a long wooden bar and wooden tables. He let Emma get settled on one of the tall stools at the bar, then walked over to join her.

"Couldn't sleep?" he asked, and tried to keep the edge of anger out of his voice.

She turned, looked up at him. "Sometimes I have trouble. Apparently you couldn't sleep, either."

"I would have come with you if you'd asked. Or maybe it wasn't my company you wanted." He glanced around the bar, saw that half the guys in the place had seen her walk in and were watching her. Hell, he didn't blame them.

"I didn't want anyone's company but my own," she said. "I'm a big girl, Luke. You don't have to babysit me every minute."

The bartender, a tall guy, built, with dark hair and a small goatee, arrived in front of Emma before Luke had time to reply. The last thing he thought was that Emma was a baby. *Babe*—hell, yeah.

"Can I get you something?" the bartender asked her.

"I usually drink Bud Light, but tonight—"

"Bud Light for the lady," Luke said, "Corona for me."

"Boilermaker," Emma said, drilling him with a glare.

The goatee twitched. "Jack Daniel's, okay?"

"Perfect," Emma said.

Annoyance warred with interest. "What's going on with you, Em?"

"It's like you said, I couldn't sleep. I thought a drink might help."

"It's more than that and you know it. We both had a helluva night."

The bartender set her Bud down on top of the bar, set a shot glass of Jack beside it. Emma picked up the glass and tossed the liquor back, squeezed her eyes closed against the burn, and took a big swig of beer.

"Impressive," Luke said. "When did you start drinking whiskey?"

"Tonight a beer's not enough." She turned to the bartender. "Hit me again."

Luke's eyebrows went up. Maybe he didn't know Emma as well as he thought.

"You got it," the bartender said.

Luke sipped his Corona and watched as Emma downed three shots of whiskey without blinking an eye and finished her Bud.

The bar was getting ready to close.

"Last call," the bartender said.

Emma swayed on the stool. "Time for one more," she said, but the words came out a little slurred.

"She's done," Luke said, and the bartender nodded. "Time to go, Em. You're gonna have a helluva headache in the morning."

Emma slid down from the bar stool. "I never get hangovers. It's a gift from my Irish dad."

When she swayed toward him, Luke steadied her. "You ready to go?" He tossed money for the drinks and a tip on the bar.

Willie Nelson sang, "*She's a good-hearted woman.*" Emma leaned toward him, slid her arms around his neck, went up on her toes, and kissed him. Soft lips melded with his in a hot, wet, kiss that had him rock-hard in an instant.

Her eyes found his, deep brown and searching. "Make love to me, Luke."

He bit back a groan. He'd dreamed of it, a dream as hot and wet as her kiss. It was all he could do not to drag her down on the floor, tear off her clothes, and bury himself to the hilt.

For a moment, he kissed her back, just to see if those pretty lips were really as soft and lush as they'd seemed. He kept on because he'd rather kiss her than breathe.

Tasting and nibbling, he lifted her into his arms and carried her to the door. Emma's arms locked around his neck as he shoved it open with his foot and walked outside. The cold night air hit him, but it didn't cool the heat boiling through his blood.

His room was just across the parking lot. All he had to do was haul her inside and over to the bed, strip off her clothes, and take her. He wanted to. Wanted her so bad, he ached with it.

But this was Emma and something was wrong.

Carrying her to the edge of the lot, he set her on her feet, broke the kiss but kept a hand at her waist to steady her.

Emma whimpered. "Luke . . . please . . ."

"Tell me what's wrong."

She leaned toward him, looped her arms around his neck. He could feel her plump breasts pressing into his chest and his dick started throbbing, trying to batter him into submission.

"I need you, Luke," Emma said. "Please don't stop." She kissed him again, as deep and wet as the first time, and it took every ounce of his will to break away.

"Something's wrong. Tell me what it is."

She clamped a hand on her hip, drawing his attention to her short little skirt, making him want to shove it up to her waist and see what was underneath. With any luck, nothing, though he couldn't really imagine that.

"Damn you, Luke Brodie," she said. "Everyone knows what a man-whore you are. What's wrong with me? Why don't you want me?"

His mouth edged up. "I'm not a man-whore, and nothing's wrong with you. If you ask me again when you're sober, I'll give you the ride of your life. Now tell me what the hell is wrong."

Her big brown eyes welled with tears, erasing some of his lust. One slipped over and rolled down her cheek.

"Tell me," he coaxed.

Emma dragged in a shaky breath. For a moment, he didn't think she was going to answer.

"Emma?"

She swallowed. Her bottom lip trembled as she looked up at him. "What happened that day . . . to . . . to Ginny and Eleanor . . . it was my fault, Luke." Her eyes swam with tears. "I was supposed to stay with Ginny that afternoon, but . . . but a friend of mine called and wanted . . . wanted to go shopping. It was only for a couple of hours and Eleanor was there. I thought . . . thought it would be okay." She brushed away another tear. "But when I came home . . . when I got back to the house . . ." Her voice broke.

"Oh, baby." Luke pulled her into his arms and just held her. Emma started crying, sobbing as if her heart was breaking. Luke held on tighter. "It's all right, honey. It wasn't your fault. It was Rudy Vance's fault."

A tremor slipped through her body. "I should . . . should have been there, Luke."

"I'm glad you weren't. If you'd been there, Vance might have murdered you, too."

Emma sobbed.

"We're gonna find him, honey, I promise you." He

kissed the top of her head. "We're gonna find Rudy Vance and we're gonna make him pay." Scooping her back into his arms, Luke crossed the lot to the motel, unlocked the door to his room, and carried her inside, then through the door into her adjoining room.

Emma looked up at him as he set her on her feet. Her eyes were big and dark and needy. "Please don't go. I'm not drunk anymore. Or not very."

His body tightened with a fresh shot of lust and what felt strangely like longing. "I'm doing my best to be a gentleman here, baby."

Emma traced a finger over his lips and a jolt of fire went straight to his groin. "You're no gentleman, Luke."

Hunger burned through him. She had no idea how badly he wanted her. "You're right, baby, I'm not." Then, right or wrong, he kissed her—and this time, he wasn't going to stop.

Chapter Thirteen

Luke kissed her and kissed her, and he didn't stop. It was the longest, wettest, deepest, hottest kiss Emma had ever known.

Kicking off her sandals, she went up on her toes and kissed him the way he was kissing her, kissing him and kissing him until she could no longer breathe. Luke peeled her tank top over her head, unhooked the front of her white lace bra, and tossed it away, then broke the kiss and took a step back to look at her.

Those amazing blue eyes were as hot as the tip of a flame, burning her wherever they touched.

"Beautiful," he said. "Prettier than I ever imagined."

Her skin flushed. She made a little sound in her throat as he cupped the fullness, ran his thumb over her nipple. *He had imagined her half naked?*

Testing the weight and shape, Luke lowered his head and took the fullness into his mouth, teased and tasted, suckled as if he couldn't get enough, as if he had all night and wouldn't be rushed.

Emma made a whimpering sound and clung to him, barely able to stay on her feet. Desire rolled through her, hot and liquid, making her skin feel tight. She peeled

Luke's Henley over his head and pressed her mouth against his granite-hard chest. Muscle vibrated beneath her tongue. She ran her tongue over a flat copper nipple and made him groan.

She swayed a little, but from Luke's attention, not from the whiskey. Her skirt and panties were gone. She didn't remember him taking them off. Didn't remember how he got naked. She was just glad he was.

He was beautiful all over, the perfect male specimen, shoulders banded with muscle, pecs that wouldn't quit, ridges of muscle across his abdomen. Narrow hips and long legs formed of lean, sinewy muscle. She hadn't expected the size of his erection, but she probably should have. He was, after all, Luke Brodie.

Luke settled her in the middle of the bed, then came down on top of her and started kissing her again. It didn't take long to figure out how much Luke liked kissing, and his were the best she'd ever known.

No part of her went unexplored. His mouth, hot and damp, traveled over her skin, kissing and tasting, driving her crazy. She wanted to taste him, too, but Luke had her moaning and squirming, riding the edge of climax.

She was breathing hard, close to begging, when he slid on a condom and positioned himself between her legs. He eased himself inside her, settled himself deep. Emma started coming the minute he began to move, her legs over his, her body clenching around him, pleasure melting like honey out through her limbs.

Luke Brodie was making love to her. She'd been half in love with him before she'd ever met him. She could probably come again just thinking about him being inside her.

"Luke . . ." His name whispered out on a sigh as she began to spiral down.

Luke shifted, moved a little deeper. "Easy, baby, we're just getting started."

Emma whimpered. *Just getting started?* Fresh heat rolled through her, and a fresh rush of desire. Her fingers dug into the muscles across his broad shoulders, and she just hung on. Time seemed to slow, as if every stroke took minutes instead of seconds. Higher and higher, he pushed her, upward and upward till she didn't recognize the sounds coming out of her mouth, spiraling completely out of control and tipping once more over the edge.

"Luke . . . !" She arched her back to take him deeper as wild, saturating pleasure rolled through her. Luke hissed in a breath, his muscles going rigid with the power of his release. He whispered her name as he buried his face in her hair.

When he gently kissed the side of her neck, Emma felt like crying. At the same time she felt like laughing. Instead, she closed her eyes and let the sweet feelings slip through her, let her body absorb the little shocks of pleasure then drift into a peaceful sleep.

In the middle of night, she awoke to the feel of Luke's hand teasing her breasts. He made love to her again, slow and easy, bringing them both to release, then once more before morning.

By the time sunlight filtered through the curtains and her eyes slowly opened, Emma was alone.

Emma glanced around the motel room, but saw no sign of Luke. Just the empty double bed and the nightstand beside it, her clothes in a rumpled pile on the floor.

Her eyes stung. It was ridiculous. She'd had her one-night stand with Luke, and it had been fantastic. She'd known his reputation, known he was famous for having a different woman in his bed every night. So what if she was one of them? It had been her decision.

Truth was she'd seduced Luke, not the other way around.

She just hadn't expected it to hurt so much when the night was over.

Raking back her tangled hair, determined to put the encounter into the proper perspective, Emma slid out of bed and headed for the shower. The warm spray helped erase the last of her self-pity and boosted her spirits.

So she'd slept with him. So what? Women had needs just like men. The important thing was to ensure that what had happened between them didn't interfere with her search for Rudy Vance.

She prayed Luke wouldn't use sleeping with her as an excuse to end their partnership. She needed him. The dead body she'd found and the shootout that followed had shown her just how much.

Padding over to her suitcase, she slipped on a clean pair of white thong panties. She pulled out a pink T-shirt with flowers on the front and slipped it on and was searching for her sneakers when the connecting door swung open and Luke walked into the room.

Carrying a cup of coffee in each hand, he saw her standing there, but instead of a smile, his features looked grim. He set the paper cups down on the dresser and walked toward her.

"I brought you some coffee. I figured you could use it. Are you okay?"

Was she okay? Not exactly. "I'm not going to burst into tears again, if that's what you mean."

"Okay . . . that's good. Because I meant what I said about Vance. We're going to find him. We won't stop until we do."

She hadn't expected this conversation, but maybe she

should have. He wasn't talking about the amazing sex they'd had last night. The night was over. Luke was done with her. He was moving on. She felt a stab of pain she'd convinced herself she wouldn't feel.

"That's good to know," she said.

"Listen . . . about last night . . . I'm really sorry, Emma. I took advantage. You were drunk. I got carried away and I'm sorry. It won't happen again."

The hurt was gone. A wave of fury hit her like a tidal wave. "You're sorry? Oh, my God, you're sorry you slept with me?" She hadn't meant to lose it so completely, but she did.

Her hand flew out to slap his handsome face. Luke's forearm shot up to block the blow so fast, she felt it but didn't see it coming. Emma swung the other hand, harder this time. Luke blocked the blow with his other forearm. Her knee drove up sharply, aiming for his crotch, a blow he blocked with his thigh. She moved, went after him with a right and left elbow jab, each of which Luke blocked.

In an instant, she was slammed up against the wall, Luke pinning her there, locking her wrists together above her head with one of his big hands.

"Okay, fine," he said, his expression fierce. "You want the truth? I'm not one little goddamn bit sorry. I loved every minute of it and I want you again right now."

Her eyes widened. Her anger slowly faded and her body relaxed. "I'm not sorry, either," she said softly.

Luke's eyes were as blue as she had ever seen them. He let go of her hands, which slid around his neck with a will of their own. Then his mouth crushed down over hers, and all hell broke loose.

He kissed her until she was senseless; then her T-shirt went flying. Luke unbuckled his belt and unzipped his jeans, lifted her up and wrapped her legs around his waist.

He fumbled with a condom, pulled her panties aside, and he was inside her, taking her against the wall, taking her hard and deep.

Climax exploded through her body. Luke drove into her again and again, lighting her up from inside, drawing a moan from her lips. Then his muscles went rigid, he ground out her name, and followed her to release.

Time passed but she had no idea how much. Finally, he set her back on her feet. He dealt with the condom, stripped off her panties then his own clothes, and carried her over to the bed. After another round of amazing sex, slower this time but no less fantastic, they lay naked, Emma curled into Luke's side.

Several long seconds passed. "It's daytime," she said. "You broke your one-night rule."

Luke shoved a hand behind his head. "I don't have a one-night rule. I just hadn't met anyone I wanted for more than one night."

"Ever?"

"Not since I left the army."

Emma leaned up on an elbow to look at him, her tangled hair falling over his gorgeous naked chest. "So . . . are you tired of me yet?"

His sexy mouth edged up. "Not even close." Luke leaned up and very softly kissed her.

"So what are the new rules?" She ran a finger down the muscled indentations over his rib cage, knowing if they didn't stop now they wouldn't get out of bed before noon and that wasn't an option, not with Vance still on the loose.

"There are no rules, okay? Why don't we just take things slow and easy, see what happens?"

"Good idea. But there is one thing."

Luke toyed with her hair, wrapping a curl around his finger. "Yeah, what's that?"

"I need to tell my boyfriend."

Luke shot upright. "What!"

Emma burst out laughing. "It was a joke. Sorry. I couldn't resist. Not when you have an army of women at your disposal."

"I don't have an army of women. If you want to know the truth, I haven't been with a woman in weeks."

Exactly what Xavier had said. "The thing is, I need to be sure that no matter what happens with our . . . arrangement, you'll partner with me till we bring Vance in."

"I told you I would. I also told you I don't break my word."

She relaxed back on the bed. "All right, so what's the plan for today?"

"The plan is for us to get some breakfast. I can't think when I'm this hungry." Brilliant blue eyes slid down to her breasts. She'd already figured out he was a boob man. Fortunately, her full breasts were one of her best features.

"Unless you want to satisfy another kind of hunger," he finished, circling a teasing finger around her nipple.

Emma just smiled. "Later, Mr. Insatiable. It's time to go find Rudy Vance."

Luke sighed and rolled out of bed. "So I guess that means we have to shower separately."

She was tempted to join him, but they had work to do. "There's always tonight," she said. "You can pretend I'm someone else."

Luke laughed and headed for the door to his room.

The shower turned cold, but Luke left it running. He needed to clear his head.

What the hell did he think he was doing? He wasn't

into relationships. Hell, he couldn't afford to stick around another night.

But he wanted to. That was the scary part. He wanted more of Emma Cassidy, and he wanted more than just sex. He hadn't felt that way about a woman since Heather.

He'd started seeing Heather Roberts in high school, proposed right after graduation. He'd been engaged to her when he joined the army. Heather had waited for him a couple of years, but by then he'd signed up for Special Forces.

She'd been engaged to someone else by the time he'd gone Delta. Luke hadn't blamed her. She deserved a guy who could make her happy. He was a different man by then, the kind who didn't have anything to contribute to a marriage.

In the years since, he'd kept his affairs light and uncomplicated, mostly a string of one-nighters. He'd burned out on that a couple months ago, finally stopped dating altogether a few weeks back.

He'd known Emma Cassidy was trouble the moment he'd seen her at Rocker's, making pulp out of Skinner Digby's head. Now he was committed to partnering with her until they caught Vance.

Which should have freaked him out, but didn't.

It could only go bad for Emma. Hell, he was bad news for any woman.

Luke sighed as he turned off the shower, stepped out, and toweled himself dry.

At least he'd tried to do the right thing.

You're no gentleman, Luke. Emma was right about that. Luke thought about the best night of sex he could recall, thought about the night ahead, and found his grim mood lifting. As he pulled on his jeans and a faded, olive drab T-shirt and headed for the connecting door, a smile flickered at the corners of his mouth.

* * *

"What do you mean things didn't go the way I planned?" Rudy spoke quietly into the phone. He rarely raised his voice, even when he was angry. And yet there was an unmistakable edge to his words.

"When Dixon and Rio got to the house last night to pick up the body, a man and a woman were waiting. They were looking for you. Dixon got away. Rio took a bullet. He's in the hospital in Coupeville."

Sitting in the living room of a nicely furnished suite at the Willows Lodge in Woodinville, just twenty miles from his office in downtown Seattle, Rudy's hand tightened around his cell phone, one of several throwaways he carried.

"What did Dixon tell them?" The room was registered in the name of Malcolm Hobbs. The fictitious Hobbs had a matching passport, driver's license, and credit cards. In the months since he'd left Seattle, Rudy had shaved his head, grown a Van Dyke beard that ringed his mouth down to his chin, and now wore a pair of small gold earrings. He liked his new look. Amazing how little effort it took to hide in plain sight.

"Dixon didn't say squat, according to him. He didn't know where you'd gone so there wasn't much he could say. I sent him to take care of the boat."

Rudy had beached the twenty-five-foot Sea Ray south of Everett near Howarth Park, a place they'd set up ahead of time should he ever need a quick getaway. Grady Kelso, one of his most valued employees, had arranged for a driver to pick him up and drop him off at whatever he chose as his destination. Even Kelso didn't know he was staying at the lodge.

"Can you count on Rio to keep his mouth shut?"

"He doesn't know anything, but even if he did, he wouldn't talk. Matter of honor and all that." Parker Levinson, the man on the other end of the line, was his partner and closest associate, one of the few people who had this number. Parker was motivated entirely by money, which was the reason Rudy trusted him.

"Any idea who was looking for you at the house?" Parker asked.

"Had to be Brodie. Riggs made the mistake of calling Kelso, telling him he'd been followed home from the Polo Club. Said some guy and a woman named Emma Cassidy were asking questions, trying to find me. After they left, Riggs found out the guy was Luke Brodie. Kelso picked Riggs up and brought him to me. Riggs admitted he'd spilled, told Brodie about my aunt. Idiot never should have opened his mouth."

"Riggs didn't know where to find you. You think your aunt told Brodie where you were?"

"Bernice wouldn't give Brodie the time of day. Besides, she didn't know I was staying on the island. Brodie's good. He was hunting me before I left Seattle. He must have gotten word I was back and started looking again."

"Sounds right. So where's the girl fit in?"

Rudy adjusted the phone as he leaned back on the comfortable beige sofa. "Riggs claimed she was a bounty hunter working with Brodie. I've got a man on the inside. He'll take a look at the police report and confirm."

"If it's Brodie, we could be in for trouble," Parker said.

"If he gets any closer, we'll bring Kelso in. He can arrange to have Brodie eliminated—and the woman." Or Rudy would do it himself—not an entirely unpleasant thought.

Silence lingered on the other end of the line. "I'll keep you informed," Parker said, and the line went dead.

Rudy set the disposable phone down on the coffee table in front of him. He pulled out his wallet and removed the photo of Cissy he still carried after all these years, ran a finger lovingly over the picture.

Cissy, no longer the girl he'd once loved, was lost to him. But he had found Ginny. She was as dear to him as Cissy had been. Now they were trying to keep her from him, but in time he would find her again. She would come to understand that her place was with him.

The doorbell rang. Knowing his guest had arrived, his body stirred. He was freshly showered. Rudy pulled the sash on his white terry cloth robe a little tighter and strode to the door, looked out through the peephole.

He stepped back and opened the door, allowing the little Japanese girl to walk into the entry. No more than five feet tall, she had a flawless complexion and long black hair. She was a prostitute, but with her slim hips and small breasts, she looked like a teenage girl.

He could always rely on Parker to take care of him. Parker understood his particular tastes, and he had done a fine job with this one.

"My name is Miko," the girl said, bowing deeply before she looked up at him. "What may I do to please you?"

Rudy pulled the sash on his robe and drew it open. "Get down on your knees," he said.

Chapter Fourteen

In a pink vinyl booth at Paula's Pantry, a small café in Freeland, Emma looked over at Luke. The man ate like a lumberjack. Pancakes and eggs over easy, sausage and hash browns, and toast.

"Your cholesterol must be off the charts." She dug into her single poached egg, cottage cheese and sliced tomatoes, dry toast with a spoonful of jam.

Luke grinned, carving a dimple into his left cheek. The man even had a dimple. It was unbelievable.

"One-fifty," he said. "I'm healthy as a horse."

Emma smiled. "I should have known."

Luke swallowed a mouthful of potatoes. "Why is that?"

"You're Luke Brodie. God wouldn't have it any other way."

Luke just shook his head and kept eating. They had phoned Aunt Bernice before they'd left the motel and given her a whitewashed version of what had happened at the house on Whidbey Island last night. Bernice didn't believe her nephew would connect her to the information she had given them.

"Even if he does," the older woman had said, "Rudolph would never hurt me. I'm the only family he has."

Emma hoped she was right.

Once both of them had finished eating, Luke shoved his plate aside and leaned against the back of the booth. His gaze came to rest on her face.

"It's quiet in here. If we're going to catch Vance, I'm going to need all the information I can get. You ready to tell me what happened the day the housekeeper was murdered and Vance attacked your niece for the second time?"

Emma tossed her napkin onto the table and sat back, too. "I knew you'd ask me sooner or later. I'm surprised you waited this long."

"I figured I'd give you a break. A lot's been going on."

A lot. Like another brutal murder. Like Luke spending the night in her bed—and the morning. She sighed, resigned to telling the story one more painful time.

"My sister, April, met Rudolph Vance through one of her girlfriends. She and her friend Carrie are both dental hygienists—apparently Rudy is meticulous about keeping his teeth clean. One day April went by Carrie's office to pick her up for lunch and Rudy had just finished his cleaning. He was attractive, only a few years older than April. I guess they got to talking."

"I can see how a woman would find Vance appealing, at least on the surface."

"My sister is very pretty. Rudy must have thought so, too."

"She's your sister. I'm not surprised."

Emma looked up at him. "She's blond and blue-eyed like our mother was."

"Was? Your mom's dead?"

"Small plane crash five years ago. Both she and my father were killed."

"I'm sorry, Em. That's rough."

An understatement. Those were the worst days of her life—until Rudolph Vance. "At any rate, Rudy asked April to accompany him to a charity event, some kind of Heart Association dinner. April said he was a big contributor."

"Rudy knows which palms to grease. The mayor is on the board of directors. He did a lot of favors for Rudy. Knowing whose pocket to climb into was one of the ways Rudy was able to stay under the radar so long."

"He must be a pretty smooth operator. April said she enjoyed herself, looked forward to seeing him again. A couple of days later, he called, and she invited him over for supper. That's where he met Ginny."

Emma bit her lip as unwanted memories crashed in.

"Just take your time," Luke said gently. "You don't have to hurry."

She took a deep breath and let it out slowly. "From the day Ginny was born, there was something different about her, something sweet and endearing. The moment Rudy saw her, he was enthralled. Of course now we know Ginny looks exactly like his stepsister, Cissy."

Luke's features darkened. "I can't wait to get my hands around that sick fuck's neck."

"Luke . . ."

"Sorry, go ahead."

"April sensed something was wrong. She said she didn't like the way Rudy was looking at her daughter. When he called for another date, she turned him down."

"Smart woman."

"She was done with Rudy, but two days later, while she was at work and Ginny was in her bedroom alone, Rudy broke into the house. He forced Ginny down on the bed and raped her. He used a condom. There was no DNA, and since he'd been in the house before, his fingerprints wouldn't hold up as evidence. It was Ginny's word against his, a teenager against a man who could afford the best criminal lawyer in Seattle."

"Elliott Markham," Luke said. "Markham tried to make it look like his client was the victim. He claimed April was using Ginny to extort Vance for money. Rudy was released on a three-million-dollar bond."

"That's right. He was out, free to do more of his evil. Three days before his court date, he went back to the house and tried to rape Ginny again. Eleanor managed to stop him, but in the process Vance killed her." Emma's eyes filled as the horror replayed in her head. "Vance escaped. The police believe he left the country. You know the rest."

Luke reached across the table and caught her hand, gave it a gentle squeeze and didn't let go. "I know how hard that was for you. Thank you for telling me."

Emma just nodded. She hoped it would help in some way. She hadn't wanted to talk about it, but now that she had, she felt as if a little of her burden had been lifted.

"Let's go." Luke stood up from the table and pulled Emma to her feet. He paid the bill; they left the café and took off in the Bronco.

"So what's our next move?" Emma asked as the battered old Ford rolled down the road toward the ferry terminal.

"We go back to the city and regroup. First we need to ID Rio, see how he's connected. Before my brother moved to Seattle, he was a Dallas PD homicide detective. He's got friends in the Seattle PD. Maybe he can convince them to let me talk to the kid. Maybe Rio has some idea where to find Vance."

"That sounds good. That reminds me . . . I've got a paper towel I picked up at the house. I'm hoping we might find some DNA."

"Great, we'll drop it at the lab. The one I use isn't far from the office."

"Are you sure we shouldn't just keep looking? Head

north and try to find the boat? Rudy's disappeared before and you couldn't find him."

"We don't even know what kind of boat it is," Luke said. "Besides, there are a hundred places he could have docked. Hell, he could have beached it and had someone pick him up. The thing is, Vance came back to Seattle for a reason. Once he killed Riggs, he couldn't risk staying on the island. He had to move to a new location, but I'm betting whatever he came to the city to do, he hasn't had time to finish."

"So the best way to find Vance is to figure out what his unfinished business is."

"Exactly."

Luke's cell phone signaled a text as he stood at the rail of the ferry, watching the water rush past the ship's white hull. Emma stood beside him, smiling as the wind played with the long dark ponytail she was once more wearing. Luke remembered how pretty those dark curls looked spread over his pillow and felt a pulse of heat slide into his groin.

Clearly he hadn't had enough of Emma yet. He didn't think it was going to happen anytime soon.

Ignoring the worrisome thought, Luke pulled the phone out of his pocket and read the text running across the bottom of the screen.

"It's from Ethan," he said. "I asked him to check on Rio's condition and see what else he could find out."

"In your line of work, having a former police detective in the family must be handy."

"E's really good at what he does."

Emma looked up as a pair of seagulls screeched over-head. In the distance, the Mukilteo terminal loomed on the horizon. "So what's in his text?"

"They're transporting Rio to Harborview Hospital. Kid's in stable condition."

"That's good news. Sounds like he's going to make it."

"Yeah," Luke said. "Good news for us. Maybe not so good for Rio."

"Vance isn't going to be happy with the way things went down."

"That's right. And Rudy isn't exactly a forgiving kind of guy—as Felix Riggs found out."

"My car's parked at your office," Emma said. "Is that where we're going?" They were back on the mainland, rolling down Interstate 5, almost to the 405 split, which could take them into downtown Seattle or along the east side of Lake Washington to Bellevue.

"That's our first stop. I want to see if the cops have ID'd Rio. If they won't let me talk to him, maybe Ethan can get in to see him. If that doesn't work, I've got a friend in the tattoo business who might be able to help find out who he really is."

"You think Rio's tats are Asian, right?"

"Be my guess. Beautiful artwork. Really professional. Didn't look like the design was finished, though." He made a lane change just before the freeway split, and took the 405 toward Bellevue.

"I didn't notice you wearing any ink," Emma said.

Luke's mouth edged up. "I hope that means you took a good long look."

Emma's lips curved into a smile. "I looked. You were naked and you really look good naked."

Luke grinned. "Thanks. So do you. And no, I don't have any tats."

"I read somewhere special ops guys don't get tattoos because they need to be able to blend in."

"So you ran a check on me?"

"Of course. Top to bottom. Didn't you run one on me?"

"What would be the fun in that? I'd rather find out for myself."

Emma liked that idea. "I didn't see anything that mentioned which branch you were in. I noticed a couple of scars, though. The one on your lower back looks like you were hurt pretty badly. Was that the reason you left the service?"

He nodded. "I was in the hospital for a couple of months, two different times. Third time I got hurt, I figured my luck had about run out. By then Ethan was working in Seattle. He said he had the perfect job for me. Bounty hunting wasn't exactly what he had in mind, but I'm flexible. I do whatever comes my way and it pays enough to be worth my time."

"You were a Ranger?"

"I was. Until I went Delta."

"Delta? No way. You're too tall to be Delta. From what I've heard, most of those guys are average height or less. Just like with the tats, they need to blend in."

"There are always exceptions. I had special skills."

She thought of last night and a flush crept over her skin. "I can't argue with that."

Luke laughed. "Not those kinds of skills. I've got a gift for languages. I hear it spoken, I remember it. The accent, the whole deal. I speak Spanish, French, Farsi, Pashto, even a little Chinese. I could probably come up with some Russian in a pinch."

"Wow. That's amazing."

"That's why I don't have much of a Texas accent anymore, at least not unless I want to."

"That's where you were born, right?"

He nodded. "Sulpher Springs. Little town east of Dallas. Still got cousins down there. We're all pretty close."

"What about your mom and dad?"

"Mom died a few years back. Hard on all of us. Dad's remarried, lives in North Carolina. He's happy. I'm happy for him."

"Seems like you've got a really nice family."

"The best."

"You're lucky to have them. With my parents gone, April and Ginny are the only family I have left."

He flicked her a sideways glance, must have caught the sadness in her face. "Hey, we're gonna catch Vance, okay? Then you'll have your family back."

She just nodded. They rode along in silence for a while. The blue water of Lake Washington appeared here and there on the right side of the highway.

"So what's the deal with the weekend get-together?" she asked. "And don't improvise. We both know you don't want to go."

Luke's hands tightened around the steering wheel as he felt a familiar surge of despair. He managed to push it away. Life was a bitch sometimes. But he'd learned that a long time ago.

"Ian, Ethan, and Nick are all married. Dirk and Meg's wedding is coming up. All of them have kids. I always feel like a spare wheel, you know?"

Emma shook her head. "I love spending time with April and Ginny. I'm sure your family loves having you with them."

They did. He knew they did. Didn't change the way he felt. Luke sliced her a sideways glance. "Might not be so bad if you went with me." The words were out before he could stop them. Now it was too late to call them back.

"Really? You'd want me to go?"

He shrugged. "Yeah. Sure. Why not?" *Why not?* Because he'd never taken a woman to a family gathering. Jesus only knew what they would think. Although having Emma there might make the whole day easier.

What the hell. They already knew he and Emma were working together. "You'd be doing me a favor. Of course there's a good chance we'll be busy following a lead on Vance."

"God, I hope so."

So did he. That way he'd have an excuse not to go to the damn barbeque at all.

Emma's cell phone chimed a text coming in. "It's Chelsea. She'll be back in town Saturday morning. I can't wait to see her."

"Maybe she'd like to go to the party."

Emma laughed. "Are you kidding? Chelsea's the original party girl. I'm sure she'd love to go. Assuming we aren't tied up."

Tied up? A hot rush of blood went straight to his groin. Emma tied to his bed, her sweet little body available for his plunder? He inwardly grinned at the thought of what Emma might do to him if he actually suggested it.

He cast her an assessing glance. Or maybe she'd like the idea as much as he did.

"I'll text Chelsea," she said, slamming his thoughts back to where they should be—catching a filthy murdering pervert who preyed on little girls. "But I'd rather find Vance," she finished.

Luke's jaw went tight. "Yeah. Me too."

Chapter Fifteen

The little house in Denver was cozy, with a white picket fence and beds filled with bright blooming flowers. April loved the small, ranch-style home. She just wished it were in Seattle.

She sighed as she sat at the white kitchen table late that morning. It looked pretty with the matching white cabinets and sunny yellow walls. FBI Special Agent Conner Danfield had chosen the place carefully.

Working closely with witness protection, Agent Danfield had gone beyond his duty and taken vacation days to help them settle into their temporary home.

Or not so temporary, depending on whether or not the police found and arrested Rudy Vance.

Or Emma did.

April knew how determined her sister was. Emma felt responsible for what had happened to Eleanor and Ginny that terrible August last year. Her sister believed if she had stayed home instead of going shopping with her friend, she might have been able to save them.

April knew it wasn't Emma's fault. Rudolph Vance was a monster. He had raped Ginny once, had tried to rape her again that day, and would have succeeded if it hadn't been for Eleanor. If Emma had been there, he might have murdered her, too.

If anyone was at fault, it was April. She'd brought Rudy Vance into their lives, even if she'd realized her mistake right away and refused to see him again. But nothing April said to Emma, younger by nearly eight years, could convince her.

In the past ten months, her sister had completely changed. She wasn't the optimistic young woman who loved puppies and children, who taught seventh grade at Central Middle School and tutored underprivileged kids on weekends.

The new Emma had put herself through a program of rigorous physical conditioning and learned how to defend herself. She had learned to shoot and become a skilled marksman. Emma was determined to bring Rudolph Vance to justice and keep Ginny safe.

April believed if there was any way to make that happen, her sister would find it.

April glanced down at the newspaper on her iPad, the *Denver Post*. Nothing new, at least nothing that involved Rudolph Vance—not that she had expected anything. Setting her iPad aside, she took a sip of iced tea.

Ginny was out of school for the summer. From the kitchen table, April could see her on the sofa in the living room, her legs curled beneath her, earphones plugged into her ears. The TV was on but Ginny wasn't watching. She was somewhere far away, in a place where she felt safe.

April's chest squeezed. After what had happened, all of them had changed. Ginny was no longer the joyful, high-spirited teenage girl who loved to dance with her girlfriends and talk for hours on the phone. Now there were long periods of quiet, times she holed up in her bedroom with a pair of headphones and didn't come out until April insisted she help with supper.

Her daughter was seeing a psychologist who specialized in troubled teens, and that seemed to be helping. Ginny liked her, and little by little she was becoming stronger, more her old self.

Still, April constantly worried about her. Recovering from two brutal attacks, the doctors warned, could take years. Add to that, April constantly feared Rudy would somehow find them and hurt Ginny again.

Silently, she thanked Agent Danfield for taking a personal interest in their situation. The handsome agent with the gray eyes and silver-touched dark brown hair had a soft smile he seemed to reserve just for her. From the moment they'd met, there'd been a spark between them. But April had Ginny to think of, and Con was working on the case against Vance.

There was no way the attraction between them could go anywhere, and both of them knew it.

Still, she thought of him often.

It was Thursday. Today and Saturday were April's days off. She had taken a job as a part-time clerk at a little boutique in a small strip mall, which had turned out to be more fun than she'd expected, and she really liked the people she worked with.

The sound of a car in front of the house drew her attention.

"Mom . . . ?"

April stood up at the trace of fear in her daughter's voice. She couldn't miss the sudden pale hue of Ginny's face.

April hurried to the window. There was a car idling out front, an older model dark blue Buick. The car started moving again, then braked to a halt in front of the house next door.

April breathed a sigh of relief. "It's okay, sweetie. They aren't coming here. It's just someone visiting the neighbors."

Ginny still looked uncertain. Her gaze returned to the window. When an older woman got out of the car, she relaxed back against the sofa.

April's throat tightened. How long would it take before her daughter would be a happy, normal, teenage girl again? How many years before she stopped flinching at every noise, stopped having nightmares, stopped being afraid just to walk down the street?

April thought of Rudolph Vance and what he had done to her family. She thought of Ginny and her daughter's uncertain future. Silently she prayed Emma would be the one to find him.

That Emma would keep her promise and make Rudolph Vance pay.

Emma felt Luke's hand at her waist as he guided her into his BOSS, Inc. office. Across the open work area, she spotted his brother, Ethan, in front of the computer on his desk.

"Glad you're here," Luke said, heading in Ethan's direction. "I'm hoping you've got a sit rep for me on Rio."

Ethan stood up, even taller than Luke, with a heavier, more muscular build. He was wearing jeans and a snug black T-shirt, his eyes dark brown instead of blue. Just like Luke, he was handsome as sin.

Ethan's gaze cut to Emma. "So my brother hasn't scared you off yet."

She smiled. "Not yet."

"You're a tough lady. Luke doesn't work well with partners. The few he's had didn't last more than a couple of days."

"I want to find Rudy Vance. So does Luke. Sometimes two people working toward a goal are better than one."

Ethan's dark eyes flashed to his brother. "Sometimes they are," he said. Whatever message those dark eyes conveyed was lost on Emma. If Luke got the message, he ignored it.

"So what about Rio?" Luke pressed.

"I've got news, but you aren't going to like it. Rio killed himself in his hospital room last night. Managed to hang himself in the bathroom."

"What the hell? Why would the kid do that? Rio didn't kill Felix Riggs. Yeah, he worked for Vance, but he had to be a low-level player. He was only there doing clean-up work. A decent lawyer could have gotten the murder charges dropped."

"The cops are looking into it. So far they haven't been able to get an ID. No record, nothing in the system."

"What about his tats? They were unusual and really good. Probably done by someone who's known for his work. They following up on that?"

"I'm sure they are. Since Riggs's murder may be connected to Vance, Bruce Hoover's the lead detective on the case. Hoover's good. He'll work the tattoo angle, hopefully come up with a name."

"I know someone who might be able to help."

Ethan smiled. "You always know someone."

Watching the exchange, Emma silently agreed. It seemed Luke could always think of someone who knew someone or could find out something useful.

"I'll stay on Hoover," Ethan said, sitting back down at his desk. "I'll try to keep you posted as much as I can."

Luke turned to Emma. "I'll make a call, see if I can track my tattoo guy down." They walked a little ways off as Luke dragged out his cell, brought up his contact list, and hit the send button.

While he was at it, Emma replied to the text she'd received, pulling out her phone to call Chelsea.

"Hey, girlfriend," her roommate said. "What's new? Seems like we haven't talked in forever."

"That's because we haven't talked in forever. I'm really glad you're coming home."

"Me too." Chelsea sounded upbeat. But then she usually did. "I've got a whole three days off and I plan to make the most of them. What about you? Any breaks on the case?"

Emma glanced over at Luke, who was back on his phone, making another call. "Actually, a couple of things have happened. I'm . . . ahh . . . working with Luke Brodie. I think I might have mentioned him."

Chelsea laughed. "Oh, you mentioned him—only a couple of hundred times. *The* Luke Brodie? Your hero? Superman?"

Emma turned away so Luke couldn't hear. "If you tell him that, our friendship is over."

"Okay, okay. I won't say a word."

"Good, because he's invited you to a party Saturday afternoon. His brother Ethan, and Ethan's wife, Val, are hosting. Some of Luke's friends will be there."

"Sounds like fun. Is Luke as hot as you thought he'd be?"

"Hotter." The minute the word came out, she realized her mistake.

"Wait a second. . . . You aren't sleeping with him, are you? You said Luke was a real Casanova. You said you felt sorry for the women he seduced."

Emma sighed. Lying wasn't even a remote possibility, not when Chelsea was such a good friend. "The thing is, aside from being hot, there's something special about him. Luke's different than I thought."

"Oh, my God, you did sleep with him!"

Emma felt a trickle of irritation. So what if she had? Why was it that other women could sleep with any man they wanted, but she was supposed to be the perennial good girl? "Do you want to come to the party or not?"

Chelsea just laughed. "Absolutely. A party with Luke Brodie and his bounty hunter friends? I can hardly wait."

"There'll be kids there, too, so you'll have to behave yourself." Emma gave Chelsea the details and finished with, "It's not a definite thing. If we get a lead on Vance, we'll have to cancel. I'll know more by the time you get home."

"Okay, keep me posted. I can't wait to meet Luke."

Emma ended the call. Now that she thought about it, maybe inviting Chelsea to the party was a bad idea. Chelsea Davenport was blond, blue-eyed, and beautiful. Luke had already broken his one-night rule. He might be on the prowl for somebody new. Chelsea would never betray her with a guy she was dating, but still . . .

The thought of Luke with another woman bothered her more than she wanted it to. She turned as he walked up behind her.

"You ready?" he asked.

"Did you talk to your friend?"

"Stuart Gibbons. He's actually a friend of Dirk's. He's the guy who did the tat on Dirk's shoulder."

"I thought I saw a hint of ink on the side of his neck."

"It's a dragon. Mostly it's hidden. It's really great work. Stu's one of the best. He didn't answer so I left a message."

Emma glanced toward the door leading out to the parking lot. "Since we don't have a meeting yet, I've got a couple of errands I need to run."

Luke nodded. "I've got a few things I need to do myself." As they headed for the door, Luke waved to his brother. Once outside, Luke walked her over to where her white Mazda was parked, then waited while she clicked open the locks.

"I'll call you as soon as I talk to Stu," he said. "Gibbons does tattoos in his spare time. He's got a job that takes him out of town so it might be a day or two before we can set up a meet."

"Maybe the cops will come up with something in the meantime."

"Yeah, maybe." Luke opened her door and waited for her to slide in behind the wheel. "Listen, Emma, I know you're going to keep working on this. You stumble on something, you call me. Don't go off on your own. That partnership deal works both ways."

"I'll call." After what had happened on Whidbey Island, she wasn't going to do anything stupid. She looked up at him as a thought crossed her mind and her stomach began to churn.

"I know we didn't make any rules about . . . us," she said, "but there is one rule I insist on."

"Yeah, what's that?"

"You don't sleep with other women while you're sleeping with me. You don't do that until we're over."

His lips thinned. "I know you find it hard to believe, but, honey, I'm not that kind of guy. I'm all yours till we're done. But I've got a rule of my own."

"What's that?"

"Same goes. You're mine till we're finished."

Relief trickled through her, and something else she couldn't quite name. "Okay," she said softly. "Same goes."

"I'll call when I hear from Stu."

Emma watched Luke walk away, his long legs eating up the asphalt on the way to his battered Ford. No matter how short their affair, Luke wouldn't end their partnership until they found Rudy Vance.

That was all that mattered, she told herself. But she was beginning to doubt it was the truth.

Chapter Sixteen

The afternoon turned cloudy. The wind kicked up, blowing leaves and trash along the gutters in the street. Luke's first stop was the North Country DNA Lab, where he dropped off the paper towel Emma had collected. For a few extra dollars, a college student named Danny Palachek, who was working two jobs to get through school, would move the item to the top of the test list.

It was late afternoon by the time Stu Gibbons returned Luke's phone call. As Luke had guessed, Stu was out of town until tomorrow. They set up a meet at the Black Owl tattoo parlor for ten o'clock Friday morning. He phoned Emma and gave her the news.

"I really hope he can help," she said. "I'm still running errands. Plus I want to stop at Oakmont and check on Booth."

Luke inwardly groaned. Booth had a way of reading people. He'd know in a heartbeat that Luke had taken Emma to bed. Booth wouldn't like it—not one little bit. He'd be sure Luke was just taking advantage.

Hell, maybe he was. If he had a lick of conscience, he would have left her alone.

Luke sighed as he drove through the one of the seedier

sections of Seattle, an area around Pioneer Square that included James Street, 3rd, Pike, and Pine. Streets he knew well.

It was late afternoon. He stopped at a couple of beer joints, talked to some of the bartenders who were always in the know, but nothing turned up. Back on the street, he made phone calls to some of his other contacts, putting out feelers, trying to dig up something new on Vance's where-abouts.

He was getting nowhere fast. Add to that, he grudgingly admitted, asking questions and running down leads wasn't nearly as much fun without Emma.

He wondered what she was doing, thought about calling her but talked himself out of it. He wondered if Booth would warn her against sleeping with him and knew he would. He didn't like the way that made him feel.

An hour later, he thought of her again, wished he'd asked her to go with him to dinner, wished he'd be taking her home with him later or spending the night in her bed.

He knew her address in West Seattle. If it didn't get too late, maybe he'd call her, see what she was up to.

If Booth hadn't convinced her never to speak to him again.

"Have you lost your mind?" Booth looked at Emma as if she was someone he'd never met. "I told you what Brodie was like. I warned you to stay away from him. If he was here right now, I'd punch Luke Brodie in the face."

They were sitting in the living area of Booth's studio apartment at Oakmont, drinking glasses of sugared iced tea. In the courtyard outside the window, wind whipped the branches of the trees and clouds had begun to gather, dark-ening the sky overhead.

"It wasn't Luke's fault," Emma said. "Luke tried to be a gentleman. I wouldn't let him."

Booth ran a hand over his thick silver hair. "So it's your fault Luke Brodie took you to bed. You're the evil seductress and Luke's just your innocent victim."

"It wasn't like that."

Booth rolled his eyes. "Spare me the details. I've heard more than enough."

"You're the one who asked. Did you want me to lie about it?"

"You could have improvised a little. Of course, if you had, I would have known."

Emma flashed him a disbelieving glance.

Booth just shook his head. "So what happened with Vance? Did Studly Do-wrong get you any closer to finding him?"

Emma couldn't stop a laugh. *Studly*. If Booth only knew. "That's a good one. I'll have to tell Luke."

"You mean you actually expect to see him again? Mr. One-night Stand?"

Her laughter faded. "We made a deal. No matter what happens, we partner till we find Vance."

Booth's silver eyebrows went up, along with one side of his mouth. "Brodie said that?"

She nodded. "He gave me his word."

"Well, that's a surprise. If Brodie gave you his word, he won't break it. Which doesn't mean he won't break your heart."

A fine thread of worry slipped through her. Booth was right. It would be easy to fall for Luke. She had to be careful. Very careful. It was probably good she wasn't seeing him tonight. Probably.

"So fill me in," Booth said. "Where are we with Vance?"

Emma settled in to tell him about her trip to Whidbey

Island, about finding Felix Riggs in the freezer, the shootout, and the police. She told him their most promising lead to Vance had killed himself in his hospital room last night.

She didn't mention what had happened at the Pine Tree Inn. But, then, Booth had already guessed.

Luke drove the dark Seattle streets. The weather was slightly improved. The wind had calmed, the temperature was mild, but the moon and stars were obscured by a thick wall of low-hanging clouds. Not far from Pioneer Square, drunks prowled the sidewalks, prostitutes plied their trade, and loud music blared through the open doorways of local bars.

At a stoplight, a familiar bleached blonde wearing long dangly earrings, a low-cut sequined top, and a gold lamé skirt too tight for her wide behind walked up to the Bronco and leaned in the passenger window.

"Hey, Luke, what's happenin', sugar?"

"Hey, Sophie—you tell me."

"You still huntin' Felix Riggs? I got somethin' that might help you find him. But if you want it, it'll cost you."

"I found Riggs. He's dead."

Sophie made a disgusted sound in her throat. "Too bad. I coulda used the money."

Luke pulled out his wallet and drew out a hundred-dollar bill. He liked to keep his informants happy. The happier they were, the more they talked. You never knew what useful tidbit they might spill.

"So what info did you have for me on Riggs?"

"Just that I seen him talking to a guy in the Red Devil bar. I thought you might be able to find the guy. Maybe he could tell you where to find Felix." She eyed the hundred. "Guess it doesn't matter now."

Luke shoved the hundred into her bulging cleavage. "What's this guy look like?"

Sophie smiled and used a heavily ringed finger to tuck the money deeper. "Fortyish. Nice lookin'. Good build. Carrot red hair. I remember he had a crooked nose, like he'd been in a fight, you know?"

"What else?"

"Felix left the bar with him."

"When was this?"

"Around noon yesterday."

The time would fit. Plenty of time to get dead, but not enough time to freeze solid. "Anything else?"

"I don't know. If you ain't huntin' Riggs, who you huntin' now?"

"Rudy Vance. He's a bad dude, Sophie. Keep your ears open, but steer clear of him. You hear anything, you know how to find me."

"I know." She ran a hand over her bosom, cupped one big breast. "You sure you don't want some of this? Be on the house for you, sugar."

Luke just smiled. "Not tonight, sweet cheeks." Luke pulled away from the curb.

By the time he drove by the Red Devil bar, the lights were off except for the blinking neon sign in the window. Tomorrow he'd come back, try to track down the man Riggs had left the bar with. Good chance it was the guy who got him killed.

Still not ready to face his empty apartment, Luke drove the dingy streets awhile longer. He had never considered the nights he spent there lonely. Tonight the belly of the city seemed to throb like an old wound that ached only part of the time. This was one of those times.

It was past time to go home. Luke turned the corner and headed the Bronco toward Bellevue.

* * *

Emma couldn't sleep. She'd closed her eyes for a while, but there was too much going on in her head. She'd finally given up, turned on the reading light over her bed, and cracked open the novel she'd started to read before she'd gotten the tip on Skinner Digby.

She was into the fourteenth chapter of a good romantic suspense when she heard the doorbell ring. She frowned. The front door leading into the lobby was locked. Anyone who wanted to visit a tenant had to be buzzed in.

A little uneasy, she grabbed her yellow fleece robe off the foot of the bed, dragged it on over the nightie she was wearing, and headed for the door. Couldn't be Chelsea. She wasn't due in until Saturday, plus she had her own key.

Emma leaned over and peered through the keyhole, saw Luke in the hall outside her door. She unfastened the locks and pulled the door open, felt her stomach clench at how good he looked in his faded jeans and soft leather moccasins.

Oh, boy, she was in trouble.

She managed to smile. "Hi. Come on in." She stepped back to let him inside the apartment. "How did you get past the front door?" A memory arose of the Whidbey Island house he'd so easily broken into. "Never mind. What's up?"

"I know it's late. I got a lead on Vance. I thought you might want to know."

She looked into those blue, blue eyes. It was a lame excuse but Emma didn't care. "I couldn't sleep, either," she said softly.

"Yeah . . ." Luke slid his hands into her hair and cupped the back of her head. Drawing her close, he settled his mouth over hers and kissed her. It was one of his long, slow, deep, toe-curling, Luke Brodie kisses, and it made her feel weak. She whimpered when he finally let her go.

"Be okay if we just went to bed?" he asked a little gruffly, his incredible blue eyes locked on her face.

"It's really late. I'm not just a booty call, am I?"

He kissed her softly once more. "Never." Sweeping her up in his arms, he carried her into the bedroom and set her on her feet. Luke stripped off his clothes, then her robe and nightie, carried her over to the bed, and followed her down.

They didn't sleep, of course. At least not right away, not until Luke had made wild, passionate love to her. She'd been pleasantly rag doll limp when she'd finally fallen asleep.

In the morning, she awoke to the smell of coffee. After a bathroom stop, brushing her teeth, then her hair, she joined Luke in her serviceable galley kitchen. A bag of doughnuts sat on the ceramic tile counter. Apparently Luke had already been to the bakery next door to her building.

He poured her a cup of coffee, walked over and pressed the cup into her hand, leaned down and kissed her.

"Peppermint," he said. "Nice." Then he scratched his gorgeous chest and turned to survey the corkboard on the wall behind her breakfast table. "So that's Vance's profile?"

Emma dragged her gaze away from all those delicious muscles and turned to the photos on the board. "It's Vance. Pictures of him at various ages. Old photos of him with his family that I ran across in some articles I found. I missed his adoption, but I've corrected it and added his aunt Bernice. I knew he had a stepsister, but I didn't have her picture until yesterday. I've got everything I could find on International Cargo and businesses that link to it."

There were subcategories, names of people connected in any way with Vance, including Lyle McCarthy and Sam

Cogan, newspaper clippings, photos of Vance at parties like the one where she'd seen Felix Riggs.

"Yesterday I added all the other stuff we've uncovered in the last few days," she said, "but now that I'm looking at it, I need to put up something else."

Walking over to the board, she picked up the pencil hanging from a string beside it and wrote a note on the tablet on the wall.

"What is it?" Luke asked, coming up beside her. She forced herself to ignore his heat, tore the note off the tablet, and pinned it to the corkboard.

"Marmite," Luke read. "What the hell is *Marmite?*"

"I didn't know either till I Googled it when I got home. I saw it written on Rudy's grocery list when we were in his house. It's a spread made of yeast extract. It's a lot like Vegemite."

"Vegemite," he repeated.

"The stuff they eat in Australia. You know the Men at Work song about the Vegemite sandwich?"

Luke smiled. "I know it."

"So Marmite's like Vegemite, a spread made from yeast. It's extremely healthy. Low sugar, low cal, has protein, vitamins, and minerals. It's supposed to taste cheesy, kind of salty and fermented."

"Sounds delicious," Luke said dryly.

"Some of the articles I read mentioned Rudy's a health nut. Likes to stay in shape, jogs, eats organic, buys his groceries at the Whole Foods store. From what I gather, Marmite isn't that easy to find." She shrugged. "Probably not important but you never know."

"That's right, baby, you never do. Catching a criminal is all in the details. Nice work."

Emma smiled. "Thanks." She glanced at the kitchen clock above the sink. "I need to shower. I better get moving if we're going to be on time for our meeting with Stuart Gibbons." Walking past Luke she headed for the bathroom, grabbing a doughnut along the way.

As she reached the bathroom door, she felt Luke behind her. He kissed the nape of her neck. "We'll save water if we shower together."

Heat curled low in her belly. "What about Stuart Gibbons?"

"What? You've never heard of a quickie?" Luke followed her into the bathroom, closed the door, and turned on the shower.

The quickie wasn't that quick. But it was worth having to hurry afterward.

Chapter Seventeen

Luke waited for Emma in the living room. She was rushing to make up for lost time. He didn't like to be late and neither did she. He appreciated that about her, though he didn't regret the shower, or the extra time he'd taken with Emma's delectable little body.

An unexpected shot of lust rolled through him. Dammit, what was there about Emma that he couldn't get enough of her? To take his mind off sex, he glanced around the living room of an apartment almost as spartan as his own.

According to what Emma had told him, before the murder and rape last year, she'd been living with her sister and Ginny. Once she'd set herself to finding Rudy Vance, she had moved from the suburbs to the city and rented the apartment she shared with her roommate.

Instead of the cozy space Luke had imagined, the place was a basic furnished apartment: beige sofa and chairs, dark brown carpet, cheap oak tables, two bedrooms, each with a dresser, nightstands, and a queen-size bed.

He smiled as he thought again of last night. Good thing he didn't mind snuggling.

Still, as they walked out of the apartment, he couldn't help wondering how the place would look if Emma wasn't so obsessed with catching Vance. He had the feeling she would make it into a real home.

It didn't take long to reach the parking lot. They got into the Bronco and Luke cranked the engine.

"I need to make up a little time," he said, warning her of his intentions. Emma hurriedly snapped her seat belt in place as Luke shoved the SUV into gear. He chuckled. She was beginning to know him.

To make up for the shower, he hauled ass to the Black Owl tattoo parlor on East Pike and Broadway, a nice clean establishment that looked more like a beauty salon than one of the seedy tat joints of the past. There were four stations, each fitted with the most modern equipment: guns, ink, needles, and medical cleaning supplies. Dozens of poster-sized examples of artwork hung on the walls.

"There's Stu," Luke said, urging Emma in that direction. Except for his tats, the guy looked more like a computer geek than a tattoo artist, with his horn-rimmed glasses, short brown hair, and a clean-shaven face.

But the scene of an eagle soaring over the mountains colored one arm, while a waterfall pouring into a tropical pool appeared on the other. Stu had done the drawings himself, then had the work completed by an artist he respected.

His friend spotted him and smiled. "Hey, Luke, how's it going?" He and Stu bumped fists, leaned in, and gripped shoulders.

"All good," Luke said, "except for the current hunt I'm on. I'm hoping you can take a look at some photos, see if you can figure out who did the tats. By the way, this is Emma. She's working with me on this."

Surprised, Stu turned to the petite woman beside him, gave her the once-over. "Nice to meet you, Emma."

"You, too, Stu."

For the first time, Luke noticed there was a client in the

chair on the other side of the half wall, the space where Stuart worked.

Dirk lifted his head, his dark brown hair curling around the nape of his neck. He sat up in the chair.

"Hey, you two. Ethan brought me up to speed on what's been going on. I figured you'd show up here sooner or later."

"Hey, bro, you getting another tat?" Luke asked.

"No, man. I'm about to become a father. My wild days are over." Dirk grinned. "Well, mostly."

He pointed at the tattoo of a broken heart on his upper left chest. He'd put it there after he and Meg had split up, a reminder never to fall in love again.

"I'm having the line removed as a wedding gift to Meg. I'm making the heart whole again." He smiled softly. "Now that we're back together, that's the way I feel."

Emma's eyes misted. "That's really sweet, Dirk. And incredibly romantic. Meg's a lucky woman."

"I'm the one who's lucky," Dirk said a little gruffly.

Luke felt the darkness begin to sweep over him. As happy as he was for his friend, he hated being reminded of the kind of life he'd never have.

He forced himself to smile. "You're one lucky S-O-B, no doubt about it. But I need to find Rudy Vance before he kills somebody else. I'm hoping Stu can help."

"Let me see the photos," Stu said.

Luke pulled out his cell and brought up the pictures he'd taken of Rio's tats. He handed the phone to Stu.

"Amazing work," Stu said, sliding the images past with an ink-stained finger.

"You know who did them?" Luke asked.

Stu nodded. "His style is really distinctive, so yeah, I know whose work it is. His name is Richard Tanaka. He's one of the finest artists in the business. The problem is, he moved back to Japan."

"Damn. You sure?"

Stu handed him back the phone. "Tanaka lived in Seattle for a while. They did an article about him in the *Times* just before he left."

Fuck, another dead end. Luke blew out a breath. "That is a problem."

"Why are you looking for him?"

"I'm trying to ID the guy in the picture." Luke pulled up a photo of Rio's face and handed the phone back to Stu. "Calls himself Rio. Early twenties, black hair, kind of a pretty boy muscle jock. I'm guessing he's at least part Asian. After what you've said, probably Japanese. He was unconscious at the time I took the pictures."

"I know him. That's Rio Sakamura. He came in here awhile back looking for someone to do more tats. I was busy at the time."

"He got any family?"

"I don't know. I only remembered him because of the work Richard did on him. It was amazing. So Rio's a bail skip?"

"No. Rio's dead. He killed himself last night. The guy I'm hunting is Rudolph Vance. Rio was working for him. I was hoping I might be able to connect the two and get a lead."

Dirk spoke up just then. "You ought to talk to your old buddy, Quan Feng. He might have something you could use."

The huge Chinese who owned the Golden Lily, a gambling casino in the International District, knew everything that happened in the Asian community. Casinos were illegal in the city limits, but Quan's family had been there for more than a hundred years. When payoffs were no longer enough to keep him in business, he'd managed to get the place grandfathered in and get a special permit.

"Exactly what I was thinking," Luke said.

"You want me to come along?" Dirk asked. "I'm on my own tonight. Meg's doing inventory at her boutique and Charlie's spending the weekend with his grandparents."

Luke smiled. "I've got Emma. She puts on one of her slinky outfits, she'll have Quan drooling, and if anything goes wrong, she can back me up."

Dirk laughed. "Handy to have—a sexy lady and a bounty hunter rolled into one."

Luke cast Emma a glance. Even in jeans and a T-shirt she was way beyond sexy. He didn't mention she was also dynamite in bed.

"Yeah, very handy," he said. Beautiful women were Quan Feng's weakness. They were always a ticket through the door. The bad news was, the guy's sexual tastes ran toward kinky.

He glanced over at Emma. Quan would be impressed, all right. On the other hand . . .

His gaze swung back to Dirk. "On second thought, I don't trust Feng as far as I can throw him—which at four-hundred pounds is not at all. It might not be a bad idea to have a little extra backup."

"Sounds good," Dirk said. "Text me with the details and I'll meet you there."

They left Dirk and Stu in the tattoo parlor, and on the way to the car, Luke phoned Bruce Hoover, the lead detective on the Rudy Vance case, a guy his brother had worked with on a number of occasions.

"Hoover, it's Luke Brodie. I got a name for you on that

suicide last night. The kid they brought in from Whidbey Island."

"Thanks, but we found him. Full name's Norio Sakamura. Twenty years old. Born in Seattle to a Russian mother and a Japanese father. Mother's dead. We're trying to run down the father, but so far no luck."

"How's he connected to Vance?"

"That's police business, Brodie, but it doesn't matter, since I have no idea. Aside from being caught with the dead body of one of Vance's associates, there *is* no connection."

"I might have found some DNA that will link the cases, but the results aren't back from the lab. If there's anything there, I'll let you know."

"I'd appreciate that. Wouldn't hold up in court without a chain of evidence, but at least we'd know for sure Vance was on the premises."

"I'll keep you posted. Any help you could throw my way would also be appreciated."

Hoover sighed into the phone. "You're a pain in my ass, Brodie, just like your brother."

"Thanks. I'll be sure to tell him you said so."

Hoover grunted. "Don't worry, he already knows."

Luke smiled as Hoover hung up the phone.

"So what's the plan?" Emma asked once they were back in the Bronco and rolling along the freeway toward BOSS, Inc.

"Lunch," Luke said. "We can't see Feng until tonight. Not much we can do before then."

"I swear you're always hungry."

He cast her a lascivious glance. "Like I said, there's not much we can do for a while. We'll be out late. Maybe we'll stop by my place after lunch and grab a nap." He went hard just thinking about spending the afternoon in bed with

Emma. Her cheeks turned pink so he figured she knew what he was thinking.

"So . . . umm . . . tell me about this guy, Quan Feng?"

"Feng runs a gambling casino. Guy's in the know on everything that happens in Seattle. I'm hoping he might know Rio. If he does, maybe he'll be able to tell us how Rio was connected to Vance."

"Are you sure he'll be there?"

"It's Friday night. Odds are he will be." Luke wanted to do a little digging on the down-low, before the cops started asking questions, ruffling feathers in the Asian community and everybody clammed up.

"Where do you want to eat?" he asked.

Emma surprised him with a slow, sexy smile. "Why don't we get takeout? Bring it back to your place."

Luke grinned. He liked a woman who knew what she wanted. "Damn straight," he said.

Chapter Eighteen

In Seattle's International District, Chinese, Japanese, Filipino, Vietnamese, and Southeast Asians all lived together. The Golden Lily on Maynard Street was a narrow establishment on the bottom floor of a four-story brick building.

As Luke drove past, Emma noticed a martial arts school next door, while a few doors down, a sign read LING'S NOODLE HOUSE. There was a Vietnamese restaurant and a place whose sign read TEA GALLERY.

Luke parked on a side street, then rounded the Bronco and helped her out of the vehicle. "Stay close," he warned. "You're not a bounty hunter tonight. You're just my woman."

His woman? After spending the afternoon in his bed—*merciful heavens!*—she actually felt like Luke's woman. Dangerous as the feeling might be.

She had never been to his apartment before, but she wasn't surprised to find it modern, efficient, and military clean and neat. There was a gun safe in the living room—*that*, she hadn't expected. His big, king-size bed made her wary. How many women had slept there? She wasn't sure she wanted to join that particular list.

"I know what you're thinking," he'd said. "I've never

brought a woman here before. I usually go to her house or we get a room somewhere."

The words stunned her. And the serious look on his face. "Why me?" she asked softly.

Luke shook his head. "I don't know. Maybe because I trust you. I know you won't get the wrong idea."

The words only stung for a moment. She wouldn't get the wrong idea. She knew what they had was only temporary, until they found Rudolph Vance. Emma intended to make the most of the time they had.

Going up on her toes, she looped her arms around his neck. "We can always reheat that pizza we bought."

Luke pulled her against him, lowered his head, and kissed her. "Yeah, baby, we can."

The next thing she knew she was naked and so was Luke. The afternoon passed in a blaze of hot need and deep, saturating pleasure, then napping curled up in Luke's arms.

They showered together, which resulted in another round of steamy sex, and ate the reheated pizza. Afterward he drove her back to her place to pick out something to wear to the Golden Lily.

Now as Luke walked next to her along the sidewalk, Emma glanced down at the red silk dress she had chosen. The dress was cut low enough to flatter her cleavage, fitted through the waist and hips, then floated out around her thighs. Matching red heels pushed her up an extra five inches.

She usually saved the outfit, one of her favorites, for special occasions like Christmas parties, but Luke had asked her to wear something sexy so she had chosen the dress.

The way he kept looking at her, as if he wanted to rip it right off her body, she was glad she had.

"That dress is killing me," he said as if he had read her mind. "I can't wait to get you home."

Her stomach melted. She felt breathless just thinking about it. She managed to smile. "I'm glad you like it."

"I like what's in it, honey." He was dressed up tonight, in black skinny jeans that rode low on his hips, a white shirt, and a black blazer. A pair of black and yellow sneakers looked chic and expensive. His sun-streaked brown hair had been stylishly moussed.

He looked more like a cover model than a bounty hunter, which was exactly the idea.

"Hey, you two." Handsome in pressed blue jeans, a white T-shirt under a navy blue blazer, Dirk strolled up as they approached. He'd arrived in a hot, metallic blue, four-door Porsche, and he looked good in it.

"Thanks for coming," Luke said. "You ready to get this done?"

"You bet," Dirk said. "Emma?"

"Anything special I need to do?" she asked.

Luke flicked her a glance. "You like to gamble?"

"Sure. I'm pretty good at blackjack. Of course I was only playing with April and Ginny and we weren't using real money."

Luke rolled his eyes. Pulling out his wallet, he peeled off five crisp hundred-dollar bills and handed them over. "Try to make it last."

Emma handed the bills back. "I can't take your money."

"Why not?"

"Because I might lose it."

He looked at Dirk and both men shook their heads. "Fine. I'll take it out of your fee." He pressed the money into her hand.

Emma relaxed. This was business. "All right." She grinned. "This way I get to keep whatever I win."

Luke chuckled. Apparently that wasn't likely in a place like this.

They rounded the corner together. Next to the front door, a big Asian stood guard, hands crossed in front of him, legs splayed. He looked like Odd Job in *Goldfinger*.

The big man studied them head to foot, but didn't try to stop them from walking inside.

Except for the glowing pink neon tubes running behind the back bar, the interior was dim. A green and red Tsingtao beer sign hung over a shuffleboard table along the wall. Emma didn't recognize the rock song playing on the digital jukebox.

The place was full but not overflowing, a mix of Asian and Caucasian, both men and women. A line of men sat on bar stools at a long black granite bar. She could feel their eyes on her as she walked past, the hem of her short dress floating around her as she moved.

One of them said something and the others laughed. Luke pulled her a little closer, making it clear that she was with him.

"Keep going," he said softly, urging her toward the back of the bar. The place wasn't seedy, yet she couldn't help wishing she had her little .380 pistol strapped to her thigh beneath her skirt.

Unfortunately, it wasn't legal for them to carry firearms where alcohol was served. She'd seen Luke slide a four-inch switchblade into the pocket of his jeans. Emma had added a mini can of pepper spray to the red handbag slung over her shoulder. She figured Dirk was probably armed in some way.

Two men played pool on a green baize table in the back of the bar. An Asian man even bigger than the one out front, arms bulging with muscle, stood next to a stainless steel elevator.

"Good evening, Fu Han," Luke said politely. "I'm here

to see Quan Feng." He peeled off a hundred-dollar bill and pressed it into the Asian's meaty hand.

"Mr. Brodie. It's good to see you." Fu Han pocketed the money and pushed the elevator button. When the door slid open, Luke urged Emma inside and followed her in. Dirk joined them, followed by big Fu Han.

On the third floor, the elevator doors slid open. Emma walked out and the men followed. A maître d' in a black suit, white shirt, and narrow red-striped tie stepped forward, a tall man with coarse black hair trimmed very short.

"Mr. Brodie. It has been quite some time. What may we do for you and your friends this evening?"

"Good evening, Louis. I need to speak to Quan Feng."

Louis turned in Emma's direction, his black gaze sliding over her like cold maple syrup. She squared her shoulders, refusing to be intimidated.

Louis returned his attention to Luke. "You have brought Mr. Feng a gift?"

A muscle ticked in Luke's jaw. "She's with me."

One of Louis's black eyebrows arched in disapproval. "Mr. Feng will not be pleased. I will tell him you are here. In the meantime, you know the rules. No weapons allowed."

A small, black-haired man stepped forward. Luke volunteered his switchblade, reluctantly handing it over. Dirk waited for the man to pat him down. The guy pointed to the slight bulge in the front pocket of his jeans. Dirk pulled out a little .22 caliber pistol and set it on a tray on the table beside the elevator door.

They didn't ask to see Emma's purse, which she kept tucked against her side.

"This way, Mr. Brodie," Louis said.

Luke turned to Emma and Dirk. "You two might as well enjoy yourselves."

Dirk tipped his head toward the blackjack tables, urging her in that direction as Luke headed deeper into the club.

Louis Chan, the manager of the Golden Lily, escorted Luke to the booth where the massive Chinese, Quan Feng, sat watching over his domain like an almond-eyed Jabba the Hutt.

"*Zhè shì hěn gāoxìng jiàn dào nǐ*, Quan Feng." Luke greeted the man respectfully in Chinese, as he hadn't done before.

Feng looked surprised and oddly pleased as Luke slid into the booth across from him. A Scotch on the rocks, the drink he'd ordered the last time he was there, magically appeared on the table in front of him. The server, a beautiful young Chinese girl, disappeared as silently as she had approached.

Quan's beady eyes swung across the room to Emma. "Louis tells me the woman is yours." He toyed with the cup of green tea in front of him. "Her looks please me greatly, a tiny woman with all those dark curls and such pretty breasts. I can think of any number of ways I could enjoy her."

Luke clamped down hard on his temper. He'd known what to expect from Quan Feng. He just hadn't anticipated his own reaction.

"I keep what's mine," he said darkly. "And I don't share."

Feng's hard gaze centered on Luke's face. "Twice you have been here with beautiful women, dangling them in front of me like succulent bits of meat. Next time I expect you to bring someone for me, someone special."

Not good. "If there is a next time, I'll see what I can do.

At the moment, I'm here for information. I'm hoping you can give it to me."

"I don't *give* anything, Mr. Brodie. Always there is a price."

"I'm aware of that. Do you know a kid named Norio Sakamura?"

Feng's heavy-lidded eyes darkened. His massive bulk shifted on the seat. "I know who he is."

"Rio killed himself last night at Harborview Hospital."

Feng just nodded. "I heard he was dead. Something about family honor."

Family honor. Interesting. "Rio was working for a man named Rudolph Vance. I need to know how the two are connected."

"You just said Sakamura was his employee."

Luke took a sip of his Scotch, rattling the ice in his glass. "So you don't know anything more than that? Nothing about him or Vance?"

"I've been told you are hunting this man, Vance."

"That's right. I lost his trail several months ago. Word is he's back in Seattle."

Feng released a deep breath. "You have come at an opportune time, Mr. Brodie. There is a problem I need to resolve and it looks as if that problem also involves your Mr. Vance."

"What sort of problem is that?"

Feng's thick lips thinned. "Yakuza."

The single word sent a chill down Luke's spine. The Yakuza was Japan's version of the mafia. Unfortunately, their membership had spread to parts of the United States, including Seattle and even Canada. Drugs, prostitution, extortion, pornography, and gambling were all part of their world.

Gambling. Luke had a bad feeling he knew the direction

the conversation was about to take. "You're telling me Rudy Vance is involved with the Yakuza."

"That is the word on the street. The Yakuza and Rudolph Vance are in the final stages of negotiations."

"Negotiations for what?"

"I am afraid I do not know. Before his disappearance, Mr. Vance was involved in the import-export business. Under one company or another, I am certain he still is. His dealings with the Yakuza most likely involve the smuggling of drugs in and out of the country, or perhaps illegal weapons. Mr. Vance has connections that could prove quite useful."

Luke took a drink of his Scotch. "So where does your problem come in?"

"The Yakuza would like to expand their gambling operation. That would not be in my best interest." Feng slanted him a greasy smile. "Perhaps the information I've just given you will benefit both of us."

Luke mentally went over the situation. "Perhaps it will," he said. The FBI was already pursuing Vance. If Luke could find Rudy and connect him to the Yakuza, the authorities would be more than happy to step in and shut down the entire operation. Luke would collect his fee. The FBI would bring down a smuggling operation, and Quan Feng could go forward with business as usual.

Luke took a final drink of Scotch, set the glass down, and eased out of the booth. "I appreciate the conversation. With any luck, we'll both be better off. Now it's time I collect my lady. By this time I'm sure she's made you five hundred dollars richer."

Quan Feng chuckled, jiggling his three chins and big Buddha belly. He spoke to Luke in Chinese. "*Hái jìdé wǒ shuō de.*" *Remember what I said.* "I will expect a woman the next time I see you."

Not likely, Luke thought. "I'll remember." Looked like he'd gotten his last lead from kinky Quan Feng.

Luke strode back across the casino to where Dirk and Emma sat on stools at one of the blackjack tables. Dirk was down to three twenty-five-dollar chips. Luke's eyes widened at the pile Emma had amassed in the time he'd been gone. Next to the chips, four hundred of the five he had given her still lay on the table.

"Time to go," Luke said. Reaching down, he plucked up the cash, then shoved the pile of chips out on the table, betting it all on one hand.

Emma whirled on him. "Wait a minute."

"Play the hand," he said, since it wasn't a good idea to leave the Golden Lily with a pocket full of money.

Emma grumbled but played the hand. When she picked up the ace of spades followed by the king of hearts, Luke softly cursed.

"Blackjack! I win!" Grinning ear to ear, so damn cute he couldn't do anything but smile, she laid her cards faceup on the table.

What the hell, she'd won the money fair and square.

"I'll cash it in," Dirk offered, sporting a wide grin of his own.

A few minutes later they were heading for the elevator, stopping to collect the knife and pistol they'd left on the tray beside the door, then riding down to the first floor.

They were outside the club, breathing the fresh night air, heading back to their vehicles. Trouble didn't rear its ugly head till they rounded the corner.

Chapter Nineteen

Six men moved toward them, one who seemed to be the leader walking a little in front. Emma heard Luke whisper the f-word.

Her heart set up a clatter as a trickle of fear slid into her stomach. All of the men were Asian, in their twenties and thirties, with coarse black hair, dressed in a mixture of jackets, jeans, and slacks, one with a shaved head, some with mustaches or beards. From the sinewy muscles in their necks and shoulders, she could tell they were in prime physical condition.

Spreading out across the sidewalk, they blocked the way forward and just kept coming.

"Take your time," Luke said softly, his eyes never leaving the men. "Wait for them to come to us."

Emma could feel the tension in his lean, hard body. On her other side, Dirk took a loose-limbed stance, but his jaw was locked, his eyes hard.

Emma mentally prepared herself. She wasn't dressed for combat—she was wearing five-inch heels! But she was fit and she knew self-defense. Inside her chest, her heart raced with the speed of a runaway train.

Her hand shook as she unzipped her purse, reached

inside, and wrapped her fingers around the little mini pepper spray can.

The men fanned out, moving to encircle them. Luke eased her a little behind him. Taking a fighting stance, long legs splayed, his face as cold and hard as steel, he let them get a few feet closer.

"Now," he said to Dirk, and the pair exploded into action as if every move had been rehearsed. Luke used his elbows, his fists, and his feet, took one man to his knees, whirled and shot a kick at another man, knocking him backward, whirled again and finished the first man, leaving him moaning on the sidewalk.

Dirk took a man down with a punch to the jaw and one to the stomach, doubling him over, whirled and kicked another man in the face so hard, he careened backward and slammed into a parked car, setting off the alarm as he crashed onto the sidewalk.

Luke centered a deadly attack on a man rushing toward him as another man raced toward Emma. He was only a few feet away when she yanked out her pepper spray and shot a stream of the vicious burning liquid into his face.

"Ahhee!" Screaming, he tried to cover his eyes with his hands. Emma sprayed him again and he yelped in pain. He swung at her wildly, unable to see, and she finished him off with a punch that sent him sprawling.

Another man lashed out, slamming a fist into her face, knocking her backward onto the sidewalk. Ignoring the throbbing in her cheek, she pushed to her feet, kicked off her heels, came up behind him and did a behind-the-knee kick. As he started to go down, he spun toward her. Emma jammed the palm of her hand under his chin, jolting his head back so hard he careened into the wall.

When he came at her again, Luke finished him with a chop to the back of the neck with the side of his hand. A few feet away, a man on the ground pulled a pistol out of his coat pocket.

"Gun!" Emma shouted. He fired a shot that zinged through the air next to Luke's head. Dirk's little .22 revolver appeared in his hand. He fired twice, the shots no louder than the pop of a champagne cork, and the guy went down.

Emma didn't see the man who came up behind her, just felt the strength of the arm that wrapped around her neck and the cold steel of the blade he pressed against her throat.

A whimper of fear escaped and Luke spun toward her, took in the scene at a glance. When he spoke, his words were as deadly as the switchblade that appeared in his hand.

"Let her go."

Emma steeled herself, forced in a deep, steadying breath. The action around her had halted, everyone frozen as if the next few seconds were a still shot instead of an action sequence. As she took another deep breath, she got a glimpse of her attacker's face in profile. It was the leader, tall, lean, with shaggy black hair and a wiry build. His button-down shirt fit snugly over a body hard with muscle. In a distant part of her brain, she noticed the top half of his little finger was missing.

"Put your pistol on the ground," he said to Dirk.

Luke made a curt nod of his head and Dirk did as the leader demanded, setting the little gun carefully at his feet.

"Now let her go," Luke said.

Even in profile, Emma could see the chilling smile that creased the leader's face. Instead of releasing her, he drew his blade in a shallow, stinging line across her throat. Emma bit back a moan as a thin trail of blood oozed out, and Luke's entire body went rigid.

Her legs started shaking. Fighting down her terror, she kept her gaze on Luke's face and clamped down on her fear. The wound wasn't mortal. At least not yet.

And Luke was there. He wouldn't let anyone hurt her. She forced her quivering muscles to relax. She had to be prepared, be ready to act when the chance came.

"What do you want?" Luke asked. His voice, cold as ice, remained deadly calm, but the hand wrapped around his knife was balled into a bloodless fist.

"You want money?" he pressed. "Is that it?" With his free hand, he reached into the pocket of his jeans and pulled out the folded hundred-dollar bills he had taken from the black-jack table. He tossed them across the sidewalk. "Let her go and I'll give you more."

The leader spit on the ground near his feet. "We don't want your money."

"What then?"

"We are here to make certain you leave Rudolph Vance alone. You will stop asking questions, stop trying to find him. You will stop making trouble for him and the Yakuza. If you want your woman to live, you will end your pursuit. Do you understand?"

Not a muscle relaxed in Luke's body. Dirk hadn't moved either.

"I understand," Luke said. "Now let her go."

One of the attackers, a big Asian in his thirties, face battered, nose bleeding, lips bloody, stepped up to Luke. "I should kill you." His shirt was torn open and bright-colored tattoos, much like Rio's, completely covered his chest.

The knife in Luke's hand quivered, betraying his quiet rage.

"Junichi!" the leader called to the man. "Take Aguri and go. He needs a doctor. Get him back to the car and I will meet you there."

Aguri—the man Dirk had shot. For several seconds no one moved. Cursing, Junichi and another man hauled Aguri to his feet. Blood dripped from the bullet wound in his side. Draping Aguri's arms over their shoulders, they dragged the injured man down the sidewalk and disappeared into the darkness.

The leader shoved Emma toward Luke, who caught her against him.

"What happened tonight is only a warning," the leader said. "Leave Rudolph Vance alone." With a jerk of his head, he ordered his men to disperse and they moved backward along the sidewalk till they disappeared out of sight.

As Dirk picked up his pistol and the hundred-dollar bills, Luke folded his switchblade and slipped it back into his pocket. He turned Emma to face him, his hard gaze assessing the darkening bruise on her cheek, the thin red line across her throat.

"Jesus, baby." Featherlight, he touched her face and a tremor ran through his hard body. Luke drew her closer, kissed the top of her head. "You gonna be okay?"

Emma nodded, unable to speak.

A muscle ticked in Luke's jaw. He slanted a glance at Dirk. "Let's get the fuck out of here."

Emma didn't even mind the swear word.

Rudy Vance sat on an expensive raw silk sofa in a penthouse apartment overlooking Lake Washington. It was late, after midnight, dark and cloudy outside. His partner, Parker Levinson, had been there earlier to handle last-minute details on the arrival of their first shipment.

Now it was Rudy's turn. He'd arrived an hour ago to ensure the partnership would continue. With his shaved head and earrings, a dove gray mock turtleneck beneath a black Ralph Lauren blazer, he looked sharp and confident, the image he needed to go up against the two men seated across from him.

John Hirada and Robert Fujita were important leaders of the Yakuza. Both wore suits, one black, the other dark blue, very businesslike and professional.

Rudy hadn't yet met the *kumicho,* Ryota Masaki, the overall boss of the Seattle syndicate, but with the money they would make from the partnership, he figured they'd soon be bosom buddies.

Hirada spoke up. "Robert and I believe our association with you and your people will be a very profitable endeavor. But it is imperative our first shipment goes off exactly as planned."

"I'm aware of that," Rudy said. "That's the reason I returned to Seattle. I wanted to make sure the delivery went smoothly and give you my personal assurance that this shipment and those in the future will be handled in a manner beneficial to all of us."

"We are satisfied with the terms of our agreement," Fujita said, "but we are not pleased by the current troubles in which you are immersed."

"If you're talking about the young man who died, there was no reason for his suicide. If he had simply done his job."

"Norio was naïve and foolish. He believed he dishonored the family. There were other, less costly ways he could have paid for his mistake. Still, the entire episode was unseemly. What concerns us more are your personal problems, Mr. Vance."

Rudy sat up straighter on the sofa. "As soon as this shipment arrives, my business in Seattle will be finished. In the future, I'll be working from out of the country. That should take care of any concerns you might have regarding my trouble with the authorities."

Hirada glanced over at Fujita, the smaller of the two with a more compact build. "Yes, I believe that would be best," Fujita said.

"So where are we with Masaki?" Rudy asked.

"Our *kumicho* poses somewhat of a problem. For the past few years he has been working to improve the image of our organization, trying to move our dealings into the legitimate business world. Some of us, however, believe it is important to take advantage of opportunities whenever they arise."

"I'm aware of his opinions." Rudy had no interest in their above-board business dealings, the real estate they'd been purchasing, the corporations they were taking over. The big money was in drugs, along with human trafficking, as the men sitting across from him clearly knew. "It's a worthy goal, but it takes money to make those things happen. That's where we come in."

Hirada's features remained impassive, yet Rudy knew he and Fujita wanted their very profitable shipping venture to continue.

So did Rudy. The government had tied up his forty percent share of International Cargo, a legitimate import-export firm, the front for his illegal activities. But his dealings with the Yakuza involved Allied Shipping, a container company that belonged to him and Parker, though neither of their names appeared anywhere in the corporate documents or on any other paperwork.

A single ship could carry ten to twelve thousand containers, even more if they weren't completely loaded. Seattle had four container terminals servicing seventeen different ocean carriers.

That meant hundreds of thousands of containers shipped through the port of Seattle every year. Policing them was nearly impossible. Even harder when the right palms were greased.

Smuggling drugs was relatively easy. Smuggling people was more difficult, but the profits, long term, were enormous.

Human trafficking was out of the authorities' control and stopping it wasn't going to happen anytime soon.

Hirada's expression changed. "One last thing. As of now, your problems with the bounty hunter are over. In a gesture of good faith, a message has been delivered. I do not believe Mr. Brodie will bother you again."

So Brodie had been dealt with, a favor that would need to be repaid. The price would be worth it. "Thank you. Shall I assume you will be able to convince your *kumicho,* Mr. Masaki, to endorse our deal?"

Hirada's gaze swung back to Fujita. They spoke briefly among themselves. Masaki pressed for legitimizing the organization. The men in the room disagreed. They wanted the money, pure and simple, any way they could get it.

Rudy was convinced the partnership would continue with or without Masaki's approval, but it would be better for all concerned if the group was united.

"We will speak to Mr. Masaki," Hirada said. "Perhaps he will agree to meet with you. If so, arrangements will be made." Hirada rose from his chair, indicating the meeting was over. Fujita stood up, and Rudy rose as well.

"You can still be reached at the number you have given me?" Hirada asked. One of Rudy's burner phones.

"Yes. I look forward to hearing from you." Rudy made the appropriate farewells and left the penthouse apartment. Downstairs, he climbed into the black Lincoln Town Car waiting for him in the garage, left the high-rise building, and headed back to his suite in Woodinville.

Everything was in order. As soon as his business was completed, he could put his personal plans in motion. He would collect his little Ginny and they could leave the country. Once he was gone, no one would find him.

Unless his business dealings demanded it, Seattle was a place he never intended to visit again.

Chapter Twenty

Luke stood in front of Emma in the bathroom of his Bellevue apartment. His hand shook as he swabbed alcohol over the thin cut across her throat. When Emma hissed in a breath, his stomach knotted.

Luke's hand dropped away. "I need to do this, honey, but I don't want to hurt you. Those bastards already hurt you enough tonight."

Emma looked up at him, her big brown eyes on his face. "I'm okay, Luke, really. I admit I was pretty scared when it was happening—I've never had to deal with a guy holding a knife at my throat. But it's over now and I'm okay."

Luke ran a finger gently over the bruise on her cheek. "You were great out there, Em, but . . ." He swallowed, his chest clamping down.

"But what?" Emma asked.

"We need to stop, baby. We have to quit looking for Vance. You could have been killed out there tonight. I can't be responsible for that."

Emma shook her head. "What happened tonight wasn't your fault. It's a hazard of the job we're trying to do and you know it. I'm not stopping, Luke. We're getting close or those men wouldn't have come after us."

"Dammit, do you know who those guys were?"

"No, but they must be friends of Rio's. They were Asian and I saw tattoos on one of them that looked like his."

"They're Yakuza," Luke said. "Yakuza is Japanese mafia. Quan Feng told me Vance is negotiating a deal with them. Probably something that involves smuggling. Either drugs or maybe gunrunning. Could be both."

"I heard that." Dirk's voice came from the living room. The bathroom door stood open. He strode down the hall and stopped outside the door. "Luke's right, Emma. You can't take on the Yakuza. Those are some really bad dudes."

"I'm not interested in the Yakuza," she said. "I'm looking for Vance. Clearly I'll have to be more careful how I go about it, but I'm not quitting."

"Fuck," Luke said.

"Luke," Emma chided.

"Christ." He raked a hand through his hair. Emma started to get up off the toilet seat, but Luke shoved her back down. "Sit still. I'm not finished." Pissed now, he didn't stop when she started squirming, just kept swabbing the alcohol around the cut on her neck. "I need to get this done. We have no frigging idea where that knife has been. You don't want to get an infection."

Emma went still.

"That's better," Luke said.

Dirk propped his shoulder against the doorjamb. He tipped up the bottle of beer he'd taken out of the fridge and took a long swallow. "What else did Feng tell you?" he asked.

"He said the Yakuza wants to expand its gambling business. He wasn't real happy about that."

"I bet he wasn't. So he's hoping your involvement might help him solve the problem."

Luke taped the bandage in place around her neck. "That's right, but now—"

Emma looked up at him. "You promised, Luke."

He ground his teeth to stop another curse. Taking a deep breath, he let it out slowly. "Fine. I'll keep looking, but you're out of it."

"No way! A deal is a deal. We do this together."

This time it was Dirk who cursed. "You two have any idea what you're getting into? I know a little about the Yakuza. Those tattoos you're talking about? Part of the Yakuza ritual involves tats that cover every part of the body—even the genitals."

"That's right," Luke said. "Rio was in the process. His tats just weren't finished. The Yakuza come from all walks of life and consider themselves family. They live by strict codes of conduct."

"If a member does something wrong," Dirk continued, "he has to cut off part of his own finger. They start with the little finger and keep moving up."

Emma's face went paper white.

"That sound like the kind of people you want to deal with?" Luke asked. He caught Emma's chin, forcing her to look at him. "You saw it, didn't you? The guy holding the knife at your throat had half a finger missing."

She turned her face away. "I saw it," she whispered.

"I can't handle you getting hurt, Em. I can't." Luke walked out of the bathroom, brushing past Dirk, heading down the hall.

Dirk said something to Emma, closed the bathroom door, and followed him into the living room.

"You're in deep, bro. You know that, right?"

Luke picked up the beer he'd left on the coffee table,

tipped it up, and took a swallow. "What are you talking about?"

"Emma." He glanced back toward the bathroom to be sure the door was still closed. "First off, you never work with partners. But you decide to take Emma under your wing and promise you'll help her find Vance."

"So what? She's a damn good tracer and I can use the help."

"I saw you tonight, bro. I read the fear in your face when you watched that guy slice his knife across her throat. I've never seen a look like that on your face. Emma means something to you. A big something. You need to figure out what and deal with it—before one or both of you gets killed."

The knot in Luke's stomach went tighter. "I'm sleeping with her. It wouldn't have lasted this long if I didn't like her. We're friends—that's it. When it's over, it's over. If Emma's okay with that, it sure as hell shouldn't bother you."

Dirk just shook his head. "Whatever you say. Just be sure you're being honest with yourself. And if you're determined to keep looking for Vance, you better keep it on the down-low."

Since Luke agreed, he nodded. "You're right about that. I need to figure my next move."

Dirk finished his beer. "Good idea." He carried the bottle into the kitchen and tossed it into the trash can. "I better get going. I told Meg I'd be home late, but I don't want to worry her. I'll see you tomorrow."

Luke frowned. "Tomorrow? What's going on tomorrow?"

For the first time in hours, Dirk smiled. "The barbeque. You aren't getting out of it, so I'll see you there."

Luke tipped his head back and released a frustrated breath. "Yeah, I guess."

Dirk made his way out the door, closing it softly behind

him just as Emma came out of the bathroom. She was wearing the white T-shirt he had loaned her to sleep in, her legs and feet bare.

She was battered and bruised. The bandage around her neck filled him with guilt. Still, with her soft dark curls and big brown eyes, she was so pretty, his chest clamped down. And bastard that he was, he went hard.

She padded toward him, stopped right in front of him. He could see the plump hills of her breasts beneath the soft fabric and closed his eyes to block the memory of her nipples against his tongue.

"You think we could just go to bed?" she asked, bringing him out of his self-imposed trance with the words he'd once said to her.

His mouth edged up. "Sure." He kissed her softly, ignoring the shot of lust that tore through him. "We don't have to have sex. We can just go to sleep. We've both had a pretty bad night."

"We don't have to have sex," Emma said, then went up on her toes and pressed a slow, lingering kiss on his lips. "If you don't think you're up to it."

Luke laughed and swept her into his arms.

Emma ached all over, which Luke must have known. She had never thought Luke Brodie could be tender, but as she felt the soft press of his lips against her temple, as she felt his hands moving gently over her body, her eyes burned with tears.

She'd told him she was okay, but if she closed her eyes, she could still feel the knife sliding across her throat, the sting of the blade, and the warm trickle of blood. She had never been so frightened.

She tried not to think of it, tried to concentrate on Luke's hand gently cupping her breast. He kneaded softly, ran his thumb over her nipple, then his mouth replaced his hand. Just the softest tug, the faintest scrape of his teeth over her skin.

Heat moved through her, settled low in her core. She slid her fingers into his hair as he eased down her body, trailing soft kisses in his wake. Desire slipped through her. Her heart beat almost painfully.

She whimpered as he moved lower, pressed a kiss against the inside of her thigh. Luke took his time, gently laving and tasting, taking her higher and higher, driving away all thoughts of the terrifying night.

Thoughts of Luke Brodie replaced them, the careful way he touched her, the pleasure he was determined to give. She came with surprising force, crying out his name, then slowly drifting back to earth.

Luke rose above her, settled himself between her legs. Bracing himself on his elbows, he very softly kissed her.

"You okay, baby?" he asked as he eased himself inside.

Her throat tightened. "Better now." And as he began to move, as she felt his power and strength, her world seemed to right itself. Luke was there, watching out for her. She always felt safe with Luke.

He made love to her with infinite care, his rhythm deep and steady, giving her body time to catch up, making her want him again. Desire spiraled out through her limbs. Need began to claw at her insides. His pace increased, driving her toward the peak, lifting her until she tumbled into freefall.

Luke followed, his muscles straining, his body shuddering with the force of his release. With a last soft kiss, he collected himself, moved off her, and headed for the bathroom.

Returning a few minutes later, he curled her against his side and kissed her temple. "Go to sleep, honey," he whispered.

The aches were forgotten as she drifted into dreams, safe once more in Luke's arms.

Chapter Twenty-One

It was a warm, sunny day in Denver, the distant mountain peaks still white with snow. April awoke early on Saturday morning, enjoying her second day off that week. After a grocery shopping trip with Ginny to King Soopers, she drove her Subaru wagon into the garage of her little ranch-style house on Cedar Lane.

"I'll get the door, Mom." Ginny jumped out of the passenger seat, pigtails flying, grabbed a couple of plastic bags out of the backseat, and headed for the back door. She stopped and called back, "Come on, Rowdy!"

The three-month-old, mostly golden retriever puppy, jumped out of the car with a yip and raced to catch up.

April smiled. Yesterday, desperate for a way to raise her daughter's spirits, she'd had an idea. On her way home from work, she'd stopped at the local animal shelter, found the darling little dog that seemed perfect for Ginny, and brought it home. Her daughter had fallen in love with the puppy on sight, and April was already attached to Rowdy, too.

Feeling more optimistic than she had in days, she started hauling the rest of the grocery bags out of the back. Last bag in hand, she followed her daughter up the steps into the kitchen and set the bags on the table next to the ones Ginny had brought into the house.

"Mom . . ." The word came out on a shaky breath that sent a tremor down April's spine. She hurried to where her daughter stood staring into the dining room.

"What is it, sweetheart? What's the matter?"

Instead of answering, Ginny pointed to the crystal vase of flowers in the middle of the dining room table, a card from the sender in the middle. A lovely arrangement of perfect pink roses.

"They're from . . . *him* . . ." Ginny said softly, her voice breaking. Her face was ashen, her brown eyes liquid with tears. "I knew he would come." The puppy whimpered at her feet.

"No . . ." Fear twisted in April's stomach. Moving woodenly, she forced herself to walk to the crystal vase in the center of the table. The roses were beautiful, each perfect bud a match to the one beside it. April pulled the card out of the bouquet with a trembling hand.

> *Beloved Ginny,*
> *Soon we'll be together.*
> *Love,*
> *Rudy*

April's gaze shot to her daughter. Ginny slid down the wall to the floor, drawing her knees up beneath her chin. Tears streaked her cheeks while her eyes stared straight ahead. The little dog crawled over on its belly and shoved its nose beneath her limp fingers.

"He's coming to get me," Ginny said. "There's no place we can hide."

April knelt and drew her daughter into her arms.

"That . . . that isn't true. We'll find a place. I'm calling Agent Danfield. . . . Con . . . Conner will know what to do."

Ginny said nothing. Even the puppy's cold nose against her hand went unnoticed. Her daughter didn't believe she would ever be safe.

April's throat closed up. As she fumbled in her purse for her cell phone, her eyes filled with tears. Rudy Vance had found them. He or someone who worked for him had been inside their house.

She bit back a sob. She had to reach Agent Danfield. Her hand trembled as she found his contact number and pushed the send button, then held the phone against her ear.

"Con . . . ?" Her voice wavered when he answered. "It's April. He . . . he's found us. Rudy Vance." A sob tore loose. "I don't know what to do."

Con's voice changed, strengthened. "I'll have the police there in minutes. I'm on my way, April. I'm coming to Denver. Just hold on, honey. I'll be there as fast as I can."

The tears in her eyes rolled down her cheeks. Protecting them wasn't Con's job anymore. He was coming because he cared about her and Ginny.

A little sound came from her throat. Con was still on the line. She could hear him barking orders. April's fingers tightened around the phone. Conner was coming.

She just had to hang on long enough for him to get there.

The Saturday afternoon barbeque at Ethan and Val's was in full swing. The weather had cooperated, a blue Seattle sky with only a light breeze blowing in off the Sound and a few fluffy clouds overhead.

The men were out on the patio drinking beer. Emma was in the kitchen with the women, helping them prepare the side dishes. She'd hoped Chelsea would be there, but her roommate had ended up having to take an extra flight, then not being able to get back in time to join them.

Emma and Luke had arrived a little late, Luke managing to stall so they wouldn't have to stay too long. He'd introduced her to his cousins, Ian and Nick, who worked with him at the office, both dedicated family men. She already knew Ethan; had fought alongside Dirk, liked and trusted both of them.

The women had been surprisingly friendly, accepting her immediately as if she belonged there. The children were adorable, their parents doting. Luke had said his family was the best. From what she could tell, he was right.

Standing in the kitchen, Emma surveyed the three women working beside her, all of them connected to BOSS, Inc. men.

Nick's wife, Samantha, about Emma's height, had a great figure, curly light brown hair, and just enough freckles to make her look cute and sexy at the same time. Next to her, Val Brodie, Ethan's wife, was a tall, gorgeous blonde, a former La Belle lingerie model like Meg, the fabulous redhead soon to become Dirk's bride. Even in jeans and T-shirts, both had perfect figures, evidence of their past modeling careers.

She had also met Isabelle and Carmen, one Italian and one a saucy Latina, both still models, both surprisingly nice. Currently they were in the living room with Ian's pretty wife, Meri, entertaining the kids: Hannah, Charlie, and Lily. Travis, Samantha's six-month-old baby, was napping in one of the bedrooms.

As Emma poured potato chips into a bowl and Val plopped scoops of onion dip into the cup in the middle, the conversation returned to the topic of the day—Meg and Dirk's upcoming wedding, which was set for July eighteenth.

"I can't believe I'm admitting this," Meg said, "but sometimes I wish we had just eloped."

Val laughed. "I bet Dirk feels the same way."

"Actually, I think Dirk's kind of looking forward to the wedding," Meg said. "Under that tough guy exterior, he's very romantic."

Emma smiled, finding it easy to believe. "I hope you liked the wedding gift he gave you. Luke and I were there when he had his broken heart tattoo changed. I thought it was the sweetest thing. He said you made his heart feel whole again."

Meg's blue eyes misted. She wiped away a tear. "I'm so lucky. I can't wait to marry him."

They talked about the wedding, talked dresses and flowers and the reception. It was going to be simple but elegant, nothing like the extravagant, overblown country club wedding Meg had endured to please her parents when she'd married the wrong man.

"Luke is Dirk's best man," Meg said to Emma. "That means we expect to see you there."

She wanted to be. She adored weddings. Before Rudy Vance, she'd dreamed of a beautiful white wedding to a man she loved. Emma didn't tell them she and Luke would probably be over by then.

She managed to smile. "That would be lovely." Just being invited brought a lump to her throat. She missed her parents, the family she'd once had. She missed April and Ginny so much. She was grateful for the warm welcome she had received from Luke's friends.

Emma was enjoying herself, having a really great day, but as the hour slipped into the next, Luke grew more and more distant.

She didn't understand why he hadn't wanted to come. She knew he loved his family. The bond between his brothers and cousins was strong. Luke would do anything for these men and the women they loved, and they felt the same about him. She wished she knew why it was so hard for him to be around them.

"Luke says you're a bounty hunter," Samantha said, snaring Emma's attention as she loaded silverware into a basket to carry outside.

"That's right," Emma said. "That's how we met."

Val grabbed a stack of paper plates. "You had to learn self-defense, right?"

"Among other things. But I've been missing my classes lately. I'm hoping to get back on schedule Monday morning."

"Those fighting techniques would have come in handy for some of us." Meg grinned as she peeled the plastic wrap off a big blue bowl of potato salad.

Samantha grinned, too. "Maybe Emma will teach us a couple of moves."

"Isn't there a move where you knee a guy in the groin?" Val asked, her blue eyes sparkling. "That'd be a good thing to know."

Emma thought of the night she had used the move on Badger and the stooges from hell. "I've used it a couple of times. If you can surprise your opponent, it can work really well."

She told them the story of the night Luke had come to her rescue at the Polo Club, then, Val, Meg, and Samantha told Emma a few of the experiences they'd had since they'd met their BOSS, Inc. men.

"I can't believe you took some guy out with a curling iron." Emma wiped tears of laughter from her eyes. "I'll have to remember that one."

"I broke a lamp over a Russian mobster's head one time," Samantha said, eliciting a peal of laughter from all of them. "In a tight spot, you never know what's going to come in handy."

"Exactly," Meg agreed, as if she were an expert on using makeshift weapons. Hey, from the stories Emma was hearing, maybe she was.

"Okay, so now it's time for you to come clean," Samantha said. "What's really going on with you and Luke?"

Unease filtered through her. Luke was already uncomfortable being there. She didn't want to complicate things by giving his family the wrong impression.

"Nothing's going on," she said carefully. "It's just like Luke said—we're working together to catch Rudolph Vance."

"First off, Luke doesn't work with partners," Val said. "That means you're special. Plus, he's never brought a woman anywhere near his family before."

That she hadn't known. Then again, he hated the whole idea of being at this gathering so it made a sort of sense he wouldn't bring a date. She was just there as a friend. Completely different . . . sort of.

"You might as well dish," Meg said. "There's no mistaking the hot looks Luke's been casting your way. Those looks say you aren't just working together. They say you *are* together. Which, by the way, we all think is great."

"You do?"

"Of course we do," Val said. "It's obvious you care about Luke. I can see it in your face whenever you look at him. And Luke cares about you—though he probably hasn't said anything like that to you."

"He wouldn't," Samantha said. "That's just not Luke."

"Besides, he probably hasn't figured it out," Meg added.

Val set a pitcher of lemonade on a tray next to a stack of red Solo cups. "Meg's right. When it comes to women, guys like ours need a little time to get their heads on straight."

"Right. So hang in there," Meg said. "Luke's worth it."

The lump returned to Emma's throat. "I know he is."

A noise came from the kitchen doorway. Ethan stood in the opening, the muscles in his powerful arms threatening to burst the sleeves of his snug black T-shirt. "We're getting hungry out here. Can I go ahead and put on the burgers?"

Val walked over and gave him a smacking kiss on the lips. "Anytime, lover. We're just about ready."

Ethan hauled her into his arms and very thoroughly kissed her. "The sooner we eat, the sooner we get to play." With a sexy wink, he walked away.

The women all broke out laughing.

Emma thought of Luke. He didn't want to be there. She felt a pang at how much he was missing.

Chapter Twenty-Two

The air smelled like smoke and barbeque sauce. Cold beer in hand, Luke stood next to Ethan, who was doing his best not to burn the hot dogs or overcook the burgers. Nick, Dirk, and Ian surrounded the grill like vultures waiting for their next meal.

The rest of the men were out on the lawn playing horse-shoes: a couple of PIs from the office, along with Walt Whizzy, Pete Hernandez, and Sandy Sandowski, security guys who had worked with Ethan on the fashion show tour. Men who now worked part-time for BOSS, Inc.

Nick tipped his head toward the kitchen window, where a gaggle of women laughed as they worked at the counter in front of the sink.

"I like her," Nick said. "Your Emma. Samantha likes her, too."

"She isn't my Emma," Luke said. "I told you we're just friends. We're working the Vance case together."

The women had been so shocked to see him with a female, they had all swooped in to immediately make her feel welcome.

"You should see Emma in action," Dirk said to Ian, tipping up his beer and taking a hefty swallow. "For a little thing, she can do some major damage. The lady can really handle herself."

Fortunately, his best friend had enough sense to keep his mouth shut about the fight last night outside the Golden Lily, at least in front of the women—an encounter that could have gotten Emma killed. Refusing to wear the bandage around her neck to the barbeque, she had covered the thin line with makeup.

Just thinking about what could have happened made Luke's stomach burn.

"I think she fits you," Ethan said, taking a swallow of beer. "You need a woman who can kick your ass."

Luke felt the faint edge of a smile.

"She definitely kicked some ass last night," Dirk said.

Ethan turned a hot dog over on the grill. "So I heard."

Luke had been keeping his brother up to date. Ethan was highly respected by the Seattle PD. Any information he gleaned on the case could be useful. Nick and Ian were family, good at their jobs and men he trusted.

"How are those burgers coming?" he asked, aiming the conversation in a different direction, his relationship with Emma not a subject he wanted to discuss.

"They're done," Ethan said. "Ian, will you find out if the women are ready?"

"I'm on it." Ian took off walking, one of the few blond men in the Brodie family. His wife, Meri, a pretty brunette, opened the back door just then, and their daughter, Lily, raced out, followed by Ethan's little girl, Hannah.

"Daddy!" Lily ran to Ian, who caught her up in his arms.

"You ready for a hot dog, kiddo?"

"Hot dogs!" Lily shouted. "Yippee!"

"Yippee! Yippee!" Hannah repeated, jumping up and down, her blond ponytail flying.

When Ian kissed his daughter's forehead and set her back on her feet, Luke looked away. The blackness was there, hovering at the edge of his mind. Having Emma there had helped for a while, distracting him from his thoughts. But as she walked out of the house, hand in hand with Meg's little redheaded son, Charlie, the bleakness swelled, threatening to overwhelm him.

He needed to get out of there. He just wished to hell this day would end.

The women started setting food on the picnic tables Ethan had shoved together and covered with red-and-white checked tablecloths. Baked beans and pickles, buns for the dogs and burgers, four different kinds of salads.

The desserts he'd seen on the kitchen counter would be coming out later: a couple of pies and a big chocolate layer cake with thick chocolate frosting, one of his favorites.

"Come on, everybody," Val called out. "Time to eat."

The guys pitching horseshoes tossed them on the lawn and headed for the patio. Luke stepped back as everyone grabbed paper plates and formed a line in front of the grill.

Standing next to Emma, Samantha handed Emma baby Travis to hold. She lovingly cradled the baby in her arms and started jiggling him, making him laugh. She smoothed the fine dark hair on top of the baby's head, clearly enamored with the six-month-old as only a woman could be.

Luke took a deep breath but couldn't seem to get enough air. The blackness was there, pressing in on him like a heavy layer of fog. He couldn't do this. He had to get out of there.

Dirk came up beside him. "You okay?"

"I need to get some air. Can you watch out for Emma? Take her home later?"

Dirk glanced back, saw Emma with the baby. "You know I will."

Luke looked at the petite woman who had been a tiger in his bed that morning, the same woman who had been so brave last night. Emotion streaked through him. He felt his chest clamp down.

"I can't do this. I can't handle it."

"You're talking about Emma."

"I've got to end things. It's getting too complicated."

"What about Vance?"

"I'll talk her out of it. It's too dangerous. If she won't listen and by some miracle manages to find him, she can call me. I'll step back in and help her make the arrest."

"You sure that's what you want? I know this isn't how you saw this going down, but however complicated it is, I have a feeling Emma's worth it."

He clenched his jaw. "I know she is," he said a little gruffly. "I gotta go."

Leaving Dirk to drive Emma home, Luke started walking toward the side yard, hoping to make a quiet escape. A last look at Emma and he saw her digging her cell phone out of the pocket of her jeans. He paused long enough to watch her press the phone against her ear.

She stumbled backward a couple of steps, came up against the wall. Even from a distance, he could see the color leach out of her face.

Something was wrong.

Luke turned and started striding back to her.

Emma ended the call, her hands shaking as she gripped the phone. She glanced up to see Luke striding toward her.

He caught her shoulders, looked into her face. "What is it? What's happened?"

"April just *.* .. my sister just called. Vance found them. Oh, God, Luke."

"What the hell? Are they all right? I thought they were in witsec." He grabbed her arm and hauled her back inside the house, sat her down in one of the kitchen chairs. "Start from the beginning. Tell me what's going on."

Emma told him all she knew. That April and Ginny had gone grocery shopping that morning. When they got home, they found a bouquet of pink roses on the dining table that Vance had sent to Ginny. Vance or someone who worked for him had been inside the house.

"The card said something about him and Ginny being together soon. I'm so scared for them, Luke." Emma took a shaky breath, fighting back tears. "How did he find them? My sister didn't tell anyone where they were, not even me."

Luke pulled out a chair, spun it around, and sat down facing her. "They'll be okay. The feds will relocate them somewhere safe."

Emma shook her head. "April won't do it. She and Ginny are convinced he can find them wherever they go. They both feel safer in Seattle. Apparently Special Agent Danfield agrees."

"He's FBI?"

"That's right. Danfield thinks there's a leak somewhere. He wants April and Ginny in Seattle where he can protect them until the FBI can figure out who it is."

"A leak. That's not good. If Vance can get to someone in the FBI, coming back might be their safest option. At least they'll have protection round the clock. When will they get here?"

"They're flying in tomorrow." She brushed a tear from her cheek. "It's been so long. I know it's selfish, but I can't wait to see them."

"It isn't selfish. They're your family." Luke's features

looked hard. He was worried. If Luke was worried, it had to really be bad.

"I've got to find Vance," she said. "I've got to find him before he hurts Ginny again."

A muscle jumped in Luke's cheek. His expression remained dark and turbulent, his incredible blue eyes, fierce. He blew out a slow breath and raked both hands through his hair.

"We'll find Vance," he said. "We'll go back to your place, take another look at that profile you made. We'll start over, work the case from a different angle. That DNA sample should come through the first of the week. Maybe we'll get a match to someone besides Vance or Felix Riggs. If we do, we'll track him down, press him for information. We'll figure out something, Emma."

She leaned over and kissed the corner of his mouth. "Thank you. I knew you wouldn't quit on me."

Luke glanced away. "I know you think I'm some kind of hero, Em, but I'm not."

"You're trying to help me save Ginny. That makes you a hero to me."

Luke stood up and paced over to the window. Clamping his hands on his hips, he stared out into the yard.

Emma came up behind him, her gaze following his. Everyone was eating. The food looked incredible.

"We need to get going," Luke said.

"You must be hungry—you're always hungry. Don't you want something to eat before we leave?" She managed to smile. "I saw you eyeing that chocolate cake earlier. Surely you aren't leaving without having a piece of it."

Luke turned back to her and some of the tightness in his shoulders eased. "We should probably go, but . . . I guess it wouldn't hurt to have a burger before we left."

Emma took his hand and led him out onto the patio.

Dirk and Meg had saved a place for them at their end of the table.

The meal was delicious. Luke and Emma didn't leave until both of them had finished a plate full of food and a piece of Val's delicious chocolate cake.

Chapter Twenty-Three

The Bronco rolled down the freeway, headed toward Emma's apartment. The perfect day had begun to fade, the sky turned a sullen gray-blue. The wind blowing in off the ocean had strengthened, tossing leaves and papers across all four lanes.

Luke's thoughts remained on Rudolph Vance. He needed to step up the hunt. Emma's family wouldn't be safe until Vance was back in jail. Luke wanted to take another look at the profile Emma had built. He'd done one of his own, but hers was more detailed. And looking at leads from her point of view might give him some fresh ideas.

Besides, it would give him a chance to clear the air between them, to have the discussion they needed to have.

His stomach tightened. After the phone call she'd received, there was no way he could abandon her. He'd keep his word, keep working with her on the case, but he had to end this thing between them.

His hands clenched around the steering wheel. He was already in balls-deep—something that was never supposed to happen. Hell, he hadn't imagined it was possible, but here he was sleeping with her as if they were a couple, leading her on when there was no way it could ever work out. It wasn't fair to Emma. It wasn't fair to him.

He took a deep breath, trying to think what he should say, hoping he wouldn't hurt her. Hell, maybe she'd be glad to be rid of him.

The thought made his chest feel tight.

Traffic whizzed by. When a little silver Prius raced past and cut in front of him, he glanced down at the speedometer and realized he was going slower than the speed limit. Dammit, he had to get his mind off Emma and back where it should be.

Luke hit the gas and ten minutes later the Bronco was pulling up in front of her apartment. They got out and walked inside, but instead of heading for the kitchen to look at the profile on her corkboard, Emma stopped in the middle of her unimposing living room and turned to face him.

"Okay, what's going on?" she asked. "Something happened today, Luke. What was it?"

He tried to brush it off. He wasn't ready to talk yet. He needed a little more time. "How about that prick Vance found a way to get to your sister and her kid? That was definitely something."

Emma jammed her hands on her hips. "That's not what I meant and you know it. Something happened that involves you and me—don't try to deny it. Are you tired of me, Luke? Are you ready to move on? If that's it, just tell me."

He thought about lying, telling her something she might accept. Hell, if he lied, she would probably know it. Which made the truth his only option.

"I'm not tired of you, Em. You're one of the sexiest ladies I've ever known. All I have to do is think about having you and I get hard. This has nothing to do with sex. It's just . . . it's . . ."

"It's what, Luke?"

He tried for a shrug. "It's just . . . women and kids, relationships and families aren't something I can deal with. Being there today, watching the way normal people behave, seeing the lives they lead—it was torture. You and me . . . this thing between us . . . it could never go where you'd want it to. I saw you with the kids, with little Charlie and Nick's baby boy. I'm not cut out for that. I just can't handle it."

"Why not?"

He blew out a breath. He should have known she'd want more. This was Emma. She always wanted answers. "Because I've seen too much, done too much."

"You have PTSD? Is that what this is about?"

He grunted. "I almost wish I had that excuse. I don't have flashbacks. I don't regret a single thing I've done. If I had to, I'd do it all over again. But the war changed me. I can't imagine having a wife and kids. What would I tell them about myself? About my past? What would I say to them?"

"You'd say you were a soldier, Luke. One of the best."

Luke just shook his head. She didn't understand. Christ, he didn't understand it himself.

She reached up and touched his cheek. "I don't expect hearts and flowers, Luke. I don't expect a happy ending. The deal we made was first and foremost a business arrangement—we work together to catch Rudolph Vance. Secondly, we enjoy ourselves for as long as it lasts. When one of us is done, it's over. Is it over, Luke?"

Inside his chest, his heart beat dully. She was saying exactly what he wanted to hear. No happy endings. Just no-strings sex for as long as it lasted. She was giving him exactly the excuse he needed to have her in his bed, to keep her with him.

And bastard that he was, he was going to grab hold and hang on for as long as he could.

"It's not over," he said gruffly. "Not unless you want it to be."

Emma's eyes remained on his face. "I don't want us to be over." Reaching up, she caught his head and dragged his mouth down to hers for a hot, mind-blowing kiss. His groin tightened, blood rushed south, and he went hard.

When she started to back away, he cupped her face in his hands and kept on kissing her. "We don't have time for this," he said, kissing the side of her neck.

"Maybe we do." Emma kissed him again. "You ever heard of a quickie?"

He almost smiled. Instead, he cupped her face between his hands. "Jesus God, lady, you make me nuts." Another blazing kiss and he reached down, unsnapped the front of her jeans, then walked her backward till she came up against the arm of the sofa. Luke pulled her sexy stretch jeans down over her hips, turned her around, and bent her over, smoothed a hand over her fine sweet ass.

She was wet. In seconds he was inside her. Emma was moaning, arching to take him deeper. He was gripping her hips and driving hard, then both of them were coming.

God, she felt good. She always felt so damned good.

He eased her back against him for several long moments, then turned her into his arms, and just held her.

Contentment rolled through him, a feeling he didn't recognize at first. *You're mine,* he thought, *no one else's.* Whatever he'd told her, whatever Emma had said—one thing was clear.

Luke was in serious trouble.

Emma wasn't sure how much time passed before they were ready to go into the kitchen and take another look at Vance's profile. As she stood next to Luke, she told herself she had done the right thing in reassuring him she could handle a no-strings sexual relationship.

It was a complete and total lie. She was surprised he couldn't tell.

The truth was, she wanted far more from Luke than just sex, but for now she was willing to take what she could get. She wasn't sure what Luke felt for her, but her feelings for him ran deep. Very deep. She wouldn't let herself think the *L* word—she didn't dare. But she cared for him greatly.

Whatever his feelings, Emma was sure all the way to her soul that Luke needed her.

Her heart squeezed to think he believed he could never have the happiness his family and friends had found. Whether he realized it or not, Luke was a hero—a man who had fought and been willing to die for his country. Luke was a hero and a hero deserved to be happy.

She was sticking with him. Aside from hunting Vance, she was staying with Luke not only because she wanted him more than any man she had ever met, but because she wanted to help him get the life he deserved. Maybe it would be with her. Maybe not.

In the end, only time would tell.

"Let's make some notes," Luke said, dragging her thoughts back to the problem at hand. Long legs splayed, hands on his hips, he studied the photos and notes pinned to the corkboard. "You got a tablet or something?"

"One second." She knew he was making notes more for her than himself. Luke had an astonishing memory. Still, it never hurt to get organized. Opening a kitchen drawer, she pulled out a steno notepad and flipped it open, then grabbed a pen and clicked the button on top. "Ready."

"First off, I don't think I mentioned a lead I stumbled onto the other night. I haven't had a chance to follow up, but apparently Felix Riggs was spotted in a bar called the

Red Devil the afternoon he was killed. The guy he was with had red hair and a crooked nose. The men left the bar together."

"You're thinking that's the guy who drove Riggs out to Whidbey Island."

"Timing's right."

She wrote down *Red Devil bar. Man with red hair and crooked nose.* "We could go there tonight."

Luke shook his head. "We'd be better off tomorrow. Day shift. Usually a different bartender. The crowd's the same way, some people hit the place in the daytime, others are night owls."

"Good thinking. I'll find the Web site, make sure they're open on Sunday."

Luke nodded.

Emma looked over at the corkboard, scanned some of the notes she'd put up there. "I need to check into the Marmite angle, see if I can find any stores in the area that carry it."

"Good idea."

She wrote down *check out Marmite.*

"Monday I'll call the lab," Luke said, "see how they're coming with that DNA."

Emma wrote down *DNA.* She glanced up at Luke. "What about the leak at the FBI? Vance has to be paying someone for information."

"Yeah. How about this guy, Special Agent Danfield? He knew where your sister was living. Is she sure she can trust him?"

Emma smiled. "I don't think Conner Danfield would do anything to hurt April or Ginny. I could see the attraction between them. He did his best to keep everything professional, but the spark was definitely there. He took personal time to help them get settled in Denver."

"If you're right, that could be good. He'll be pushing to find out who the mole is and he'll be determined to keep your sister and Ginny safe."

"Agent Danfield is arranging for the three of us to get together sometime late tomorrow afternoon."

Luke smiled at her softly. "That's good, Em. I know how much you've missed them." He was looking at her in that way he had, his eyes gentle on her face and so incredibly blue. Emma felt a little pinch in her heart.

The sound of a key turning in the lock ended the moment. Rudolph Vance had murdered at least two people. Luke moved toward the door, then stepped behind it as Emma ducked behind a wall in the kitchen.

The lock turned, the door swung open, and Chelsea Davenport walked into the apartment. Emma grinned. "Hey, lady!" She hurried across the living room and the two of them hugged. "I didn't think you were coming home till tomorrow."

"I was able to close the sale early and catch a flight home."

"I'm really glad to see you." Emma smiled but when she looked at Chelsea, her friend was staring at Luke, who stood a few feet away.

Chelsea gave him a slow, knowing appraisal. "So I guess you must be the infamous Luke Brodie."

Luke just smiled. "I'm Luke. Nice to meet you, Chelsea." She reached out a hand and Luke shook it.

Emma wasn't sure what she had expected. Chelsea Davenport was blonde, beautiful, and sexy, the kind of woman men were instantly drawn to. Chelsea had a body that wouldn't quit and Luke loved women. She didn't expect his nonchalant, clearly uninterested glance as he assessed her best friend.

She didn't expect the little thrill that shot through her

when his gaze slid past Chelsea, landed on her, and went blue-hot.

Emma didn't expect that to be the moment she fell in love with Luke Brodie.

Emma stayed at her apartment with Chelsea that night. She hadn't seen her friend in what felt like ages, and Chelsea would only be in town a few days. They ordered pizza, then sipped a glass of Chianti while they waited for the delivery to get there. As soon as the food arrived, they refilled their glasses and curled up on the sofa with big gooey slices of pepperoni and cheese with olives and mushrooms, Chelsea's favorite.

"So anything new and exciting going on in your life?" Emma asked.

"Well, I met someone."

Emma smiled. "You're always meeting someone. The problem is he usually lives hundreds of miles away."

"True, but not this time. This guy actually has a house in Seattle."

"Good for you. What's his name?"

"Dennis Winston. Denny. He's in his late thirties, good-looking, and smart. We started talking and sort of hit it off. He asked for my number. He's supposed to call sometime this week."

"That's great, Chels."

Her smile faded. "You want to know the truth? I really don't want to go out with him. I'm tired of the rat race, you know? Meeting some guy you think you're really going to like. Finding out he's no different from the rest, mostly self-centered and boring. I think I'm going to skip this round. Take a break from men for a while."

Chelsea's luck with men had never been great. Maybe a

break would be good, give her time to decide what she really wanted. "If you really feel that way, it might not be a bad idea."

"I think it's a great idea." Chelsea set her half-finished slice of pizza back down on the paper plate, picked up her wineglass, and leaned back against the sofa. "So now it's your turn. What about you and Luke? You were right—that guy is smokin' hot. And he is really into you."

"You think so?"

"Oh, yeah. He didn't even know I was in the room."

"Well, I don't know about that. Pretty hard for a guy not to notice you, Chelsea."

"Your guy didn't."

Emma sighed. "Luke's just passing through. He's made that clear more than once."

Chelsea took a sip of wine. "You never know. Maybe he'll figure out what he wants. Sometimes it takes awhile for a guy like that."

"What kind of guy are we talking about?"

Chelsea shrugged. "I don't know . . . a man who's been on his own for too long. You said he was a soldier, right? Now he's a bounty hunter. Same deal. They aren't used to having a woman around, at least not one who matters. Sometimes they discover they like it. If they do and you're the one, they're usually in for the long haul."

Chelsea knew a lot about men. As a female sales rep, she had learned to deal with them. In her personal life . . . not so much. But still . . .

"I suppose it's possible."

"Come on, Em. You're the kind of girl who takes in stray dogs and rescues lost kittens. I figure you're planning to stick around long enough to rescue Luke."

Since it was true, it was hard to argue. "You think he needs rescuing?"

Chelsea sipped her wine. "The way he was looking at you?" She shook her head. "I don't know . . . there was something in his eyes . . . I'm not sure exactly . . . but yeah, I do."

Could she rescue Luke? Emma had no idea. So far, Luke had been doing most of the rescuing, like at the fight outside the Golden Lily. Though she had held her own remarkably well.

Tomorrow they were going to the Red Devil bar, which, after Luke had left her apartment, she had confirmed was open seven days a week. She'd texted him the information. Luke had texted back that he would pick her up at noon for the trip downtown.

"So tell me more about him," Chelsea said.

Emma swallowed her bite of pizza. It seemed there was a lot to tell. Emma smiled and started talking. It was going to be a long girls' night in.

She hadn't expected to already be missing Luke.

Chapter Twenty-Four

The Red Devil bar sat on a street near Pioneer Square. Peanut shells crunched under the soles of his moccasins as Luke guided Emma inside. She was wearing a peach-colored scoop-neck top and a pair of those stretchy jeans he liked, the ones that hugged her curves and reminded him how he'd peeled her out of them yesterday in her apartment.

The thought sent his blood rushing south and his groin tightened. Dammit. He had to clench his teeth to keep from getting hard. When she walked up to the bar and climbed up on a stool, the guy on the bar stool next to her gave her a slimy appraisal then a horny smile.

"Buy you a drink, sweetheart?" He winked. "Gonna be a long, lazy afternoon. I can be real good company."

Luke felt a surge of heat at the back of his neck. He wanted to jerk the guy off the bar stool and shove a boot in his randy ass.

"The lady has all the company she needs," he said. "Be in your best interest if you worried about your own drink and left her the hell alone."

The guy grunted. "Asshole."

Luke's jaw tightened. One quick tug on the back of the

prick's plaid shirt and he'd be lying on the ground sucking peanut shells. He reached out . . .

"Luke!" Emma's voice jolted through him, making him feel like a fool.

What the hell was he doing? He was there on business, not to fistfight some loser at the bar. He sat down on the stool on the other side of Emma. "Sorry."

She looked like she was fighting a smile. She turned to the bartender, a guy with longish blond hair beneath a Seattle Seahawks baseball cap. "I'd like a beer, please. Bud Light is fine."

"Corona," Luke said.

The bartender twisted the top off a Bud and set it in front of Emma, set a Corona on the bar beside it. Luke took a long swallow, hoping it would tame the adrenaline still pumping through him. What the hell had just happened? He wasn't the jealous type. At least he kept telling himself he wasn't.

Emma took a sip of beer, set it down, and smiled at the man behind the bar. "Hi, I'm Emma. What's your name?"

The bartender smiled back. "I'm Joey."

"Hi, Joey. We were hoping you might be able to help us out. Were you working on Wednesday afternoon?"

Joey grabbed a dish towel and started wiping down the bar. "Thursday's my day off, so yeah, I was here on Wednesday. Why?"

Luke pulled out his silver money clip with the head of an eagle on the front. He peeled off a twenty-dollar bill and tossed it onto the bar. "We're looking for a guy who was in here that day. Might be a regular. Red hair, crooked nose like maybe it was broken."

Joey mopped the bar in front of them. "Now that you mention it, I remember seeing the guy. That carrot top hair kind of stuck in my head."

Luke peeled off another twenty. "What's his name?"

The bartender stared at the money. "I don't know his name. I saw him talking to one of the regulars, guy named Felix Riggs."

"Riggs is dead. What can you tell me about the other guy?"

The bartender's blond eyebrows went up. "Riggs is dead?"

"Died the same day. What else can you tell me?"

"You think that guy killed him?"

"No. But I think he might have had a hand in it. What else?"

The bartender eyed the money. The towel moved in a circle on the bar. "I wish I had something. The red-haired guy came in. He and Riggs talked, then left a few minutes later. That's all I know."

Luke pulled a business card out of his wallet and stuck it into the bartender's pocket. He shoved the second twenty across the bar. "He comes in again, give me a heads-up. There's a Benjamin with your name on it if he's still around when I get here."

The bartender nodded. "I'll keep an eye out."

Luke tossed down enough money to pay for the beers. Emma's bottle was barely touched. Luke took a long draw on the Corona, set the bottle back down, and they left the bar.

"We didn't get much," Emma said as they walked down the sidewalk.

"Not enough. We can hope the guy comes back in, but I have a feeling he was just there to pick up Riggs and deliver him to Vance."

"You think Vance killed Riggs because he gave us information?"

"It could have been anything. Something Riggs said.

Something he didn't say. Whatever happened, it's Vance's fault, not ours."

Emma made no reply. He wondered if she believed him. Seemed to him Emma had a little too much heart to be a bounty hunter.

"You got that meet set up with your sister?" he asked.

"Agent Danfield called this morning. April and Ginny were just getting on a plane, a private jet, I think. He's calling me later to tell me where we're going to meet."

"He isn't taking any chances. That's good. You think Danfield will be there?"

"I have a feeling he will but I don't know for sure."

"What would you think about me coming along? I'd like to meet this guy, get a take on him."

"You don't trust him?"

"Someone told Vance where to find your sister and her daughter. We need to be sure they're safe."

"You're right. We can't take any chances."

"I'll just stay long enough to size him up, see where he stands."

Emma bit her lip. "If I bring you, the FBI isn't going to like it."

"Yeah, well, I don't give a flying—"

"Luke!"

"*Fig.* They're the ones who leaked the information."

She nodded. "Okay. As soon as I hear from Danfield, I'll call and tell you know where to go."

Luke cast her a glance. "You had lunch yet?"

"Not yet."

"How about Chinese? Then we'll wait for the call at my place."

Emma laughed. "You are so transparent."

Luke dipped his head and kissed her. "You know, you

have me at a helluva disadvantage, lady—you being so damned smart."

He watched the amusement fade from her pretty face. His plans for the afternoon might keep her worries away for a while. But until Rudy Vance had been stopped once and for all, it would only be a temporary fix.

Flanked by two men in dark suits, April walked past Special Agent Conner Danfield into an unassuming two-story tract house in an out-of-the-way neighborhood in Kirkland. Rowdy, the mostly golden retriever, trotted along next to Ginny, who held on to his leash as the puppy began to sniff his way around his new temporary home.

Or at least April hoped it was temporary.

"Three bedrooms, two and a half baths, living room, kitchen, and utility room," Conner said. "All the comforts of home." He waved a hand toward the stairs. "You and Ginny will have the upstairs all to yourselves. The men will be down here."

Ginny reached down and scratched Rowdy's ears. "I'd really like to visit a couple of my friends," she said. "Will we be able to leave the house?"

"We're going to need some time to get things worked out," Con told her. "I know this is hard for you, Ginny. At least it's summer. You don't have to worry about missing school."

Ginny glanced away. "I guess so."

April could feel her daughter's pain. At fifteen, Ginny missed her friends, missed being a normal teenage girl. At least being underage had kept her name out of the media. Few people knew she was the young girl who had been in the house when Eleanor Harris had been murdered or that she had been victimized by Rudolph Vance.

"Is it okay if I go upstairs and check out my room?" she asked, raking back her hair. April had gotten her blond hair and blue eyes from her mother while Emma had inherited their dad's dark brown hair and warm brown eyes. Ginny had fallen somewhere in between, with the same brown eyes Emma had, April's features, and Grandma Cassidy's light brown hair and gentle disposition.

"The house has been cleared," Conner said. "Go ahead. One of the guys will bring up your luggage."

"Thanks, Agent Danfield." Ginny tugged on Rowdy's leash and the two of them raced upstairs. April heard a door close down the hall.

The good news was, Ginny seemed to be recuperating from her ordeal very well. Maybe it was the help of the psychologists she had been seeing, a woman in Colorado Ginny adored, and before that, one who was here in Seattle.

Maybe it was the resilience of youth or simply Ginny's valiant, indomitable spirit. Whatever it was, April was grateful to see the light sparkling once more in her daughter's eyes.

April's gaze went to Con, who stood nearby in conversation with one of his men. From the start, she'd tried to ignore her attraction to Conner Danfield. But with his perceptive gray eyes, dark brown hair silvered at the temples, strong jaw, and straight nose, Con was a handsome man. She'd tried not to notice his toned, athletic build, the way his shirt fit over his wide shoulders and very solid chest.

But she was a woman and Con was a good-looking man. A good-looking single man who had obviously also noticed her. The attraction had been instant and mutual. Why things like that happened, April had no idea, but eventually they'd been forced to acknowledge the pull between them.

"I've got a job to do, April," Conner had said before they'd left for Denver. "Whatever my feelings for you, this can't go anywhere until Rudolph Vance is in prison and you and Ginny are safe. After that . . ." He cupped her face between his hands and looked into her eyes. "Then it'll be up to us."

April appreciated his honesty. There had been no personal phone calls, no e-mails or texts. Still, the moment she had heard his voice on the phone, telling her he was coming for them, all her hidden feelings had rushed forward. They had strengthened when he'd arrived on her front porch. For a single moment, Con had weakened and held her while she cried in his arms.

A noise drew her back to the present. One of the FBI agents, a forty-something blond man named Quentin Melrose in a dark, well-tailored suit, walked back in from outside, followed by a brawny young African-American agent named Lester Wills. They carried the last of the bags from the car.

Sometime that week, the movers would be bringing their clothes and the few belongings they had accumulated while they were in Colorado.

"Okay if we take these bags up?" Melrose asked.

"Sure, go ahead." The men trooped up the safe house stairs, their polished wing-tips thumping on the carpet.

April had sold her own home in Seattle right after the murder. Too many bad memories. Once Vance had been found and dealt with, she hoped to buy another house in the area. April wished all of this was over and she and Ginny were in their own home right now.

She sat down in the living room. It wasn't fancy, but the ceiling was vaulted, giving the room an open feel. The sofa and two matching chairs, rental furniture, were plain brown tweed. A dining table and six chairs sat at one end of the room, next to a wide opening into the kitchen.

Con followed her in and sat down in one of the living

room chairs. "I need to call your sister, tell her what time we'll be picking her up. I'll give you a chance to unpack, get settled a bit before then. Does that work for you?"

"Absolutely," April said. "I've really missed Emma. When she lived with us, we were a real family. None of us was ever lonely."

"I could tell the two of you were close." Con's beautiful gray eyes fixed on her face, and her heart took a leap, which was a little surprising since she wasn't a heart-leaping kind of woman, not after the disastrous marriage she'd had with Ginny's father.

"We're going to find this guy, April," Con said. "We're going to put him away for the rest of his miserable life."

Or maybe his miserable life would end in a hail of gunfire. She hated herself for the thought, but it was there just the same.

It was late Sunday afternoon. Emma sat on the sofa in Luke's living room, her cell phone on the coffee table as she waited to hear from Special Agent Danfield.

"Relax, the guy's going to call," Luke said. "He's FBI. If he said he'd call, he will. They're all a little anal."

Amusement curved her lips. She glanced at Luke, and as if he had ESP, her cell phone started to ring. Hooking a long curl behind her ear, Emma grabbed the phone and pressed it against her ear.

"Hello, Emma," a man's deep voice said. "This is Agent Danfield. Your family is anxious to see you. Are you ready for a visit?"

Anticipation shimmered through her. "More than ready. I know the circumstances aren't good, but I'm so glad they're back. Give me an address and I'll be right there."

"I'm sending a car to pick you up. Where are you?"

She looked at Luke and rattled off his Bellevue address, adding, "Unit three-sixteen." The number on the door of his third-floor corner apartment. High enough, she figured, to keep out intruders and low enough Luke could get out if he needed to make an escape.

She was learning a lot from Luke Brodie, a thought that reminded her of the afternoon she'd spent in his bed and sent color flooding into her cheeks.

"The agents will be there in twenty minutes," Danfield said.

"I'll be ready." Emma hung up the phone. "They're picking me up. I didn't get the impression Agent Danfield would be coming himself."

Luke dropped down on the sofa beside her. "Then I guess I'll have to tag along."

But when the FBI came knocking at the door, it was clear that wasn't going to happen. Emma invited them inside and the men introduced themselves.

"This is Luke Brodie," she said. "If it's all right, I'd like for Luke to come with me."

The taller man, Special Agent Melrose, blond, early forties, just shook his head. "I'm afraid that's not possible. Sorry."

Standing at her side, Luke surprised her with a shrug. "Maybe next time," he said.

Unease rolled through her. This was Luke. He didn't take no for an answer.

"Are you ready, Ms. Cassidy?" Agent Wills asked. He was dark-skinned, good looking, and built like a brick house.

"So I guess I'll see you tomorrow," Emma said to Luke.

"Sure," he said. "Maybe sooner."

She cast him a warning glance as the agents hustled her out the door and they took the elevator downstairs.

A plain brown four-door Buick sat on the street out in front. Melrose walked around to the driver's side and climbed in while Wills opened the back door, waited until she slid inside, then closed the door, rounded the car, and got in on the opposite side.

Once her seat belt was fastened, Wills pulled a white handkerchief out of his pocket, folded it into a triangle, and handed it over. "You'll have to wear this, I'm afraid."

"You're kidding, right? You think I'm going to tell someone where you're hiding my sister? You think I would do anything that would cause her or Ginny harm?"

"Not on purpose, but that kind of information has a way of slipping out."

Emma grabbed the handkerchief. "Fine." She tied it around her head, covering her eyes, and leaned back in the seat.

"Make damned sure we aren't tailed," Wills said to Melrose as the agent pulled the Buick away from the curb.

Emma felt the swaying motion as the vehicle made a series of turns, stops, and accelerations that said the driver was using evasive maneuvers to ensure no one followed them to the safe house.

A couple of jarring stops, more turns, speeding up and slowing down. She was about half carsick by the time they finally arrived. She pulled off the makeshift blindfold as Wills came around and opened her door.

As she climbed out of the car, she surveyed her surroundings: a two-story, nondescript tract house with an attached two-car garage. There was a big pine tree in the yard and the lawn needed mowing.

"Let's go," Wills said, urging her up the sidewalk toward the front door.

Before they had time to reach it, a tall familiar figure in

jeans and a Henley sauntered out from behind the evergreen
tree, hands in the air.

"Luke!"

Two semiautomatic pistols flashed as the agents jerked
weapons from their shoulder holsters. Emma shook her
head, only a little surprised to see him.

"Don't shoot," Luke drawled as he walked slowly toward
them, hands high in the air. "I need to talk to Danfield, then
I'll go."

Melrose was furious. "The only place you're going,
Brodie, is to jail. You're interfering with a federal investigation. Put your hands behind your back."

Just then the door swung wide and Conner Danfield
stood in the opening. "All right, what's going on?"

"He's a friend," Emma said hurriedly. "His name's Luke
Brodie. H-he's a bail enforcement officer. Show them your
badge, Luke."

Luke carefully reached into the pocket of his jeans and
slowly drew out his badge wallet. He flipped it open and
the metal flashed in the sun.

"Brodie, you and Emma get inside," Danfield said. "We
don't need half the neighborhood speculating on what the
hell is going on out here." He tossed a glance at the other
two men. "I thought I told you to be sure you weren't
tailed."

"We were careful," Melrose said. "We never saw a
damned thing."

"Luke has . . . umm . . . special skills," Emma said.

Danfield jerked his head toward the house. "Inside, you
two. Now."

Emma walked ahead of Luke into the house, followed by
the other two agents. The door closed solidly behind them.

Chapter Twenty-Five

Luke watched Emma cross the living room to her sister and Ginny, one a pretty blonde with blue eyes, the younger girl with warm brown eyes that reminded him of Emma and long hair several shades lighter. As the women hugged, then wiped tears from their eyes, Luke felt a soft pang for the troubles the family had suffered.

First the death of the sisters' parents, then the terror brought on by Rudy Vance. His resolve hardened. He needed to make it end.

Danfield motioned for his men to go into the kitchen, then urged Luke toward the far end of the living room.

"Who the hell are you?" Danfield asked.

Luke sized him up, approving of the man's confident authority and no-bullshit approach. "Like Emma said, I'm her friend. That means I'm a friend of the family. I'm also ex-military. I'm a bounty hunter and I'm good at what I do. I'm here to make sure Emma's family is going to be safe."

Danfield made the same assessment of Luke that Luke had just made of him. "You're good or you wouldn't have been able to track Melrose and Wills, but I need more than that."

"Talk to Special Agent Ron Nolan. He'll vouch for me."

"How do you know Nolan?"

"We've worked together a couple of times, recently on an Interpol investigation that ended up in Argentina."

"Gertsman?"

"That's right."

"So you were the one who went down there."

"Me and couple of other guys. Officially we were never there."

"Well, you aren't supposed to be here, either. You realize you're interfering in FBI business."

"Maybe, but we both know you've got a leak. I came to make sure that leak isn't you or one of your men."

Danfield's jaw went tight. "I'm not the leak and I hand-picked Melrose and Wills and everyone else on the task force." He looked across the room to where April and Ginny were sitting at the dining table. Emma was holding on to Ginny's hand. Beneath the table, a golden lab puppy rested its muzzle on the young girl's sneaker.

"I'm not going to let anything happen to them," Danfield said. "I'll do everything in my power to keep April and Ginny safe. I give you my word on that."

Luke looked into the agent's worried eyes. "I believe you. But it might not be that easy. If you need some help, let me know."

"You hunting Vance?"

"That's right." He didn't mention Emma. He had no idea how much she had told her family or the FBI.

"Big fee involved," Danfield said, watching Luke's face.

"Sure is. I could use six hundred thou, just like anyone else, but I'd rather have Emma and her family safe."

Danfield relaxed, even managed the faintest smile. "Then I guess we're on the same team."

Luke returned the smile. "Looks like."

"I'd appreciate it if you'd keep me in the loop. Finding

Vance is turning out to be a helluva lot harder than we thought."

"I'll do my best." Which meant he wasn't giving the FBI jack shit until they plugged the leak. They exchanged cell numbers. "I'll come back for Emma whenever she's ready to leave," Luke said. "Doesn't matter how late. Tell her to give me a call."

Danfield seemed to mull that over. The FBI had gone to great lengths to keep Emma from knowing the location of the house. Luke had seen them blindfolding her for the trip over.

Danfield finally nodded, apparently deciding he either had to arrest Luke or trust him, and that included trusting Emma.

The agent turned to the men standing in the kitchen doorway. "Brodie's leaving."

Melrose's whole body went stiff. "You're just letting him go?"

"That's right. He wouldn't be here if you two had done your jobs."

Luke grinned as he walked out the door.

Emma was finally alone with her sister. Special Agent Melrose had left, his shift over. He'd be returning again in the morning. Conner Danfield was in the living room while Agent Wills prowled the house and kept an eye on things outside.

Ginny was upstairs with Rowdy. There was a TV in her bedroom and she had gone up to watch. The puppy was adorable. Emma could see how much the teenager loved the little dog.

Emma thought of her sweet niece and what she had been through and a soft pang throbbed in her heart.

"How's Ginny holding up?" she asked. "She seems good, but I know how hard this has been on her."

"She's doing a lot better than I expected. After the flowers showed up and she knew Vance had found us, I was sure she'd break down, but she didn't. She just got angry and even more determined not to let him ruin her life."

"That sounds like Ginny."

"The psychologist in Denver says that sometimes a younger person can deal with trauma better than an older one. They're able to focus on the future, look forward to what's ahead in life instead of dwelling on what's happened in the past. Sometimes it goes the other way, but it seems like Ginny is looking forward."

Emma felt a sweep of guilt. She'd been sure she would have found Vance by now, sure Ginny would be safe. "She was talking to me about going to college, trying to decide which school she wanted to attend. She's always been so smart."

"She was a straight A student until . . ." April let the sentence drop. "She was getting good grades again in Denver."

Emma's heart tugged. "That's great. I've been so worried about both of you." She shoved away the half-eaten ham and cheese sandwich and chips on the paper plate in front of her. Agent Wills had gone to the deli and brought back what was meant to pass for supper, along with a six-pack of Diet Coke.

"We're holding up okay," April said. "Con isn't sure how long we'll be staying in the house, but Ginny and I are determined to make the best of it. Tomorrow I'm making a grocery list. Agent Melrose volunteered to go shopping for us."

Emma smiled. "You're a great cook. Their meals will definitely improve."

April looked down at her mostly unfinished, rapidly drying-out sandwich. "That's for sure."

"So what about you and Conner?" Emma asked quietly, tipping her head toward the man on the sofa.

"Con's been great. As far as the two of us, I guess we'll have to wait and see. Nothing's going to happen until Vance is . . . out of the picture."

A look passed between them. "He will be," Emma promised. "Either the FBI will find him or Luke and I will."

"Luke Brodie. That's his name, right? I heard what you said out on the lawn."

"I would have introduced you and Ginny but the timing wasn't the best."

April shook her head. "I can't believe he followed you here. I mean, these guys are FBI."

"Luke was special forces before he became one of the best bounty hunters in the country."

"He's very protective of you."

Emma shrugged. "He's just that kind of man."

April smiled. "He's gorgeous. He has the most incredible blue eyes I've ever seen. And the way he was looking at you . . . like he wanted to go caveman and carry you out of here over his shoulder. If I had to guess—which I don't because I'm your sister and you're going to tell me—I'd say the two of you are sleeping together."

Emma fiddled with a potato chip on her paper plate. "We're . . . umm . . . together until we find Vance. I don't know how long it'll last after that. Luke's not a permanent kind of guy."

April sipped her Diet Coke. "Maybe he didn't have a reason to be until now."

Emma took a sip from the can in front of her. "I'm falling for him. It's stupid, but that's the way it is."

April leaned over and hugged her. "We don't get to

choose who we love. I didn't really choose Con either. Who wants to love someone who risks his life every day?" She glanced toward the living room. "You never know . . . maybe it'll work out for both of us."

Emma forced a smile, though thinking of Luke, it was hard to believe.

It was early Monday morning. They were waiting for the DNA sample, which Luke was hoping would come in that afternoon. Last night after her reunion with April and Ginny, Luke had picked her up. Wordlessly, he had headed the Bronco back to his apartment instead of taking her home.

Feeling a little guilty for abandoning Chelsea again, Emma had called her from the road, only to discover she was partying at the Alibi Room in Belltown.

"Sounds like you're having fun," Emma said, talking loud enough to be heard above the noise in the bar. "Hot date?"

"No date. I'm with friends. We're having a great time."

The guilt slid away. "I just thought I'd let you know I won't be home tonight."

"Hey, no problem. If I had a guy as hot as Luke, I wouldn't be coming home, either."

Emma smiled into the phone. "Thanks, Chelsea. Have fun."

Once she and Luke had arrived at his place, he'd managed to keep her mind off Rudy Vance, her sister, and Ginny, at least for the rest of the night.

Now it was morning. Since Luke couldn't phone the lab until it opened, Emma had enough time for her self-defense class. She'd missed too many lately. It was important to stay in shape.

"If it's okay with you, I think I'll tag along," Luke said

as he ambled bare-chested into the kitchen, looking like an ad for fantasy sex. "I could use a good workout."

He flashed a cheek-dimpling grin. "Not that I haven't been getting some mighty fine calisthenics every night, thanks to you."

Emma flushed but couldn't help smiling. "You are so bad."

Luke just laughed. They left his apartment and he drove her back home to change and pick up clean clothes, then they headed for the gym. In yoga pants and a pink tank over a black sports bra, her hair pulled into a ponytail, Emma walked into Easy Fitness.

Walking in behind her, Luke caught more than one female eye in a pair of gray sweats that hung low on his hips and an orange tank that showed the iron-hard muscles in his chest and shoulders, a pair of biceps that made her mouth water.

As they entered the classroom, Nita Castillo was warming up, her cocoa skin glinting with a light sheen of perspiration, toned body moving gracefully as she kicked an invisible opponent.

Nita waved her over. "We've missed you. I thought maybe you'd forgotten the whole bounty hunter gig and gone back to teaching." She flicked a glance at Luke. "I'm guessing that hasn't happened."

"This is Luke Brodie, Nita. Luke and I have been . . . umm . . . working together."

Nita grinned at Luke. "Is that what they call it these days?"

Luke grinned back while Emma did her best to ignore the remark. "Nita is Xavier Castillo's sister."

"Hi, Nita. Tell X I said hello."

"Oh, I will," she said, casting Emma a knowing glance.

Fortunately, Len walked into the classroom just then, sandy-haired, buff, and good-looking.

Luke walked over to greet him. "Hey, Len, good to see you, man." The pair leaned in and did the one-shoulder man-hug thing. "Emma said you were her instructor."

Emma inwardly sighed. She should have known they'd be acquainted.

"It's a semiprivate class," Len said, "just her and Nita. They're both excellent students."

"If Nita's as good as Emma, you've done a great job."

Emma tried not to feel pleased at the praise.

Luke turned toward her. "I'm gonna check in at the front desk, then hit the weights for a while. Have fun." To Len he said, "Don't let 'em off too easy." Luke winked at Emma.

"Hey, wait a minute," Len called after him. "I've got an idea. How about we run a few moves for the class before you start lifting."

Luke shrugged. "If you want."

Emma felt a tug of excitement. She had seen Luke in action, but at the time, her adrenaline had been pumping so hard, his movements had been mostly a blur.

Nita walked up beside her as the men took positions opposite each other on the big rubber mat.

"So . . . you and Luke Brodie? I guess my brother's advice blew past you like dust in the wind."

"Luke and I are hunting Rudy Vance. Aside from that, I'm a grown woman. I can do whatever I want."

Nita's black eyes went to the men circling each other on the mat, paused for a moment on Luke. "If I had a shot at a guy who looks like that, I'd do the same thing."

Emma followed Nita's gaze. Luke's relaxed expression was gone. He was all business now, assessing every move Len made. Her trainer was in top condition, a former Marine who practiced self-defense every day.

Both men went into a shoulder-wide stance, legs splayed, lead foot forward, weight on the balls of their feet. Len came at Luke, throwing a punch at Luke's jaw, at the same time delivering a kick aimed at his midsection.

Luke dodged the punch, blocked the kick with the back of his arm, whirled, and came at Len with a roundhouse kick Len blocked. Both men attacked, delivering a series of blows using their elbows, fists, and knees.

It happened so fast, Emma barely saw the knee that shot up, stopping just short of Len's groin, the arm that wrapped around his neck, the body twist that took him down on the mat.

Luke held the position for a moment, then let go and both men rolled to their feet.

"Nicely done," Len said.

Luke nodded at the compliment.

The men started circling once more, each keeping his loose-limbed, shoulder-width stance. Len waited only moments before going into attack mode again, going after Luke with his fists, using his elbows, driving forward with a kick; Luke defended, blocking the attack, then going on the offensive.

Luke shot out an elbow, followed by a knee kick Len blocked; Luke dodged a kick, then his palm shot out, slamming up beneath Len's chin, tipping it backward, halting just short of a death blow.

Emma's heart thundered. Luke stepped back, and so did Len.

"You okay?" Luke asked, his arms once more loose at his sides. He was calm on the outside, but Emma recognized the feral instincts the match had aroused. So did Luke.

"I'm okay," Len said. "Nice work. You want to go again?"

"I've had enough. I think I'll go hit those weights." Turning, Luke strode past Emma without a glance and walked out of the classroom.

"Wow, that was amazing," Nita said.

"Luke was special ops," Emma explained, feeling a need to defend him. "His training was a little different from Len's."

Len walked up just then. "Yeah, no question of that." He ran a hand beneath his chin down over his chest. "I'm glad he's got such good control."

Emma thought of the fierce look on Luke's face as his combat instincts took over. "People think he enjoys fighting, but he doesn't."

Len's gaze went to Luke's retreating figure, then back to her. "Sometimes it's necessary," Len said. "Which is why we need to get to work. Ladies—a hundred push-ups should be a good place to start."

Emma silently groaned. Flicking a last glance at the doorway, she dropped down on the mat and went to work.

Chapter Twenty-Six

Luke's tank stuck to his chest, the effect of a hard hour's workout. Lying on his back on the weight bench, he shoved the heavy bar up one last time, the muscles straining in his arms and shoulders, held it for the count of five, then set the bar into the rack above his head and rolled up off the bench.

His mind returned to his match with Lenny Fox. Len was a former Marine and a damned good competitor. A little too good. He'd pushed Luke just hard enough for him to go into the zone. He'd stayed in control, as he had been trained, but he didn't like being that close to the edge.

He wondered what Emma had thought, wondered if that glimpse of wildness she had seen in his face had given her a better understanding of the kind of man he was. The kind who could never be someone she deserved.

The bleak mood threatened. Luke managed to push it away. Using the towel he'd draped around his neck, he wiped the sweat from his forehead and looked up to see Emma approaching. She didn't stop, just walked up and slid her arms around his waist, rested her head on his chest.

"Hey, I'm all sweaty." But he liked the way she felt wrapped around him.

"So am I." She smiled, making him smile in return.

"Guess we better hit the showers," he said.

"Yeah, too bad they aren't unisex."

He laughed. It felt so good, his bleak mood slid completely away. "Meet you back out here in ten."

"Better make it fifteen." She disappeared into the women's locker room, and he went into the men's.

Ten minutes later, in clean jeans, a navy blue long-sleeved T-shirt and sneakers, he stood waiting.

"Let's get to work," Emma said.

Luke nodded. April and Ginny were back in Seattle, and as long as Rudolph Vance was on the loose, they were in danger.

Once they were outside sitting in the Bronco, he dialed the North County DNA Lab and asked for Danny Palachek.

"This is Danny," the kid said.

"Luke Brodie. How's that DNA sample coming, Danny?"

"I'm glad you called, Luke. I came in on Saturday and worked a few hours, just finished running your sample this morning. I got something for you. When can you stop by?"

"I'm on my way now." Luke ended the call and fired up the Bronco's big V-8 engine.

"The lab found something?" Emma asked as he pulled out of the lot.

"Looks that way. We're just about to find out."

The North County DNA Lab sat in a strip mall in Bellevue, not far from the BOSS, Inc. office. Emma walked past Luke, who held open the door, into a white-walled, linoleum-floored waiting area with a gray vinyl sofa and chair.

Luke walked up to the counter and rang the bell, the light *ding* echoing across the empty room. When an older woman walked up, Luke asked to speak to Danny Palachek. A few minutes later, a young man with kinky brown hair and tortoiseshell glasses strolled up.

"Hey, dude, good to see you," Danny said.

"You, too, man. Danny, this is Emma. She's working with me on the case. What have you got for us?"

Obviously proud of his work, Danny smiled. "I found DNA on the paper towel you brought in—skin cells work great. I ran the sample through CODIS and came up with a match. DNA belongs to a guy named Grady Kelso."

Emma felt a tremor of excitement. It was a lead, one they needed badly.

Danny opened a large manila envelope and pulled out a sheet of paper. "I printed this for you, along with some miscellaneous info I thought you could use." He shoved the paper across the counter and Emma moved close enough to see.

The first page was a rap sheet with a photo of an attractive man with red hair in an orange jumpsuit. Grady Evan Kelso was the name printed on the page, followed by the details of his arrest.

"That's got to be the man from the Red Devil bar," she said, "though his nose wasn't broken back then."

"Probably a prison fight," Luke said. "But I'm betting it's him. And now we've got a name."

"So I guess you can take it from here," Danny said.

"You bet we can. Good work. Send the bill to me at the office. Thanks, Danny."

"Will do. Glad I could help." Danny walked away and Luke looked down at the information.

"Grady Evan Kelso, born in nineteen seventy-six, twenty-nine years old when his mug shot was taken. Graduated UCLA in ninety-seven. Went to work for Century Capital as a stockbroker. Arrested eight years later for his part in a Ponzi scheme that bilked investors out of millions."

"Sounds like Vance's kind of guy."

Luke kept reading. "Kelso spent three years in the federal prison in Lompoc—got out early for good behavior. Moved to Seattle in two thousand eight after his release."

"Amazing. All that from a paper towel."

Luke smiled down at her. "You did good."

They walked out of the building, heading for the Bronco.

"Does it give Kelso's address?" Emma asked as they crossed the parking lot.

"12809 Lincoln Avenue in Lakewood, apartment fourteen. At least that was it when he moved up here in o-eight. Let's go see if our boy Grady still lives there."

By the time they got back to the Bronco, Emma had Googled Kelso on her smartphone. "Grady E. Kelso. No address, nothing on Facebook, but he's got a profile on LinkedIn. No photo. Just says he's a financial consultant."

Luke flicked her a glance. "Yeah, I'd love to have a guy who spent three years in the can for stealing money giving me advice on what to do with mine."

Emma chuckled.

They drove to the address, a gray, two-story building with a hip roof and small windows, a low-rent apartment complex called the Lanai. When they knocked on the door to unit fourteen, an old man with thinning white hair, still wearing his bathrobe, answered the door.

"We're looking for a guy named Grady Kelso," Luke said. "We were hoping to find him here."

"Never heard of him," the old man said. "I been livin' here more'n two years." He looked over his shoulder at the TV. "Sorry, I couldn't help. Gotta go. I'm missing *The Bold and the Beautiful*." The door closed in their faces.

"So much for that," Luke grumbled as they walked back toward the Bronco.

"If we're going to find Kelso," Emma said, "I need to get my laptop out of the backseat. I've got some great software programs."

"I've got a better idea." They reached the Bronco and Luke pulled open her door. "Let's go talk to Sadie."

As they walked into the office, Luke spotted Ethan sitting at his desk, talking on his cell phone. His brother lifted a hand in greeting. Luke waved back and so did Emma.

At a desk nearby, Dirk pounded away on his laptop keyboard. He did a quick chin lift and kept working. Luke urged Emma up the stairs.

In the glass-enclosed office, Sadie sat behind her three computer screens, head down, platinum curls jiggling around her shoulders, immersed in the game of digging up information, a job she seemed to relish.

Luke knocked on the jamb beside the open door. Sadie glanced up and motioned them inside, her gaze going straight to Emma.

"I heard you were still around. Good for you. Most of Luke's partners are down the road by now."

Emma just smiled. "Actually, he isn't all that bad—once you get past the *do as I say, not as I do* phase."

"Hey, wait a minute," Luke said, offended.

One of Emma's dark eyebrows went up. "You deny it?"

Luke grinned. "Hell no."

"All right, you two," Sadie interrupted. "I'm busy. What do you need?" Her features were stern, but amusement crinkled the lines at the corners of her pale blue eyes.

"We need to find an ex-con named Grady Kelso," Luke

said. "We could probably track him ourselves, eventually, but we need to find him sooner rather than later."

"What have you got?"

Luke handed over the info he'd picked up at the lab. "He's been gone from that address for at least two years."

Sadie studied the paper. "Give me a minute and I'll see what I can do." As she started typing in the information, Luke eased Emma out into the hall, giving Sadie a chance to work.

They headed downstairs and Luke led Emma into the break room for a cup of coffee. It wasn't too old so he poured each of them a Styrofoam cup. They sat down at the small round table in the corner.

Emma took a sip of coffee. "Once we find Kelso, what's our approach?"

Luke stretched his legs out in front of him. "We find him, get him to give us what he knows about Vance. DNA links Kelso to the house on Whidbey Island. It's likely he delivered Riggs up to Vance on a silver platter. Riggs is dead. Kelso is connected to the murder. That gives us leverage."

"You make it sound simple."

He shrugged. "We find him, we make him talk. That's our strategy."

Before Emma could say more, Nick walked into the room. "Hey, Luke. Emma." He grabbed a cup and filled it, crammed a lid down on top.

"Looks like you're in a hurry," Luke said.

"Got a meeting with an informant on a case I'm working. I'm hoping it'll lead to something. Then I'm meeting Samantha for lunch." His smile said he was looking forward to it. When it came to his pretty little wife, his cousin was a goner.

Luke felt a sweep of something he didn't want to feel and stood up from the table. "Let's go see what Sadie's got."

"Tell Samantha I said hello," Emma said as she rose from her chair.

"Will do." Nick grabbed his cup of coffee and headed out the door.

Luke and Emma followed him out. As they climbed the stairs to the second floor, Luke forced his mind back to the job. When they reached Sadie's office, he summoned his courage and stuck his head through the open door. "How's it going, darlin'?"

"I found him," Sadie said. "Come on in and I'll show you."

Emma walked past him into the office. Luke ignored the soft scent of her perfume.

"That was fast," he said. "I knew this was a good idea."

"Kelso's trying to appear legit so most of what he's done since he got to Seattle is on the record. After leaving his apartment on Lincoln, your boy made a couple of moves, all of them upward. At the moment, he lives in an expensive condo complex called the Park."

"Address?"

"Six eighty-eight Bell Street. Unit thirty-six ten. Phone number is five five five three one two two. I don't have his cell."

Emma made a note on her smartphone.

"What else?" Luke asked, watching the monitor as Sadie continued to search.

"DMV records say he drives a dark silver, two thousand fourteen Porsche Carrera."

Luke whistled. "Nice ride."

"Oh, and you're gonna love this," Sadie said. "Kelso wasn't in Seattle long before he started working for a company you may have heard of—International Cargo? He's listed as an outside consultant. I took a look at his college records. The guy is smart—straight A's in business at UCLA. If he hadn't gotten greedy, he might have been a very successful stockbroker."

Luke shook his head. "Now he's working for Vance. Three years in the pen and he still hasn't learned his lesson."

"So he does work for International Cargo," Emma said, getting him back on track, "a company connected to Vance."

"That's right." Sadie snorted. "Must pay him big money to afford what it costs to live at the Park."

Luke summed up what they knew. "Kelso's DNA proves he was at the Whidbey house. According to his aunt, only a few people knew the place existed. That makes Kelso more than just an associate. That makes him one of the higher-ups in Vance's food chain."

"I'll keep on him," Sadie said, going back to work. "If anything interesting turns up, I'll let you know."

Luke leaned down and pressed a kiss on her forehead. "You're the best, sweet pea." Setting a hand at Emma's waist, he urged her out of the office.

"I gather we're off to the Park." Emma adjusted the purse strap on her shoulder as they crossed the parking lot.

"That's right. Except I'm starving. It's after two and we haven't had lunch. How 'bout we hit Burger King on the way?"

Emma sighed as he helped her into the Bronco. "I swear, if you keep this up, I'm going to put on twenty pounds."

Luke grinned. "You don't have to worry, you look great. Besides"—he sliced her a look so hot, she couldn't mistake his meaning—"I'll help you work it off tonight."

Emma's cheeks turned pink, which made him smile. She didn't have to worry about her weight. Along with the sex, she worked out all the time. Add to that, they were constantly on the run, following one lead after another.

Luke just hoped one of them would finally pay off.

The Park on Bell Street was architecturally beautiful, twin towers that rose forty stories above the city with views out over the ocean. They walked inside and Emma tilted her head back to look up at the two-story lobby, which was spectacular.

"Not bad for an ex-con," Luke said as they headed over to the front desk. Emma spotted a pretty brunette in a white uniform jacket and navy blue skirt behind the counter. Her name tag said Lisa.

She smiled as they approached. "May I help you?"

"We're here to see Mr. Kelso," Luke said. "He's in thirty-six ten."

"I'll see if he's home." Lisa picked up the phone on the desk and punched his residence number. It rang a few times, but apparently no one picked up. "I'm sorry. It doesn't look like he's in."

Luke went into charm mode, leaning toward her across the counter, flashing the brunette one of his lopsided sexy dimpled smiles. "I don't suppose you'd have any idea when he might be back?"

"I wish I could help, but I'm afraid I don't know. Most of the residents go in and out through the garage. The elevators take them straight up to their floors."

"That's too bad," Luke said. "Maybe I can catch him later."

Hope sprang into the woman's dark eyes. Emma figured she was thinking that if Luke returned, maybe he would come back alone.

"Would you like to leave a message? If you give me your phone number, I'll be happy to see he gets it."

And even happier to call you myself, Emma thought darkly as the brunette's gaze slid from Luke's gorgeous blue eyes to the rock-solid body beneath his snug long-sleeved T-shirt.

"Not necessary," he said, "but we appreciate your help."

"Anytime," said the brunette, a slightly husky note in her voice.

Hearing it, Emma felt a shot of jealousy. Luke had his choice of women. He specialized in one-night stands. Surely he was getting tired of her by now.

But when she looked at him, he wasn't paying attention to the brunette. His mind was clearly somewhere else. He crossed the lobby, shoved open the heavy glass door, and waited for her to precede him into the damp city air.

"If we come back," he said as they walked away from the building, "we're going to have to sign in before they'll let us go upstairs. There are cameras all over the lobby. Security's tight. I think we need a different approach."

Emma paused on the sidewalk. "What are you suggesting?"

"Kelso's a consultant. That means he comes and goes as he pleases. No way to know exactly when he'll be here. I'll take you home, come back, and stake the place out. I'll make sure he's alone, then go up and pay him a little visit."

"You just said there were too many cameras."

"I said there were too many cameras in the lobby. I'm not going in through the lobby. I'm going in through the parking garage."

The garage had a security gate. She didn't bother to ask how Luke was planning to get past it. Emma had no doubt he could handle the job.

Chapter Twenty-Seven

Luke needed to get into the garage. He needed to make a preliminary survey of the parking structure, check out the camera situation, figure the best approach. Getting in wouldn't be much of a problem. He had some pretty good software himself.

"Wait for me in the Bronco," he said to Emma. "I'll be back in a few minutes."

"You're going in there now? I thought you were going to wait till dark."

"I need to know the layout, get a take on what I'll be facing." That said, he headed in the opposite direction, making his way to the partially underground garage. Besides the vehicle entrance, there was a door on one side. Standing next to it, he plugged a cord into his smartphone, then used the sensor attached to digitally discover the numbers for the keypad along the wall.

When they appeared on his screen, he manually punched them in, opened the door, walked down the half flight of stairs, and wound up inside. It was mostly empty this time of day, but a couple of Caddies, a few BMWs, two Mercedes, and a Bentley took up spaces. The faint smell of rubber and gasoline drifted across the cement floor, though it had recently been swept.

Best of all, no cameras aimed toward the door he'd come in through. A lens pointed at the vehicle entrance and several cameras surveyed the parking spaces. Keeping his head turned away, he moved close enough to check the brand. Kyoto. Newer but surprisingly not the top of the line and already becoming outdated. Looked like the builders had hoped to save a few bucks, probably not the best idea.

Pulling out his iPhone, he upgraded his software, then, head down, crossed the garage to the elevator. Camera outside the elevator door, same brand. He was betting they were the same throughout the building.

Bringing up the screen, he pressed a key on his smartphone and the cameras in the garage blinked off. When the elevator door dinged open, he saw that the camera inside was also turned off.

Piece of cake. He crossed the garage back toward the door he'd come in through. As soon as he was out of lens range, he turned the cameras back on, headed up the half flight of stairs, and walked outside.

Now all he had to do was wait for Grady Kelso to come home.

Emma watched as Luke approached the Bronco and slid in behind the wheel.

"Getting inside won't be a problem," he said.

"So we're waiting here for Kelso?"

"I need to talk to him alone—without his girlfriends or golfing buddies—so yeah."

"By '*I* need to talk to him alone,' you mean, '*We* need to talk to him alone,' correct?"

Luke sliced her a look. "This might get nasty, Emma.

Let me take you home—then I'll come back and deal with Kelso. You really don't want to be there when I do."

"Oh, I want to be there. You have no idea how much I want to be there when Grady Kelso tells you where to find Rudolph Vance."

Luke made no reply, but a muscle ticked in his cheek. She could see he didn't want her there, but they had made a deal. It was her decision.

Luke started the engine and moved the Bronco to a vantage point where they could watch the garage and see all the way down the block without being spotted.

"Kelso might not be home till late," Emma said. "Sitting for hours out here in the cold isn't going to be a whole lot of fun."

Luke shrugged. "Just part of the job." He glanced at Emma and his eyes gleamed. She recognized the sensual curve of his lips.

"On the other hand, since you're determined to stay, maybe we can find a way to make it fun."

Heat slid through her. She knew what he was thinking. Emma had no doubt Luke Brodie could make the waiting fun.

It was almost midnight. Yawning, Luke leaned back against the seat. "My turn." Emma had slept for the past two hours. "Wake me if Kelso shows up."

It had been a long afternoon. Even with Emma walking down to the corner and returning with sandwiches and soft drinks, an even longer evening. And Emma had been right about the weather. The afternoon had gone from breezy to downright cold, with a drop in temperature as a damp fog rolled over the city.

Luke closed his eyes. He'd kept watch earlier. He felt the

tug of a smile. Once it was dark, they'd gotten creative. Emma had fallen asleep after she'd reached a squirming orgasm sitting on his lap.

Hey, they'd kept an eye out for Kelso, hadn't they?

At least Luke's eyes had been open. He liked watching Emma reach her peak. He liked making it happen, liked the way just hearing her soft cries of pleasure turned him on like crazy.

He drifted off, fighting not to get hard again just thinking about it, slipped just below the surface into the zone he had perfected in the army. He'd been asleep maybe fifteen minutes when he felt an excited nudge.

"It's him," Emma whispered. "Luke, it's Kelso."

He came instantly awake. Looking down the block, he spotted a dark metallic gray Porsche rolling along the street toward the towers.

Luke was armed. Both of them were: Emma's Glock and his M-9 Beretta, plus the eight-inch Ka-Bar knife strapped to his thigh. Grabbing the night-vision goggles he'd retrieved from his gear bag in the back, he verified that Kelso was the only one in the Porsche, waited until the car disappeared into the parking garage, then nodded to Emma and both of them exited the vehicle.

Earlier, he'd dug into his go-bag and was now completely dressed in black. Emma's bag held black jeans and a lightweight black turtleneck. She'd pulled her hair into a ponytail and jammed on a black baseball cap.

They moved with purpose, weaving in and out of the foliage. There was enough shrubbery along the road to help them stay out of sight. Hurriedly, they crossed the road and made their way toward the door leading down into the garage. Luke punched in the code on the panel outside, shutting down the alarm, and they slipped inside just seconds after Kelso had parked his Porsche.

A hard smile surfaced as Luke watched the man climb out of the car. Standing at the bottom of the stairs they'd come in through, he used his phone to blink out the cameras, pointed to the elevator, and Emma headed in that direction while Luke moved toward the Porsche, pulling his semiauto out of the holster at his waist. As Kelso crossed the floor of the garage, Luke moved silently up behind him.

Luke shoved his gun into Kelso's ribs. "You want to be very quiet, Grady. Just keep walking toward the elevator. You're having unexpected company tonight."

Kelso's muscles went rigid.

"Don't do anything stupid," Luke warned, nudging the barrel a little deeper. "I won't kill you—but I won't hesitate to hurt you."

Kelso didn't back down. "Who are you? What do you want?" He was six feet, barrel-chested, with a solidly muscular build. Luke nudged him forward, rethinking his strategy. This guy might be a white-collar criminal, but he was no pussy.

"We'll talk upstairs."

Kelso started walking. By the time they reached the elevator, Emma had the door open and was waiting for them to join her inside.

"What the hell is going on?" Kelso asked when he spotted her.

"That's Emma. She's joining us for our friendly little chat."

"I hope you know the kind of trouble you're bringing down on your head."

Luke sighed. "I've got a pretty good idea," he said as the elevator doors swished closed. *Seemed like lately trouble was Luke's middle name.*

The conveyance shot up thirty-six floors in seconds; then the doors quietly slid open. They moved along the corridor, Kelso in front of them, stopped in front of unit 3610, Kelso cooperating so far.

Luke held the gun steady as Grady opened the door and they followed him inside. Luke checked for cameras, found none, clicked the cameras back on in the corridor, and Emma closed the door.

"Beautiful place," she said, glancing around at the floor-to-ceiling plate-glass windows, the deck that wrapped around the living and dining areas, the view of a thousand lights sparkling all over the city below.

Except for the dark wood cabinets and wide planked floors, the entire condo was white: walls, drapes, white leather sofas, bar stools, and chairs. It shouldn't have looked masculine but it did.

"I looked at the brochure for this place on the Internet," Emma said. "The upper floors cost over a million dollars. Rudy must pay you very well."

Kelso looked at Luke. "Who are you?"

Luke ignored the question. "We're looking for your employer. You help us find him, you won't have a problem."

"I don't know what you're talking about."

Emma shoved him forward, over to a low-slung chair. "Sit down."

Kelso's jaw tightened.

"Do what the lady says."

Kelso sat down.

"Put your hands in front of you," Emma commanded.

Kelso humored her. Emma slid on a nylon tie, tightened it around his wrists. Slipped one around his ankles and pulled it snug.

"Look, I don't know anything," Grady said. "I'm a consultant at International Cargo. I'm a businessman. You have me mixed up with somebody else."

"Cut the crap, Kelso. We found your DNA at Vance's

house on Whidbey Island. We know you picked Felix Riggs up at the Red Devil bar and drove him out to the island so Vance could slit his throat."

Kelso blinked. His features remained unreadable, but he moistened his lips. "I didn't know he was going to kill the guy. I don't think it was planned. That stupid fuck, Riggs, just kept talking, saying the wrong things, talking about Rudy's aunt, telling him how sorry he was for screwing up. The next thing I know, Riggs was flopping around on the kitchen floor, bleeding all over the linoleum."

"Ceramic tile," Emma corrected.

Kelso's eyes swung to hers. "Whatever."

"We need information, Kelso. You give it to us, no one has to know you were involved. You don't, we go to the police."

"You want to go back to jail, Grady?" Emma asked. "This time it won't be three years in a cushy white-collar prison. You'll be in for murder. Riggs is dead. He can't tell them you weren't the one who killed him."

"Where's Vance?" Luke pressed.

Kelso shook his head. "I don't know. I really don't. I haven't heard from him since he left the island."

"What did you do for him?"

"Fixed things. Helped him manage whatever problems came up. I gave him a little financial advice and found the right people to handle things, that's it."

"If you don't know where he is—what *do* you know? And it better be good."

Kelso's gaze went from Luke to Emma and back. "Wait a minute. You're that bounty hunter—Brodie. You're the guy who got Riggs killed."

"Riggs got himself killed."

Kelso released a slow breath. "Can't argue with that."

"I want Vance. Give me something and we're out of

here. Keep your mouth shut and no one will know we ever talked. What's Vance into? What deal is he here in Seattle to make?"

Kelso said nothing.

"The FBI is after him, Grady. They're looking at him for smuggling, gunrunning, you name it. We go to the police, you're going down right along with him. Tell me what you know."

Kelso shook his head, the track lights making his red hair gleam. "He'll kill me. Just like he killed Riggs."

"All right. Then tell me about the Yakuza." Kelso's head jerked up. "You think I don't know they're involved in this? What's the deal?"

When Grady didn't answer, Luke reached down and gripped the handle of the knife strapped to his thigh. Emma made a sound in her throat when he slid out the serrated eight-inch blade.

"I won't kill you," Luke said. "But you're gonna have a helluva time getting the blood out of all this white furniture."

"You're bluffing."

Luke jerked Grady's bound hands up and rested them on the arm of the chair. He set the blade across the last digit of Kelso's little finger.

"You'll fit right in, Grady. Whenever something goes wrong, the Yakuza cut off part of their fingers as punishment. Unless you tell me what I want to know, that's what's going to happen to you."

The vein in Kelso's neck pulsed with the rapid beat of his heart. For several tense moments, he studied Luke's face. "You'll do it, won't you? I can see it in your eyes. You'd probably cut off my whole damned hand if that's what it took to get what you wanted."

Luke shrugged as if cutting off a guy's hand meant

nothing. He forced himself not to look at Emma, not to worry about what she was thinking. "Talk," Luke said.

Unwilling to press his luck, Kelso gave up a sigh. "You're right, Vance is doing a deal with the Yakuza. They've got something in the works, but I'm not sure what it is. Rudy's here to make sure the deal gets done right and everybody's happy. Aside from his interest in International Cargo, he owns a shipping container company. I don't know the name. Vance is secretive about it. I don't think he's listed on any of the ownership records."

"Who is?"

"I don't know."

"Shipping containers . . . so what's he smuggling?"

"Like you said, guns, drugs, whatever else he gets paid for."

There was something in Kelso's eyes. It almost looked like guilt. "And?" Luke pressed.

"Bodies. At the moment, that's the main attraction. Big money in human trafficking these days."

"Always has been." Luke moved the knife away from Kelso's hand. "I need to know where to find him. Keep in mind, Grady, once Vance is off the street, you can breathe a whole lot easier."

"Like I said, I don't know where he is, but I heard him talking. He mentioned a guy named Ryan Masaki. He's a big man in the Yakuza. Vance said something about Masaki not wanting to go along with the deal. That's the main reason he's here. That's all I've got."

Luke gave him a last hard appraisal. Satisfied he'd gotten all he was going to, he leaned down and sliced the nylon band around Kelso's ankles. He left the band on Grady's wrists and sheathed the knife.

He turned to Emma. "Let's go."

Emma crossed the room and waited at the door. Luke opened it, used his cell to blink off the cameras, then they were gone.

A few minutes later, Luke had Emma back in the Bronco and they were roaring down the highway toward his apartment.

"Would you really have cut off his finger?" Emma asked softly.

Luke's chest clamped down. He tried to sound nonchalant. "I was hoping it wouldn't come to that. Kelso seemed like a pretty smart guy. I always try to gauge the situation."

Emma didn't say more.

Luke thought of things he'd done in the past and the blackness shifted inside him, threatening to surface and drag him down. Then Emma reached over and gently rested a hand on his leg.

"I think we made some progress tonight," she said. "I'll be glad when we get home."

Luke's throat felt tight. "Yeah," he said, covering her smaller hand with his. "Me too."

Chapter Twenty-Eight

A heavy mist hung in the air, cloaking the house in murky darkness. The hour was late, well after midnight. Except for the hum of insects and the wind luffing through the trees, the neighborhood was quiet. No lights burned in the rooms upstairs.

Ginny would be asleep by now, curled up with her mutt of a dog. Rudy wondered if she thought of him, if she remembered those moments they had spent together. He knew he had frightened her. He hadn't meant to. She was sweet and innocent. Knowing it was her first time, he had tried to go slow, but then she had fought him and her struggles had aroused him. He had taken her roughly, unable to control himself.

He regretted that now. But he would make it up to her. Once they were together, he would make it good for her, find ways to please her, show her how to please him.

A single light glowed through the curtains in the living room. The TV was playing downstairs. His informant said two agents guarded the house round the clock. Getting Ginny out wouldn't be easy.

But he knew the men's names, knew their schedules. In time, he would come up with a plan. First he needed to conclude his business. Once that was finished, he could turn his full attention to Ginny.

Quietly slipping through the shadows, Rudy disappeared out of sight. When the time was right, he would return. He wouldn't have to wait much longer.

Luke wasn't in bed when Emma awoke the next morning. Padding over to the dresser, she snagged one of his T-shirts and pulled it on, reminding herself it was time to make a trip back to her place for clean clothes.

The smell of coffee beckoned her down the hall. As she walked past the bedroom that Luke had converted into an office, she spotted him sitting at the desk, his laptop open in front of him.

He was wearing headphones, mumbling words she couldn't make out so he didn't hear her approach. Sneaking up behind him probably wasn't a good idea. She walked around to where he could see her and smiled.

"Good morning."

Luke smiled back and removed the headphones, paused the program he was running on his computer. "Morning."

"You let me sleep. Thanks."

He just shrugged. "I figured you could use the rest."

They'd gotten home late from the stakeout. After the tense moments in Kelso's condo, she'd been exhausted. Curled up against Luke, she'd slept the sleep of the dead.

She glanced down at the headphones lying on top of the desk. "What are you doing?"

"I thought I'd pick up a little Japanese."

Emma's eyebrows went up. "Just like that? You're learning Japanese?"

Luke picked up the headset, slung it around his neck.

"Just enough to understand a few phrases here and there. I thought it might come in handy."

She knew he had an aptitude for languages. He'd said he had used it during his years in the army. Under the circumstances, they needed every advantage they could get.

"By the way," Luke said, "I called Sadie this morning. She's digging around, trying to find out which shipping company Vance owns."

"Great." Emma turned and started for the door. "I need to shower and get dressed. I'll let you get back to practicing your Japanese."

Luke smiled. "I wish I could join you, but once in a while, I actually have to work."

She smiled at him over her shoulder. "Your loss." Tossing her dark hair, she paused. "Before I go, what's on our schedule today? I imagine hunting down Ryan Masaki, right?"

"Already found him," Luke said. "His first name's Ryota, Americanized to Ryan. He's a pretty big deal in Seattle. Get dressed and we'll talk about it."

Curiosity piqued, she headed for the shower, spent a little extra time washing and drying her hair, giving Luke a chance to work on his Japanese.

She couldn't help thinking what an amazing man he was. Tough and smart, and yet there was a tender side most people missed.

Half an hour later when she walked back down the hall, dressed and ready to face the day, Luke was still working, still mumbling, going over Japanese phrases. She wondered if the smattering of Chinese he'd learned helped him with the pronunciation.

Thinking of how much she had to do, she sighed as she continued past him into the kitchen for a cup of coffee. She hadn't been back to her apartment since Luke had picked her up Sunday, so she didn't have her car. She meant to remedy that today.

Besides collecting her vehicle and clothes, she wanted to check on Booth. He'd been doing better each time she visited. She thought maybe he'd be moving back to his own apartment soon.

She wondered how April and Ginny were holding up, but in order to talk to her sister, she would have to go through the FBI. Better to wait until she had something to report. She wondered if Agent Danfield had found the mole in the department. Until he did, even with round-the-clock protection, April and Ginny wouldn't be completely safe.

Fidgeting with so much on her mind, she poured a mug of coffee and paced over to the window in the living room. Three stories below, cars rolled by on the Bellevue streets. In the distance, she could see a patch of green in the shape of a rectangle, a small nearby park.

She was sipping her coffee, getting antsy, anxious to get on the road, when Luke walked out of his office and ambled down the hall in her direction.

Her gaze ran over the snug T-shirt and jeans that defined the hard muscles and sinews underneath. She couldn't help remembering what it was like to be in bed with him, how good that amazing body felt, pressing her down in the mattress.

Emma glanced away, trying to hide her thoughts, but Luke must have recognized the lust in her eyes, because she clearly recognized it in his.

"I guess I should have nudged you awake this morning," he said as he came up behind her, leaned down and nibbled the side of her neck. "My mistake."

Heat rolled through her. She tried to pretend she wasn't interested. "We don't have time for that—at least not right now."

Luke sighed and backed away, apparently deciding to behave himself. "You're right. We need to talk to Ryan Masaki."

"Tell me about him."

"Masaki's the head of the Yakuza family in Seattle—he's their *kumicho*. His subordinates, the *kobun*, report directly to him. There are a number of different factions in the area—the whole organization is set up in tiers."

"Interesting."

"In the articles I read, Masaki claims the Yakuza is going legit."

She cocked an eyebrow. "Legit? You mean no guns, no drugs, no human trafficking?"

"Masaki has a different vision for the organization. Apparently the idea started in Japan in the seventies and eighties. The Yakuza got into the building business, then tapped into distribution and transportation, long-haul trucking, that kind of thing. Easy credit in the eighties allowed them to get into real estate. In the past few years, they've taken over huge corporations that have earned them millions of dollars. Masaki claims the days of intimidation and violence are over."

"So I guess they weren't using violence and intimidation outside the Golden Lily the other night."

Luke chuckled. "Supposedly Masaki holds a view different from some of the other family members."

"I can't wait to hear what he has to say."

"Good, because I called his office this morning. I told his secretary I was with the Seattle *Times*. I made an appointment for an interview with one of the paper's journalists and her cameraman—that would be us—at four o'clock this afternoon."

"Are you crazy? We don't have any credentials. No way are they letting us in without them."

"I've got software that can create press badges. We print them, get them laminated, and we're set."

Mug cradled between her hands, Emma took a sip of coffee. "Once we get into the office, you aren't going to threaten to cut off his finger, are you?"

Luke shot her a look. "In this case, I don't think that's the best approach. Hey, the guy is the president of a big retail clothing chain—just your ordinary successful businessman. At least that's what he claims. He isn't going to do anything to us while we're there. We'll just ask him a few questions, see what he has to say, and play it by ear."

"You aren't worried the Yakuza will come after us? I thought we were going to stay off their radar."

"I'm banking on the split within the group. If what I read is true, then Vance is on one side with certain Yakuza members, and Masaki's on the other. We just need to convince the guy it's in his best interest to help us."

Emma shook her head. "You are one scary dude, Luke Brodie."

Luke's laughter rolled over her. "You in?"

"Sure. Why not? Oh, that's right. I might wind up missing one or all of my fingers, or—wait for it—I might end up dead."

Luke didn't seem to think that was funny.

With hours to spare, Emma asked Luke to take her back to her apartment to pick up her car. She told him she'd be at his place by three, plenty of time for them to reach the headquarters of Pacific North Clothing in Renton, southeast of Seattle, by four P.M.

Emma hadn't been home much lately. With Chelsea off on another sales trip and the nights being spent with Luke, the place seemed strangely empty and unfamiliar.

Emma shook off the thought. Considering Luke's history with women, she couldn't be sure she would be spending another night at his place, but just to be safe, she packed a few changes of clothes before grabbing her car keys and heading downstairs to her Mazda.

She drove over to Oakmont, wasn't surprised to find Booth sitting outside in the courtyard beneath the shade of a sycamore tree, talking to Nurse Wilson.

"Hi, Barbara." Emma smiled as she walked up.

"Hi, Emma, nice to see you." The nurse patted Booth on the shoulder. "It's almost time for lunch. I'll see you then."

Booth nodded and winked at her, giving the attractive older woman a lascivious glance as she walked away.

"You're terrible. You know that, right?"

"What do you mean? I'm a guy. I had a stroke—so what? I'll be back on my feet in no time, and once I am—"

Emma laughed. "I get it. I just came by to bring you up to speed on Vance, see if you had any ideas on where we should go from here."

"We? So I guess you're still sleeping with Mr. Wrong."

She ignored the quick flush that rose in her cheeks. "I told you—we're working together until we find Vance."

"Yeah, that's what you said. So where are you so far?"

She filled Booth in on everything that had happened since the last time she'd seen him, including the mole in the FBI, their run-in with the Yakuza, and Vance's connection to the group. She finished by giving him the details of their conversation with Grady Kelso.

"You're in deep water here, Emma," Booth said, frowning. "The Japanese mafia—Christ Almighty. Brodie's going to get you killed."

Irritation trickled through her. "It's not Luke's fault. He pressed me to quit, but I can't. I told you about the mole. April and Ginny won't be safe until we find Vance. At least now we know the Yakuza's the reason he came back to Seattle. He's trying to finalize some kind of deal with them."

She didn't mention the interview she and Luke planned to have with Ryan Masaki. She knew Booth would go off the deep end if she did.

"I wish I could talk you into letting the cops handle this," he grumbled. "You don't have enough experience to deal with people like these. Hell, I don't have enough experience."

"Luke's good—you know that. Better than good. So far, we're working very well together."

Booth shook his head. "I still don't like it."

Emma pulled out her cell and checked the time. She had to get back to Luke's. Leaning down, she kissed Booth's cheek. "I've got to run. If you think of anything, call me."

Booth just nodded.

"Here comes Barbara with your lunch." Emma smiled. "Don't do anything I wouldn't do." Waving at Barbara, she headed to her car.

After leaving Oakmont, she decided to make a stop at the Hide and Seek. Maybe the X-man or Bobby Grogan, another bounty hunter friend, would be there. She could grab a sandwich and catch up on the local gossip, see if she might learn something useful. Or maybe the owner, Mattie Jackson, would have heard something juicy, something related to Vance.

It was amazing how fast bail skip news traveled.

The Hide and Seek was noisy with the lunch crowd when Emma walked in, her sneakers squeaking on the worn board floors. There was a pool game going on. The cue ball hit the striped fifteen, which slammed into the eight, sending it into a corner. One of the players groaned.

Emma spotted the X-man's huge bulk spilling out of a

chair at a table against the wall, sitting next to his überfit sister, Nita. Emma walked over to join them.

"Hey, X, Nita. Good to see you guys."

"You, too, lady," Xavier said. He and Nita had almost finished their lunch, meat loaf, it looked like, the Tuesday special.

As Emma pulled out a chair and sat down across from them, Nita grinned.

"So how's that hottie you showed up with at the gym?" The question drew Xavier's shrewd attention.

"Luke's . . . umm . . . fine."

Xavier's black eyes narrowed. "Luke? You don't mean Luke Brodie?"

"Well . . . umm . . . yes. We've been working together to find Rudy Vance."

"He was with you at the gym? That class starts at eight in the morning."

She tried for nonchalance. "So what? Luke's an early riser."

X shook his head. "I warned you about him. You better be careful, lady."

"I need to find Vance. Luke's helping me. You know how important that is."

Xavier sighed. "Yeah, I know." He frowned. "Come to think of it, I haven't heard any gossip about Brodie lately. Maybe he's keeping it in his pants for a change."

"Nope, not Brodie." Mattie sailed up to the table to take Emma's order and collect Nita's and X's empty plates. "I heard he's got some hot babe moved in with him. Looks like he's off the market for a while."

Xavier's suspicious gaze shot to Emma.

"I'll have a burger, no fries, and a Diet Coke," Emma said, hoping to send his attention in a different direction.

"You got it." As Mattie took off to fill the order, X opened his mouth to say something, but Nita cut him off.

"Leave her alone, big man. Emma knows what she's doing." Nita patted Emma's hand and smiled.

But Emma didn't have the foggiest notion what she was doing when it came to Luke, aside from setting herself up for a broken heart.

"So . . . any new gossip I should know about?" she asked. "Anything that might help me find Rudy Vance?"

"I guess you heard Felix Riggs got himself fried," Xavier said. "Got his throat cut ear to ear."

She swallowed back a thread of nausea. She had learned that bit of news firsthand. "I heard." Her mind ran over the night Riggs had been murdered, which made her think of Vance, and an idea arose.

"You haven't heard any rumors about a dirty cop lately, have you? Someone taking payoffs in the SPD or the FBI?"

Xavier's thick fingers wrapped around the beer bottle in front of him. He tipped it up and took a drink. "If I'd heard, it wouldn't be the kind of news I'd be repeating. Info like that could get a fella killed."

"You'd tell *me,* though. Right?"

"I wouldn't tell anyone I wanted to keep breathing."

Emma narrowed her eyes at him. "You know something, don't you? I can see it in your face. All right—give. What's his name?"

Xavier sighed and shook his big head. "I don't have a name. I don't even know if it's true. It could just be the guy who said it's a malicious a-hole with a grudge against the cops."

"So someone mentioned something." Her heart was pulsing, shooting adrenaline through her veins. "Who'd you hear it from?"

"Bobby picked up a skip. On the ride downtown, the guy

said he'd just delivered a payoff to a lawman, said he could get money for Bobby if he'd turn him loose."

"Did the guy say if the payoff went to an FBI agent or a cop in the SPD?"

Xavier rubbed a hand over his face. "Shit, he said it was a fed."

Excitement poured through her. "Do you know the fed's name?"

"No."

"Okay, so what's the skip's name?"

"Dammit, Emma, even if you get the name, you can't go making accusations against an FBI agent. That could cause you all kinds of trouble."

"I need the skip's name, Xavier. I'll be careful how I use it."

Xavier sighed. "Terry Garcia. He's in lockup down at King County."

"Terry Garcia," she repeated as she rose from her chair. "Sounds a little like an ice cream flavor—you know, *Cherry Garcia*."

Xavier nodded. "Yeah, that's how I remembered it."

Emma leaned down and grabbed Xavier by the ears, bent, and kissed his forehead. "I owe you big-time." She dug her wallet out of her purse and dropped enough money on the table to pay her lunch bill. "I gotta go. I'll see you guys later."

"What about your burger?" Nita asked.

"Tell Mattie to sell it to someone else, or let X have it."

"Yeah," X said, grinning.

Nita leaned over and socked him. "Another burger is the last thing you need."

"Be careful, Emma," Xavier called out, watching over Nita's shoulder for Emma's burger to arrive. She laughed as she hurried out the door.

Chapter Twenty-Nine

Luke checked the time on his iPhone. During the hours Emma had been gone, he'd started working a different angle. He and Conner Danfield had exchanged cell numbers. Luke had called the FBI agent to see if the feds had made any progress in finding the leak.

"Not so far, but we're on it," Danfield had said.

Not good enough, Luke thought, but didn't say it.

"I'll let you know if I hear anything." Luke hung up the phone. Since the feds had nothing, he decided to talk to some of his informants, see if there was any word on the street that might lead to the dirty cop on Vance's payroll.

He made a handful of calls, came up with zip, then left the apartment and drove downtown to Pioneer Square. There were a couple of bars he haunted for information. At a lounge on James Street called the Sportsman, he talked to the bartender, a guy named Freddy Reeves.

"How about a Corona?" Luke asked as he sat down on a red vinyl stool at the bar.

"You got it." Freddy was older, tall and skinny, had worked there for as long as Luke could recall. Freddy popped the top on an icy bottle of beer and set it down on the counter.

"You still looking for Rudy Vance?" Freddy asked. The place was mostly empty, just a few regulars sitting at the far end of the bar, an old guy in a battered felt hat and seedy wool jacket and a wide-hipped woman with bleached blond hair.

"Looking, not finding," Luke said, tipping up his beer, taking only a swallow. He had work to do this afternoon. The beer was just a way to connect. "You heard anything lately?"

"Not a word."

"Too bad. Maybe you can help me with something else. I'm looking for a cop on the take, most likely a fed. The info could make you a nice chunk of change."

"A fed, huh? How much?"

"Say . . . a thousand?"

The bartender gave a grunt of approval. "I haven't heard a whisper, but for that kind of money, somebody might know something. I'll put the word out. If I hear anything, I'll let you know."

"Do that and there'll be something in it for you, too." Luke slid a hundred across the bar. "Thanks, Freddy."

The kind of information Luke wanted didn't come cheap. But he wanted Emma's sister and her daughter safe. Finding Vance was the only way to make that happen.

He headed back to his place to wait for Emma. By two-thirty he was pacing the floor. He reminded himself Emma was rarely late, which meant she should be there any minute.

At ten minutes to three she arrived, bubbling with such excitement, he found himself smiling.

"Looks like you had a good day," he said.

"I've got something, Luke. I got a lead on the leak in the FBI."

Luke's smile widened. "Great minds," he said. "I started working that angle this morning after you left. What have you got?"

"There's this guy in lockup down at King County. Skipped bail on a warrant—I don't know what for. Bobby Grogan brought him in. The thing is, the guy tried to bribe Bobby into letting him go, said he'd just delivered a payoff to a fed, said he could get money for Bobby, too."

"What's the skip's name?"

"Terry Garcia."

"Jeez, I've picked up Garcia a few times myself. The guy's always fucking up. If Vance is involved, this could be his first real mistake."

"I don't know if the payoff actually happened, or if it's connected in any way to Vance, but it's worth checking out."

"You bet it is. Good work, baby."

"I guess we don't have time to talk to him till we finish with Masaki."

Masaki. Luke glanced away. "Yeah, about that . . . I've, ah, been doing some thinking."

"And?"

"And I think it'd be better if I talk to him alone."

Her features tightened. "Why is that?"

"I might get more out of him, you know? Might get him to open up more if we talked man to man."

Emma planted her hands on her hips. "That's bullshit, Luke Brodie. You're improvising again. I thought we'd gotten past that."

Luke said nothing because it was true.

"You're just worried that if the interview goes wrong, it could bring the Yakuza down on our heads. That's what you're thinking about."

He clamped down on his temper. Sometimes he wished

Emma wasn't so damned smart. "Look, there's no way to
know if my take on the situation is correct. If I'm wrong,
we could have the Japanese mafia breathing down our
necks. I don't want you involved. I don't want to take the
risk that something might happen to you."

"Well, I don't want to take the risk that something might
happen to *you*."

Luke blinked. It wasn't the answer he'd expected. It
wasn't that often someone worried about him; it was usually the other way around.

Emma reached up and cupped his cheek. "We're good
together, Luke. We watch each other's backs. You've given
this idea a lot of thought—you always do. I trust your judg-
ment. We go in, talk to Masaki. We figure out where we
stand as we go along and proceed from there."

"I'd rather you stayed out of it."

"I'm going. That was our deal. We do this together."

Luke raked a hand through his hair. "I ought to leave
you here. I could cuff you to my bed—at least I'd know you
were safe."

Instead of anger, interest filtered into her pretty brown
eyes. "That might be . . . umm . . . fun sometime, Luke. Just
not today. We need to get going."

A shot of lust hit him like a brick. Pulling her into his
arms, he very thoroughly kissed her, then finally let her go.
"You're amazing—you know that, right?"

Emma smiled up at him. "Come on. We don't want to be
late."

Shaking his head, thinking thoughts he should be saving
until later, Luke followed her out of the apartment.

In the parking lot of the Pacific North Clothing headquarters building in Renton, a two-story cement block

structure with the company logo of a pine tree in a circle out in front, Emma climbed out of the passenger seat. They had decided to drive the Mazda, which looked more professional than Luke's battered Ford.

She accepted the laminated press pass he handed her, the fake Seattle *Times* badge he'd had made that morning. Emma clipped it on the pocket of her white cotton blouse. Along with a navy skirt, matching blazer, navy high heels, a briefcase, and her purse, she hoped she looked like a hardworking journalist.

Luke wore his jeans, a Henley, and sneakers. A Nikon camera with a Tamron lens he used for PI work hung around his neck.

They walked through the front door into the lobby, which was well appointed with brown leather sofas and chairs, the walls painted a soft cinnamon beige. Lots of wood and a mountain landscape tapestry hanging on the wall.

With a nod, Luke gave her the lead and she walked up to the counter where a small, fine-featured Japanese man in his early twenties worked as a receptionist.

"May I help you?" the young man asked.

"I'm Emily Lang. This is Lucas Bonner." Names Luke had printed on the badges. "We're here to interview Mr. Masaki for an article about him in the *Times*."

The young man smiled. "You're his four o'clock. Please follow me."

The receptionist left them with Masaki's personal assistant, a beautiful, black-haired Japanese woman, slender and very businesslike.

"Right this way." She opened the door to the president's office, which was done in the same outdoors motif as the rest of the building, and stepped back out of the way.

The company specialized in sportswear: down jackets, rain gear, snow boots, as well as pants, sweaters, and vests for men, women, and kids.

Masaki rose as they walked inside and the receptionist closed the door behind them. In a navy pin-striped suit and red power tie, he appeared to be exactly the corporate executive he claimed to be.

But there was a dark glint in his black eyes and a hard set to his features, the high cheekbones and blade-sharp nose. He was in his mid-fifties, fit, and from the way he looked them over, the man was no fool.

As he walked toward them from behind his desk, Emma caught a glimpse of ink at the neck of his starched white shirt. He was Yakuza. She wondered if his lean body was completely covered with tattoos.

"Ms. Lang, I presume."

For a moment, her courage faltered. He was going to know instantly she was a fraud. She flicked a glance at Luke, whose jaw was as hard at Masaki's. She couldn't fail. She couldn't let Luke down.

She summoned a smile and extended a hand. "I'm Emily Lang. This is my cameraman, Lucas Bonner."

Masaki relaxed a little, accepted the hand she offered, and gave it a firm shake. "Perhaps we could sit at the table."

"Yes, that would be good." She preceded him toward a round mahogany table and both of them pulled out chairs. Luke busied himself snapping photos of the two of them together.

"I'd like to know a little about you, Mr. Masaki," she began. "But before you start, I should tell you I've already read a number of articles. Besides you being the president of Pacific North Clothing, I know you're the leader of the

Yakuza here in Seattle. I'm particularly interested in your vision for the future of the organization."

Apparently used to this line of questioning, Masaki launched into the same sort of spiel Luke had read on the Internet, mainly that he wanted to rebuild the group's image and bring the organization into the twenty-first century.

"We are no longer the criminals people once believed," Masaki said with conviction. "We are simply members of an extended family with the goal of wanting to flourish and prosper."

Luke let the camera drop down on the strap around his neck and moved toward the table, walking with that pantherlike grace she had noticed when she had first met him. His strides ended in the predatory stance he took in front of Ryan Masaki.

"You say you're no longer involved in illegal activities, Mr. Masaki. You say you have no interest in pursuing the sort of business that made your group so much money in the past. But not all of your members are in agreement with you. Isn't that correct?"

Masaki's dark, assessing eyes ran over Luke. "I thought you were a photographer."

"I know how to take pictures. That isn't why I'm here. But before we continue, I need an answer to my question. Not all of your members agree with your vision of the future. Isn't that true?"

Masaki's features tightened. "Change is never easy, Mr. Bonner. So the answer is, no, not everyone in our organization agrees."

"How strong are your convictions?" Luke pressed.

Masaki rose from his chair. "You are not with the newspaper, are you?"

"We don't work for the paper," Luke said. "We're here

on something more important. I ask again. How strong are your convictions?"

Masaki's jaw hardened. For a moment, Emma didn't think he was going to answer. "It is quite simple, really," he said. "I do not intend to fail."

Luke's rigid posture eased. "There's a man, his name is Rudolph Vance. He's an escaped criminal wanted for murder."

Masaki did his best not to show recognition, but a slight tick leaped in his cheek.

"At the moment, Vance is attempting to solidify a deal with some of your people, a business venture that involves human trafficking, among other illegal activities. I'm hoping you'll be willing to help me bring Vance to justice before his association with the Yakuza unravels everything you've been working to achieve."

"Who are you?" Masaki asked with soft menace. He was several inches shorter than Luke, but the man emanated power and strength.

"My name is Brodie. I'm a bail enforcement agent. I'm hunting Rudy Vance. I need your help to find and arrest him, bring him to justice."

Several long seconds passed. As if a great clock ticked inside her chest, Emma counted every heartbeat. If Masaki balked, they would be on the Yakuza hit list.

His black eyes swung toward Emma, pinning her in her chair. "It took great courage to come here. Or great stupidity. Which is it, Ms. Lang?"

Emma's mouth felt dry. She had to force out the words. "I'm hoping you'll agree to help us. If you do, then our coming here won't be stupid. But it will take great courage on your part to do what is right for your people."

Luke's glance held a hint of respect. "What's it going to be, Masaki?"

The man turned the full force of his gaze on Luke. "Leave a number where you may be reached. I will let you know my decision."

That said, Masaki walked past Luke to the door, pulled it open, and disappeared out into the hall. The door closed firmly behind him.

Chapter Thirty

At the worried expression on Emma's face, Luke left a business card on Masaki's desk, set a steadying hand at her waist, and they walked out of the office, out of the building and back toward the Mazda at the rear of the lot.

He could feel her trembling. "You were great in there, Em. You did everything right. Now we just have to wait and see what Masaki decides."

"What if he tells the Yakuza we're still hunting Vance?"

"Then we find a way to deal with it. I'm hoping he'll stand by his convictions and give us the info we need."

"You think he will?"

He wanted to say yes. He even considered lying, but as Emma had said, those days were past. "I don't know. Depends if what he's telling us is the truth."

They reached her car and Luke pulled open the passenger door.

"Oh, darn it," Emma said. "I was so freaked out in there, I left my purse. I've got to go get it. I'll be right back."

"I'll get it for you," Luke said. Both of them turned away at the same instant. Two steps later, a deafening explosion ripped through the air as Emma's car erupted in a million fiery pieces, the blast so strong it sent both of them into the air, then slammed them down onto the pavement.

Hot metal and burning debris rained down as Luke crawled toward Emma. He covered her with his body, held on tight while car parts and shattered glass crashed down around them. He felt the hot bite of burning rubber searing through his shirt, felt the sharp edge of a chunk of metal slicing into the top of his arm.

A second explosion erupted, the gas tank blowing up, engulfing what was left of the car in a fresh round of flames. The smell of smoke and fuel filled the air.

Adrenaline pumping, Luke surveyed the parking lot, searching for the man who had detonated the bomb, the man who had been watching, waiting for them to come out of the building. Luke knew enough about explosives to be sure it was a manual detonation. No way for the bomber to know how long they would be inside and not enough time to attach a more sophisticated device.

Or maybe he just liked the high of watching someone burn.

Employees were streaming out of the building, people gathering to watch the flaming pile of rubble, but he couldn't pick out the bomber, probably long gone by now.

As soon as the debris had mostly settled back to earth, Luke pulled Emma to her feet and urged her farther away, out of danger. They sat down on a curb around the base of a tree at the edge of the lot. Emma was trembling, sucking in deep breaths of air.

"It's over, baby." He did a quick bone check, but nothing seemed to be broken. "You okay?"

"I'm . . . I'm okay." Her voice shook with the remnants of adrenaline and fear. "Just bruises and . . . and scrapes, but . . . Oh, God, Luke, they tried to kill us." She swallowed. "If I hadn't . . . hadn't forgotten my purse . . ." She didn't finish the sentence. If they hadn't taken those few steps away, both of them would be dead.

Luke's hand unconsciously fisted. "I guess we know Masaki's decision." Guilt swirled through him. He should never have brought her with him. "I'm sorry, Em. I shouldn't have let you get in this deep."

"You didn't have any say in it, Luke."

Several people ran over to make sure they were okay. Emma glanced down, saw the blood soaking the sleeve of Luke's shirt. "You're hurt!"

He had another gash on the back of his leg she couldn't see, painful but not as deep.

"We need to stop the bleeding."

Just then, one of the employees, a tiny Japanese woman, hurried forward, pulling a soft yellow scarf from around her neck. "Here." She handed the scarf to Emma. "You can use this."

Emma's voice shook. "Thank you." She wrapped the scarf around Luke's arm and pulled it tight. "You're bleeding pretty badly. You're going to need stitches."

Luke just shrugged. "Won't be the first time."

"I was bringing your purse," the tiny lady said. "Mr. Masaki said you left it in his office."

Emma took the purse and held it like a treasure, which it was, since it had saved both their lives. "Thank you."

Sirens wailed in the distance. Emma glanced over at the Mazda, no more than a burning heap of twisted metal. "I really liked that car."

Luke's gaze followed hers. "I'll get you another one, honey, I promise."

She just looked at him.

He tried to lighten the moment. "Hey, I know how you feel. I lost my favorite gun in that car. My Beretta was under the driver's seat." He was wearing his ankle gun, a little Glock .27 subcompact, but no way could he carry the Beretta into Masaki's office.

She sighed. "My pistol was in there, too." She opened the purse and looked inside. "At least I still have my .380."

So both of them had been carrying. Luke gave Emma another mark of respect.

Just then a fire truck careened around the corner, sirens blaring. It turned and bumped its way into the parking lot. A black and white police car drove in behind it, followed by a second smaller fire truck. Firemen in full turnout, heavy coats and big billed hats, jumped out and began unloading hoses.

"The cops are going to want answers," Luke said. "This is going to take awhile." He raked a hand through his hair and his fingers came away black with soot.

"We don't really know what happened," Emma said. "We just need to stick to that."

Luke nodded. "You're getting pretty good at this, honey."

"Yes, well, bounty hunting isn't going to be my long-term career choice. I can guarantee you that."

Luke didn't argue. At the rate things were going, they might not live long enough to have long-term careers.

His cell phone rang. He pulled the phone out of his pocket, saw the screen was cracked from hitting the ground so hard, cursed, and took the call.

"I had nothing to do with what just happened," Ryan Masaki said. "That is not how we do business. I will help you in any way I can."

"If it wasn't you, who's responsible?"

"I do not yet know."

"The bomb was detonated by hand. Someone had to be watching. How did they know we were here?"

"I cannot tell you that, either, but I will have answers very soon. Do we need to provide you with protection?"

Like he would feel safe with the Yakuza doing the protecting?

"Just find out who tried to kill us and make sure they don't do it again."

"You may be certain that I will. In the meantime, I would appreciate if you would not voice your suspicions about who planted the bomb."

"That should be easy enough, since I don't have a clue."

"Expect to hear from me soon." Masaki hung up the phone.

"Masaki's going to help us?" Emma asked.

"That's what he says. Says he wasn't involved and as angry as he was on the phone, I tend to believe him."

Emma looked relieved.

Luke hit the contact button for his brother's number, relaxed a little at the deep rumble of Ethan's voice. "E, there's been some trouble. I'm in Renton." He rattled off the address. "Someone blew up Emma's car. Can you pick us up?"

"Sonofabitch, little brother. Are you two okay?"

"So far, so good. Like I said, we got trouble. The cops are going to want answers. It might take awhile."

"Maybe I can help. I'm a ways from Renton, but I'll be there as quick as I can." The line went dead. Being a former detective, Ethan had an easy rapport with police.

As Luke pocketed the phone, he spotted the officers who'd gotten out of the patrol car walking toward them, one six inches taller than the other, both of them fairly young.

Luke shoved himself up from the curb and so did Emma. Sliding an arm around her waist, he drew her against his side. Both of them were pretty banged up and covered with grit and grime from rolling around in the parking lot. He had burns on his back and his arm hurt like hell. A chunk of metal had sliced through his jeans, cutting into his calf, but it wasn't bleeding all that much.

The tall cop looked at the blood-soaked scarf tied around his arm and the stream of red trailing down his sleeve.

"Ambulance is on the way," the guy said. "I'm Officer Benson. This is Officer Aiello. What's your name?"

"I'm Luke Brodie. This is Emma Cassidy."

"Can you tell us what happened?"

"Aside from the fact that Emma's car blew up, we have no idea."

Officer Benson looked over the cuts and bruises on their hands and faces. "Ambulance ought to be here any minute. Let's take this one step at a time. Why don't you start from the beginning?"

Luke started talking.

The ambulance arrived five minutes later, putting the conversation on hold. Besides the EMTs, there was a PA on board. She cut off his shirt and put fifteen stitches in his arm. They treated the burns on his back and the slash on the back of his leg, treated the cuts and scrapes on Emma's hands and face.

One of the EMTs gave him a green scrub top to wear, since his shirt was in pieces. By the end of the hour, he and Emma had given their statements, which were basically two versions of *Duh, we have no idea who blew up the car or why*.

Luke told the officers they were bounty hunters, which meant they had enemies. Could have been anyone.

Which was true, though the Yakuza or Rudy Vance was clearly at the top of the list.

About the time they finished, Luke spotted Ethan striding across the parking lot. His jaw was set in a grim, hard line, but when it came to dealing with the cops, it was always a relief to see him.

"Hey, big brother."

Ethan took a good long look at the smoldering vehicle now bathed in fire retardant foam, at the bandage on Luke's arm and the abrasions on his face. "How you doing?"

"I'm okay . . . considering."

Ethan's worried gaze went to Emma, who looked pale and shaken, the bruise on her forehead standing out against the pallor of her skin. She still had a faint yellow bruise on her cheek from their fight outside the Golden Lily. Luke felt a fresh shot of guilt.

"How're you holding up, sweetheart?" Ethan asked.

For whatever reason a female might have, she looked up at Ethan and burst into tears. Luke pulled her into his arms and just held her.

"She'll be okay," he said, kissing the top of her head, which his brother didn't miss.

"It's all right, Emma," Ethan said, resting a hand gently on her shoulder. "I know you feel like you need to be strong for Luke, but it's okay once in a while just to be a woman."

What the hell? So now that Ethan was married, he was an expert on women? Worst of all, Luke had a feeling his brother was right.

Emma made a little sound in her throat, cried a few seconds more, then shuddered and pulled herself together. Luke knew how strong she could be when the going got tough.

"I'm sorry," she said. "I didn't mean for that to happen."

Luke caught her chin and tipped her battered face up to his. "It's okay, baby. Getting almost blown up has a tendency to screw with anyone's head. Just remember, Masaki's going to help us. That means everything's going to be okay." *He hoped.*

Ethan walked over to the cops, who were still taking notes, spoke to them briefly, then returned.

"We can leave. They know how to reach you. Let's go back to the office."

"I'd rather just go home," Emma said, looking up at him with pleading brown eyes.

Luke tightened his hold. "Sorry, honey. We need to be somewhere safe. We'll go to the office and figure things out from there." They were going to BOSS, Inc. first, but ultimately, they would be staying at his cabin till this was over. The place wasn't luxurious, but it was extremely secure.

Emma took a deep breath and squared her shoulders. "You're right. I just . . . I wasn't prepared for anything like this to happen."

"No one's ever prepared for an attack like that," Ethan said as they headed for his big black Jeep.

Luke had the selfish thought he was glad they hadn't blown up the Bronco.

Chapter Thirty-One

There was already a meeting under way when Luke walked Emma into the BOSS, Inc. office. On the way to pick them up in Renton, Ethan had phoned the other guys and brought them up to speed on the bombing. Dirk in turn had filled them in on what he knew about the Yakuza and Rudy Vance.

Dirk, Ian, Sadie, and Nick were sitting in the conference room when Ethan, Emma, and Luke walked in.

"You two look like you've been hit by a garbage truck," Sadie said, her assessing gaze going over their bloody, torn, and filthy clothes, their scraped and battered faces.

Luke's mouth edged up. "Yeah, feels like it, too," he said.

"You both okay?" Sadie asked.

"We're fine," Luke said.

"Emma?" Sadie pressed, which told Luke she had passed some kind of test.

She managed a lackluster smile. "I admit I'm a little shook up, but I'm okay."

Sadie nodded.

Once they were seated, Luke updated them on the situation, briefly and with the calm focus that made him good at his job.

"So now you know the basics," he said. "I think we can count on Masaki to hold up his end of the deal. No way to know for sure, but my gut says he's heavily committed to taking the Yakuza legit. That means he'll take some kind of action to keep the dissenting faction in line."

"Finding the guy who detonated the bomb would be a good start," Ethan said darkly.

"With any luck," Luke agreed. "Someone had to have been surveilling my apartment. He wasn't there last night or I would have noticed. Whoever it was tailed us to Masaki's and put the bomb under Emma's car."

"Maybe he was watching my place," Emma said. "He could have followed me from there to your house."

Luke felt a chill. It was possible. Even probable, since his training kept him more aware. From now on, Emma wasn't going anywhere by herself. "Result's the same. Guy followed us, nearly ended us."

"Was the device on a timer?" Ian asked.

"Manual detonation," Luke said. "Looks like the plan was to wait till we came out of the building and set off the bomb once we got in the car, but we turned back at the last second and it threw off his timing."

Ethan swore beneath his breath.

"We need to get a look at the security cameras," Luke said. "See if the guy shows up somewhere."

"I'm on it." Ethan rose from his chair. He'd talk to the police, who would be checking the cameras already, try to find out what showed up on them. He was pulling out his cell as he left the conference room.

"Maybe Kelso gave you up," Nick suggested. "He's the guy who came up with Masaki's name, right?"

"Could be," Luke said. "Looks like the Yakuza got wind we were still hunting Vance and decided to do something about it."

"Maybe the bomber wasn't Yakuza," Emma said. "Maybe he works for Vance."

Luke's gaze swung to her. "You're right. That's another possibility we need to run down."

"Okay, so we let Masaki look at the Yakuza to find the bomber," Dirk said. "In the meantime, we check the security cameras and follow the Rudy Vance angle."

Luke nodded. "That sounds like our best option." He turned to Sadie, who still wore her worried, mother hen expression. "You've been working the shipping company angle. Have you had time to come up with anything?"

"I've narrowed the possibilities down," Sadie said. "At the moment, I'm focusing on a corporation called Allied Shipping. But I can't be a hundred percent sure it's the right company till I find a link to Vance. So far that hasn't happened."

"What do you know about the company so far?" Luke asked.

"That's part of what makes it interesting. Allied Shipping Corporation is owned by another corporation, owned by another corporation. Seems a little cloak and dagger, if you know what I mean. There are a lot of names, but so far none of them connect to Vance. I have a hunch he isn't anywhere on paper."

"That fits with what Kelso said. I need a list of every name you come up with. Maybe one of them will ring some kind of bell."

"We'll all take a look at the list," Ian suggested. "One of us might pick up something."

Luke nodded at his blond boss/cousin. "That'd be great, Ian. Thanks."

"I'll send the list to your inbox," Sadie said.

"Print it, will you?" Ethan asked as he walked back into the conference room, always happier working old school.

"Will do." Sadie started to pack up her laptop.

"Before you go," Luke said, "what kind of merchandise does Allied Shipping handle?"

"I looked at their manifests. It's a container company. Seems like they take just about anything they're paid to carry."

"Where do the shipments come from?" Emma asked. "Is there any place in particular?"

"I noticed a lot of containers coming in from Southeast Asia, mostly Indonesia, Thailand, and Vietnam."

"What was in them?" Emma asked.

"Let me take a look." Sadie sat back down, opened her laptop, and began her rapid-fire keyboard typing. She leaned back and studied the screen. "Looks like lots of electronic equipment and motor vehicle parts." She skimmed the pages. "Shipments of plastic products and clothing."

"Only maybe that isn't what's in the containers," Emma said.

Luke's gaze swung back to her. "Grady Kelso said Vance was trafficking with the Yakuza. Southeast Asia is a snake pit when it comes to the slave trade."

"That's it," Dirk said. "Got to be. Some of those shipping containers are bringing in people, not goods."

People locked inside forty-foot steel boxes. Ten days to two weeks for the ship to reach the States. No sanitation, very little food and water, jammed together in the darkness. Then the brutality they faced when they reached their destination: sold into sweatshops or pimped out as prostitutes. The thought made Luke's stomach turn.

Emma's eyes held the same look of horror he was feeling. In fact, all of their thoughts ran very much the same.

"We need to stop him," Nick said darkly, having dealt with a different sort of trafficking in Alaska.

"That's exactly what we're going to do," Luke said.

Sadie folded up her laptop and rose from the chair. "I'll keep digging. I'll get you those names and let you know what else I find out." She marched across the conference room and disappeared out the door, heading back upstairs to her office.

Luke checked his watch. It was getting late, after nine; day was sliding into darkness. At least the heavy traffic would be mostly gone by now.

His gaze went to Emma. She was a mess, her forehead bruised, her heavy dark curls in a tangle around her face. Her hands were scraped, her navy blue blazer torn. His chest squeezed. He should have kept her out of this.

"I need to get Emma home and get her to bed," Luke said.

Several pairs of eyes shot to his at his proprietary tone. Luke ignored them.

"She's exhausted," he said. "She's had more than enough excitement for one day."

"You're heading up to the cabin?" Dirk asked.

"Safest bet right now."

"Anything else we can do for you?" Nick asked.

"Not tonight. Tomorrow I'm going over to King County. I need to talk to an inmate named Terry Garcia. Apparently he recently delivered a payoff to a fed. Whoever it is may be the guy feeding Vance information on Emma's sister."

"I hate a dirty cop," Ethan grumbled. "Want me to talk to Garcia?"

Luke smiled thinly. "You think I'm letting you have all the fun?"

"I'm going with you," Emma said. "You think I'm letting *you* have all the fun?"

Ethan chuckled. Dirk just shook his head.

"Maybe we should let the FBI know about this," Emma

said seriously. "If the agent who took the payoff actually is on Vance's payroll, he may already know April and Ginny are back in Seattle. Maybe he's even given their address to Vance."

"She's got a point," Ian said.

Luke blew out a breath. "First we need to be sure the money Garcia delivered came from Vance. I figure there aren't many dirty federal agents in Seattle, so odds are it's Vance's guy. But if we give the feds Garcia's name and they go after him, he might clam up."

"He may be scared to roll on one of their own for fear of retribution," Nick said.

"I'd say you've got a better chance of getting the information than the feds do," Ethan said. "As for April and Ginny, the FBI already knows they have a mole. They'll be doing everything in their power to keep the safe house location a secret."

"Danfield has two worries at the moment," Luke said to Emma. "Keeping your sister and Ginny safe and finding the mole. If we tell him about the bomb, he's going to want answers we don't have. He's going to insist we stand down. I'd like to talk to Garcia before we go toe to toe with the FBI." Luke kept his gaze on Emma's face. "That work for you?"

It was her family that was at risk. The decision had to be hers.

"I'm not quitting, so we talk to Garcia before we go to the FBI."

He nodded. "Okay, then we stick to our plan. We can't get in to see Garcia tonight, but tomorrow, as soon as we can make it happen, we pay him a visit. We find out if Vance is behind the payoff. We get the name of the agent, then talk to the feds."

Luke shoved up from his chair. "Okay, that's it for now."

"Before you leave, you need to disable your cell phones," Ethan reminded them.

Luke nodded. "I've got a burner in the Bronco. I'll call you with the number."

"If you need backup—" Dirk started.

"I won't hesitate to call," Luke finished. He and Emma took the batteries out of their smartphones and made their way out of the conference room, returning to Ethan's Jeep for the short trip back to Luke's apartment, where the Bronco was parked.

He needed his ride, but now that his Beretta was history, he needed the Nighthawk .45 he kept as a backup weapon. There was a Glock .23 at the cabin, an easy gun for Emma to handle.

On the drive back to Luke's apartment, Ethan was careful of a tail. He circled the Jeep around the block to be sure the place wasn't being watched before pulling over in front of the building.

"Watch your six on the way up to the cabin," his brother said as Luke and Emma climbed out of the Jeep onto the sidewalk. "You run into any trouble, just call and I'm on my way."

"Will do," Luke said.

Ethan stayed in the car, keeping watch while Luke and Emma went up to his apartment to collect their gear. Luke told Emma to wait in the hall as he checked for any kind of tampering with the door and looked for any sign of explosives. Pulling his ankle gun, he went inside and cleared the rooms. Once he was sure it was safe, he motioned for Emma to come inside and both of them started collecting their gear.

Luke had plenty of clothes at the cabin so he didn't have to worry about that. And plenty of weaponry up there, too, but he liked the Nighthawk, and you could never have too much ammunition.

Emma packed whatever items she'd brought over to his place. He noticed her toothbrush missing from the holder in his bathroom. He hated to admit it, but he kind of liked seeing it there.

As soon as they were done, they took the elevator downstairs to the garage. He was careful again to clear the area, then spent some time with the Bronco, making a thorough check for any kind of explosive device that might have been attached.

Finding nothing, they climbed inside the vehicle and he fired up the engine, called his brother on the burner in his glove box, and gave him the number, told him they were on their way.

Luke glanced over at Emma as he drove out of the garage. She didn't relax until she was sure the Bronco wasn't going to explode.

April stood next to Special Agent Conner Danfield out on the patio behind the safe house. Ginny was up in her room with Rowdy, watching TV. She loved the little dog so much. They were practically inseparable. Adopting the puppy had been one of the best decisions April had ever made.

Along with April and her daughter, two FBI agents were on duty round the clock in the house, currently a man and a woman. Conner had arrived to check on them, had spoken to his agents, then, satisfied the house was secure, walked April out onto the patio for a few moments alone.

April glanced over at Con, who stood staring out past the yellow glow of the solar lamps at the edge of the patio, into the darkness beyond. Tension tightened the muscles across his shoulders and dug lines into his forehead. The muscles in his jaw looked taut.

She wanted to reach out and touch him, wipe away the worry she read in his face. Instead, she listened as he turned to her and started talking, filling her in on the progress he and his team had been making, which didn't sound like nearly enough.

"We're moving in the right direction," Con said. "But it isn't happening as fast we'd hoped. We need to find Vance before he leaves Seattle."

"I know you're doing your best," April said.

Con's sigh held a note of frustration. "I wish I could be here to protect you and Ginny, but I can't. I need to work this case and I can't do it if I'm here at the house."

"I know. I appreciate everything you've done for us, Con, everything you're doing to keep us safe."

"We're going to find him, April. Once we do . . ." He was looking at her in that way he had, as if he could see into her heart. If he could, he would see the deep respect she held for him, and the desire she fought whenever he was near.

He was so damned handsome. Lean and fit, with that tiny cleft in his chin. The well-tailored suits he wore only made him more attractive. At night she dreamed of him, imagined what it would be like to have him make love to her.

Maybe he was reading her mind, because he moved closer.

"I've only kissed you once," he said, reminding her of a single moment of weakness in Denver. "But I replay it over and over in my head. All I can think of is doing it again."

"Con . . ."

"I tell myself if I kissed you just one more time, I could put it out of my mind, at least for a while."

Her heart was racing, thrumming beneath her breastbone. She reached up and rested her palm against his cheek. "I want you, Con. I think about it all the time. I know that's a terrible thing to say, but—"

She gasped as he pulled her into his arms. His mouth came down over hers in a devastating kiss that burned right through her. Her insides turned liquid and her knees felt weak. When she gripped his shoulders, he deepened the kiss, taking it to a whole new level.

His kisses grew softer, more gentle, just a melding of lips, coaxing now, tasting and caressing. Con groaned as he pulled away.

"I shouldn't have done that," he said. "It's highly unprofessional." He stroked her cheek. "But I'm not sorry I did."

A little embarrassed, April shook her head. "It was my fault. I shouldn't have told you the way I feel."

A beautiful smile broke over his face. "I'm glad you did. I'm glad I'm not in this alone." He kissed her lightly one last time. "Let's just call what happened motivation. The sooner I catch Rudy Vance, the sooner we can be together."

April laughed, the sound so rare, it seemed foreign. She smiled up at him. "Okay, then, Special Agent Danfield, go to work. Catch Rudolph Vance and come back to us. Come back to me."

He reached down and caught her chin. "What I feel for you, April . . . it's more than just physical attraction. I want you to know that." Con dipped his head and kissed her one last time. Then he walked her back into the house and just kept going, heading out to his car, going back to work.

For several long seconds, April's smile remained in place. Then she thought of Rudy Vance and her daughter and the danger they still faced, and her warm smile slid away.

Chapter Thirty-Two

This time of night, there wasn't much traffic. Emma figured the drive out of the city to Luke's cabin in the hills wouldn't be too long, but he was taking evasive action, making sure they weren't followed.

Weaving in and out of traffic, Luke seemed to have one eye glued to the rearview mirror and one on the cars in the lanes around them. All the while, his hands gripped the wheel, making a series of high-speed maneuvers, then slowing, turning, roaring down an off ramp, then getting back on the freeway somewhere else and starting the process all over again.

Eventually he seemed satisfied they were in the clear and slowed to the speed limit, a change from his usual too-fast driving.

Luke had told her the cabin was off May Creek Road above the small town of Gold Bar, on sixty acres of evergreen and deciduous trees.

"We'll be safe there," he said as the Bronco rolled through the darkness. "The property is completely enclosed, but the ten acres around the house have additional security. Along with an eight-foot chain-link fence, the perimeter has a state-of-the-art alarm system and first-rate security cameras."

Emma sighed. "After what happened, that sounds amazingly good."

"It's off the beaten path for sure, but the good news is the area has cell service. That's one of the reasons I bought the property."

At the thought of Rudy Vance or the Yakuza being able to track them through the GPS on their smartphones, a little shiver ran through her.

"Good thing we disabled our cells," she said.

He sliced her a glance. "I've got a couple of extra burners at the cabin." Luke's gaze locked with hers. "I have to warn you, the place is pretty rustic. I built a lot of it myself after I left the army. Kind of a personal retreat, you know?"

Her gaze went to his hands, thought of them wielding a hammer, thought how strong and capable those hands were. How gentle they could be sometimes.

"Rustic," she repeated. "So not a place you bring your lady friends, I don't imagine."

He laughed. "Not if I ever want to get laid again."

Emma managed to smile, though thinking of Luke with someone else wasn't the least bit funny. "So I should feel privileged?"

He cast her a look. "It's different with you."

She didn't press him for more. She understood what he meant. They'd gotten so close lately. Luke could say anything to her and she felt the same about him. It was starting to scare her.

She knew Luke well enough to know that sooner or later he was going to start feeling boxed in. If it weren't for the danger they faced, he might already be gone.

Her heart throbbed. She was in love with him. Which

was bound to end in disaster, at least for her. But she couldn't think about it now, not with so much at stake.

The Bronco turned off the main road and climbed higher into the hills. There weren't many streetlights out here, just the yellow glow through the windows of an occasional farmhouse. A black and white dog ran into the road, barking and racing toward the moving wheels. Before she could shout a warning, Luke had swerved around the dog, leaving it in the darkness behind them.

Her heartbeat slowed and she relaxed back in her seat. "That was close."

"I'm used to it. Lots of deer out here."

She didn't see the property until they had almost reached the gate. Luke pulled an electronic opener out of his glove box, clicked it, and the gate swung slowly open. Once inside, he got out and slid a heavy chain around the two gate halves, padlocking it closed.

"Ethan would call that *old school,*" he said as he climbed back inside. "No way can they jam the signal, but if by some miracle they did, at least the chain would slow them down a little."

"You think they can find this place?"

"Be pretty damned hard. The property is owned in a fictitious name. After I started working as a bounty hunter, I began taking extra precautions."

They reached the cabin, which appeared as rustic as Luke had said, constructed of logs, with a small covered porch out front that looked down into the valley below.

He opened the front door and she walked inside. "Security cams right here." He tipped his head toward a row of screens on the wall next to the door.

"Bedroom's in there." He pointed down the hall, tossing her a look filled with enough heat to make her stomach contract. "Only got a queen bed. Like I said, I usually come here by myself or with some of the guys. They toss their sleeping bags down on the floor in the living room."

"I'm used to a queen," she said. And snuggling with Luke? She remembered what had happened in her apartment and felt like fanning herself.

He went back to his tour. "There's a small bath with a shower at the end of the hall, nothing fancy. The kitchen has a propane stove and refrigerator. Windmill and solar run the generator, which powers the lights and the well. Wood-burning stove in the living room provides the heat."

"So you're pretty much self-contained."

He shrugged. "Pretty much."

One of her eyebrows went up. "You aren't one of those survivalists, are you?"

Luke smiled. "If that means, can I survive up here if the world turns completely to sh . . . worms? Then I guess you could say that. It wasn't the reason I built the place, but being so far off the grid has come in handy more than once."

"Like right now."

His features darkened at the reminder of the bomb. "Yeah."

He went back out to the SUV and brought in their gear, tossed it on the floor of the living room. "I've got one of those instant hot water heaters. Why don't you go in and take a shower? Make you feel better."

"I won't argue with that. A shower sounds wonderful."

"While you're in there, I'll fix us something to eat."

"Are you sure? You're the one who got hurt today. I should be taking care of you. Your arm has to be hurting like crazy."

He glanced at the bandage around his bicep. "I'll just open us a can of soup or something. Tomorrow we'll get some real groceries in here."

"All right." Since she wasn't a martyr and she felt pretty crappy herself, she disappeared down the hall.

After a steamy shower that went longer than it should have, she came out in a pair of blue sweatpants and a gray short-sleeve sweatshirt with a Seattle Mariners logo on the front. Not exactly glam, but she was going for comfort tonight.

As she walked toward the kitchen, the smell of vegetable soup hit her and her stomach growled, reminding her how long it had been since she'd eaten.

Luke filled a bowl for her and set it on the small oak kitchen table. They both sat down and started eating, both so tired they didn't say a word.

"It's your turn to shower," Emma said when they had finished. "I'll clean up in here."

For once, Luke didn't protest, just turned and headed down the hall, which said how bad he was really hurting.

"Be careful not to get your bandages wet," she called after him.

Luke just kept walking. A few minutes later, she heard the shower go on. She had the kitchen cleaned up, the dishes washed and put away when he walked back down the hall.

A clean pair of dark green sweats with a U.S. Army star hung low on his hips. His beautiful muscled chest was bare, the bands of sinew moving as he towel-dried his sun-streaked brown hair.

Emma felt a ridiculous shot of lust. She glanced away, hoping he wouldn't see. "How's . . . umm . . . your arm? I think we should change the bandage before we go to bed."

His head came up at the word. His gorgeous blue eyes held the same lust Emma was feeling.

"Oh, no," she said. "You have stitches in your arm, a cut

on your leg, and burns all over your back. You need to take a pain pill and go to sleep."

"What about you? You're exhausted, baby. I told the guys I was going to take care of you. You need to get a good night's rest."

A minute ago sleep was exactly what she wanted. Now looking at all that male virility wrapped in such a tempting package, sex was the only thing on her mind.

"I don't feel like sleeping right now," she said, walking toward him.

Luke's eyes darkened. "You sure?"

"I say we sleep later—on one condition."

"Yeah? What's that?"

"First I change your bandage. Then you let me . . . umm . . . handle things. You were hurt trying to protect me. You took care of me after what happened at the Golden Lily. It's my turn to take care of you."

His eyes sparked with interest. "I know I should argue. You're in pretty bad shape yourself."

"Now that I've had my shower, I'm feeling much better." She didn't tell him she felt good enough to rip off his sweatpants, drag him down on the sofa, and have her way with him. That just would not do.

A sexy smile broke over his lips. "All right, we do it your way. I want you, and the truth is my damned arm is killing me."

Emma took his hand and led him over to the sofa. "Okay, then, sit down and let's get this done."

He eased down on the sofa a little more slowly than she had expected. Earlier, as Ethan had driven them back to his office, he had stopped at a pharmacy to pick up some ointment and the prescription Luke had been given for pain pills. The dose called for two, but Luke had only taken half of one, in case they ran into trouble.

Under the sink in the bathroom, she found an emergency kit, along with bandages of every shape and size. In minutes she'd finished re-dressing the gash on the top of his arm—which wasn't that easy with Luke massaging her breasts through her sweatshirt and biting the side of her neck.

She slapped his hand away. "Will you behave? I need to get this done and you, Luke Brodie, are not helping."

He flashed a wicked grin. "I'm going to give you all the help you need just as soon as you're finished."

Her stomach melted. All the man had to do was look at her and she went hot all over. Forcing her mind back to her work, she replaced the bandage on the back of his leg. The burns on his back were covered, the bandages surprisingly dry and still looking good.

She smiled. "You're all set."

Before she could move, Luke reached up and slid his hands into her hair. Pulling her mouth down to his, he claimed her lips in one of those slow, deep, Luke Brodie kisses that seemed to have no end. Beneath his soft cotton sweats, she could feel his hardened arousal, and her whole body went warm. Emma moaned into his mouth, but before things went too far, she pulled away, determined to take charge.

"Just sit there and try to relax," she said. Bending down, she kissed the corner of his mouth, placed soft kisses along his throat and across his powerful shoulders.

Luke pulled her sweatshirt off over her head, cupped and massaged her breasts, caught her mouth in another steamy kiss—and sweet Lord, the man could kiss.

It took all her will to ease away. Trailing kisses lower, she pressed her lips against the muscles on his lovely naked chest, down the hard ladder across his stomach.

Luke hissed in a breath as she knelt on the floor in front of him and pulled the cord at the waist of his sweatpants.

She had never done this for him, never used her hands and mouth to give him the kind of pleasure he had given to her.

She did it with great relish now, loving the power she held, making him fight for control. His breathing grew ragged. A low growl rumbled in his throat.

She was well on the way to bringing him to climax when his hands spanned her waist and lifted her astride him.

"I want to be inside you when I come," he said, burying his face in her hair.

"I want that, too," she whispered. Wrapping her legs around his waist so he wouldn't hurt his back, she eased herself down on him, took him deep, and started to move. Luke filled his hands with her breasts and she arched backward to give him better access.

She loved the thick feel of him, loved the way he gripped her hips and took charge. She loved the way he looked at her as if she were the most desirable woman in the world.

God above, she loved everything about Luke Brodie, and as she reached her peak and hot pleasure speared through her, as Luke groaned and reached his own release, Emma knew, no matter what happened, she would never regret giving her heart to Luke.

Chapter Thirty-Three

A light rain formed puddles on the ground outside the cabin. The sullen sky warned it could be a long, rainy day. Luke grabbed his brown bomber jacket off the rack next to the door, then helped Emma into her raincoat.

In concession to the cool mid-June weather, she was wearing black leggings beneath a long, cable-knit sweater and a pair of low-heeled boots. They were on their way down the mountain, headed for the one-thirty visit with Terry Garcia that Ethan had arranged at King County Adult Detention, the earliest time they could get.

Garcia had been arrested for burglary—this time—skipped bail, and thanks to bounty hunter Bobby Grogan, was now back behind bars.

The guy was a complete loser.

Luke hoped Garcia was Vance's delivery boy. If so, he hoped they could find a way to get the rat to fink on the rat in the FBI.

"Do we know which unit Terry's in?" Emma asked as the Bronco headed for downtown Seattle. The day had worsened, the sky dark with the threat of even heavier rain. As the SUV wove through the downtown streets, people hurried along beneath umbrellas, some on bicycles, ignoring the dampness in the air. Seattle folks were used to the wet Pacific Northwest weather.

"According to Ethan," Luke said, "Garcia's on the ninth floor, N-wing, upper tier, tank C. Ethan talked to a guy named Andrew Monroe. He'll be expecting us."

"I know Andrew. He's the assistant administrator."

There was something in her voice. Luke flicked her a sideways glance. "How do you know Monroe?"

"We met through friends. He's . . . umm . . . asked me out a couple of times."

A fine thread of jealousy slipped through him. He knew Monroe. Good looking, smug, believed he was God's gift. "You sleep with him?"

Her gaze shot to his and a spark of anger flashed in her eyes. "Not that it's any of your business, but no. He isn't my type and even if he were, I've been too busy to date."

Relief trickled through him. She was too busy to date. But not too busy to spend her nights in his bed. He relaxed back against his seat.

Her words came back to him. *Too busy to date,* she'd said, and he supposed that was true. Aside from the bar-beque at Ethan's where she was mostly doing him a favor, they had never actually been out on a date. It didn't seem right somehow.

Their destination neared. Up ahead on Fifth Avenue, King County jail was a complex of multistoried buildings. Parking the Bronco in a nearby parking structure, they made their way inside, up to the front counter.

The receptionist smiled at him, a redhead named Susan Barry. He'd forgotten she worked there.

"Hello, Luke, good to see you."

"Hey, Susie. Been awhile. Sue, this is Emma Cassidy. We're here to see a prisoner named Terry Garcia. Andrew Monroe set it up."

She glanced down at the screen. "Yes, it's right here on my computer. You'll be in a private room in the visitor section." She rattled off Garcia's location, the same info he'd gotten from Ethan.

Susie handed Emma a badge, then one to him. "You've been here before. You know where to go."

"Thanks." Luke clipped on his visitor pass. Emma clipped hers on, and they started off down the hall.

"Susie, huh?" Emma's voice held a thread of irritation. "Who was she? One of your women?"

His mouth edged up. He liked that she sounded a little jealous, too. "She wasn't one of my women. In case it's slipped your mind, you're the only woman in my bed. Susie's happily married to one of the corrections officers."

She gave a little huff that made him smile, and picked up her pace.

They made all the right turns and ended up where they were supposed to be. Monroe had a guard waiting to meet them—short, sandy hair, a few extra pounds around the middle. Rosetti was printed on his name tag.

"They just brought him in," Rosetti said, pointing through the window of the glassed-in private room where Terry Garcia, in an orange jumpsuit, sat in a chair on one side of the table.

Luke held the door for Emma, then walked in behind her. Both of them sat down across from Garcia, a little guy with jet black hair and the cocoa complexion of a Latino. A couple of jailhouse tats covered the backs of his hands and the side of his neck, but they were mostly for show, since Terry was the furthest thing from a tough guy.

Luke gave him a friendly smile. "Hey, Ter. How's it goin', man? I can't believe you're back in here again."

"I was framed, man," Terry said.

"That's too bad. Terry, this is Em Cassidy. She's a bounty hunter. You might have heard of her."

He looked her up and down, taking in her small stature, underestimating her the way most men did. "I thought you was a man."

Emma just smiled. "Nope, never have been."

"The reason we're here, Terry, is we got a tip you've been working for Rudy Vance."

Garcia's black eyebrows shot up. "I don't know nothing about no Rudy Vance."

"Well, we think you do, Ter."

Garcia's eyes shifted back and forth between Luke and Emma. "You hunting him?" Garcia asked.

"That's right."

"Who told you about me and Vance?"

Bingo. Garcia never did have a brain. "Guy's a bad dude, Ter. Cops know you work for him. You could be looking at some serious time."

"I'm in for burglary, man. With good behavior, I'm outta here in six months."

"That's what I'm sayin'. That burglary charge is nothing. Now this thing with Vance—you don't do something to save yourself, you're going away for a very long time."

Garcia squirmed in his chair, looking more and more worried.

Emma smiled at him. "We can help you, Terry, but we need your help in return. We know you were just doing a favor, just delivering some money to a guy Vance owed. We need to know the name of the guy who took Vance's money."

"I'm not talkin'. I know my rights."

"The thing is, Ter, we know the guy's a fed," Luke said. "We just need a name."

"No way, man." Terry's handcuffs rattled on top of the

table. "I don't want those guys coming down on my shit, man. You know what I mean? A guy could get killed that way."

"Look, Terry. The FBI wants this guy. They don't like a dirty cop any more than anyone else. They'll be grateful to you for giving him up. Now what's his name?"

Terry looked everywhere but at Luke. Finally he turned back, his eyes dark and scheming. "I give you his name, what do I get in return?"

Luke had been expecting this. Garcia wasn't the kind of guy to do anybody a favor. "That's a fair question, Terry. I'll tell you what I'll do. I'll talk to my contact at the bureau, see if he can get you some kind of deal. Would that work for you?"

"I want witness protection. I'm not going against Vance and the FBI. Not unless they're willin' to protect me."

Garcia was right. If he testified against Rudolph Vance and an FBI agent, he was definitely going to need protection. "All right, I'll talk to them, see what I can do." Luke rose from his chair and Emma stood up, too.

"You get them to help me, you'll give you the name."

Luke nodded. "I'll be back in touch as soon as I can."

The door at the rear of the room opened and the guard who'd brought Garcia in came back to get him. Terry tossed a last glance over his shoulder. In a flash of orange, he disappeared out the door.

"You're going to call Danfield?" Emma asked as they left the visitor area and walked back to the reception room to return their badges.

"Yeah. I'll call, see if we can get him to meet us somewhere."

"Somewhere besides FBI headquarters."

"Copy that," Luke said.

* * *

Emma and Luke waited for Special Agent Danfield in a little café called Aurora on Third Avenue not far from the jail. The interior was stark, mostly scattered round mesh tables with wood-and-wire chairs. Luke was almost finished with the slice of blueberry pie he had ordered. Emma was enjoying a cup of cappuccino when Danfield walked in.

He spotted them immediately and started toward them, his khaki raincoat flapping around his long legs. He sat down in a chair across from them and a waitress hurried over, a pretty little blonde with a ponytail.

"Hi, I'm Dottie," the blonde said, giving Conner the once-over, though he didn't seem to notice. "What can I get you?"

"Just coffee," Con said with a non-smile that hurried her on her way.

"How are April and Ginny doing?" Emma asked, anxious for any news.

"April's worried. She's terrified Vance will find them again. Ginny's hanging in there. She's a brave kid." He sighed. "We need to get Vance off the streets."

"We're hoping we can help you with that," Emma said.

The waitress returned with a porcelain mug filled to the brim. "Cream and sugar?"

"No, thanks," Con said absently, cradling the warm cup between his hands as she walked away. "On the phone you said you had something. What is it?"

Luke shoved his empty plate aside. "I'm afraid it's not that simple. We've got a lead on your mole. I can get you a name, but the guy wants witness protection."

"Christ. Making that happen isn't easy." He rubbed a

hand over his face. "What makes you think the guy's for real?"

"He's for real, a bail skip named Terry Garcia. He got picked up by a bounty hunter friend of Emma's. Garcia bragged to him about paying off a fed."

One of Danfield's dark eyebrows hiked up. "When you called, you said you'd talked to him. Are you convinced he's telling the truth?"

"He's a lowlife. In a roundabout way, admitted to working for Vance. I think he made the payoff."

"We need that name, but witsec . . ." Conner shook his head.

"Look, Danfield, the guy's not suicidal. You want him to testify against Rudy Vance and an FBI agent. He's going to need protection."

Luke was right. Emma knew it and Conner did, too.

"You've got nothing to lose, Danfield," Luke pressed. "If the lead doesn't pan out, you don't have to keep your end of the bargain."

Conner seemed to mull that over, then started nodding. "All right, I'll see what I can do."

"If you don't want him changing his mind, you better do it quick."

"Like today," Emma added.

Con started digging for his phone.

"One more thing," Luke said, stopping him. "Vance is in bed with the Yakuza. They're running some kind of smuggling operation."

"That's not exactly news. We got word yesterday, been trying to figure out how Vance fits in."

"Yeah, well, here's something that is news. Yesterday, one of the Yakuza tried to blow us to kingdom come. Damn near succeeded."

"Jesus!" For the first time Conner noticed the bruise on Emma's forehead. "Are you two okay? What happened?"

"We're lucky to be alive," Emma said.

"Someone followed us," Luke said, "put a bomb under Emma's car."

"Luke got the worst of it. He protected me with his body while fire and metal rained all over the parking lot."

"Jesus," Conner repeated, his gaze going back to Luke. But most of Luke's injuries were on the back half of his body, since he had been on top of her. She ignored a little shiver.

"You sure it was Yakuza?" Danfield asked.

"Odds are," Luke said. "We were talking to Ryan Masaki just before it happened. Claims he had nothing to do with it. I think he could be telling the truth. Could be a different faction, at odds with where Masaki believes the group should be headed."

Conner nodded. "Trouble's brewing inside his organization, one faction against the other."

"That's right. So . . . anything you want to tell us that might keep us from getting dead?"

Con sighed. "We figure they're into human trafficking, probably a lot more than that. We don't have any specifics."

He turned in Emma's direction, his coffee untouched and growing cold on the table. "You need to back off, Emma. You and Brodie both. This is FBI business. Aside from that, your involvement could get you killed."

Emma made no reply. She wasn't quitting till they found Rudy Vance. Which Luke clearly knew, since he didn't try to convince her.

"We need to get back to County and talk to Garcia," Luke said. "Get him to give you that name."

Conner pulled out his cell phone, stood up from the

table, and walked away where he could speak privately. A few minutes later, he returned.

"If Garcia gives us a name and it looks credible, we'll protect him."

Luke rose, dropping enough money on the table to cover the check. Emma stood up, too. "Let's go," Luke said, setting a hand at Emma's waist.

"I can handle Garcia," Conner said. "The FBI will take it from here. You two need to stay out of it."

"I told you it wasn't that simple. Maybe you can get Garcia to talk, and maybe he'll clam up. Garcia knows me. He trusts me to keep my word." He tipped his head toward the door. "Let's get this done."

Conner's jaw went tight. He said something beneath his breath, then reluctantly, started walking.

Outside the café, they had headed for their vehicles just as Luke's cell phone rang. He held up a hand and Danfield paused.

Emma couldn't hear what was being said, but Luke's fingers went tight around the phone.

"Thanks for the call." His gaze went to Danfield as he disconnected.

"What's going on?" Conner asked.

"That was my office. Andrew Monroe, assistant admin at King County called there looking for me. He knows the situation with Garcia. He said to say our source just dried up. Garcia got shanked on the way back to his cell. He's in surgery. It doesn't look good."

Con swore softly.

"Fuck," Luke said.

Chapter Thirty-Four

Con Danfield stepped out of the elevator on the surgical floor at Virginia Mason Medical Center, where Terry Garcia had been transferred. Emma and Luke Brodie followed in his wake.

After Brodie had shown up uninvited at the safe house, Con had run a check on him. Born in Texas. Mother deceased, father remarried and living in North Carolina. Moved to Seattle a few years back and went to work for Brodie Operations Security as a bounty hunter, just like he'd said.

Before he'd been wounded and left the military, he was Army Special Forces. Con had to go deep to find out he'd been a Delta operator. Con figured the guy was way too arrogant and used to being in charge, but he was also beyond capable of taking care of April's younger sister, which was comforting. Con wanted Emma safe. April and Ginny had suffered enough already.

Unfortunately, he had also discovered Brodie's rep as a first-class womanizer. The guy was a real heartbreaker, and the way Emma looked at him, she was going down hard.

Or at least that was how it seemed.

But there was something else going on, something

happening with Brodie that didn't quite fit. Con knew what it was like to fall for a woman. He was half in love with April and he'd only kissed her twice.

With the awful circumstances of her daughter's rape, it hadn't taken long to see what a caring mother she was, to understand she was smart and determined and stronger than she first appeared. Con hadn't realized he was looking for a woman like April until he had found her.

He wondered if the same thing could be happening to Luke. The possessive gleam in Brodie's eyes whenever he looked at Emma made him wonder if the guy had finally met his match. Emma had trained hard to become a bounty hunter, and according to what he'd heard, she was damn good at her job. But Emma had a soft, feminine side that reminded him of April.

For a tough man like Brodie, it was a combination that might be impossible resist.

Striding along the corridor, Con spotted a white-coated doctor, clipboard in hand, stethoscope around his neck, brown hair and a small goatee, walking in his direction.

"Special Agent Conner Danfield," Con said, flashing his badge. "I'm here for an update on an inmate named Terry Garcia. He was brought in a little over an hour ago."

"I'm Dr. Cardwell. We spoke on the phone. Mr. Garcia is still in surgery. He suffered stab wounds to the stomach, groin, and liver. He's in critical condition."

"I need to speak to him. How long before he's out of surgery?"

Above the goatee, the doctor's mouth thinned. "If he survives, Agent Danfield—and that remains to be seen—Mr. Garcia won't be speaking to anyone for quite some time."

"It's extremely important," Con pressed. "I just need a few moments."

Cardwell shook his head. "I'm sorry. You're welcome to call, check on his status."

Con shoved aside his irritation. It wasn't the doctor's fault Garcia was lying near death, that he might not even survive the surgery. Cardwell was only doing his job.

"I'll check back," Con said.

The doctor walked away, passing Emma and Brodie in the corridor.

"You heard?" Con asked them.

"Yeah," Luke said. "This case sucks."

"Did they catch the man who knifed him?" Emma asked.

"They caught him. Lifer named Bull Thompson. Looks like Vance got to him, offered him something he wanted. Guy had nothing to lose."

"Poor Terry," Emma said softly, and Con caught Luke's glance in her direction.

"You two might as well go," Con said. "Nothing's going to happen here."

Luke's gaze met Emma's as if he knew her thoughts. "We're in this thing till it's over, Danfield. Be better if we helped each other."

"You're right," Con said, meaning it. "The last thing I want is for something to happen to Emma. April and Ginny have been through enough already. If anything new turns up, I'll let you know."

Brodie just nodded. As he and Emma walked off down the corridor, Con glanced at the doors leading into the surgical ward. Maybe Garcia would surprise them and come through okay. Maybe the guy would give him the name of the mole.

He blew out a slow, frustrated breath. And maybe rats would stop eating garbage.

* * *

The rain had let up, dark clouds hung over the city, and a thick mist choked the air. Luke pulled up the collar of his leather jacket and shoved his hands into his pockets. His cell phone signaled a text as he and Emma crossed the hospital parking lot.

Pulling his phone out, he read the message at the bottom of the screen. Got news. Call when you can. Sadie. He showed Emma the screen.

"I wonder what she found," Emma said.

"Let's go find out. We need to regroup, anyway, figure our next move."

"Maybe Ethan will have something off the cameras in the parking lot."

Luke hoped so. The attack on Garcia was a helluva setback.

As he had been doing since the explosion, when they reached the Bronco, he bent down and examined the undercarriage, checked for anything that shouldn't be there, then checked beneath the hood.

He'd been careful of a tail, but still . . .

Satisfied it was safe, he and Emma climbed into the vehicle and he headed for Bellevue. Once he reached the office, he circled the block a couple of times, looking for anyone who might be surveilling the place, waiting for him to show up.

Seeing no one, he drove into the BOSS, Inc. lot, but saw no sign of Ethan's black Wrangler. Luke figured his brother would call when he had something. They both cracked open their doors and got out of the vehicle. As they started across the lot, he spotted one of the neighborhood kids riding his bike along the sidewalk, a tall skinny teenager Luke shot hoops with once in a while. The boy recognized him and waved. "Hey, Luke!"

"Hey, Beau! You got a minute?"

"Sure." The kid wheeled his bike in their direction. "What's up?"

"Beau, this is Emma."

"Hi, Emma."

Emma smiled. "Hello, Beau."

"There's ten bucks in it if you'll watch the Bronco till I get back," Luke said. "We won't be that long."

"Sure, man, no problem."

"If you see anyone around the car, come and get me. Don't say anything. Don't try to talk to him. Okay?"

"Okay, sure."

They walked toward the glass rear door and Luke held it open. "You think someone might have followed us?" Emma asked.

"No. I've been watching for a tail. But I think they could be watching the office, waiting for us to show up. One bomb's one too many. I'm not taking any chances."

Emma flicked a glance toward the Bronco. He could read the worry in her face.

The place was empty when they walked in, none of the guys sitting at their desks. The real work a PI did took place outside the office. Luke led Emma upstairs.

"Got a second?" Ian called out as they headed down the hall past his open office door.

"Sure." Luke led Emma into the roomy interior. They walked over to where Ian sat behind his big black granite-topped desk. A chrome desk lamp reflected pale highlights in his cousin's thick blond hair.

"I've been going over those Allied Shipping ownership records Sadie sent me, about twenty names in all."

"Any luck?" Luke asked.

"Well, if you take out the half who are dead and eliminate the ones who don't exist, there aren't actually all that many."

"Tell me you recognized someone."

Ian smiled. "Actually, I did. Guy named Toby Reeves. Tobias Reeves went to jail for armed robbery back in two thousand three. I'm the cop who arrested him." At the time, Ian had worked for the Seattle PD. He turned the computer around and brought up Reeves's mug shot, a big ugly dude with a flat nose and pitted complexion.

"Back then, I'd never heard of Rudolph Vance," Ian said. "But I know Toby Reeves. He'd sell his mother's soul if the price was right."

"You think Reeves and Vance are connected?"

"Somehow, some way—yeah, I do. I was just about to give the info to Sadie, let her see if she could run it down."

"That's where we're headed," Luke said. "Tobias Reeves. I'll fill her in."

"Tell her I'm accessing his file through a friend in the department. I'll send whatever comes through to her inbox as soon as I get it."

"Thanks, Ian."

"So how'd your interview go with Garcia?" he asked. "He give you anything?"

"Basically admitted to working for Vance. Wouldn't give us the name of the mole until he got a deal. While we were working on it, someone decided to shut him up. Garcia's in surgery. Doc says he might not make it."

Ian shook his head. "Bad timing, that's for sure."

"Bad for us," Emma said. "Worse for poor Terry." She turned to Luke. "How do you think Vance found out we were talking to him?"

"I don't think he knew. I think Vance was just tying up loose ends. Garcia had information Vance didn't want him spilling. It's as simple as that."

Ian's phone rang, which Luke took as a cue to head on down to Sadie's. As usual, she was typing away on her keyboard when they walked in.

"Got your text, darlin'," Luke said. "Whatcha got for us?"

Sadie rolled her chair back from her three computer screens. "I found the schedule for the Allied ships coming in and out of the port. There's four in the fleet: *Vagabond, Monarch, Argonaut,* and *Westwind.* I still haven't confirmed the company belongs to Vance."

"Ian has something on that, guy named Tobias Reeves. He's one of the names on the Allied ownership list. Ian thinks he's acting as a straw man for Vance in one of Allied's corporations. Ian's sending you the info."

"I'll watch for it."

"So what about the Allied ships?" Emma asked. "When are they coming in?"

Sadie swung the screen around so Luke and Emma could read the schedule.

"The *Vagabond* is in at the end of the week," Emma said excitedly. "Do you think it could be trafficking human cargo?"

Luke tapped the screen. "Kelso said Vance came back to Seattle to finalize his deal with the Yakuza. I'm betting the *Vagabond* is the ship we want. Vance is here to make sure the cargo arrives without a hitch."

"Unfortunately, we don't have any proof," Emma said.

"Twelve thousand containers on that ship." Sadie brought up another screen with pages and pages of ship's manifests. "Finding one—maybe more—filled with people won't be easy."

Emma gripped Luke's arm. "We have to find them, Luke. We have to get to them before Vance does."

He knew she was thinking of the terrible conditions they were suffering inside that forty-foot steel box, and worse yet, what would happen to them after they arrived. Vance or the Yakuza would pimp them out or sell them into some kind of bondage, whatever paid the most.

Luke clenched his jaw. "We'll find them, baby. We're getting closer all the time. I can feel it."

He was scenting blood, closing in on his quarry, his senses becoming hyperaware. Trouble was, the closer they got, the greater the danger.

He looked down at Emma, fought an urge to kiss the top of her glossy dark hair. What if something happened to her? What if she got hurt or killed and it was his fault? He had always worked alone until now. Until Emma. If something happened to her . . .

His mind went to his days in Special Forces, to Big Jack Mullen and Max McArthur, guys who had died in the line of duty. Men he had served with, brothers closer than blood. He'd been with them the day they'd died, watched the life drain out of them and been helpless to save them.

He knew what it felt like to lose someone you cared about that much. He'd been able to deal with it before because it was part of the job. Death was a possibility they had all accepted when they had put on the uniform.

Emma was different. Her intelligence, grit, and determination had won his respect. And though he'd tried to pretend it wasn't true, her concern and caring had won a place in his heart. If something happened to Emma, he didn't think he could handle it.

Even as they walked back downstairs, he was thinking about her, thinking about Emma instead of the mission.

He was losing his objectivity, losing his ability to focus. He was too close to Emma, in too fucking deep. He needed to get a handle on his emotions, get himself back under control.

To do that, he needed some space, needed time away from her. But with Vance and the Yakuza breathing down their necks, leaving her was something he absolutely could not do.

Luke steeled himself. He needed to find Vance. He needed to get his life back in order. He prayed something would break and he could make all of this end.

Chapter Thirty-Five

Chapter Thirty-Five

Luke was quiet as they walked across the BOSS, Inc. parking lot. Emma was coming to know his moods, to recognize when he was starting to feel boxed in. He had told her his black moods came from things that had happened in the past. It was the reason, he'd said, he didn't get involved in relationships.

But Emma had begun to wonder if part of the reason Luke kept himself apart was fear of losing someone he cared about. His mother had died not that long ago. In a family as close as the Brodies, it had to have been a terrible loss. As a soldier, he must have lost close friends in war.

He was afraid for her. Emma believed he would end their relationship now if he didn't feel obligated to protect her.

In a way, Emma felt the same. She would run from her feelings for Luke if she could. If she didn't need his help to find Vance.

More than that, Luke was a good man, a hero. Emma refused to abandon him. Luke deserved to be loved. She could give him that love if he would let him.

She glanced up as a black Jeep Wrangler pulled into the lot and parked. The five o'clock rush hour was over; only the occasional blast of a horn blared through the air.

In a black leather jacket similar to the brown bomber jacket Luke wore, Ethan climbed out of his Jeep into the damp drizzle and strode toward them. He was a big, heavily muscled man, and the jacket made him look even bigger. Emma could see the faint bulge of his shoulder holster under his arm.

"What's up?" Luke asked.

"I talked to Detective Hoover. He managed to get me a look at the images on the cameras at the time of the bombing. Guy was Yakuza, Luke."

"You sure?"

Ethan shook his head. "Couldn't see his face. He was careful about that. But he had tats, Luke. Once they brought the image up close, they were visible around his wrists and neck. They looked Asian, very distinctive. Had to be Yakuza."

Luke ran a hand over his hair. "I don't know if that's good news or bad. Might be easier if the guy worked for Vance. I need to talk to Masaki."

"What else can I do?"

"I'll let you know."

Ethan started to walk away, then turned back so quickly he bumped into Emma. He picked up her purse and handed it back to her. "Sorry. I was just going to say be sure and let me know what Masaki has to say."

"I will." It took a lot to shake Ethan, but Luke couldn't miss the worry in his brother's face.

As Ethan strode off toward the office, Beau rode up on his bicycle. "I didn't see anybody," the boy said.

Luke held out a ten. "Thanks, Beau."

The teenager grabbed it. "Are you working a case or something?"

"Or something," Luke said.

The teenager grinned. "Cool." The boy rose back up on

his bicycle seat and pedaled away. The air was heavy with mist, but the rain had stopped, at least for now. Emma climbed into the Bronco to get out of the cold and Luke slid in behind the wheel.

"I need to make that call," he said. "I want to hear what Masaki has to say about the bomber."

"You think he'll admit it was one of his people?"

"No idea. Maybe what he doesn't say will give us the answers we need." Luke called information and got the number for Pacific North Clothing, then hit the send button.

"Can you put it on speaker?" Emma asked. She wanted to hear the tone of Masaki's voice, see what she might be able to read into his words.

"Sure." Luke pushed the button and set the burner phone on the seat between them.

Emma recognized the educated voice of the fine-featured man behind the front desk. "Pacific North Clothing. How may I help you?"

"This is Luke Brodie. I need to speak to Ryan Masaki."

"Mr. Brodie. Mr. Masaki left word that you might call. I'll put you right through." The line rang twice before Masaki picked up.

"Mr. Brodie. I have been trying to reach you. Unfortunately, your phone seems to be turned off. My calls go directly to voice mail."

"An unfortunate but necessary precaution after someone tries to kill you."

"Yes, about that . . . I can tell you're on speaker. I presume your friend is listening."

"That's right," Luke said, flicking her a glance.

"I was calling to let you know the problem you mentioned has been handled."

Emma caught Luke's eye.

"You found the bomber?" he asked.

"That is correct. The man has been dealt with severely. The punishment will be worse should he disobey the orders I have given him. I assure you he will give you no more trouble."

Emma swallowed.

"What about others in your organization who might be a threat?"

"They are a threat only as long as they are aligned with the man you seek, Rudolph Vance."

"Then we both have reason to want him dealt with."

"So it would seem. There is a saying . . . the enemy of my enemy is my friend."

"I know it well," Luke said.

"This man, Rudolph Vance, has snakes in his heart. We will both sleep more easily when he has departed this earth."

Luke made no reply. Emma didn't miss the hard look on his face that said he wouldn't mind being the one to send Vance on his way.

"If you need to reach me," Luke said, "call my office. That number is also on the card I left for you. Someone there will see I get the message."

"As you wish. Good hunting, Luke Brodie." Masaki hung up the phone.

Emma looked at Luke. "What do you think?"

"I think Masaki lives by a different set of rules, but within those rules, he's a man of honor."

"So you think we're safe from the Yakuza?"

"No. Not from the faction Vance is in league with, not until that association ends."

The rain had started again by the time they had finished the hour-long trip back to the cabin, Luke being careful they weren't followed. It was almost dark, a few scattered lights down the mountain in Gold Bar beginning to flicker on.

"I'm going to build us a fire," Luke said, stripping off his jacket and hanging it up on the hook next to the door. "Won't take long to get the place warmed up."

Emma shed her raincoat and hung it on the hook next to Luke's. She liked the way they looked hanging there together. She sighed, feeling suddenly bone-weary. "I can't wait to curl up on the sofa and just relax."

"Yeah, me too. It's been a helluva day."

Luke knelt in front of the heavy iron stove and busied himself laying down old newspaper and kindling, shoving in logs from the wood bin, then lighting a match. The paper curled to life and the tinder caught. In seconds the wood was ablaze.

Emma loved watching him work, loved the way the muscles and sinews bunched and shifted beneath his snug-fitting shirt. Crouching as he was, his muscular behind flexed when he moved and a little tug of heat curled in her womb, like the flames licking the grate inside the stove.

Luke closed the heavy iron door, but she could still see the orange and red blaze through the thick glass window. She felt warmer already. But perhaps it was simply looking at Luke.

His eyes caught hers, vibrant blue and suddenly intense. "The room'll be warmer soon," he said, his voice a little gruff, and she knew his thoughts were close to her own.

Luke took his cell phone out of his pocket and set it on the coffee table, then sat down next to her on the sofa. Sliding his arms around her, he drew her back against him and the chill began to fade. Both of them had just begun to unwind when Luke's cell started to ring. He leaned over and grabbed it, recognized the number.

"It's Sadie," he said. "Hey, darlin', what's up?"

"I found something."

"I'm putting you on speaker so Emma can hear." He set the phone back down on the coffee table. "Go ahead."

"Tobias Reeves shared a cell with Rudolph Vance during a stay in juvenile detention. Records were sealed since they were both underage. I guess he figured no one would be able to make the connection."

So Sadie had hacked into Vance's juvenile record. Emma wasn't surprised. No one at BOSS, Inc. seemed to consider it hacking.

"Great work, darlin'. So now we're sure Allied Shipping is Vance's company—or at least, as sure as we're going to get."

"Which means," Emma said, "the ship coming into port the end of the week is likely the one Vance has been expecting."

"He's smuggling something," Luke said. "All we need to do is narrow twelve thousand containers down to one or two."

Sadie scoffed. "Yeah, no big deal. Let me know if I can help." The line went dead.

Luke leaned back on the sofa. "We'll figure out something. In the meantime . . ." He snuggled her back in his arms and just held her. Every once in a while, she felt the warm press of his lips against the back of her neck, but neither of them was in the mood to hurry. Not after the awful day they'd had.

They were relaxing, enjoying a comfortable silence that allowed them to hear the crackle of the fire inside the stove, the shifting of the logs against the hot metal. Luke eased her down in his arms and kissed her softly just as his phone rang again.

He sighed and they both sat back up. Few people had the number of the disposable phone. They both knew the call would be important. Luke hit the button and pressed the phone against his ear. "Brodie."

"Con Danfield. Garcia made it out of surgery. He's awake off and on. He's asking for you, says you're the only one he'll talk to."

"I'm an hour away. Emma's with me. We'll be there as fast as we can."

"I'll be waiting." The line went dead.

"What is it?" Emma asked.

"That was Danfield. Garcia made it through surgery. Says he won't talk to anyone but me." His glance went to Emma. "I'll have to drive back down the hill. You'd be safe enough here, but—"

"No way," she said, and he grinned.

"I didn't think so. We're both tired, but with any luck, the trip'll be worth it. Looks like we might finally be catching a break."

"I'm glad Terry's going to be okay," Emma said.

Luke cast her a glance. "Let's just hope he's got the info we need."

The corridor leading to the intensive care unit at Virginia Mason Medical Center bustled with activity. Nurses in scrubs pushed rattling carts along the hall, passing doctors in scrubs or long white coats. The smell of alcohol and antiseptic made Emma's nostrils burn.

Luke walked on one side of her, Conner Danfield on the other.

"Right this way." A heavyset nurse shoved open the double swinging door that led into the intensive care unit. Emma spotted Terry Garcia lying in a sea of tubes and wires. A heart monitor beeped in rhythm to the pulsing of his heart.

Her footsteps slowed. She tried not to remember seeing Ginny in a place like this after Rudy Vance had raped her, tried not to see her niece's sweet face bruised, her soft pink lips swollen.

She tried not to remember the day two weeks later that she had returned from a shopping trip to find Ginny huddled on the bed, her eyes bleak, her mind numb with shock and fear. She tried not to remember Eleanor Harris lying dead and bloody in the hall.

"Em, honey, are you okay?" Luke's worried voice reached her, pulling her back from the horror.

"Sorry. I'm okay. I just . . . I don't like hospitals."

"Yeah, neither do I." The rigid set of his features said he was remembering horrors of his own.

They walked over to the man lying on the bed, his black hair matted and stuck to his head, his dark complexion bleached pale from pain and loss of blood. Emma felt a pang of sympathy for a guy who had made so many mistakes.

"Terry . . ." Luke spoke the name softly. In the army, he had been hospitalized for months. Emma could tell by Luke's face, he knew exactly how bad the poor man felt.

"Terry, can you hear me? It's Luke Brodie."

Both Terry's eyes were black and blue, one completely swollen shut. His lips were puffed and torn. His good eye slowly cracked open.

He looked so pitiful, so alone, Emma couldn't help reaching down to catch hold of his hand. Terry looked up at her and his good eye filled with tears. When he blinked, a drop rolled down his cheek.

"Will you . . . help me?" he asked, his split lips barely able to move.

She wanted to say yes. Sympathy for the poor man made her heart hurt. She looked up at Luke for an answer.

"We'll help you, Terry," he said. "This is FBI Special Agent Conner Danfield. I trust him to do what he says. We just need that name. Once we have it, Agent Danfield will make sure you're safe."

Terry's eye remained on Luke's face. "Do you . . . give me your word?"

Luke nodded. "You've got my word."

Emma bit down on her lip to keep it from trembling. She looked at Con Danfield, who nodded.

She squeezed Terry's hand. "As soon as you're well, they'll take you somewhere safe."

Danfield moved up to Terry's bedside. "The name, Garcia. Give us the name, then you're home free."

Terry swallowed with difficulty, his Adam's apple moving up and down. ". . . Ryman."

Emma caught a flash of surprise before Con's features darkened. "Ryman? That's his last name?"

Terry gave a nod.

"What's his first name?"

Garcia managed to wet his split lips. "Richard."

"Richard Ryman. You're sure that's the guy?"

Terry gave a faint but unmistakable nod of his head. "Works . . . for . . . Vance."

Con loomed over him. "If you're telling the truth, you have nothing more to worry about. If you're not . . ." He let the words hang in the air.

"The . . . truth," Terry said.

The nurse arrived just as Terry's open eye drifted closed. "I'm sorry. You'll have to leave now. Mr. Garcia needs to rest."

Emma set his hand very gently back down on the bed. She felt Luke moving up beside her.

"Time to go, honey," he said softly.

The trip back down in the elevator passed in a blur. By the time they reached the hospital entrance, Con had his cell phone out and was madly giving orders.

"I want ten men at the safe house—now. I want Rick Ryman in custody. Nobody leaves the premises till I get there." Con kept talking as they exited the building, Emma hurrying to keep up with the two men's long strides.

"Richard Ryman," Luke said as they crossed the parking lot beneath broad circles of white from tall LED lights. "What do you know about him?"

"*Rick*. That's what we call him. I considered him a valued agent, as well as a friend." He scoffed. "Rick's got a thing for expensive suits, drives a new Caddy every year. He's got a wife with a good job and no kids so I figured he could afford it." His jaw clenched. "Now I know he's been supplementing his income."

"How's he getting his info?" Luke asked.

As they reached Conner's plain brown Chevy, Emma noticed one of his hands unconsciously fisted. "He's on the task force."

Luke's head shot up. "You don't mean he's one of the agents protecting the house?"

Conner jerked open his car door. "That's exactly what I mean." Danfield jammed in behind the wheel, slammed the door, and fired the engine.

Luke and Emma ran for the Bronco.

Chapter Thirty-Six

The pitch-black night, heavy with mist, surrounded him, making him invisible in the darkness. Not even the hint of a moon. Just inky blackness and the lights glowing in the windows of the house below. Upstairs in Ginny's bedroom, he could see movements behind the curtain, the outline of her soft young curves.

He was so near, he could imagine the sweet scent of her skin, the soft, silky texture of her light brown hair. So near, and yet far enough away, they had never even suspected he was out here.

It was almost time to take her away with him. In three days, the shipment would arrive. Once Fujita and Hirada were satisfied with their arrangement, he would leave the country. He would hire a private jet, have it sitting on the tarmac when he got there, ready to fly him and Ginny off to a new life.

He was thinking maybe Brazil. He did some shipping business there and the climate was warm.

He would have to drug her—just this once—to ensure her cooperation, but as soon as they were safely away, he would begin his seduction. He would do it properly this time, woo her and win her affection, buy her expensive trinkets, jewelry, and clothes, things young girls liked. In time she would forgive him his harsh treatment of her. She would understand how deep his feelings for her ran.

In time she would be completely his.

He looked back at the house, watched her light wink out, knew the puppy was in there with her.

The dog was the key. He had figured that out awhile back. Ginny took the puppy out in the yard every evening. He would go in through the back gate and hide in the foliage, be ready when she walked past. A little chloroform on a rag over her mouth would keep her quiet.

His informant would be on duty that night. He would look the other way. Just in case, Rudy would take a couple of his men with him, but he didn't think it would be necessary. In a matter of minutes, he would be safely away and Ginny would be his.

He was just about to leave his hiding spot when he saw the cars, a battalion of them, careening around the corner, slamming to a halt in front of the house. Car doors jerked open and men poured out. Rudy hissed in a breath. *FBI.*

He sank back into the foliage, watching as some of the agents ran around to the back while others rushed to the front door. It was immediately pulled open and the men ran inside. More of the agents spread protectively out around the home.

Rudy just stood there, his jaw locked, his breathing harsh in the chilly night air, furious as he watched the destruction of his plans. It didn't take a scholar to realize the FBI had discovered the identity of his informant, Richard Ryman, to know they would now move Ginny to a new location. It didn't take a genius to know he would have to find her all over again.

A fresh round of fury swept through him. He'd thought Garcia had been dealt with, believed the man would never survive the attack. As usual, his expectations had not been met by the idiots who worked for him.

Rudy glanced back at the house. It was time to leave. Though his vantage point was completely hidden, soon they would be spreading out, checking the area to see if the house was being watched. He'd been careful. Once he was gone, they wouldn't find any trace of him.

He started to leave just as two more vehicles shot around the corner, a brown unmarked Chevy and a beat-up Ford Bronco. He knew the owner of the Bronco and his mind went dark with rage.

Brodie. Always it was Brodie. The man was like a bad stink you couldn't get rid of. Brodie should have been dealt with by now, both Brodie and the woman. Another failure.

He would handle the problem himself, do what the others hadn't. He was a powerful man. He could assemble a small army on a moment's notice. He'd start the process now.

He'd gather his men and have someone he trusted watch the house, find out where Ginny was being taken. She'd be his, just the way he planned.

In the meantime, he'd take care of Luke Brodie.

Clenching his teeth in an effort to control his rage, Rudy slipped quietly off into the trees, making the two-block walk to where his driver waited in a black Lincoln Town Car.

He slid into the deep red leather backseat. "Drive," he said, pulling his burner phone out of the pocket of his trench coat.

"Back to the inn, sir?"

"Yes. And don't waste time. I've got things I need to do." Rudy leaned back in the seat. His first phone call went to Grady Kelso. He ground his teeth when Grady didn't pick up, but it didn't really matter. Kelso was just one of his minions. Rudy started dialing again.

"I can't believe this. You think I'm the mole?" Rick Ryman sat on the sofa, his hands cuffed behind his back. He was a lean, well-built, sandy-haired man, his expensive brown suit immaculate, at least when Con had arrived. Ryman and a female agent named Janine Whitelaw worked this shift, both people Con highly trusted. Janine was shaken and Con didn't blame her.

It took all his years of training not to punch Rick Ryman in the face.

"How many years have we been friends, Con?" Ryman asked, still playing the game. "You know me. You can't believe—"

"Cut the bullshit, Rick. The minute your name fell out of Garcia's mouth, I knew it was you. You're finished in the FBI. You won't be driving your fancy new Cadillac or walking around in thousand-dollar suits. You'll be spending your days in jail."

"I don't believe this," Ryman repeated, shaking his head as if he were the victim.

"You really want to continue this charade? You're actually going to sit there and play innocent until we have your bank account records? You don't think we're going to find the deposits you made that were way out of line with your salary? Sums of money you received from Rudolph Vance?"

Ryman's face looked ashen beneath his sandy hair.

"Tell me the truth and I'll do my best to help you. But you have to do it now. You can help yourself here, Rick. But if you wait, it's going to be too late."

Ryman looked at him and his head drooped forward.

The house was overflowing with agents, both inside and out. Ginny and April were upstairs with Emma. Brodie lounged a few feet away, one wide shoulder propped against the wall. He looked calm. Too calm. Con recognized the seething anger hidden behind those intense blue eyes.

He should send Brodie away. Or at least make him go upstairs with Emma. But Con figured Luke had earned these few minutes with Ryman. Beyond that, Luke Brodie was extremely intelligent. He'd been hunting Vance for weeks. He knew everything about the man, his past, his habits, his intentions. Maybe he'd be able to contribute in some way.

"This is your last chance, Rick," Con said.

Ryman looked up at him from his place on the sofa. His expensive suit was wrinkled and beads of sweat rolled down his forehead. He gazed around at the men and women in the room, agents he had worked with, people he had betrayed.

Releasing a breath that seemed to deflate him like a pin-pricked balloon, Rick started talking, telling him how he had never met Rudy Vance. How an intermediary had contacted him—he didn't know his name—but the man said he would pay for information, pay big sums of money.

"How did it work?" Con asked.

"He gave me a number. I called and gave him the info. In exchange he gave me an address. A guy there handed me an envelope full of money." Rick admitted he'd understood the information was for Vance. The contact had told him the job would only last a couple of weeks. He'd be financially set and his part in it would be over.

"Has Vance got men watching the house?"

"I don't know. I don't think so. I've never seen any sign of them."

Con glanced up as Brodie shoved away from the wall and ambled over to Ryman.

"You knew it was Vance? Did it occur to you that you were helping that sick fuck molest a little girl?"

"Easy," Con warned.

"I didn't see it that way at the time," Ryman said, his eyes pleading. "Later, I was in too deep. I didn't know how to get out."

"You gave Vance Ginny's location in Colorado?"

He nodded bleakly.

"And he knows where the girl is now?"

"He knows."

Con's own anger shot up. "It's a miracle he hasn't already figured a way to get his hands on her. It's a goddamned miracle!" He stalked away. "Get him the hell out of here. I can't stand the sight of him."

Two agents grabbed Ryman's bound arms and lifted him up off the sofa.

"Hold on a minute," Luke said, his gaze swinging to Con. "I've got an idea."

Con held up a hand, signaling the agents to wait. "All right." He and Luke walked a few feet away.

"Ryman's going down," Luke said. "No doubt about it. But maybe there's a way you could use him first, figure a way to set a trap for Vance."

"I'm listening."

"Vance wants Ginny. If Ryman sends him a message telling him you're moving Ginny to a new location, say in a day or two, maybe he'll come after her here."

"Ryman would have to tell him he's being taken off the detail, that he won't know where Ginny's being taken."

"Yeah. So Vance is forced to come after her before he loses track of her. Except when he shows up, April and Ginny won't be here."

"But the FBI will be," Con said harshly.

"Won't work if he's got someone out there tonight."

"My men are sweeping the area. If they don't find anything, we'll set the trap."

"From what I know of Vance, he's got a lot of men at his disposal. He might come straight at you."

Con felt a surge of anticipation. "I hope he does. You can bet we'll be ready." He focused on Luke. "We'll need a day to pull it together, get the message to Vance. But if he bites, we'll make it work."

Con looked over to where Rick Ryman stood between two federal agents up against the wall. "Bring Ryman into the kitchen. *Richard* and I need to talk."

Sitting on the bed next to Ginny, Emma held on to her niece's hand. "We're going to catch him, sweetheart. They've found the man who gave him your address in Denver. Agent Ryman has been arrested. They'll move you and your mom again and this time no one will tell them where you are."

On the twin bed across from them, April sat on the edge of the mattress. "Your aunt Em's right, honey. Agent Danfield will move us into another house and this time we'll be safe."

Ginny's eyes welled. She shook her head and tears spilled onto her cheeks. "He found us in Denver. He found us here. We'll never be safe—not until he's dead!" She turned away, threw herself down on the bed, and started sobbing into her pillow.

Emma thought of Rudolph Vance and what a cunning monster he was. How he had deceived the judge and gained his freedom after the rape, how he had come back and attacked Ginny again, how he had murdered poor Eleanor

Harris. She thought of how he had used his power to reach into the depths of the FBI and find Ginny here in Seattle and how she and April would be forced to run from him again.

Ginny was right. Con Danfield and his men might find Vance and arrest him, but with the help of the powerful attorney he'd used before, he might get out of jail again. As long as Rudolph Vance was alive, Ginny was in danger.

She reached over and rubbed her niece's slender back. "We'll think of something, sweetheart, I promise."

From the start, Emma had known what she had to do. She needed to find Vance before the FBI got their hands on him.

She needed to make sure, once and for all, that Ginny was safe.

They didn't get back to the cabin until almost four in the morning. As they walked through the front door, Luke could read the exhaustion on Emma's face. The fire in the stove had burned to cinders, but the heavy cast iron was still warm enough to keep the chill away.

Luke shoved in a couple more logs to restart the blaze, then they went into the bedroom, curled up together in bed, and fell asleep. Neither of them awoke till late the next morning.

Luke was sitting across from Emma at the breakfast table in his tiny kitchen, feeling the warmth of the sun streaming in through the window. Since they still hadn't made it to the grocery store for fresh food, Emma had managed to scrounge a couple of cans of Spam out of the emergency cupboard. She'd cut the meat into slices, rolled them in crackers and fried them, then served them with canned peaches and plenty of hot coffee. Luke thought the meal tasted surprisingly good.

"They'll have moved April and Ginny by now," Emma said, her coffee mug cradled between her hands. "Danfield is going to arrange for me to see them once they get settled. I think he's worried about Ginny—she's really scared, Luke." Emma's troubled look made his chest clamp down.

"They're gonna catch him, honey. The plan's going to work."

She glanced away. "Maybe it will, maybe it won't. Even if they catch him, Vance has plenty of money. With his fancy, high-powered lawyer, he might be able to get out again. Even if he goes to jail, eventually, he'll be free. April and Ginny will have to spend their entire lives looking over their shoulders, watching for Rudolph Vance. I can't let that happen."

There was something in her voice, a steely determination unlike anything he'd heard before. "What are you thinking, Emma? You aren't thinking you're going to end this guy?"

Her chin firmed. "Don't ask me that question, Luke. You might not want to know the answer."

"Jesus!" Luke shoved out of his chair, stalked around behind her, hauled her out of her chair, and whirled her around to face him. "You don't know what killing does to a person. You aren't made for that kind of thing! You think I didn't see you with that creep, Terry Garcia? Holding on to his hand? You think I don't know what a soft heart you have?"

Her eyes filled. "It doesn't matter. If I get a chance, I'll do it. I'll do it to save them."

Luke gripped her shoulders. "We don't even know where he is."

"Sooner or later we'll find him."

"Are you willing to give up your life, Emma? You kill him, they'll put you in prison."

"Not if it's self-defense."

"That's your plan? You draw Vance out, kill him, and make it look like self-defense? Was that your plan all along?"

"Yes."

Anger and worry filtered through him. She didn't understand, couldn't know how killing Vance would haunt her. Luke knew. He'd faced his demons, mostly conquered them. Still, the things he'd done had changed him, taken something from him. He looked at Emma, thought how hard it was going to be to let her go, and he knew the price he would still have to pay.

"I'll tell you what. You want Vance dead that bad, I'll kill him for you."

Emma sucked in a breath. "No, Luke—you can't. It's different for me. I'd be doing it to protect my family."

"You'd be doing it to protect your family, Emma? Well, I'd be doing it to protect *you*."

Silence fell. Emma's pretty features softened. She went up on her toes and kissed him. It was the sweetest, softest kiss he'd ever had. Luke cupped her face between his hands and deepened the kiss. Then he let her go.

Emma laid her hand against his cheek. "Let's not talk about killing anymore. Like you said, we don't know where Vance is. If the trap works, the FBI will arrest him. There won't be anything I can do."

"That's right," Luke said, relieved. "The feds are going to catch the bastard and put him away for the rest of his life."

Emma nodded. "For now, we let Danfield worry about Vance."

"Yeah. In the meantime, we've got our own problems

to solve. We need to figure out what's going down with Allied Shipping."

Emma looked up at him. "How do we do that?"

"I have no frigging idea. When that happens, I usually head down to the office to talk to Sadie, see if she can use her magic to find something that'll help."

Emma started nodding. "Okay, that sounds like a plan. Let me get my stuff and we're out of here."

She hurried into the living room and grabbed her canvas gear bag off the floor. The Glock .23 he'd loaned her was holstered inside. She found her purse, pulled the little .380 out and checked the load while he walked into the bedroom to collect his Nighthawk .45.

Out of habit, he dropped the clip and shoved it back in. He slid the pistol back into its holster and clipped it onto his belt.

All the while, his mind kept going over what Emma had said about killing Vance. He'd known she was desperate to protect her family. He hadn't realized how far she was willing to go. Though he admired her conviction and her courage, he'd never let her go through with her plan, even if she got the chance.

But he'd meant what he'd said. He wasn't stupid enough to kill the rat bastard in cold blood, but if their paths crossed and he got the slightest opening . . .

He'd do what was necessary to make sure Emma's family was safe.

Chapter Thirty-Seven

They timed the trip from the cabin to the city to miss the traffic, so it didn't take long. It was a beautiful day, the first in a while, the sun shining down through the leafy branches of the trees, just the faintest nip in the air from the breeze blowing in off the Sound.

Emma spotted the two-story brick BOSS, Inc. office up ahead, saw Luke glance in the rearview mirror, checking for a tail as he had been doing all the way to the city. He'd said he didn't believe Vance could find the location of the cabin, but he was playing it safe.

It was the middle of the day when they arrived, the parking lot empty except for Sadie's little white Toyota. Luke parked the Bronco a few spaces away and Emma got out. As she rounded the car, Luke joined her and they started toward the back door of the office.

She was still a little tired after their late hours last night, her mind wandering absently, when she heard the screech of tires and the roar of engines. Four black SUVs slammed into the parking lot from different directions, hemming them in where they stood.

"Emma!" Luke shouted, his big black semiauto already in hand as car doors flew open and a dozen men poured

out, weapons drawn. Emma had the little .380 out of her
purse, her arms extended, pointed at the men moving into
position around them.

Her aim held steady though her heart thundered, fighting to tear through her ribs. She thought of Luke's Glock,
shoved under the passenger seat of the Bronco, and felt a
pang. She backed up a few steps and so did he, bringing
them together, back to back.

The men moved closer—Vance's men, she had no
doubt—the circle tightening around them. They were out-
numbered twelve to two, not good odds. Luke held his fire
and Emma waited for his signal. If gunshots erupted, they
would be dead.

One of the men stepped forward. She recognized Tobias
Reeves's big, homely, pitted face from the mug shot Ian had
shown them. Dressed in a plaid shirt, jeans, and heavy
leather boots, he was built like a boxer, thick-shouldered
and square through the torso. The men were all different
ages and nationalities: Asian, black, white, Hispanic.
Clearly Vance was an equal-opportunity employer.

She caught a glimpse of red and blue ink at the base of
the neck of an Asian man on her right. *Yakuza.* Emma shiv-
ered. It was Junichi, she realized, one of the men who'd
attacked them outside the Golden Lily, the man who had
threatened Luke.

A tremor passed through her hand and she steadied
her aim.

"Mr. Vance wants to see you," Reeves said. He tipped
his head toward one of the black SUVs, indicating they
should get in. "He doesn't like to be kept waiting."

"You think we're just going to go with you?" Luke said.
"You're in downtown Bellevue. Sooner or later someone's
going to notice what's happening and call the police."

"Put your weapons down and get in the car or we shoot

you right here. You can kill some of us, but you and your woman will be dead."

With Luke's hard body at her back, Emma could feel the tension in his muscles, the way his legs were splayed, his weight on the balls of his feet. She could feel his iron control.

He was weighing the odds, deciding whether the men would kill them as soon as they were unarmed, or take them to Vance. She knew the answer and so did Luke.

Vance would want payback for the trouble they'd caused. He'd want revenge. He'd want to make it personal. She remembered what he'd done to Eleanor Harris for trying to stop him from getting to Ginny, what he'd done to Felix Riggs for divulging his secrets, and a chill slipped through her.

"All right, you win," Luke said, as Emma had known he would. The odds might be better somewhere else. "But we go together."

Reeves nodded, the breeze ruffling his shaggy brown hair. "All right. Put your weapons on the ground."

Luke lowered his pistol, set it on the pavement. Emma took his cue and set hers down beside it.

The men swarmed around them, found Luke's ankle gun and pulled it out of its holster, dragged their arms behind their backs and slid on nylon cuffs. Booth had taught her the trick of making your wrists as big as you could and turning them a little so the cuffs weren't as tight as they seemed, and she used that trick now. She could tell by the fit as they shoved her forward that with a little work, she'd be able to free herself.

Her purse slid off her shoulder as they pushed her into the backseat. One of the men snatched the bag up and threw it into the rear of the SUV. She thought of her mini pepper spray can and wished she'd had time to replace it, wished she had it in her hand right now.

A fair-skinned man slid into the vehicle from the opposite side and pressed his gun into her ribs. One of them shoved Luke in beside her, wedging the three of them together, and slammed the car door.

She glanced down. They hadn't cuffed Luke's ankles. They didn't know he was Delta. They didn't know a Delta operator could take half of Vance's men down with his hands bound behind his back.

She thought he might make a move as he settled in the seat, but he didn't. He was trying to figure Vance's next play, examining the setup from every angle, looking for the right opportunity.

She had to be ready. Had to stay calm. Together they might have a chance.

Luke turned toward her. "You with me, Em?" he asked, his beautiful blue eyes on her face.

"All the way," she said, and the SUV shot out of the parking lot.

No blindfold. Luke watched their surroundings fly past as the line of SUVs rolled along the freeway, heading south on the 405. They took the 90 west, then veered south again on Interstate 5. When the driver took the exit for the West Seattle Street Bridge, followed by the one toward Harbor Island, Luke knew where they were going.

Vance owned a shipping company. There were dozens of warehouses in the Port of Seattle area. Rudy didn't care if Luke saw where they were being taken, didn't care if he saw the faces of the men who had brought them there, including his buddy, Tobias Reeves.

Vance didn't intend to let them live.

But Luke had known that the minute the black SUVs had roared into the parking lot. No way to avoid the confrontation. At least not then.

In a way he was glad the hunt was finally coming to an end. Like Emma, he didn't want to be looking over his shoulder, watching for Rudy Vance for the rest of his life.

He glanced in her direction. A hard-faced man sat on her left, a high-caliber semiauto shoved into her ribs. Nothing he could do without the man pulling the trigger.

The worst scenario he could have imagined had occurred— Emma in Vance's hands, her life in extreme peril. With her there, his hands were tied in more than just the literal sense. On his own, he could find a way to deal with Vance and his men, but he couldn't risk getting Emma killed.

It was the reason he never worked with partners. He didn't want one of them ending up dead.

Especially not Emma.

He took a deep breath, forcing his thoughts away from her, getting himself back in the zone. Didn't matter what he wanted; he had to work with the hand he'd been dealt. The good news was, he trusted Emma. They had come to know each other, to act in sync when they had to, to read each other the way men learned to do in battle.

He would trust her now, count on her to do what he said when the time came. To do her part, to be ready when they made their move.

He glanced out the rear window. One of the SUVs had peeled off on the 405. The vehicle had not reappeared. Four men inside the car. That cut Vance's army down to eight. No piece of cake, but manageable if everything went perfectly.

Which it never did. And if more men weren't waiting for them when they arrived.

He moved his wrists, twisted a little, flexed, moved. The nylon bands bit into his wrists, scraped along, abrading his skin. He twisted again, flexed, ignored the fine thread of pain. A grim smile touched his lips. His hands were free. He could lose the cuffs whenever he wanted.

Vance's men were street-tough, but they weren't well trained. Not like he was. Didn't mean they weren't dangerous. Didn't mean you couldn't wind up dead.

The SUV rolled along a road lined with warehouses. In the distance he could see a wide expanse of crystal blue water. A ship plunged through the current on its way to the Strait of Juan de Fuca and the open sea.

The SUV made a turn, turned again, slowed, and rolled into a paved area in front of a big metal building surrounded by a high chain-link fence. The other two vehicles followed.

A couple of minutes later, the door beside him jerked open and a big brawny bastard with a mustache hauled him out and stuck a gun in his middle. Men poured out of the other two vehicles, one he'd recognized earlier, the Yakuza, Junichi. Only a few drew their weapons.

He felt a dark surge of anticipation—the odds were better already.

A heavyset man in cargo pants started toward the gate, planning to roll it closed. Junichi and another man disappeared inside the warehouse, while Reeves and five other men milled around, relaxed now that he was in their custody, helpless, they believed.

He flicked a glance at Emma, saw they were on the same page, gave a slight nod, and erupted into action, spinning, knocking the gun out of closest man's hand as he shed the nylon cuffs, lashing out with his feet, kicking, slamming a foot into a man's knee before he could pull his pistol, hearing the crunch of bone, whirling, kicking, punching.

From the corner of his eye, he saw Emma. Her cuffs were gone, her hands moving, elbows, knees, feet. He felt the edge of a hard smile as he watched her drive a knee into her attacker's balls and drop him moaning to the ground.

He heard the ratchet of slides, men cocking their pistols, grabbed a guy around the neck and twisted the gun out of his hands, aimed, and pulled the trigger, saw the man go down. A double tap took a second man down.

Luke crouched and fired from behind the open car door. Emma ran, then crouched beside him. He center-shot a man, took another out with a bullet to the head. Four men completely down. Emma had one down, left one of them unconscious, and had his gun in her hand.

Two men rushed out of the warehouse firing. Damn, more of the bastards inside. Shots slammed into the car door, splintered the windshield. Luke rose up to take a shot at one of them, felt the sharp sting of a bullet creasing his side from another location. He whirled and pulled the trigger and the shooter went down.

"That is quite enough, Mr. Brodie."

Luke froze. He didn't have to look to know the voice behind him belonged to Rudolph Vance, to know that Vance held the one bargaining chip he could not ignore.

Slowly raising his hands, the barrel of his weapon pointing skyward, he turned to see the gun Vance pointed at Emma's head.

Chapter Thirty-Eight

No matter how hard they'd fought, more men appeared. Emma watched as one of them grabbed the gun out of Luke's hand, then punched him hard in the stomach. He grunted but didn't go down. Emma bit back a cry as she spotted the crimson stain spreading across his shirt just above the waistband of his jeans.

"Take them inside," Vance ordered, tossing a pair of metal handcuffs to Reeves, who clamped them around Luke's wrists behind his back.

Gun in hand, one of the men shoved her forward. Reeves shoved Luke. He stumbled and her heart lurched. How badly was he injured? How much blood was he losing?

They walked into the warehouse, which was big and empty, their footsteps sounding on the concrete floor, echoing against the metal walls. There was an office at one end. A big African American opened the paneled glass door and shoved her inside, pushing Luke inside so hard, he crashed into the wooden desk, moving it back several inches. The papers on top went flying.

"Well, here we are," Vance said. Emma almost didn't recognize him, with his shaved head and earrings, his black

T-shirt beneath a tweed sport coat over a pair of black jeans. He looked younger than his photos, more hip.

"I was hoping it wouldn't come to this," he said to her, shaking his head as if he actually cared. "You are, after all, Ginny's aunt. I hate to think of your death causing her further grief."

"Why can't you leave Ginny alone? What kind of a pervert are you? She's only a young girl."

"Ginny has reached womanhood. For thousands of years, women her age and younger have been married or mated in some fashion to older men. It's nature's way. Your rules mean nothing."

"You're sick."

His lips thinned. "So high and mighty. You're just like the rest. Ginny and I are soul mates. We're meant to be together. Nothing you do is going to change that."

"I'll make you a deal," Luke said, drawing Vance's attention back to him. "Let Emma go and I'll give you whatever it is you want."

Vance chuckled. "Surely you know that isn't going to happen. I will, however, promise that if you give me the information I need, I'll make the ending quick—at least for her."

Emma's stomach knotted. A fine thread of tension tightened the muscles across Luke's shoulders.

"You can do what you want with me," Luke said. "But think of Ginny and leave Emma out of this."

Vance scoffed. "I'll do what I want with both of you." He signaled to Junichi, who walked up beside Emma and pressed the barrel of his gun into her ribs.

Vance pointed toward two of the men in the office. "You and you—hold his arms." They moved forward, the big African American and a beefy man with flat black eyes, a barrel chest, and a scar above his lip. Luke stiffened as they grabbed hold of him. The stitches in his upper arm had started to bleed and Emma's chest ached with fear for him.

She thought he might take the men on, make a move toward freedom. She was ready, adrenaline pumping like fire through her veins. Instead, his intense blue gaze went to Junichi and the gun the man pressed against her.

Vance's gaze fixed on Tobias Reeves. "Don't stop until I tell you."

Luke seemed to prepare himself. Held firmly between his captors, his hands cuffed behind his back, he braced his feet apart to absorb the first heavy blow Reeves delivered. One punch followed another, Reeves's big blunt fists driving into Luke's lean body with the force of a hammer. His grunts of pain tore at Emma's heart.

"Let him go!" Jerking away from Junichi, she rushed forward, only to be grabbed and hauled back. She tried to kick free, but a second man, a thick-lipped, bald-headed Asian, grabbed her and spun her around, pinned her against the wall with his big hard body.

"Get her out of here," Vance commanded. Junichi and the bald Asian dragged her into the inner office and closed the door.

She could hear the thud of fists pounding into Luke's body and his deep groans of pain. Fear for him made her tremble. He was bleeding! They could be killing him! She had to do something!

Standing in front of Junichi, Emma lowered her head, then jerked up hard, coming up beneath his chin. The crack of bone against bone made a loud pop in the quiet room. Junichi bit his lip, slinging blood, and cursed foully. The bald man spun her around and backhanded her across the face so hard, she crashed into the chair beside the desk.

Pain shot into her head. When she lifted her chin, fury glittered in Junichi's black eyes. He grabbed the front of her shirt, jerked her up, and threw a punch that smashed into her jaw. For an instant the room went dark.

The bald Asian was on her, slamming her down in the chair, her head spinning, her vision blurring. She didn't feel the rope around her waist, binding her to the chair, until she tried to move.

Emma thought of Luke, desperate to help him. With cold hard certainty she realized there was nothing at all she could do.

Luke steeled himself against another painful blow. His lips were split, his eyes swollen, his body beaten and battered. Hell, he still had stitched wounds from the car bomb, which had torn open and started to bleed.

He didn't think the injury in his side was as bad as it looked, but as Tobias Reeves pounded away at him, every punch sank into him with an agonizing bite of pain.

"You can make this end, Mr. Brodie," Vance said. "Just tell me where they've taken my Ginny." Rudy's lips curled into a morbid smile. "I saw you at the house last night, you see. You didn't know that, did you?"

Luke forced his head up to look into Vance's face.

"I saw the FBI pull up in front of the house and I knew they had discovered the name of my informant, that they would be forced to move Ginny. When I received Agent Ryman's message this morning, I knew it was a trap and that Ginny had already been moved."

At least the girl's safe, Luke thought.

Vance strolled toward him, his pistol gripped loosely. Luke's hand unconsciously fisted. *Just a little closer,* he thought. Just a few more inches and Vance would be within reach. Now that Emma was out of the way, he could make his move without putting her in immediate danger. Just a few seconds was all he needed.

"I want to know where she is," Vance said, idly playing with his weapon, an S&W nine mil, it looked like. "I want to know where the FBI has taken my Ginny."

Luke shook his head, blood trailing from the corner of his eye, his vision narrowed by the swelling. "You played this all wrong, Rudy. I don't know where they took Ginny. Neither does Emma." The corner of his mouth edged up. "We aren't exactly on the FBI payroll—unlike your friend, Ryman."

The man with the scar jerked him upright. He and the black guy tightened their grip and Reeves threw a punch to the stomach that doubled Luke over.

Head down, he glanced around the room, just Vance, Reeves, the two big bruisers holding on to him, and a man by the door to the inner office. Behind the door, the two Yakuza were with Emma. The rest of the men were out in the warehouse.

Vance gave a nod and Reeves stepped back in, big, beefy and solid as a brick. The punches he delivered were brutal. Luke had to make his move soon or he wouldn't be able to. He just needed Vance a few steps closer.

He was spitting blood, panting hard when Rudy held up a hand.

"I don't have time for this. I can see that your military training has paid off." Rudy spoke to Reeves. "I don't believe Mr. Brodie will give us the information, no matter what we do to him."

He motioned toward the door to the inner office and the man standing beside it pulled it open.

Luke could see Emma bound to a chair next to the desk, her head hanging down, her pretty face mostly hidden by her long dark curls. One of the men had her left arm positioned on top of the desk, her wrist pinned down, her fingers splayed.

A vicious smile rose on Junichi's face as he held up a big steel-bladed knife. *"Watashi wa kanojo apartm, sukoshizutsu o katto shimasu,"* he said.

"No!" Luke recognized enough Japanese to know what Junichi had said. *I will take her apart piece by piece.* "Don't do it! Don't touch her! I'll tell you what you want to know! I'll tell you where they took Ginny!" It didn't matter that he had no idea. Nothing mattered but saving Emma.

Vance just chuckled. Emma's shrill scream tore loose as the blade came down, the sound of a wounded animal crying out in excruciating agony. Horror streaked through him, reached inside his chest, and unleashed the beast he thought he had conquered.

"Emma!" Luke charged, head-butted Reeves with enough force to shatter his jaw and send him flying across the room. Whirling, he kicked the feet out from under the black guy on his left. The man landed hard and Luke kicked him in the head. Luke spun around backward, grabbed the scarred man's crotch with his shackled hands and jerked, tearing his testicles inside his cargo pants. The man screamed in pain and went down, holding on to his crotch.

Luke swung his shackled arms beneath him and jumped, putting the steel cuffs in front of him, turning them into a lethal weapon. Vance fired his pistol with shaking hands, missing by inches. Luke kept going, bashing the man at the door in the face with the cuffs, slamming him into the wall a few feet away. He didn't get up.

Rushing through the door of the inner office, Luke saw Emma's small hand still resting on the desk in a spreading pool of blood, the end of her little finger missing.

Fury burned through him so fierce it blinded him. He kicked the bald Asian aside, dodged Junichi's blade, grabbed his wrist, and twisted, turning the knife against him. The Yakuza fought with all his strength, but Luke was stronger, fueled by a deep black rage. The cuffs rattled as with one hard thrust, the knife found its mark and sank into Junichi's chest.

Luke freed the blade, whirled, and plunged it into the bald Asian rushing toward him. He pulled the knife out and made a clean slice through the rope binding Emma to the chair. She made a little sound in her throat as she slumped forward.

Luke turned at the sound of footsteps coming toward them, spotted Vance, and leaped aside just as Rudy pulled the trigger. The shot plowed into the wall a few inches away and Luke strode toward him.

Luke managed to shove the barrel of Vance's pistol aside just as the gun went off. He stared into Vance's evil eyes, spun and looped the cuffs over Rudy's neck and began choking the life out of him.

Vance fired again, but Luke's black rage drove him on. Vance struggled and the gun dropped out of his hand. Luke's hold tightened. In seconds Rudolph Vance lay dead on the floor.

More gunshots split the air. Reaching down, he searched Vance's pocket for the key to the handcuffs, unlocked them and tossed them away. Grabbing Vance's pistol, Luke raced back to Emma, expecting the outside door to shatter in a storm of bullets any minute, expecting to be overrun by the rest of Vance's men. He wouldn't let them touch her. He would kill every one of them, rip their hearts out with his bare hands, before he would let them touch her again.

He gathered Emma into his arms, blood running down her hand, and held her close against him.

"Luke . . ." she whispered.

"It's okay," he said softly. "I'm right here, honey." He

swallowed past the lump in his throat. "I won't let them hurt you again."

Peeling his bloody T-shirt off over his head, he wrapped it around her injured hand, turned toward the sound of shots ringing out, growing into a steady barrage.

It took a moment to realize the gunfire was coming from the paved area in front of the warehouse. Luke's gaze shot through the aluminum blinds at the window. A big black Jeep Wrangler was parked crosswise in the lot. A BOSS, Inc. black SUV blocked the gate, and a sea of FBI vehicles filled the area around the warehouse. The *whop* of a chopper battered the air overhead.

Relief hit him so hard, he felt dizzy. "Ethan's here. Dirk and the rest of the guys. The FBI is taking down Vance's men. You're gonna be okay."

Emma looked up at him, tears streaking her face. "What . . . what about you? You've been shot. How . . . how badly are you injured?"

Luke didn't answer. Instead, he spotted the severed end of Emma's little finger, carefully picked it up and ran to the small fridge against the wall. Finding an icy can of soda inside, he grabbed it, wrapped the can and the finger in a paper towel from the roll on top, and hurried back to Emma.

"FBI!" someone shouted as the front door burst open and half a dozen men in black body armor rushed into the outer office.

"We're in here!" Luke called out. "Don't shoot!" The men rushed in, guns drawn, Con Danfield among them. Luke had no idea how the men had found them.

"Jesus," Con said, taking in the sight of them, both covered in blood.

"We need to get Emma to the hospital," Luke said. "They cut off part of her finger. If we get there in time, maybe they can sew it back on."

Emma whimpered.

"We'll take her in the chopper." Danfield urged them toward the door.

"Luke's been shot," Emma said, clutching Luke's bloody shirt around her hand, tears sliding down her face. "Please help him."

Danfield looked at Luke, then down at Rudolph Vance. The blood vessels in Rudy's eyes were broken, the twin orbs an eerie shade of crimson staring up at nothing, a silent scream frozen on his lips.

"We're going to help you both," Con said, returning his attention to Emma. "Can you make it?"

She swallowed and nodded. Luke fell in beside her, limping now, the pain beginning to worsen as the adrenaline wore off. He slid an arm around her and they moved together toward the door.

As they crossed the outer office, he surveyed the carnage he had created. Three men dead inside, the others seriously injured. More injured and dead outside.

He wished he could cover Emma's eyes, wished he could protect her from the horrors he'd created, wished she didn't have to see the killing he had done, see the kind of man he was inside.

He swallowed. No matter what it cost him, he would do it again to protect her. He would do anything for Emma.

Anything but allow her to tie herself to a brutal, unholy man like him.

Chapter Thirty-Nine

Emma lay in a private hospital room, her left hand wrapped in bandages. Next to her bed, a heart monitor beeped a steady rhythm. Hospital smells made her nauseous. Her mind was fuzzy, fading in and out, odd images flashing through her head.

Rudy Vance lying dead, his eyes bulging, his mouth hanging open. A man covered with red and blue Yakuza tattoos, the flashing silver blade of a knife. She jerked wide-awake, biting back a scream, realized where she was, and let her head fall back against the pillow.

"It's all right, Em, honey. You're safe." April's voice drifted toward her, pulling her away from the painful memories. "You're going to be okay."

She remembered it all now. How Luke had killed Vance and the others. How he had stormed into the room like a wild man to save her. She remembered the carnage, the blood all over them, all over the floor. She would never forget the look on his face as he had come for her, a look that said nothing was going to stop him from reaching her. Nothing and no one.

Her gaze went to her sister, sitting in a chair next to the bed. "Where's Luke?" Her pulse kicked up with worry as she remembered the bullet wound in his side. "Is he here? Is he going to be all right?"

"Luke's going to be fine," April said. "The bullet creased his side. It went all the way through and didn't hit anything vital. He had to have stitches, but he's going to be okay."

"Where is he?"

A man's voice answered. "He left, Emma." She hadn't seen Dirk standing just inside the door. "He waited until you were out of surgery. The doctor told him the operation went very well. He took off as soon as he knew you were going to be okay."

She swallowed. She needed to see him. She remembered the look on his face and she was afraid for him. "Where did he go?"

"I'm not sure exactly. The cabin, maybe. Wherever he is . . . I don't think he'll be back. He said you'd understand."

Her throat closed up. Luke was gone. She understood everything and nothing at all. Luke had told her from the beginning it wouldn't last. He had told her he couldn't be the kind of man she would want him to be.

But Luke was exactly the kind of man she wanted. A man she admired more than anyone she had ever met. A man who would fight to the death to protect her. A man she loved with her whole heart.

But Luke was gone and he wouldn't be coming back.

Her eyes welled. She blinked and tears slid down her cheeks. She swallowed against the lump in her throat and settled back against the pillow. The drugs were keeping the pain away, but nothing could lessen the ache in her heart.

She looked up at her sister. "I'm sorry, but I'm feeling kind of . . . tired. If you wouldn't mind . . . I think I'll try to sleep."

April reached over and smoothed back her hair. "That's

a good idea. Get some rest, honey. I'll be back for visiting hours tomorrow."

She just nodded. As her sister walked out of the room, Dirk walked up beside the bed. "You gonna be okay?" His hazel eyes ran over her face. "He'd want you to be okay."

She nodded, her throat so tight she could barely speak. "I'll be all right." She looked at Dirk, read the pity.

"Maybe he'll figure it out," he said softly.

Emma glanced away. Luke had figured it out a long time ago. He had tried to warn her but she wouldn't listen.

She didn't hear Dirk leave, but she knew he was gone. Just like Luke. Emma let the tears come. She'd known better than to fall in love with him. She had known the day would come when he would leave. She'd risked everything for Luke. He was gone now and she was left to deal with the heartache.

Her chest heaved in silent sobs as a flood of tears washed down her cheeks. For the first time, Emma realized the high price she would pay for loving Luke.

Con Danfield stood on the sprawling ship's dock on the Duwamish Waterway not far from Rudy Vance's warehouse on Marginal. The water was crystal blue, reflecting the clear blue sky. Seagulls circled overhead, hoping for a scrap of food, screeching their irritation at the men on the dock below.

Around him, FBI agents swarmed the area, watching for any sign of trouble as the *Vagabond* settled into its berth. After the roundup of Vance's men, Con didn't really expect any problems, but smuggling was a big money operation. With stakes that high, it was better to be prepared.

Dressed in their tactical gear, the agents waited impatiently to board the ship. In his pocket, Con carried a warrant to search the vessel. As soon as their job was finished, cranes could begin to unload the twelve thousand containers the ship carried, a process that would take several days.

He glanced down at the numbers written on the piece of paper in his hand. If the info was correct, two containers on the deck were different from the rest of the cargo, the metal boxes modified to let in enough air for the occupants inside to breathe. Con pitied the poor souls trapped in the boxes, men and women suffering the harshest, most brutal conditions imaginable. There might even be casualties.

Even before Luke Brodie had given him the information, the FBI had uncovered Vance's connection to the *Vagabond*. Then last night, Luke had called with more news. An informant had phoned and told him which containers smuggled human cargo.

"What's your informant's name?" Con had asked.

Brodie just laughed. "You know I'm not going to tell you. The guy got hit with a stab of conscience, okay? He called and gave me the numbers because he trusts me. That's the reason I don't burn my sources."

Con hadn't pressed him. Brodie wouldn't give him his informant's name, but Con had a feeling he knew who it was. One of Vance's employees had completely disappeared, a man named Grady Kelso. His phone had been disconnected, his expensive Belltown apartment vacated. Con figured Grady had left the country.

Officially, Kelso had worked as an outside consultant for International Cargo. He was on Vance's payroll as a financial advisor. He handled things, made arrangements, solved problems; he was not one of Vance's murderous thugs. If the info Kelso had given Brodie was correct, they could get people out a lot faster, get them medical attention, water, and decent food.

Finding them would save people from being brutally victimized in the underworld. It might even save lives. Con didn't care if Kelso spent the rest of his life on a beach in the south of France.

Interestingly, during the sweep of Vance's men, they had run across a connection to a man named Parker Levinson. Turned out Levinson was the brains of the whole operation. They didn't have enough to arrest him—not yet. But Levinson was now on the FBI's radar and sooner or later he was going down.

The breeze kicked up, ruffling the piece of paper in Con's hand. It was almost over.

Tomorrow night he planned to see April. He'd be taking her and Ginny out to supper. After that, he and April could have the talk they'd been hoping to have for months.

They were free to start seeing each other, spend time together, find out if the feelings they shared were as real as Con believed. He smiled. Maybe they'd do more than just kiss.

A crane lifted the gangway into place. His men moved into position. Con looked up at the stacks and stacks of containers sitting in towering rows on the deck of the *Vagabond* and anticipation poured through him. He knew where to search now, looked forward to putting an end to the suffering inside the metal boxes, prayed they wouldn't be too late.

Con tapped the search warrant in his pocket and started walking.

Days passed, then a week. The weather changed, turned from sunny to overcast and windy. As Ethan walked into the office, he spotted his brother sitting behind his desk, his laptop open in front of him. It was the first time Ethan had seen Luke since the violence at the warehouse.

"I've been worried," Ethan said as he approached. "You haven't been answering your phone."

Luke's head came up. "I left you a message. I told you I was up at the cabin. I said I needed a little time off." There were dark circles under Luke's eyes, the blue somehow faded. His face was battered, but beginning to heal, turning from black and blue to an ugly yellow-gray.

"A message isn't the same. How are you feeling?"

Luke shrugged. "I'm healing. Stitches are starting to itch like hell, so I must be getting better." He cocked an eyebrow. "I still haven't figured out how you knew what had happened. How'd you know where to find us?"

If Ethan hadn't been so worried about Luke, he might have smiled. "I planted a bug in Emma's purse. Remember that day in the parking lot?"

Luke started nodding. "Yeah, now that you mention it, I remember you bumping into her. She dropped her purse and you picked it up. But why did you bug—"

"You may be tough, but I'm still your big brother. Vance and the Yakuza were a deadly combination."

Luke's jaw hardened. "Yeah."

"Once I had the bug in place, Sadie kept track of you. She was in the office when Vance's men drove into the parking lot. She saw what was happening and called 9-1-1 but it was too late. She phoned us and kept tracking you. I called the FBI on the way to the warehouse. We got there as quick as we could."

Luke made no reply. Ethan figured his brother was thinking that if their arrival had been sooner, maybe there wouldn't have been so much killing.

"Speaking of the Yakuza," Ethan said, "have you talked to Ryan Masaki?"

"We had a little chat. Masaki says he dealt with the men who tried to break away from the organization and align themselves with Vance. He says there won't be any more trouble."

"I wonder what he did to them."

"Personally, I don't want to know."

Ethan silently agreed. "How's Emma?" He said her name just to see Luke's reaction. When his brother didn't even flinch, Ethan worried even more.

"Dirk says she's doing okay. The doctor said she was the perfect candidate for the operation. She's young and healthy. The cut was made between the joints so there wasn't any damage there. And the finger wasn't crushed or anything. I guess she's back at her apartment, taking it easy while she's healing."

"So you haven't gone by to check on her yourself."

Luke glanced away. "I didn't think it was a good idea. We're over. I told you we were only partnering until we found Vance. It's better for both of us if I just stay away."

"It's over," Ethan repeated. "So you're tired of her and you're just moving on?"

Luke's whole body went rigid. "I'm not just moving on! Don't you get it?" He shot up out of his chair. "I don't have any choice! You were there! You saw what happened. I'm a killer, for chrissake! I'm not fit for a woman like Emma."

Ethan felt such a strong sweep of pity, it made his chest clamp down. "My God, that's what you think?"

Luke turned away and walked over to the window, stood there staring outside. Flat gray clouds lay heavy over the city. Intermittent rain glistened on the pavement behind the building.

"Leave it alone, E," Luke said softly. "It's over between us and that's the way it's going to stay."

Ethan released a slow breath. He ached for his brother, ached for Emma. But he knew Luke. He knew when his brother's mind was made up, he wouldn't change it.

There was nothing Ethan could do.

Chapter Forty

Three weeks had passed, three long, lonely weeks with nothing for Emma to do but wait for her hand to heal and brood. Chelsea had come back to Seattle, which made the apartment feel a little less lonely. Emma's blonde, blue-eyed friend was in the kitchen making soup and sandwiches for lunch, humming a tune as she worked.

Chelsea walked into the living room and set a tray down on the coffee table in front of the sofa, where Emma had curled up to watch a movie. Since the show was over, she clicked off the tuner and turned toward the steaming mug next to half a tuna salad sandwich.

With a brace on her left hand, Emma picked up the mug with her right hand and took a sip. Chicken vegetable. Chelsea had made it with fresh ingredients and it was delicious. Emma wished she had more appetite.

Chelsea sat down on the sofa beside her and Emma took a bite of her sandwich: whole grain bread with tuna, mayo, and sweet pickle relish. A single bite and she was no longer hungry.

She didn't feel much like talking but she didn't want to be rude. She started chatting about the weather, which was rainy and damp, not much to discuss.

She told her friend that as soon as her finger was healed, which would take two to three months, she was going to work with Leonard Fox, teaching women's self-defense classes. She was sure they could build up enrollment. She and Len eventually hoped to open their own school.

Emma took a sip from her mug of soup. "Anything new on the dating front? Or are you still off men?"

"Officially I'm still off men, but I've been e-mailing back and forth with that guy I mentioned meeting, Dennis Winston? Denny seems to have a great personality, at least online. But I'm not ready to go out with him yet. I'm kind of enjoying the chance to get to know him a little, find out if he's for real, before we get into a dating situation."

"I think it's a good idea," Emma said.

Chelsea seemed to ponder that as they went back to eating, while Emma's thoughts returned to Luke as they had off and on since that terrible day at the warehouse.

Was his bullet wound healing? Was he on a new case, pursuing a bail skip or working as a private investigator? Did he ever think of her? Did he miss her?

At the burning behind her eyes, she glanced away.

Chelsea leaned over and hugged her. "It takes time," she said softly. "But eventually you'll get over him."

Emma released a shaky breath. "I don't want to get over him. That's the problem. I want to be with him."

"It seems like we always want what we can't have."

"I know."

"If you really love him, maybe you should talk to him, try to find out if—"

"Don't. Just because I want to be with Luke doesn't mean he wants to be with me."

Chelsea fell silent. After the bad luck she'd had with men, Chelsea wouldn't be surprised it hadn't worked out with Luke. She got up from the sofa and carried the dishes into the kitchen. Emma could hear her loading them into the dishwasher.

"Will you be okay if I go out for a while?" Chelsea asked as she walked back into the living room.

"Of course. I'm feeling better all the time. I just have to take it easy."

"Absolutely. Think of it as a long vacation."

Emma scoffed. "I'd have more fun at Sandals."

Chelsea laughed. "Anything I can bring home for you?"

"How about a six-foot-two, sexy, blue-eyed male?"

Chelsea just smiled. "Good to see you're getting your sense of humor back."

Emma faked a return smile, wishing it was real.

By the time her friend had left the apartment, Emma couldn't even pretend any longer. She was glad Chelsea hadn't mentioned the brand-new Mazda hatchback Emma had found parked in front of her apartment with a note from Luke under the windshield wiper.

Sorry about the bomb, L. Nothing more, nothing the least bit personal. She thought about giving the car back, decided she would send him the insurance check when it arrived, which would pay for some of it, and let it go at that. She figured it was what Luke would want.

Over the past few weeks, she had talked to Dirk a few times when he had called to check on her. She thought about calling him again or calling Ethan to ask how Luke was doing, but she didn't. The men would just feel sorry for her and she couldn't handle that.

She was working up the energy to phone her sister to see how she and Ginny were doing when the doorbell rang.

Hope surged through her. Emma jumped up from the sofa and ran over to look through the peephole. There was only an instant of disappointment when she saw three familiar faces in the hall: a tall blonde, a slinky redhead, and petite and sexy Samantha Brodie.

Glad for a break from her dismal mood, Emma smiled as she opened the door. "Well, hi. Come on in."

"It's so good to see you." Val Brodie engulfed Emma in a warm, careful hug. Hugs followed from Meg and Samantha.

"How are you feeling?" Meg asked, looking down at the brace on Emma's finger.

"Pretty good, actually. I'm going to physical therapy a couple of times a week. The doctors think my recovery will be at least eighty percent."

"That's great news," Samantha said. "We've been worried about you." Carrying a narrow silver bag with *Get Well Quick* written in pink and red glitter on the side, Samantha and the other two women walked into the living room.

"Would you like something to drink?" Emma asked. "A cup of coffee or a Diet Coke or something?"

Val grabbed the silver package from Samantha. She grinned and waggled the bag. "How about a glass of wine?"

Emma felt the pull of a rare, sincere smile. She wasn't supposed to drink alcohol while her finger was healing but just this once wouldn't be any big deal.

"Sounds perfect." Way better than moping around all day yearning for Luke.

Meg went into the kitchen to find wineglasses while Val opened the bottle.

"A nice crisp Pinot Grigio." Samantha held up her glass and Val filled it. She poured one for each of them and they sat down in the living room to relax.

"I appreciate you all coming to the hospital to see me," Emma said.

Samantha took a sip of wine. "Are you kidding? After what you went through? We're just so glad you and Luke are okay."

At the mention of Luke's name, a rush of longing went straight to her heart and tears sprang into her eyes. Emma glanced away, hoping the women wouldn't see.

"Oh, my God, I knew it," Meg said, setting her wineglass down on the coffee table. "You're still in love with him."

Emma swallowed. She'd made a good show at the hospital, pretended she and Luke had ended on friendly terms. But she couldn't pretend any longer. "Why wouldn't I be in love with him? He's the best man I've ever known."

"Oh, honey . . ." Samantha set her glass down next to Meg's. "That's the way I felt after Nick and I broke up. Like my heart was being ripped out and crumbled into pieces."

Emma's throat ached. She missed Luke so much.

Val's honey blond hair swung forward as she picked up her wine and took a sip, then leaned back against the sofa. "If that's the way you feel, you have to do something about it. You can't just let him walk away."

Emma wiped a tear. "Luke has my phone number. He knows where I live. If he wanted to see me, he would."

The women exchanged glances. "He hasn't forgotten about you," Meg said. "He's been keeping track of you through Dirk. Ethan's worried about him. He says after what happened, Luke doesn't think he's fit for a woman like you."

Emma went still. "What does that mean? What are you talking about?"

"Luke killed men that day," Samantha said. "He thinks that makes him . . . I don't know . . . somehow not worthy of you."

Emma's throat tightened. "If you had been there . . . if you had seen what those men did to him." Fresh tears welled. "Luke waited. He tried to find an opening, a way to get us out of there. They beat him bloody, but he didn't try to escape. He could have done it, or at least he could have tried. He didn't do anything because he was afraid of what would happen to me."

Emma blinked and more tears rolled down her cheeks. "When he saw what those men were going to do . . . when he saw the knife slice through my finger, he went crazy. He killed those men to get to me. To save me. He didn't have any other choice."

The room fell silent.

Emma closed her eyes, trying to block the horror, the sharp bite of the blade, the scent of blood dripping onto the floor.

"You have to tell him the way you feel," Meg said, wiping tears of her own.

"Ethan says he's never seen Luke this way," Val added, leaning forward. "You have to do something."

"He loves you," Samantha said, with a sniffle. "I know he does. You have to go to him."

Emma's heart beat dully. They had no idea what they were asking. She just looked at them. "What if you're wrong? What if he doesn't love me at all? What if he'll just feel sorry for me?"

The women made no comment because there was a chance it was true.

Emma shook her head. "Even if he loves me, it might be too late. By now Luke's probably been with half a dozen women. One-night stands are what he does. It would never be the same between us."

The two taller women looked at each other over the top of Samantha's head, then down at their shorter friend.

Val set her wineglass back down and sat up straighter on the sofa. "You have to find out. You'll always wonder what would have happened if you had talked to him. You'll never know if the two of you might have found happiness if you'd just taken the risk. You have to be strong, Emma—for both of you."

Chapter Forty-One

Luke sat in a chair in his Bellevue apartment, staring at the darkness outside the window. Only a single lamp burned in the living room. He couldn't remember the last time he'd eaten; he just wasn't hungry.

Yesterday he'd accepted a contract to find a skip named Bernie Suthers. Ten percent of the fifty-thousand-dollar bond was way less than he usually worked for. He didn't care. He just needed something to do. Something that would take his mind off Emma.

God, he missed her. He hadn't realized how bad it could hurt when you let a woman so deep into your heart. It was like your guts were being torn out, like your heart was being shredded a little more every day.

He never should have done it, knew from the moment he had agreed to help her it was a bad decision. Now he was paying the price.

Still, he didn't regret the time they'd spent together. Emma was special. She was different from any woman he had ever met. He thought of the first time he'd seen her, dressed to kill in her tight skirt and low-cut sparkly top.

He remembered the way she'd surprised him and taken

down Skinner Digby. The way she'd stood up to Badger Stovall and the creeps at the Polo Club and won his respect.

He remembered how determined she'd been to protect her sister and her niece, how she'd been willing to sacrifice everything for them. How she'd risked her life to stop Rudy Vance.

Her image appeared in his head, those big dark eyes and soft pink lips. He remembered the feel of her long dark curls in his hands, the scent of her soft perfume. He remembered her laugh, the way she smiled, the sweet way she felt moving beneath him, the way she whispered his name.

He remembered . . . everything.

His chest ached. He rubbed his eyes as he forced himself up from the sofa and started into the kitchen to get another beer. He wished it was a straight shot of whiskey, but he had to work tomorrow.

He was halfway to the fridge when he heard a light, insistent knock at the door. His stomach instantly knotted. He recognized that knock, knew who was out there. *Emma.*

He told himself not to answer it, that if he ignored her, she would go away. He wouldn't have to look at her and remember. Instead, he found himself moving across the room, turning the lock, and pulling open the door.

Emma stood in the hall, so beautiful, he yearned to reach out and touch her. Her features looked achingly familiar, as determined as he remembered and at the same time more uncertain than he had ever seen her.

Luke steeled himself. "What are you doing here, Emma?"

"I . . . need to talk to you." She glanced behind him. "Are you . . . alone?"

He knew what she was asking. He could lie, but she would know. "There's no one here." He forced himself to smile. "You're not an easy woman to replace, honey."

He wondered if she understood that he didn't want

another woman. Hadn't wanted anyone else since the first night he had met her.

"May I come in?" she asked politely.

He wanted to say yes, wanted her to come inside so much, his chest clamped down until it was hard to breathe. He wanted to haul her into his arms and just hold her. He looked down at the brace on her finger, thought of that bloody day. "Be better if you didn't."

She ignored him, walked past him into the living room, left him to close the door. He couldn't help thinking how good she looked in her short black skirt, the peach blouse cut just low enough to reveal a little cleavage. A pair of high black heels showed off her pretty legs.

His groin tightened. *Fuck.*

"What do you want, Emma?" He needed to get her out of there before he did something stupid. He'd hurt her enough, hurt them both enough. "You know this isn't going anywhere. What are you doing here?"

The determined look returned, a look he knew only too well. She tilted her head a little to the side as she looked at him. "There's something different about you."

In a way she was right. He felt like a completely different man from the one he'd been before he'd met her.

"What is it?" she asked.

"Nothing's different. I'm the same man I've always been. Why are you here, Emma?"

Her eyes ran over him, seemed to be searching his face. "That's a fair question." She wandered a little away, stopped, and turned to face him. "I'm here because I decided to take a chance, the biggest risk of my life."

"What are you talking about?"

"I'm taking a gamble, Luke. I'm betting that in the weeks we've been apart, you've had time to figure things out. I'm betting you're smart enough to realize what you really want out of life. I'm betting you aren't going to let the past ruin your future."

His heart was beating oddly. Of all the things he'd expected her to say, none of that had entered his head. He had to make her understand, make her realize the kind of man he was.

"It's not the past I'm worried about, baby, it's the present. You saw what I did at the warehouse. I killed men that day. I've done it before. The kind of work I do, it could happen again. You know the Ten Commandments? 'Thou shalt not kill'? You saw what happened that day."

Emma looked at him with a trace of pity. "The commandment says thou shalt not murder, Luke. It isn't the same." She moved closer, her eyes on his face. "Have you ever set out to murder someone? Or were you protecting your country? Did you enjoy killing those men at the warehouse? Or were you forced to do it to save my life, to save both our lives?"

Luke said nothing. His chest felt tight. He'd done a lot of things. He'd killed men in battle or in self-defense, but he'd never murdered anyone. Not even Rudy Vance.

She reached up and cupped his cheek and longing burned through him.

"So this is what I'm doing here, Luke. I'm betting that deep down inside, you know that I'm what you really want. That I'm exactly what you need. I'm betting you're brave enough to grab what you want, hold on to it, and never let go."

"Emma . . ."

"I'm betting on you, Luke. I'm betting you love me. Because I'm desperately in love with you."

Something tore open inside him. His brave Emma had come to him. She loved him. She was his. All he had to do was reach out and claim her.

Luke looked down at her injured hand, reached out, and gently lifted it to his lips. Beneath her warm skin, he felt the rapid flutter of her heart. Sweeping her into his arms, he just held her. "Emma," he said against her cheek. "Emma . . . I love you so much."

A little sob escaped. "Luke . . ." He tightened his hold, felt her arms go around his neck. "Luke . . ."

"Stay with me," he said, burying his face in her hair. "I need you, Emma. I need you so much."

"I'm right here, Luke. I'm not leaving you again."

Luke just held her, absorbing the feel of her in his arms, thinking it was exactly where she belonged. He'd been a fool not to see it. What if she hadn't come to him? He wouldn't have had the courage to go to her. What if he had let her go?

His chest squeezed. He couldn't stand to think of it. He eased her a little away, let his gaze run over her face, leaned down, and very softly kissed her. He'd never felt like this, never felt this soul-deep yearning. He wasn't quite sure what to do, what to say.

"So . . . ahh . . . maybe we could, you know, go out sometime . . . on a date, I mean. Go to a movie, or to dinner, or something. We've never really been on a date."

Emma wiped away a tear and smiled up at him. "A date. Okay, we could do that."

"Then after we go out a few times, maybe you could, you know, think about marrying me."

Another little sob slipped out. She went back into his arms, went up on her toes, and kissed him. "I love you, Luke Brodie. I'll marry you anytime you say."

Something warm and sweet that felt a lot like relief settled in the area around his heart.

"Thank God you were brave enough to come, baby."

Her eyes flashed. "You're a good man. You deserve to be happy. You aren't always right, Luke Brodie."

Luke grinned down at her. It was the last thing Emma had a chance to say before he swept her up in his arms and carried her off to his bedroom.

Epilogue

Epilogue

Three Months Later

Emma stood in the middle of the living room of the house she shared with Luke, a three-bedroom, two-bath home on a secluded street with views out over Lake Washington, a property Dirk had bought not far from his own lake house, remodeled, and sold to Luke at a very reasonable price.

The backyard, a story below, was surrounded by leafy foliage, the setting very private. She and Luke loved the house and the future it represented.

"Luke, can you come in here a minute and help me hang this picture?"

"Sure, baby." He sauntered out of the bedroom in a pair of jeans and those sexy knee-high moccasins he'd been wearing the first time she'd seen him. Her stomach did the same little curl it had that night.

"We need to measure where it goes and mark where to hammer the nails," she said.

"No problem." Luke leaned down and kissed her as he took the measuring tape out of her hand.

They were decorating the house together and having a terrific time. They'd bought the picture on the sidewalk in front of Pike Place Market, an Impressionist painting of Seattle at night, the lights of the city reflecting on the waterfront.

The glittering lights in the painting had Emma glancing down at the beautiful diamond engagement ring sparkling on her left hand, the ring Luke had bought her as soon as the brace was off and she could wear it comfortably. The marquis cut fit her small hand perfectly and she loved it.

Luke had taken her out to El Gaucho, the most romantic restaurant in Seattle. After they got home, he'd gone down on one knee and made a very formal marriage proposal that was so out of character, she started to cry. Luke thought she was saying no and the fear in his eyes made her heart clench.

"Oh, Luke," she'd said. "I want to marry you more than anything in the world."

Relieved, he'd pulled her into his arms and kissed her and of course they had ended up in bed.

The tape measure whispered out. Luke measured the space and marked where the nails should go, held up the painting so they could be sure it was exactly the right spot.

They'd moved in together three days before Meg and Dirk's wedding. Chelsea and Denny were getting along so well they had decided to take over the apartment lease, which made Emma's decision even easier.

She and Luke had gone to the ceremony together, a simple but elegant outdoor wedding beneath an arch covered in white roses set among the foliage in the backyard of Meg's parents' home.

In a tea-length antique white Vera Wang gown trimmed with Belgian lace, Meg looked stunning but no more amazing than Dirk in his perfectly tailored black tuxedo. Meg only had eyes for her husband and Dirk couldn't stop grinning. It was clear how happy both of them were.

Little redheaded Charlie wore a smaller version of Dirk's black tux, and of course Luke, as best man, and Ethan, Nick, and Ian, as groomsmen, all wore tuxes.

The men looked yummy, especially Luke, who made it clear to his friends and family that he and Emma were a couple, a very happy couple with plans for the future. It was a dream come true.

Luke started hammering, pounding the nails into the wall in just the right place, hanging the picture above the sofa, perfectly centered. He was, after all, Luke Brodie.

Luke set the hammer aside and his gorgeous blue eyes swung to her. She was wearing old jeans and a red flannel shirt, but the heat was there, the way it always was when he looked at her.

"What do you think?" he asked.

"It looks perfect." But then everything felt perfect now that they were together.

After Rudy Vance's death, it all seemed to fall in place. Grady Kelso's information had shortened the FBI's search for the people being trafficked aboard the *Vagabond*. They were dehydrated and suffering from malnutrition, two had died just days before the ship reached port, but the rest were alive and safe.

Luke walked up behind her, slid his arms around her waist. He pushed her curls aside and kissed the nape of her neck. "I forgot to tell you your sister called while you were out. How's she doing these days?"

She turned into his arms. "She and Con are madly in love and Ginny's crazy about him, too. I have a feeling they're going to move in together."

"Good for them. I can tell Danfield from personal

experience, having a woman to come home to is great." He kissed her lightly. "Of course it has to be the right woman."

Emma smiled. "Which reminds me . . . from now on, I won't be home as much as I have been. My finger's completely healed and Len has a place picked out for us to open our school."

One of his dark eyebrows arched up. "So what do I have to do, get you pregnant to keep you home?"

Emma laughed. "At the rate we're going, it wouldn't take much."

Luke grinned, digging in his dimple. Now that he'd conquered his demons, she thought he liked the idea more than he let on. And he was constantly pressing her to set a date for the wedding. Which she loved. She'd give in eventually, but what woman wouldn't enjoy being pursued by Luke?

"Speaking of work, I got a contract this morning," he said. "A big one."

Uneasiness slid through her. The bigger the payoff, the more dangerous the job. "Not a serial killer, I hope."

Luke just smiled. He was so much more relaxed these days, as if he had finally figured things out and was exactly where he wanted to be.

"I told you I'm being more careful. The guy's a white-collar criminal. Worked for the government. He's wanted for embezzling. Bilked the public for millions. I was hoping you'd help me trace him."

She smiled, relieved. "You bet I will. Every once in a while, I find myself missing the hunt."

Luke frowned. "You can hunt from right here where I don't have to worry about you."

Emma chuckled. She wouldn't tell him for all the money in Vegas that she'd never really wanted to be a bounty hunter, not when he'd told everyone how good she was at it.

The diamond on her finger sparkled. Emma thought of the day she had gone to his apartment, the courage it had taken to face him. She thought of how happy she was.

She went up on her toes and kissed him. Sometimes no matter how slim the chance, the risk was worth taking.

AUTHOR'S NOTE

I hope you enjoyed Luke and Emma's story, *Into the Firestorm*. If you haven't read the first two BOSS, Inc. novels, I hope you will. In *Into the Fury*, bodyguard Ethan Brodie is hired to protect sexy lingerie model Valentine Hart from a vicious killer.

Into the Whirlwind finds PI Dirk Reynolds helping Megan O'Brien, the woman who broke his heart, when the son she loves is ruthlessly kidnapped.

Up next for me is *Beyond Reason*. From the small town of Iron Springs to the bright lights of Dallas, Carly Drake clashes with megarich businessman Lincoln Cain. Cain is a man used to being in charge. With a shady past and years in prison, Linc dragged himself up by the bootstraps, carved out a place for himself in the tough world of commerce, and made a fortune in the process.

He isn't about to take orders from a sexy blonde trying to force her way into a man's world, even if he admires her courage and finds himself insanely attracted to her.

It's a high-stakes game of money, power, passion, and intrigue. I hope you'll watch for *Beyond Reason*, out in June 2017.

Till then, very best wishes and happy reading.

Warmest,
Kat

Read on for an excerpt from
Kat Martin's exciting new thriller,

BEYOND REASON,

coming soon!

New York Times *bestselling author Kat Martin
raises chills as danger stalks a woman determined
to make it in a man's world . . .*

Five weeks ago Carly Drake stood at her grandfather's
grave. Now she's burying Drake Trucking's top driver,
and the cops have no leads on the hijacking or murder.
Faced with bankruptcy, phone threats, and the fear of
failure, Carly has to team up with the last man
she wants to owe—Lincoln Cain.

Cain is magnetic, powerful, controlling—and hiding
more than one secret. He promised Carly's granddad
he'd protect her. The old man took a chance on him
when he was nothing but a kid with a record, and now
he's the multimillionaire owner of a rival firm.

But Linc's money can't protect Carly from the men
who'll do anything to shut her down, or the secrets
behind Drake Trucking. If she won't sell out,
the only way to keep her safe is to keep her
close . . . and fight like hell.

Iron Springs, Texas

For the second time since her return to Iron Springs, Carly Drake stood in a graveyard. A harsh Texas wind whipped the blades of grass around her legs as she waited in front of the rose-draped casket.

Between the rows of granite headstones, the Hernandez family huddled together, a wife weeping for her husband, children crying for their father.

Carly stood with her head bowed, her heart aching for the loss of a man she had known only briefly. Still mourning her grandfather's recent passing, she understood the pain Miguel's family was feeling. Joe Drake, the man who had raised her, the only father Carly had ever known, had died just five weeks ago.

But unlike her grandfather, whose heart had simply worn itself out, Joe Drake's number one driver had been shot in the head, and the criminals who had committed the truck hijacking were still on the loose.

In the weeks since her grandfather's death, Carly had been doing her best to run Drake Trucking, to keep the company afloat and its employees' checks paid. She was doing the best she knew how, but Miguel had been killed on her watch and Carly felt responsible.

The wind kicked up. The end of September weather was fickle, hot and humid one day, rainy and overcast the next. The breeze plucked fine blond strands from the tight bun fashioned at the nape of her neck. As she smoothed the hair back into place, her gaze came to rest on a man on the far side of the mourners, a head taller than Miguel's Hispanic family, taller than most of the other men in the crowd, big and broad-shouldered, with dark brown hair and a strikingly handsome face.

Carly leaned over and spoke quietly to the woman beside her, Brittany Haworth, a willowy brunette who had been her best friend in high school, a friendship that had resumed the day Carly had returned to Iron Springs, as if they'd been apart just days instead of years.

"That man across from us," Carly said. "The tall one? He was also at Joe's funeral service. I remember him going through the line to pay his respects, but I was so upset I barely paid attention. Do you know who he is?"

Brittany, a little shorter than Carly's five foot seven inches, looked up at her. "You're kidding, right? You don't recognize him? Obviously you don't read the gossip rags. He's in the newspapers all the time. That's Lincoln Cain. You know, the multimillionaire?"

Carly's gaze went across the casket on the mound above the grave to the big man in the perfectly tailored black suit and crisp white shirt. "That's Cain?"

As if he could feel her watching him, his eyes swung to hers, remained steady on her face. Carly couldn't seem to look away. There was power in that bold, dark gaze. She could actually feel her pulse accelerate. "So what's Cain doing in Iron Springs?"

"He owns a ranch here. He was born in Pleasant Hill,

left to make his fortune, came back a few years ago megarich. It's a fascinating story. You'll have to Google him sometime."

"I still don't understand why he was at Grandpa Joe's funeral, or why he's here today."

"For one thing, he was Joe's competition. Texas American Transport is one of the biggest trucking companies in the world."

She nodded. "TexAm Transportation. I know that, but—"

"Cain credits Joe Drake as one of the people who put him on the path to success. The Iron Springs *Gazette* published a couple of articles about him and Joe."

Guilt swept over her. She'd been away so much. Off to college at the U of Texas in Austin ten years ago, which her grandfather had paid for, then a job in Houston as a flight attendant.

She had always wanted to see the world, so instead of coming home to help Grandpa Joe, she'd gone to work for Delta. She'd been transferred here and there, worked out of New York for a while, came back to Iron Springs a couple of times a year, but her visits never lasted more than a few days; then she was gone again, flying somewhere else, off on another adventure.

Five weeks ago, she'd quit her job, given up her apartment in Seattle, and come home to stay. Joe's heart condition had worsened. She'd started worrying about him, decided to come back and help him run Drake Trucking, take over some of the responsibilities and lessen the stress he was under.

She'd only been in Iron Springs a week when Joe had suffered a massive heart attack. He'd died in the ambulance on the way to the hospital. By the time she'd received the call, rushed out of the office, and driven like a maniac to Iron Springs Memorial, Joe was gone.

She hadn't been there for him when he needed her.

Just as she had so many times before, Carly had failed him.

"Carly . . ."

She glanced up at the sound of Brittany's voice. The service had ended, the mourners breaking up, people walking away.

"He's coming over," Britt whispered. "Lincoln Cain."

Carly honed in on him, about six-five, a man impossible to miss. She straightened as Cain approached.

"Ms. Drake? I'm Lincoln Cain." He extended a big hand and she set hers in it, felt a warm, comforting spread of heat. Since being comforted only made her feel like crying, she eased her hand away.

"We met briefly at your grandfather's service," Cain said, "but I doubt you recall."

His eyes weren't brown, she realized, but a sort of dark gold. He had a slight cleft in his chin and a jaw that looked carved in stone. "Yes, I remember seeing you there. I don't recall much else. It was a very bad day."

"Yes, it was."

She turned. "This is my friend, Brittany Haworth."

He gave a faint nod of his head. "Ms. Haworth."

"Nice to meet you," Britt said. She'd always been shy. The way she was looking at Cain, as if the sexiest man alive had just dropped by for a visit, Carly was surprised her friend was able to speak.

Cain's gaze returned to Carly. "I realize how difficult it must be, going through all of this again so soon. Once more you have my condolences."

"Thank you. It's been difficult. But my grandfather lived

a long full life. I can only imagine how painful this has been for Miguel's family."

A muscle in Cain's jaw tightened. "Maybe catching his killers will ease some of their pain."

"You think the police will catch them?"

"Someone will."

There was something in the way he said it. Surely he didn't intend to involve himself in catching the men who'd killed Miguel.

"I didn't realize you were a friend of my grandfather's."

His features relaxed as if a fond memory had surfaced. "Joe Drake was a good man. One of the best. He gave me my first job. Did you know that?"

Her eyes burned. That sounded so like Joe. Never a hand-out but always a hand-up whenever one was needed. "I wasn't around much after I got out of high school. I should have come home more often. You'll never know how much I regret that."

His expression shifted, became unreadable. "We all do things we regret." Up close he was even better looking than she had first thought, his dark hair cut a little shorter on the sides, narrow brackets beside his mouth that only appeared once in a while, not dimples, but something more subtle, more intriguing. "Your grandfather loved you very much."

A lump swelled in her throat. She had loved him, too. She'd never realized how little time they would have. "Thank you for saying that." She needed to leave. She was going to cry and she didn't want to do that in front of him. "I'm sorry, but if you'll excuse me, I need to say good-bye to Conchita before we go."

He nodded. "There's something I need to discuss with you. After Joe died, I waited. I wanted to give you time to grieve, but after what happened to Miguel, it can't wait any longer."

She tried to imagine what Cain wanted. Something to do with Joe, she thought. "All right. You can reach me at the office. I'm there every day."

"I know the number. I'll be in touch."

She watched as he turned and walked away, wide shoulders, narrow hips, long legs striding across the grass as if he had something important to do. What could one of the wealthiest men in Texas possibly want to talk to her about?

Carly watched as Cain slid into the back of a shiny black stretch limo waiting for him at the edge of the graveyard.

"I wonder what he wants," Brittany said, voicing Carly's thoughts.

"He's in the transportation business, so it must have something to do with Drake Trucking."

"Cain owns half of Texas American. It's a huge corporation, so you're probably right. Or maybe it's something personal, something to do with your grandfather."

"Maybe. I guess I'll be finding out." Carly started making her way through the tombstones. Up ahead, the family stood on the church steps, accepting condolences. Carly squared her shoulders and kept walking.

She wasn't what he'd imagined. Oh, she was as beautiful as the pictures her grandfather had proudly shown him: late twenties, taller than average, with big blue eyes and golden blond hair past her shoulders. Joe had shown him a photo of her playing volleyball on the beach so he knew what she looked like in a bikini, knew she had a dynamite figure.

She didn't seem concerned with her appearance the way he'd expected. He'd thought she'd be more aloof, more self-absorbed. He hadn't expected her to be grieving her grandfather so deeply.

He'd been sure he wouldn't like her. Not the young woman who had accepted so much and returned so little.

And yet, as he had watched her with Miguel's family, as he read her sorrow, the depth of her concern, he had been surprisingly moved. She felt responsible in some way for her employee's death. She blamed herself and he couldn't allow that to happen.

Linc had made a vow to her grandfather. He'd promised Joe Drake that if the worst happened and his heart gave up, he'd look after Carly, make sure she was okay.

Linc planned to do just that.

And the best way he could take care of her was to buy her out of Drake Trucking. The best thing he could do for Carly was to send her packing—before she ended up as dead as Miguel Hernandez.